A FISTFUL OF EVIL

A MADISON FOX ADVENTURE - BOOK ONE

REBECCA CHASTAIN

This book is a work of fiction. Names, characters, dialogue, places, and incidents either are drawn from the author's imagination or are used fictitiously. Any resemblance to actual persons, living or dead, business establishments, locales, or events is entirely coincidental. Any resemblance to an actual cat is 100 percent intentional and approved by Mack Fu, who shamelessly insisted on being immortalized in the pages of this novel.

A FISTFUL OF EVIL

Mind Your Muse Books
PO Box 374
Rocklin, CA 95677

ISBN: 978-0-9906031-4-6

1st Edition

Also by Rebecca Chastain

Madison Fox, Illuminant Enforcer
A Fistful of Evil
A Fistful of Fire

Gargoyle Guardian Chronicles
Magic of the Gargoyles
Curse of the Gargoyles
Secret of the Gargoyles

Tiny Glitches
(paranormal romance)

Never miss any novel news:
Sign up for Rebecca's newsletter to receive emails
regarding future releases and behind-the-scenes information at
www.rebeccachastain.com/newsletter

To Cody, whose support and encouragement makes all things possible, all dreams achievable.

<h1 style="text-align:center">1</h1>

Don't Follow Me: I'm Lost, Too

THE INTERVIEW WAS A CATASTROPHE. It started out fine—better than fine. Kyle, the sales manager for the bumper sticker company Illumination Studios met me in the warm confines of a nearby Starbucks, purchased me a grande green tea, and selected a table in the corner, away from the door and the cold blast of November air every customer brought in with them. Soft music, cappuccino-machine clacks and whirs, and the murmur of conversation created a cocoon of privacy.

I handed Kyle a copy of my résumé, determined to prove myself to be the mandatory employee for the boring junior sales associate position. I wasn't particularly qualified and I would normally have rather peeled hangnails than perform cold calls—which is what I strongly suspected the position entailed—but four weeks of unemployment, seven failed interviews, and escalating credit card bills proved very strong motivators.

Strong enough for me to ignore the desperate reason I'd applied for the job in the first place. *Never trust your soul-sight,* I told myself for the thousandth time. But my imminent eviction trumped mistrust of my bizarre, mutant vision.

Kyle dropped my résumé to the table without glancing at it. He scrutinized me over the top of his dry cappuccino. Kyle exuded salesman, from his maroon button-up shirt and khaki trousers to his thinning brown hair with its frosted tips. His face was pinched, as if someone had pressed his baby flesh between their hands and pulled, extending his nose and pulling his lips and eyes in tight. He couldn't have been much older than me, despite the sullen brackets around his mouth and deep grooves between his eyebrows. Maybe his expression fell into disapproving lines naturally.

"How many years' experience do you have, Madison?" Kyle asked.

"Specifically in the bumper sticker business, none, but I believe my time at Catchall Advertising will—"

"I don't care about the bumper sticker crap. I care about your experience in the field."

My weirdo radar, dulled by the overpowering mix of desperation and determination, flickered to life now.

"I honed my sales skills while working as a saleswoman at Sundage Cars. My experience there taught me how to connect with people from all walks of life." Though it hadn't taught me how to sell a car. In the six months of my employment as a used-car saleswoman, I sold a grand total of zero cars, which is why David Sundage, my cousin-in-law and owner of Sundage Cars, had fired me at the beginning of September. But I wasn't going to concern Kyle with that minor detail.

Kyle set his cappuccino down on the table and leaned back in his chair. "How old are you?" he asked.

"I'm not sure I understand the relevance—"

"What regions have you worked in before this?"

Regions? "I've worked mainly in Roseville since I—"

"With who? Not with Brad or Isabel." Kyle leaned forward, his dark eyes intense.

Who? I eased my tea to the table and ran my palms down the sides of my black knee-length skirt, telling myself it was only nerves that were making Kyle seem so volatile.

"Um, most recently with David Sundage," I said.

"Where are his headquarters?"

Headquarters? What is this, the FBI? Hadn't he bothered to read my résumé?

"Down Douglas," I answered, pointing vaguely west toward Douglas Boulevard and the car lot.

"Before that?"

"Also in Roseville, at Catchall—"

"Look, we can both stop playing this game. I don't care about what jobs you've had to take between IE positions." Kyle deflated into his chair with a gusty sigh. "To be honest, you're the only qualified person to apply for the job—my job. I've been ready to transfer for months now, so I'm not going to make this interview hard on you. I want you to take this job as much as you want it. I just need to make this interview look good so Brad signs my walking papers, okay?"

I nodded and tried to look like I understood more than the English words he used. I didn't know what he meant by "IE positions," and I knew I wasn't qualified for his sales manager position. I wasn't even qualified to be a junior sales associate, but who was I to argue? Managers probably didn't have to make cold calls, which automatically made the job more appealing. Plus, a management position would pay better, and I was pretty sure I could fake it until I got caught up on my bills. By then, I could find a more suitable job. Something more Indiana Jones and less Bridget Jones.

"Okay, let me make this perfectly clear," Kyle continued. "Which wardens have you worked with?"

"Wardens?" As in prison?

Kyle leaned forward, placing his hands on the table. "What's the largest evil you've ever tackled? A wraith? A pissed-off dryad?"

I cast a quick glance around for a candid camera, noting the nearest exit in case I needed to make a run for it. I'd been nervous on interviews before, but never because of a mentally unstable interviewer. Was that why Kyle had insisted we meet away from the company office? Did he even work for Illumination Studios?

I eased my hand through the strap of my purse and slid it onto my shoulder, careful not to make any sudden movements that might spook the deranged man. "I don't think I'm the right person for the job, after all," I said, and pushed away from the table.

This is why I never used my soul-sight, never followed its false leads. I shouldn't have made an exception for this job. To the marrow of my bones, I knew soul-sight was untrustworthy.

"Hang on, Madison," Kyle said, grabbing my arm as I started to stand. I froze. "You're definitely the right person for the job. You're the first enforcer to walk through that door in nearly two weeks."

"I don't even know what that means. I'm going to save us both some time and leave now." I tugged to free my arm.

"Holy crap! You're a rogue." Kyle jerked away from me, shaking his hand like I'd given him cooties. Unbalanced, I fell back into my chair.

"That explains your age," Kyle said, speaking more to himself than me. "And your job history. You haven't been playing games with me—you really don't know . . ."

I stood again as he trailed off, and his gaze snapped to focus on my face. "It was nice to meet you," I said by rote. "Good luck with—"

"One question." Kyle stood, cutting off my escape. He towered over my five-foot-ten frame by a good eight inches. Despite his wiry build, the odds weren't in my favor that I could knock him down before he could grab me.

Taking a deep breath, and reminding myself that I was in a safe public place filled with people, I said, "Okay. One more."

"Did you apply because you thought you could pretend to be qualified for a sales position or because the ad glowed?"

My breath caught. The fact that the job description in the "Help Wanted" section had glowed in soul-sight had been an inexplicable anomaly. Dead, mashed pulp couldn't glow. It wasn't alive. It didn't have a soul. But hearing that Kyle knew about the glow set my arm hairs on end. No one knew about soul-sight except my best friend, and that was only because I'd told her. Soul-sight was my own personal aberration.

Seeing my hesitation, Kyle plowed on.

"Three decades as a rogue has got to be a new record. I'm not sure why you chose to come out of hiding, but I'm not letting you get away now, not when I'm this close"—he pinched his forefinger and thumb together—"to escaping this puny region for some real action."

"I haven't been hiding. I think you're mistaken—"

"Come on. We both know you're not qualified for a sales position even if it did exist," Kyle said, flicking my résumé. The crisp white paper skittered off the table to the floor. "But if you could see the glow, you *are* qualified to be an enforcer. Hmm, let's see, how to explain this to a thirty-year-old rogue?"

"I'm twenty-five," I corrected softly, wondering why I was still standing there, why I hadn't stepped around Kyle and walked out the door.

"You have the ability to see the world differently than this 'real world,' right? Black and white? Plants and animals glow all pretty and clean. People look like they're wearing snowy-weather camouflage. Is this ringing any bells?"

There was definitely a ringing in my ears. He'd just described soul-sight. My knees wobbled and I sank disjointedly into my chair.

Kyle sat across from me, shaking his head with amazement. "I can't believe you've maintained a rogue status for so long. I mean, I understand the appeal of not having a boss, but you're also not on anyone's payroll. Why not become a real enforcer and get paid for it?"

Paid to use soul-sight? Has he infected me with his insanity?

"I, um—"

"Trust me, this region's not hard at all. It's a good place to cut your teeth, but it gets monotonous real fast. Still, let's see what you've got. Tell me what you see here."

"A coffee shop," I said, not quite willing to believe he and I were talking about the same thing.

"Fine. I'll go first." He twitched his long, pointy nose and grinned at me. "You've got great color. Very pure. Which is how I knew you were an enforcer. No *atrum* in sight."

I shifted in my chair, irrationally pulling my suit jacket tighter to cover myself, but Kyle had already turned away.

"Now, that guy behind the counter, he's not the honest type. Look at the way *atrum* coats his fingertips and wrists. Disgusting."

Kyle grinned at me. I tried to remember to breathe. He was truly talking about soul-sight. I wasn't the only person with the ability. All brain activity got jammed up between that thought and his statement that people—*he*—got paid to use soul-sight. Once I could formulate a complete thought, I was going to have a lot of questions.

"Go ahead, look around in Primordium. I'm going to see if I can attract us a little fun," Kyle said.

For the first time in ten years, I intentionally blinked in public.

I gripped the edges of the table for support against the wave of dizziness that broadsided me whenever I switched between visions; then I purposely examined my surroundings. The coffee shop was slate gray, all color nonexistent in this vision. From the floor (which I knew was tiled white) to the wooden tables to the chrome espresso machine, every inanimate object was shades of charcoal. The overhead lighting didn't exist in soul-sight—*in Primordium,* I corrected myself. Shadows didn't exist in Primordium, either, not traditional light-created shadows. Something worked in this vision to give depth to objects, but trying to focus on it was a recipe for a migraine. The only bright spots in the room were the people.

I forced myself to examine the man behind the cash register to verify Kyle's description, fighting against soul-sight-avoidance instincts honed over the last ten years. My fingers tightened on the table. The barista's fingertips and wrists were smeared black, like he'd had a run-in with a dirty chimney. The rest of his arms were pale gray, as was his face. I knew from experience, those dark patches represented some immoral choices and actions. Light gray was normal for a human; black was pure evil. Only animals and plants were pure white in Primordium. The barista's smudged wrists meant he'd made some bad choices, but I couldn't tell what. That was only one of the flaws of soul-sight.

The only person's soul I'd ever seen that was as pure as an animal's was my own. Since I was far from perfect, I figured I couldn't see my own flaws. That was fine by me. Seeing my soul felt like looking inside myself, and it was a sure way to induce stomach-churning vertigo.

I swiveled my head to look at my companion, fully expecting him to look like a variation of every other human I'd ever seen.

Kyle, the plain-looking salesman, glowed brighter than most searchlights. I lifted my hand to shield my eyes, but it was as impractical as shining a flashlight in my eyes to shield them from the brightness of the sun.

"Aha! There are a few curious imps. Figured there would be with the traffic in here," Kyle said. He was too bright to see his facial features, almost too bright to see a solid outline. When he talked, I couldn't tell if his lips moved. It was one of the creepiest things I'd ever seen.

I had a thousand questions for this man—why had we never met before? Why did he refer to me as a rogue? Could he please dim himself?—but what came out was, "A curious what?"

"Imp." His glowing head swiveled toward me. "You have killed evil creatures before, right?"

I shook my head. "What evil creatures?"

"Amazing. Truly amazing. It's like you've been hiding under a rock, invisible to both sides." He shook his head in wonder. "You've not imploded a single imp? Not even a small one?"

"Maybe I have," I said, belatedly offended and not sure why. "What do they look like?"

Kyle laughed loud enough to draw several stares. "No shit. A rogue with zero experience." He chuckled again. "The best Brad can attract to his puny region is an untrained nobody with no clue. I'd love to see his face when—" He raised his hand to forestall my next question. "Never mind. You've got the ability; you're trainable. Brad won't turn you away, not when he's so desperate for an IE. Ah, that stands for *illuminant enforcer*, which is the job I'm leaving to you. So let me give you your first demonstration of what a true enforcer does. Watch carefully."

I tore my eyes from his shining aura. There was no after-image like with real light, which was a good thing, because I'd have been blind for a half hour after staring so hard. Logic said the bright light of Kyle should have cast shadows all over the room, but in this strange sight, logic didn't apply.

I wasn't sure where I was supposed to look, so I scanned other customers.

The coffee shop was busy but not full, with groups of two and three people scattered around the free-floating tables—mostly college students or businesspeople escaping the office. People firmly rooted in reality, not looking at dirty souls and talking about illumi-something enforcers and Primordium.

I focused on the group of four people to my right. Like everyone else in the room, they had gray dollops peeking through the V-necks of their shirts and flecks of black soot defiling their hands and wrists. I could see their features faintly through their bodies' natural light, and I flushed with embarrassment when all four turned to stare back at me. I rarely let myself use my soul-sight around people; despite my discomfort, it was heady to use it so blatantly now. Of course, to them it just looked like I was staring rudely.

"Do you see the imps?"

I swiveled back to Kyle and blinked against his brightness. Unobtrusively, I leaned against the table while the world spun back into color.

"They're the smallest of the evil creatures, little blobs of pure evil. Hardly enough brain matter to function. Just enough to recognize food and attack it."

Not good. This is so *not good.* I wished I were back at home with my cat, Mr. Bond, and a good book or a TV show. Something ordinary. I did not want to be talking with the only other known person with soul-sight who kept insisting there were evil creatures visible to only us. I felt like a character in a horror movie right before they slowly turn around and come face-to-face with a monster. Seeing evil on people's souls was bad enough. I didn't want to see—let alone come into contact with— something purely evil.

And yet, how could I *not* look?

I blinked, carefully focusing away from Kyle first.

I scanned the room again. Baristas. Customers. Books and CDs. Coffee bags. "What am I looking for?" Kyle didn't answer me. Movement under the nearest table caught my attention. An inky black chinchilla-like blob sat on the table's base, its glowing eyes watching me.

"What the hell is that?" Anything with life was always a version of white. Even the sullied souls of the sadistic still glowed with light undertones. Nothing living was all black—it was life that made everything glow. Furthermore, animals were never tainted by ambiguous moral choices like humans; animals were *always* white. The tiny fluff ball of blackness was darker than the inanimate objects around it. It was black—solid black. Impossibly black. Either there were varying degrees of life I'd never encountered and this was the zombie equivalent of life, or this creature—this pile of dust with bright eyes—was pure evil.

"Madison, meet your first imps," Kyle said.

The imp cocked its head at me, clearly curious. Curious meant it could think. Curious meant it was trying to puzzle me out. A thinking *evil* creature was interested in me. Abandoning my job hunt and moving back in with my parents suddenly seemed like a great idea.

The imp hopped toward me.

I lurched to my feet, sending my chair careening into the people behind me. Scrambling around the table, I put distance between myself and the creature. Its eyes tracked me. It hopped out from under the table until it was less than two feet away from me. I tensed to flee.

Kyle waved his radiant hand in front of the imp the way a matador waves a cape for a bull. Like a bull, the imp charged. I squealed. The imp disappeared.

He'd said imps, *right? With an* s? I spun around, looking for more.

I spied three behind Kyle's chair. Like the first one, the dark creatures were fixated on him. In a group they lunged. I jumped back, tripping over a chair. Windmilling my arms, I fought for balance while trying to keep the evil creatures in my sight, but gravity won. In a cacophony of wood and metal and flesh, I crashed to the floor. When I looked back at Kyle, the imps were gone.

"Miss? Are you okay?"

Reality popped like my ears had just unplugged. I blinked. The world swam. I rolled to my side. From my position on the gritty floor, I could see a circle of black-clad feet, and more approaching. Baristas. Everyone in the coffee shop had gone deafeningly quiet, making the cheerful jazz sound like it was blaring. I realized three things simultaneously: (1) *everyone*—from the patrons to the dishwasher—was staring at me; (2) I must look like I had gone absolutely, start-raving mad; and (3) my skirt was hiked up to my hips. *Shit. Can you die from embarrassment? Please?*

I untangled myself from the rungs of the chair I'd tripped over; stood faster than I should have, assisted by the adrenaline of embarrassment; and yanked my skirt down so that it covered me to my knees. I patted at my hair, pulling a bit of muffin out of a clump and wiping my hand on a napkin. And I assured everyone that I was fine, convincing no one.

How could I be fine? I'd just learned that I wasn't the only person with soul-sight—or the ability to see in Primordium. Worse, there were evil creatures that lived alongside us, visible only in Primordium. Creatures that gazed upon me and Kyle with the same loving look I reserved for triple chocolate fudge cake. Somehow Kyle had made them disappear, but for all I could tell, it was magic, because how did you use a sight to make something vanish? I wouldn't have believed it if I hadn't just seen it. It was the equivalent of a person using their normal sight to move an object; it just didn't happen.

Only it had.

2

I Didn't Sell My Soul, but I Did Hammer Out a Rent-to-Own Deal

THERE WAS MORE TO SOUL-SIGHT than judging people's souls. Something proactive. Something that involved sentient evil fluff balls. My mind stuttered over the next logical thought: Did I want to know more about it?

Kyle assured everyone that I was fine, that I'd seen a spider and had been frightened, and they believed him. The employees went back to work and the patrons pretended to ignore us once more, though they cast frequent nervous glances at me—and a few at the floor in search of the mysterious spider.

I righted my chair and sat. Sitting meant I was less visible to everyone's curious eyes.

"No," I said softly, then more resolutely. "No, I don't think I'm interested in becoming an illumination enforcer after—"

"*Illuminant* enforcer," Kyle corrected.

"Right. Well. I'm clearly not cut out to do this. You said that was the smallest, ah, evil creature, right?"

"Yes, but you saw how easily it was killed."

I thought he'd made it disappear. No. He'd killed it. Fabulous. "It may have been easy for you, but I don't have what it takes—"

"Nonsense. I'm leaving you a spotless region. You simply need to practice . . . while you get paid."

"But—"

"It is imperative that you assume the role as the region's IE. The position cannot be vacant. Illumination Studios needs you. Otherwise, the region will succumb to evil."

The absurdity of the situation was catching up with me. I leaned back in the chair and crossed my arms. "You're saying that I need to take this job, and if I don't, the world is doomed."

"Hardly doomed. There *are* other people with the ability to use *lux lucis*; it would just take time to find them. In the meantime, you and everyone else in Roseville would be helpless fodder for unchecked evil."

"I'm sorry. I don't think I'm ready for that kind of responsibility." Translation: *I'm not sure I believe this isn't a delusional dream.* I wasn't even going to bother to ask what *lux lucis* was.

Kyle dusted his hands, shrugging his shoulders in good-natured defeat. "Fine. You are free to leave, but just so you know, once the darkness has noticed you, it doesn't forget. You've been coasting up until now, with no region to protect and no need to engage the enemy. But today you did. Tell me, did the imps seem interested in you?"

There was no menace in the question, but his eyes were knowing. I thought of the imp's glowing stare as it crept closer, head cocked to the side in curiosity, and I shivered.

"You killed all the imps who saw me," I reasoned, standing and glancing eagerly toward the door, my ticket back to reality.

"I killed all the ones who saw you *today*. You have the soul of an enforcer, which is very attractive to evil. You've survived this long with no formal training only because I'm incredibly good at keeping my region clean. And you've been lucky. I don't expect you're going to make it much longer. Despite their diminutive size and strength, imps are dangerous. They're the messengers and lackeys of more powerful dark creatures. If they see someone who interests them, they'll be sure to report it."

"Report it?" I sat down heavily. I pictured a large "mommy" imp the size of an elephant, able to leap small buildings to attack to me.

"Just as our side has a hierarchy of . . . people with different and stronger abilities, so, too, does their side. They're not fond of enforcers, with good reason: You can destroy them."

I let that absorb. "Are you telling me my life's in danger?" *Was I actually believing all this?* The answer, unfortunately, was yes.

"Maybe not yet, but it will be soon. Unless you protect yourself."

I'd been successful over the years in convincing myself that I chose not to use soul-sight because I wanted to be normal, or at least not be a metaphysical Peeping Tom. Confronted with the possibility of actively using soul-sight, I could no longer pretend what I felt was anything but fear. It was an ugly truth, and one I didn't want to scrutinize. Especially now that I had a bigger problem.

Kyle must have seen me weakening, and he pressed his point. "You might as well get paid while you learn, right?"

I didn't know if following Kyle back to the office of Illumination Studios was one of the smartest or stupidest things I'd ever done. The final straw that convinced me to take the job—if only until I could figure out how to eradicate my soul-sight, which looked like the only conceivable long-term option—was seeing the sleek two-door Mercedes Kyle drove. I liked everything that implied about my future salary and very little about what it said about my priorities.

Illumination Studios was located among the plethora of two-story, two-tone beige office buildings that had spawned across the Roseville landscape in the early nineties. It came complete with traditional blue-tinted windows that worked like mirrors in the day and turned the building into a fishbowl at night. I discreetly checked my reflection as I walked toward the lobby doors where Kyle waited. I'd brushed the majority of grit from my black skirt during the drive to the office and had done a decent job fixing my shoulder-length walnut brown hair, readjusting the clip that held the top half back from my face.

My green eyes still looked a little wide around the edges and my hands trembled, but if I tucked one hand around the strap of my black purse and made the other stop fidgeting with my suit jacket, I could fake calm.

Kyle led the way across a tiled lobby and down a long carpeted hallway. We passed the doorways to a temp agency and a mortgage company, both bustling with quiet office energy behind tall cubicle walls. The hallway dead-ended at Illumination Studios, with double doors opening to the left into a modest lobby complete with the requisite tall receptionist desk and the company's name spelled out in large, top-lit silver letters across the wall behind the desk. It looked like a normal office, not like the front of some mysterious evil-fighting organization.

"Good day, Sharon," Kyle said, nodding a greeting at the high counter of the receptionist desk without pausing.

When I passed the desk, I spied the short lady seated behind it. Limp brown hair hung in sheets on either side of Sharon's thin head, and the fluorescent lighting made pasty lines of her homely face. She tracked our progress past her workstation with only her flat brown eyes. Her body remained perfectly motionless and she did not return Kyle's greeting or my overly bright, nervous smile.

The office was modest, with a wide hallway defined by beige and rose high-walled cubicles on the left and a glass-enshrouded unlit conference room on the right. At the end of the hallway was a bank of offices, their glass fronts closed off by mini-blinds. Kyle stopped in front of the middle office and knocked on the closed wooden door. I stood discreetly to the side and read the plastic name placard beside the door.

Brad Pitt.

Even as I told myself it couldn't be *the* Brad Pitt, I gleefully ran through several scenarios in which the hunky actor greeted me with a warm handshake, our conversation an easy flirtation followed by his insistence to introduce me to his younger, long-lost, even-more-handsome brother, or possibly his proclamation that I had a face that must be seen on the silver screen, or—

"I think you'll be very pleased with Madison Fox," Kyle said, interrupting my ludicrous fantasies. He held the door half open and remained in the doorway, filling the space so I couldn't see around him. "She's eager and capable. I feel confident handing the enforcer reins of the region over to her."

Brad Pitt's response was muffled by the glass between us. I edged forward to peer around Kyle, but the meat of his words registered, freezing me in place. *Eager? Capable?* Had we been at the same interview?

"Sure thing. Let me leave you to it," Kyle said. He started to turn away from the office but then spun back as if he'd just remembered something. "Would you mind sending my approval off first, though? It's— Well, if I can leave today, I'll be able to get this flat in the Marina District I've had my eye on." Another response from the unseen Brad Pitt. This one made Kyle grin. "Thanks! We should have drinks next time you're in Frisco."

Kyle turned and shook my hand. "It was a pleasure to meet you, Madison. I'm sure you'll be up to speed in no time. Best of luck."

I opened my mouth to point out that I was in no way capable or eager, but Kyle was already walking away.

He ducked into a cubicle, hoisted a messenger bag over his shoulder, and strode out of the office with a cheery wave in my direction and a farewell nod at Sharon. There was a touch of urgency behind his steps. In fact, it looked like Kyle was fleeing—in a controlled, businesslike manner, but fleeing nonetheless.

With dread pooling in my gut, I pivoted to face Brad Pitt's doorway. "Please, come in."

I stepped into the office. My gaze went immediately to the man sitting in the guest chair near the door. If ever Brad Pitt had a dark-skinned, more attractive younger brother, this was him. My brain stumbled over itself to admire him—his broad shoulders and bare forearms, his perfectly rounded and smooth-shaven head, his roasted-almond skin and even darker eyes that swept over me with an almost tangible caress, his lips firm and sculpted, begging for a closer, physical inspection.

"As long as you're not basing your decision on strength, this could work," he said.

I had almost gathered my wits enough to introduce myself when he moved. He stood fluidly, and my eyebrows rose with him. He was over six feet tall, and a lot of that was leg. All of it was muscle.

He stalked out of the office with a single nod to me. I inhaled as he passed; he smelled delicious, like something I hadn't known I'd been craving. I turned to watch his firm ass disappear.

He moves like danger, I thought. A small voice in my head scoffed at the idiotic description; the rest of me made nummy noises in agreement. *Why is he leaving?*

A throat cleared behind me. I spun, cheeks flaming, to notice for the first time the man seated at the desk. He stood and extended his hand across the clean surface to me. I rushed to pump Mr. Pitt's hand.

His hand in mine was small and meaty, much like the rest of him. The top of his shiny balding head barely cleared my shoulders. What hair he had left was gray and clung around the edges of his blotchy white head like a fallen halo.

"It's a pleasure to meet you, Ms. Fox. Please, have a seat," he said with a smile that stretched red lips wide across a pasty face.

I sat in the chair Mr. Dark and Deadly had just vacated. It was still warm from his body and smelled delicious. None of which helped me concentrate on gnomelike Brad Pitt. Pretending that I wasn't blushing bright enough to put Rudolph to shame and that I hadn't been thinking about sex, I set my purse beside me and tried to exude confidence.

"I imagine Kyle went over the particulars of the job, right?"

"Um, yes, the illuminant enforcer position."

"Good."

I opened my mouth to explain that Kyle had misled him in regards to my actual skills, but Mr. Pitt pushed a small stack of papers across his desk, saying, "This outlines the starting pay and benefits. We, of course, need you to begin work immediately."

I glanced down at the top sheet and my mouth clicked shut. The starting pay was more than any of my previous salaries, and definitely more than I'd expected as a junior sales associate. It was more than enough to keep a roof over my head, my car in my possession, and expand my wardrobe substantially.

I knew I should give the job more thought, but if I were honest with myself, I'd already made my decision when I'd left the coffee shop with Kyle. I'd found people who knew what soul-sight was. If there was anyone who could teach me how to eliminate my unwanted ability, it was these people. Kyle had spoken of protecting myself, but the best protection I could think of was not having soul-sight. Without it, evil creatures wouldn't be curious about me and I could lead a normal, oblivious life. And, yes, I'd happily get paid while I learned how to eradicate it.

"You'll find that I'm very fair with my raises, but what you'll be most interested in are the bonuses," Mr. Pitt continued. "I understand the risks that you'll take and the danger that you'll be in. This salary covers the basics. Anything more dangerous gets you a bonus. It's my form of hazard pay."

My doubt, briefly squelched, rose to a fever pitch again. I drowned it with visions of paying rent and a promise to myself that I'd be free of soul-sight long before there was any call for hazardous, bonus-worthy work. "What are 'the basics'?"

"Your daily duties. The basic cleansing of the region."

"What qualifies as more dangerous?"

Mr. Pitt gave me a small smile. "Does this mean you're interested?"

I was well aware that he hadn't answered the question. He hadn't answered either question, really—not to my understanding.

I should have been walking for the door by now. I should have thought the whole experience was some loony joke. I should have gone back to pretending that Primordium didn't exist. Instead, I said, "Kyle already left. You need me. I need to pay rent. I'll take the job if you can offer me a starting incentive."

"Five thousand dollars, and you'll start today."

I reached across the table and shook Mr. Pitt's hand. "Done."

There was all the usual mundane paperwork to fill out and photocopy. It was so ordinary, it made my previous conversation with Kyle seem like a fanciful daydream.

"Is everyone here . . . ?" I trailed off. I didn't even have the terminology to finish the question.

"Everyone here actively works for the CIA," Mr. Pitt said with a froggy smile.

"Hang on, this is a CIA operation?" I was flabbergasted. Maybe I should start believing the *Enquirer*'s government-conspiracy stories about Area 51 and other bizarre "alien" encounters. If Uncle Sam knew about soul-sight—I mean, about Primordium—maybe there was some truth to those stories. After all, if the *Enquirer* had printed stories about imps, I wouldn't have believed them—until today.

"We're active members of the Collaborative Illumination Alliance," Mr. Pitt said. His tone implied anyone who wasn't a member wasn't worth his time. "You're the only enforcer in the office, but we all do our part to eradicate *atrum* and promote *lux lucis*. And, of course, we're a bumper sticker company as well, and we make a small profit from it every year."

"Will I be doing anything with the stickers?"

"Not unless we're incredibly busy and need an extra hand, but that's rare. Standard business hours here are nine to five, Monday through Friday, but enforcer hours are more free-form, as you know. I'll let you judge how much you need to work once you get a feel for our region. Kyle had it down to about fifty hours a week. We're a small region, but not an inactive one."

This may have been the strangest, most bizarre, out-of-this-world job I'd ever had, but it was starting to sound like the best one I'd ever had, too. I was going to do something for the good of humanity, ridding the world of evil—literally. Plus, I was making good money with flexible hours. Best of all, there'd been no mention of used cars, coffee and dry-cleaning pickup, or photocopying and collating—all things I'd learned to loathe in my previous jobs. Maybe using my soul-sight for a few weeks would actually be fun.

"Rose will take you around the region." Mr. Pitt walked me to his office door. "If you have any questions, ask Rose today or me tomorrow. Why don't you show up here at nine tomorrow?"

I found myself nodding. I could do this. It was like any other job, just with a different skill set. A skill set I'd been born with. I should be more than qualified for anything tossed my way.

Feeling a surge of confidence, I followed Mr. Pitt into the heart of a clump of cubicles. Sitting amidst a tropical oasis of plants was a petite Latina. She was all curves and red lips, with long, straight, dark hair. The computer screen behind her was open to a celebrity-gossip Internet page.

"Rose, this is Madison Fox, our new IE," Mr. Pitt said.

"So I gathered."

Rose stood and delicately placed her hand in mine, removing it almost immediately, leaving me with a vague impression that we might have shaken hands, but her welcoming smile put me at ease.

"Will you get her settled in and then show her the boundaries?" Mr. Pitt asked. "She needs to be up and running tomorrow."

"Certainly, boss. Let me shut down."

Mr. Pitt scuttled back to his office while she closed ten different Internet windows and shut off her computer. I watched him over the tops of Rose's cubicle, then peered into the vacant adjoining cubicles.

"Oh, those are Joy's and Will's. They should be in tomorrow." Rose's voice was high and a little nasally, but not off-putting. "Did Brad give you the office tour?"

"Not yet."

"There's not much to it. Here's where all us grunt employees work." She winked. "You've seen Brad's office." She pointed at two cubicles standing alone on the right side of the hall. "The one on the left is yours. Or it will be, once we clean out all of Kyle's extraneous office leavings. The other one is used by the optivus aegis when he's in town."

"Opti-what?"

Rose gave me a curious look. "Optivus aegis. You know, the head honcho enforcer for half the state." When she saw my blank expression, she continued. "I guess every region's got their own name for the position. We call it optivus aegis, and when Niko's working in this area, that's his home base. But he's only here when we've got some baddies too big for our britches."

I tried to look like I was following along.

"Something tells me we'll see him around here soon," Rose said. She pointed toward the bank of offices along the back. "The office to the left of Brad's is for visiting dignitaries."

I didn't even ask.

"The one on the right is for our accountant. She's a part-timer. The skinny door on the far left leads to our break room; it's small, but it has a microwave and a fridge. The door on the far right leads out the back. Let's go out the front."

Sharon watched us leave, her dour look apparently the only expression in her repertoire. It was eerie the way she didn't blink or so much as twitch a finger, only tracked us with her eyes.

Rose held her fingers to her lips when we were around the corner in the public hallway. She was shorter than me by almost a head, even with her red-leather, three-inch-heeled boots. When we exited the lobby, she turned to me.

"Be nice to Sharon. *Always*. You don't want to get on her bad side."

"That was her good side?"

"Yep. You drive. My beast sucks down the gas." Rose patted the chrome bumper of a large yellow Hummer as we walked by.

"Where are we headed?" I asked once we were settled in my green two-door Civic.

"Let's go out Douglas to the freeway. Hand me your phone and I'll input everyone's numbers while we drive."

"Ah . . ." I cast her a quick glance. "I don't have a cell phone. That's not going to be a problem, is it?"

"Do you have bad credit?"

"No." I frowned at her.

"A stalker?"

"No."

"Are you a technophobe?"

"Would I know if I was?"

"What reason could you possibly have for not having a cell phone?"

Confessing that I didn't have anyone I felt I needed to be in constant contact with (read: boyfriend) seemed rather lame.

"Money's been tight."

"Time to let loose."

"We'd better stop by my bank first," I said, picturing my two-digit account balance and then, much more happily, the signing bonus check Mr. Pitt had handed me minutes earlier.

As I drove, it occurred to me that I wasn't going to have to avoid my parents' calls any longer—my previous mature plan. My parents' well-meaning monetary offers, partially suppressed concerns, and unsolicited advice while I was unemployed made me feel guilty—guilty that I hadn't followed in their footsteps, launching a successful career right out of college, and guilty that they still felt they needed to be my financial crutch. Plus, with all their free time now that they were both retired, they were geared up to take on my life as their next fix-it project. The thought made me shudder.

Now that I had a job and money in my bank account, I could confidently assure them I didn't need their support or their master plan for my future. I simply couldn't tell them what the job was.

Maybe this needed a little more thought.

Forty minutes later, I'd deposited my check and was the proud owner of the prettiest phone I'd ever seen. It was sleek, had a screen half the size of my laptop, and the frame was a flashy metallic green. I was in love.

I really wanted to call a bunch of people, or at least my best friend Bridget, and be properly welcomed to the twenty-first century, but Rose and I still had to tour the realm of my new employment.

"We'll get that modified soon," Rose said as we settled back in my Honda. She used her chin to gesture at my pretty phone. I petted it discreetly to soothe its hurt feelings at being so rudely referenced. *You need a name, my pretty,* I thought to my phone. *Sally? Simone? Silly Pants? Oh no, wait: That's me.*

"Modified?"

"Sure. We've got a guy who can load standard enforcer apps. Don't worry about it. Let me program a few numbers you'll need during emergencies."

Just like that, my bubble popped. I kept forgetting about the whole fighting-evil part of my job. *If Kyle said I could do it, then I can. I just have to believe,* I thought as I handed her my phone and started the car. I wasn't reassured that my mental pep talk sounded like it had been copied from the script of a Disney cartoon.

3

I Brake for Firemen

DON'T WORRY, HONEY. YOU'LL DO fine," Rose said. "Head toward I-80 on Douglas. This boulevard is the dividing line of our region. Everything south of it is not our problem."

"Oh. I live over there." I pointed back toward my apartment complex on the south side of Douglas. "I thought I lived in this region."

"Nope. Of course, near the boundaries, things overlap, so you're close enough to count if it matters to you."

"Who is the illuminant enforcer over there?" The title sounded corny when I said it.

"The IE? Summer's been there a few years, and I don't think she has plans of going anywhere soon."

"How many regions are there?"

"In Roseville? Two. East and west. We're east. That's considered Citrus Heights," she said, pointing toward my apartment and Summer's region. "Our region is kind of small, which if you know what's good for you, you won't mention to Brad. Where are you from anyway?"

"The Bay Area." Looking like a fool in front of my new coworker was less appealing than letting her believe I was new in town. Plus, I hadn't exactly lied. Even though I'd lived in Roseville for almost four years now, I'd grown up in Berkeley.

"Huh. Get on the freeway here." I merged onto I-80 going east. "We're everything that side of the freeway," Rose continued, gesturing expansively at the back of Fry's, Home Depot, and the entire eastern horizon.

"Just how much smaller is this region?"

"To give you a comparison, Jacob's region is nearly three times as large as ours. He's the IE for West Roseville—and most of Lincoln and Rocklin, too. His warden holds several regions."

"Did you say 'warden'?"

Rose gave me a long once-over, then touched a fingertip to the back of my hand. "Well, crap." She wiped her fingertip on her skirt. "You haven't worked a region before, have you?"

So much for hiding my ignorance. I tried to sound nonchalant. "Nope."

Her eyebrows shot to her hairline, but all she said was, "A warden is the boss of a region. In your case, that's Brad."

That had an ominous sound to it. I vaguely remembered Kyle mentioning wardens in our surreal interview, back when I thought he was insane. Maybe he still was and I'd merely joined him.

We rode in silence while Rose finished programming a slew of numbers into my phone; then she slipped it into my purse in the backseat. I drove past the Eureka exit, then the Highway 65 exit. The farther we went, the more nervous I got. *If this is considered a small area, I hope the ratio of imps to humans is very, very low.* I eyed all the shops, the huge hospital, and all the houses on the Sierra College hill. My stomach fluttered. Why did I feel like I was in way over my head? *Because you are,* a small voice screamed. I drowned it out with happy thoughts about paying rent, eating out, and buying a new pair of shoes—or twenty.

"What exactly do you do for Illumination Studios?" I finally thought to ask. We'd exited the freeway at Rocklin Road and were cruising past the junior college and the bisecting Sierra College Boulevard named after it.

"I do most of the design and some of the sales, but Joy and Will are a lot better at sales than I am. . . . Oh, you meant non–bumper sticker duties, the stuff I do for the CIA. I'm an empath."

"As in you can tell what I'm feeling?"

"Yep."

"Okay, maybe this is rude or hypocritical, but . . . prove it."

She laughed. "Take a right on Barton Road. Hmm, how can I prove it?" She hummed "Do You Believe in Magic" while she thought. "Well, for starters, you're feeling really skeptical right now." She winked at me. I laughed.

"Okay, that's true but not good proof."

"How about before I met you, I knew the exact moment you saw Niko."

"Who?"

"The *optivus aegis*. Niko Demitrius. Tall guy, skin like Belgium dark chocolate, eyes that could melt your soul. Aha, I see this is ringing a bell."

Mr. Dark and Deadly. Which meant he was an elite enforcer. That wasn't difficult to believe.

"You've got a lot of lust packed into that skinny little body," Rose said.

I blushed to my roots. "You could *feel* that?"

"Mmm-hmm."

"No, wait. That's still not proof. Any woman would have reacted the same."

"Good point. How about this: When I told you we were going to modify your phone, you got protective."

I chanced a glance at her expression. We'd left the city of Rocklin a few miles back, and our surroundings had transformed into rolling rural country landscape. Apartments and shopping centers had given way to white-rail fences and large, sprawling ranch-style homes. We'd passed horses, goats, a few llamas, and more mansions, RVs, trailered boats, and Corvettes than I could count. This was Granite Bay at its finest: big money and coveted acreage.

"You don't have to believe me," Rose said. "I can't see the Primordium dimension and I can't work with *lux lucis*, but I can feel it through my empathy. I can feel the darkness or sickness in people."

I was getting the feeling that *lux lucis* was important, but before I could ask Rose what exactly it was, she switched back to driving directions.

Dutifully, I turned south onto Auburn-Folsom Road, a two-lane major thoroughfare, and kicked my speed up to fifty. "The region continues all the way to Folsom Lake"—Rose gestured east through the million-dollar housing division—"but there's no other connecting road. From here, it's back to Douglas, and we've completed our loop." She paused. "Now you're nervous again. Girl, you gotta trust me. You'll do fine."

Easy for her to say. She wasn't the one who had to root out all the evil in this not-at-all-small-by-my-standards area. It was a hodgepodge of a region, too, with everything from office parks to horse ranches, a college, strip malls, suburban sprawl, and two hospitals. All it needed was a nuclear power plant and it'd be complete. *Good job. Now you're thinking positively.*

Rose pulled a cell phone out of her purse. It was a generic black phone. Nothing like my beautiful phone. *Maybe I should name it Gaea, the green goddess of all cell phones.*

A hideous screech erupted behind my seat, dying down to a metallic warble. I swerved and ducked, frantically checking the backseat for a Godzillaesque creature of evil attached to that predatory roar.

"Watch the road, crazy!" Rose shouted.

I jerked the car back into my lane. "What was that?"

Rose started laughing and reached behind me. She held my phone in front of my face. "Ringy-dingy. Your new lifeline. I was making sure I had your number correct. Sheesh, you're jumpy."

I glared at the phone, then back at the road. How could something so pretty sound so awful? *I dub thee Medusa, you obnoxious, gorgeous thing.*

"Ringtones, that's what you need. I've got my phone programmed with a different ring for each person. So, have you seen any evil lurking around?"

"What? You mean while I've been driving?"

"Yeah. When else?"

"I can't look around in soul—in Primordium while driving! I would crash."

"You're definitely going to have to get over that," Rose said with absolutely no compassion. "Not while I'm in the car, though. Pull over here. You look for evil, I'll look for firemen."

"That's hardly fair," I grumbled. I pulled over in a turn-around space near a fire station. We both got out. I studied the scenery. A few homes across the road. A lot of BMWs, Corvettes, and Cadillacs zooming past on Auburn-Folsom Road. A field behind the fire station with a couple of hedges and a patch of blackberry brambles. I did my own quick search for firemen. I could really do with a dose of handsome.

"Is there some evil, maybe over there?" Rose gestured to the fire station. "Maybe we should take a closer look."

"What should we tell them we're doing?"

"I think your car was sounding funny."

"No, it wasn't— Oh. I see where you're going with that."

"You're a quick one." She rolled her eyes at me.

I blinked. Primordium replaced color, daylight, and familiarity. I braced my hands on my knees and stared at the gray dirt at my feet until gravity rebalanced itself. I took a quick peek at the sky. The cerulean cloudless expanse had been swapped with black—solid, unrelieved black. I could still feel the sun on my face, though I couldn't see it in the sky. For all I knew, I was looking straight at it.

I shuddered and made a point not to look up again. Instead, I scanned the firehouse. There were people upstairs and something small and white just inside the bay doors. *A cat?* I turned to look at Rose. She glowed a pretty, opaque white. It was nice to know that not everyone who worked for the CIA looked like they had a sun stuck up their ass. Unlike Kyle, Rose's features looked like they were cast out of pure white marble, not radiating light. She was also in possession of one of the cleanest souls I'd seen in a long time, aside from my own and Kyle's. Even if I was dangerously deep in a world I knew nothing about, it was reassuring that I was on the good side.

Now why hadn't I thought to look at Mr. Pitt's soul?

Because you're trying not to use this sight, remember?

Too late for that.

I scanned the field. Only the blackberry brambles glowed. They were bright white, a mound of light with tendrils stretching across the dead field. Normally blackberry bushes tended to look sinister with all their thorns and the tenacious, mindless way they choked out other plant life. Now they looked like a beautiful oasis in a field of death.

I knew there had to be wildlife moving among the dead grasses, but the dark stalks were too dense for the small white bodies of rodents and birds to be visible from a distance.

I was about to switch back to normal vision when I saw it. Close to the edge of the fire station, hopping along unaware of my presence, was an imp. It was a little field mouse of an imp; I would have missed it if I hadn't been looking so hard.

"There's an imp over there." I pointed.

"Oh, goodie. Maybe I can peek in a window. And maybe they'll be having a naked wrestling contest."

Rose sashayed across the gravel, heading straight for the imp.

"You can't see it, right?"

"Nope. Take your time."

I trailed after her. In its own dark and sinister way, the imp was remarkably cute. The ones in the restaurant had looked like chinchillas, and this one was a baby. Adorable. I flashed back on the prominent memory of the creatures jumping at Kyle. Maybe I'd overreacted. He hadn't seemed the least bit frightened. Maybe they were just cute. All I would have to do was . . . whatever Kyle had done. Squint or something. Instinct would kick in and, *poof*, no more imp.

Unfortunately, the only instinct babbling in my head was telling me I needed to go the other way, not toward the harmless-looking fluff of evil. *Don't quit before you try,* I scolded. *You got this job because people knew you could do it. Get busy proving them right.* I tiptoed closer.

Rose was oblivious in her hunt for more tangible prey. I was starting to believe my own hype, too. *It's so small. How bad can it be?*

Then the imp turned, cocked its head, and started to bounce straight at me, ignoring Rose.

"Shit. Kyle was right. It recognizes me." I froze.

Rose turned to look at me, incognizant of the fluffy bundle of evil bopping our way. "Of course it does, silly. You're staring at it."

It slowed and came to an alert stop near Rose's feet, but its little glowing eyes never left me. I forced myself to kneel.

"What are you trying to do? Get all buddy-buddy with it?"

"It's very small. I can't do my thing standing." *My thing?* If only I knew what that was.

I gave the imp my best squint. Nothing happened. I pictured laser beams of goodness shooting from my eyes, melting the imp to a puddle of goo. Still nothing. How *had* Kyle done this? I should have spent less time rolling on the coffee shop floor and more time watching.

I tried a wide-eyed glare, a blink, a wink. Nothing.

"Are you flirting with it?"

The imp shuffled forward. Up close, it was even cuter. I'd been right when I thought of a baby chinchilla. It was covered in soft down and had dainty ears and delicate feet that seemed too small to support its weight. I reached out for it very slowly.

"Hi, little fella."

"Don't go getting crazy ideas about taming the bugger. You're not an Illuminea."

"A what?"

I glanced at Rose. The imp opened its mouth in a perfect round circle the size of my wrist. Row after row of ebony shark teeth glinted, impossibly long. *Oh shit.* Piercing little eyes blinked at me. We jumped at the same time. The imp aimed for my throat. I aimed for a few miles straight behind me. We both missed—me by a much larger margin.

"What's happening?" Rose demanded. She backed up quickly. The imp pounced again, and this time I saw tiny razors at the tips of its paws.

"Get back! It's attacking!" I'd landed on my butt in the dirt when I'd jumped. I didn't have time to stand now. Scrambling on all fours, I scooted back, avoiding several pounces. With the third pounce, I kicked it. When my foot connected with the scrap of hell spawn, the imp slowed, like it was moving through water. Only the water was my foot. I screamed.

"That's it. Get it!" Rose cheered.

I rolled frantically to my knees and leapt to my feet. The imp was a few feet behind me.

"Get in the car," I yelled. I grabbed Rose's arm and pushed her in the direction of the safe haven known as my Honda.

"What's here? I don't feel anything. What is it?"

The imp jumped at me. I lurched to the side, swinging my hips out of its high-flying reach.

"Are you dancing?" Rose gawked. She was half in the car. Good enough for me. I sprinted for the driver's side. "Shoot. I hate being in the dark." Rose slid into the car and we slammed our doors at the same time. I watched the imp hop toward the bumper in the rearview mirror. I fumbled blindly with my seat belt, starting the car with the other hand.

"Hey, look. There's a fireman," Rose said.

The bright glow of a man came into view in my mirror. I thrust the car into gear and peeled out onto the road. Gravel sprayed up under the car. I remembered to look for traffic at the last possible second as we bounced onto pavement. Then I glued my eyes on the rearview mirror and watched until I could no longer see the wee evil creature.

"You totally dusted him! And he was cute!"

Shaking, I blinked. The world rushed at me like a sci-fi time warp, all color and lights and nausea. It took me a moment to realize the effect was not derived solely from vertigo, and I eased the car from seventy back down to fifty.

"What happened back there?" Rose demanded.

"It tried to bite me! It was so cute and soft and then there were all these teeth—oh my God, I've never seen so many teeth—and it jumped at me. It went *through* my friggin' foot! Through it!"

"Whoa, calm down there, chica. Are you telling me we dusted one of the finest firemen I've seen because you were afraid of an imp? A tiny little fuzz ball of darkness that can hardly think for itself?"

"You don't know what you're talking about," I said stiffly. I had to focus to relax my death grip on the steering wheel and quell the last of the nausea. "It was pretty intense."

"Was there a vervet or something?"

"A what?"

"Please tell me there was at least a horde of imps."

Heat crept up my neck, washing away the adrenaline. "There was only one—but it had a horde of teeth."

"Was it larger than your new cell phone?"

"Are you making fun of me?"

"Hell yes! So that show—all that rolling around with your panties in the air—wasn't for the firemen?"

Arrggh. Not again!

"No."

"Why didn't you dissipate it?"

"I tried, but I couldn't figure out how to give it the right look."

"The right *what*?"

"You know, how to squint my eyes right."

"How to *squint* . . . Wait. You mean you've never . . . ?" She waggled her fingers like a magician making a rabbit disappear.

"It's my first day!"

Rose groaned and dropped her head into her hands. "We are so dead."

4

CLEVERLY DISGUISED AS A RESPONSIBLE ADULT SINCE 2007

I DON'T UNDERSTAND," BRAD PITT SAID for the third time. "You're twenty-five. You found the ad. You must know something. What did Kyle tell you?"

I sat in the same chair I'd accepted the job in—gosh, was that only two hours earlier? I glanced down at myself. Yep, still wearing my very expensive, dry-clean-only interview suit that was now hopelessly ruined. I'd done landscaping projects at my parents' house without getting this filthy.

Focus, I reminded myself. Mr. Pitt had come around to the front of his desk and was standing over me, as only a short, fat, bulging-eyed, ruddy-faced man could. *This is it. One day on the job and I'm already fired. That's a new record for me.*

"He didn't tell me anything," I answered honestly. It sounded insolent to my ears, so I rushed to add, "We talked a bit, and he had me look around in Primordium." I hated how *Star Trek*–fake *Primordium* sounded when I said it.

"Nothing else?"

"Um . . . he called some imps to him. I guess they couldn't resist." I thought about the imp, about its circular maw of teeth, about the way it felt as it had slid through my foot.

Sitting in the well-lit office and rationally weighing the possibility of relinquishing my advance and the nice salary—even if I'd had it for only two hours—against facing off against the tiny imp, the money definitely came out on top. And, of course, there was the guiding beacon of hope that I could figure out how to get rid of soul-sight and never see another imp again. "Kyle did something to them, but I wasn't in the right position to see."

"What position were you in?"

"I . . . I was on the floor."

Rose, who was sitting beside me in a matching chair, raised her eyebrow at me.

"I had, uh, tripped."

"Sort of like you 'tripped' at the fire station?" she asked, making quotes with her fingers.

"Yeah."

Rose rolled her eyes.

"Crap on a corn dog!" Mr. Pitt shouted. "Of all the enforcers to walk through my door, I get the village idiot."

I cringed in my seat to avoid the flying spit. I eyed Rose, wondering if she could feel my emotions. I still wasn't sure if I believed her, but if she really was an empath, I didn't want her to feel my growing humiliation. It was bad enough that she could see it.

"Tell me again what happened," Mr. Pitt demanded.

"Do you want me to reenact it?" Rose asked.

"We were driving the region," I said loudly, giving her a glare, "and Rose wanted to pull over to ogle—"

"To let Madison impress me with her skills." Rose tossed me her own dirty look and I gave her a sweet smile.

"Then the imp saw me and attacked. It was ferocious. It had more teeth than could fit in a body its size. It wasn't logical."

"They're not logical. They're coalesced bits of evil. So what did you do when it attacked?"

Rose and I shared a glance. "Well, I wanted to get Rose to safety. Then I tried to kick the imp, but it passed right through my foot."

"And your *lux lucis*?"

"You mentioned that earlier and I meant to ask—"

"You don't know how to use *lux lucis*? The energy that destroys *atrum*?"

"Uh, *atrum*? Maybe you can show me how to, you know, use *lux lucis*?" Though I was trying my best to behave like a proactive employee, judging by the deepening purple shade of Mr. Pitt's face, I was saying the exact *wrong* thing.

"This is . . . I felt you . . . We can't run a region with a . . ." He waved his hand toward me, sputtering and spitting his way to the back corner of his office. I thought he was going to punch the wall, but instead he dropped his hands to his sides and stilled. With his back to us, he took several long, loud breaths, fists clenching and unclenching. Then he strode to his desk, jammed a stubby middle finger down on the speakerphone, and punched zero. "Sharon, get me Doris!"

We all sat in silence for a minute. I wasn't sure where to look. I couldn't stare at Mr. Pitt, and every time his gaze settled on me, my whole body wanted to curl up. Rose gathered her large purse and stood.

"My work here is done," she announced. "I'm hungry."

Mr. Pitt shooed her out of the office as Sharon's voice droned from the phone: "Doris. Line one."

Another button crunched under a stubby-fingered jab. I watched Rose leave with envy.

"Doris, it's Brad Pitt."

"I figured. No one else I know has a gargoyle secretary." Her voice was gravelly and deep through the speakers.

"I've got a little problem here." Mr. Pitt flopped back in his chair, propped his elbows on the armrest, and steepled his hands together. "Kyle got recruited and I've got a new IE here who doesn't know bubkes."

"I'm retired, Brad."

"I'm up shit creek. You'll be up shit creek soon, too, if we leave this region in our new IE's hands."

"You've got Niko. Let her learn from the best."

Yes, please, I thought, casting my vote with Doris.

"Niko's in Redding, and he doesn't have time to babysit a rookie."

"And I do?"

Mr. Pitt didn't say anything.

"What about spunk?" Doris finally asked. "I'm not interested in the ones without spunk."

Mr. Pitt made a noncommittal sound. "Rose said she can move pretty fast. In the wrong direction, but fast."

"How does she compare to Kyle?"

"I think it's safe to say she shares no qualities with Kyle."

"I've got plenty of spunk," I interjected, feeling the need to stand up for myself.

"That remains to be seen," Mr. Pitt said.

"Humph. Sounds weak to me. What you need is another enforcer."

I was in something—I still wasn't sure what—way over my head, and I was scared. This wasn't just looking at people's souls. This was dealing with creatures that had razor teeth and the ability to move *through* solid matter—mainly, me. If Kyle was to be believed, these horrid little creatures were going to be seeking me out soon. I'd announced myself today, unwittingly, and apparently there was no going back. I didn't want to think about what would happen if Mr. Pitt changed his mind, and it wasn't my financial problems that had me worried now.

But it wasn't fear that made my hands tremble. My pride was stinging. I'd humiliated myself in front of dozens of people at Starbucks and again in front of an untold number of cute unseen firemen. My clothes were filthy. My hair desperately needed to be washed. And my world had been turned on its head just hours earlier with the realization that not only was I *not* the singular person on the planet with soul-sight, but also there were legions of others and I was supposed to be battling against evil like some comic book hero. My normal life—the one I'd possessed just that morning—was slipping through my fingers, and Mr. Pitt had the audacity to be upset with *me*?

"What I need is *training*!" I shouted, anger overriding caution—and professionalism. "I haven't even been here a full day. How can you expect me to know everything?"

"You said she was new, Brad. She sounds old. And needy," Doris said.

"You sound ancient and unhelpful," I shot back.

Mr. Pitt glared at me. "It's a special circumstance. She doesn't know how to use *lux lucis*."

There was a pause. "Are you sure she's an IE?"

"She's not yet. Can you do it?"

"I'm leaving for LA tomorrow. It'll have to be tonight, late. Around ten," Doris said.

"Good." Mr. Pitt snatched up my résumé and rattled off my address. "She'll be ready for you."

"You better make this worth my while."

Mr. Pitt sighed. "Of course, Doris." He disconnected the call with a jab of his middle finger.

I sat back in the leather chair, spine stiff, not sure what had just happened.

"That's that."

"What's what?" I asked.

Mr. Pitt gave me a withering look. "Go home. You wanted training, you're getting training."

"But tonight?"

"You heard her. She's leaving tomorrow. We can't wait. I knew I should have tested you, but I assumed . . . I mean, you're in your twenties!" He sighed. "You're a walking target of weakness. It's like advertising that we want evil to move into our region."

"Thanks," I grumbled, feeling all warm and fuzzy. He gave me a sharp look, and I belatedly remembered he was my boss. "For the training. Who's Doris?"

"She used to be an illuminant enforcer. One of the best."

I stopped by Miabella Gelato on the way home. If ever there was a day that I deserved a tub of tiramisu gelato for dinner, it was today. When I got home, I took two steps into my apartment, locked the door behind me, tossed my purse and leather résumé folder onto the lone gray recliner, and flopped to the floor. Mr. Bond, my obese Siamese cat, greeted me with a loud meow and took full advantage of my prone position to drape across my torso, repositioning himself with painful jabs of his feet until he lay completely on top of me, his face inches from mine. He purred happily and head-butted my chin. I struggled to breathe beneath his twenty-two pounds. I considered pushing him off me—this was my nice interview outfit, after all—but after the abuse this skirt, shirt, and jacket had seen today, a few cat hairs and puncture marks from his claws weren't going to be noticeable.

"I had quite a day."

Mr. Bond meowed encouragingly.

"Do you know there are little evil creatures called imps?"

He meowed again. I scratched his chin.

"Then why didn't you tell me?"

Mr. Bond launched from my chest, and I gasped air into my compressed lungs. He trotted to his empty food bowl. Groaning, I got to my feet and obediently scooped some dry kibble into his bowl.

My phone rang as I was peeling off my jacket. I considered not answering until I checked caller ID.

"How'd the interview go?" my best friend, Bridget, asked without bothering with a proper greeting.

"Oh my God. You're not going to believe me," I said. Or maybe she would. Bridget was the only person I'd ever told about soul-sight. Perversely, she thought what I could do was a good thing and she didn't understand why I didn't use it more often. My definition of a good thing was a pint of triple-chocolate ice cream or no-strings-attached buckets of cash, not soul-sight.

"That bad?" Bridget asked.

"Worse. But I got the job."

"You're not making any sense."

"It's a long story."

"Well, I'm getting out of here in about an hour. Meet me at the Golden Goose. I want all the details."

I walked down the hall with the cordless phone and glanced at my reflection in the bathroom mirror. "That ought to give me enough time to get cleaned up."

"Okay, now I'm really curious. See you then. Oh—and congratulations, right?"

"I think so. Bye."

I did my best not to think for the next hour. A hot shower helped. So did blasting Lorde while I dressed. By the time I left, I was feeling almost normal again.

I drove a route that happened to take me past the veterinary clinic Mr. Bond loved. I tried to catch a glimpse of the people inside as I flew by at forty-five miles per hour. Okay, so maybe Mr. Bond didn't love going to the vet—that'd be like me saying I loved to go to the gynecologist. Maybe I was the only one who looked forward to our visits to the Love and Caring Veterinary Clinic.

The name was a charming play on the main vet's name: Dr. Alex Love. There were three things I knew about the doctor: (1) he was delectable—tall, fit, and unmarried, with a smile that could be used as a defibrillator for women of all ages; (2) he had devoted his life to helping animals, instantly earning him my adoration; and (3) he had graduated from UC Davis two years before me. I berated myself yet again for not having the foresight to run into him on campus my freshman or sophomore year.

I'd met him only twice: once to get Mr. Bond fixed, the other time to have Mr. Bond's shots brought up to date. Both times I'd left feeling more dazed than my drugged cat. There's something about a confident, animal-loving, incredibly handsome, single male that gets my juices going. Frankly, I think I'd have to be dead to not feel a flutter in my pulse just at the sight of him.

I spent the rest of my drive daydreaming amusing bedroom puns on the doctor's last name and erotic situations in which they wouldn't sound corny.

Bridget's silver Prius was parked under a lamp in the nearly empty parking lot in front of the Golden Goose. I pulled into the space next to it. Although it was just the two of us, I'd still dressed up in dark skinny jeans, low boots, and a green cotton scoop-neck shirt that had enough gathers to create an optical illusion of cleavage—if you didn't look too close. I felt cute without being slutty, but the outfit wasn't exactly cold-November-weather wear. I jogged to the door and shivered when I slipped into the warm interior.

The Golden Goose was a cross between a swanky lounge and a dive, with pool tables and a jukebox on one side, couches and leather chairs on the other, and a U-shaped bar that protruded into the middle of the room to act as a natural divider.

I waved to Bridget, who had snagged a couch, and wound my way through the seating to her side. Aside from a few men bellied up to the bar and a group of college students at the pool tables, we had the place to ourselves.

"Bridget, I'm doomed," I said, flopping down on the sofa next to her.

Bridget rolled her green eyes, familiar with my melodrama. "Did your freshman spring break photos finally get posted on Facebook?"

"Worse."

"I thought you said you got the job?" She signaled the bartender, who indicated he'd be right over.

"I did."

"Then what's the problem, Dice?"

Dice was Bridget's nickname for me, stretching the verisimilitude of an abbreviation of my name: Ma-Dice-on. She'd started calling me Dice when we were still in college together, saying I ran my life like every decision was made by rolling a die. I guess that was her way of saying I was flighty. I didn't take it personally. I knew how it looked. Changing majors four times in as many years doesn't lead people to think you're on a stable path to anywhere. The nickname had stuck— partially because I liked it. It fit, though not for the reasons Bridget thought. My life had always felt a little out of my control, like the gods were toying with me—the fantasy of them playing dice with my fate was a fittingly humorous, melodramatic thought.

"I need a drink first." I ordered a peach margarita, and Bridget ordered a Long Island iced tea and a plate of nachos for us to share. I had training tonight, but that was several hours away. One drink wasn't going to impair me.

Despite the fact that Bridget had been at work for her usual ten-hour day, she looked refreshed. Her bright red hair hung around her shoulders in waves, still kinked from being trapped in a bun all day. Her gray pencil skirt had subtle cream pinstripes that perfectly matched her blouse. Her feet were strapped into shoes that, while sexy, would have murdered my feet in minutes. She looked exactly like what she was: a woman who had her life together.

If we hadn't been roommates in college, I knew we never would have met or become friends. We'd bonded over boys and music tastes and shared activities, but there wasn't much else we had in common. Bridget had always had her life in order, even as a freshman. She'd had a four-year plan followed by a master's plan, and she'd never strayed off course. Now, at twenty-six, she was on the fast track to becoming partner at Cable and Weintraub law offices, owned a home in a posh subdivision just outside of Roseville, drove a Prius, and had a closet full of shoes two sizes too small for sharing. Compared to my unsuccessful career and paycheck-to-paycheck lifestyle, it was a wonder I didn't hate her.

"All right. Tell me what's distressing you," Bridget said, settling back into the couch with her drink.

"We could start with how many people saw my underwear today. Or would you prefer to start at the point where I realized that the job advertised had been a front for a position with a wacky society of people who like to refer to themselves as the CIA? Or maybe we should begin at the point where I nearly got fired."

"*The* CIA?"

"The Collaborative Illumination Alliance."

Bridget was leaning forward now, expression intent. "Hang on. You have the job and you want to keep it?" I nodded. "And you don't want to sue?" I shook my head. "Not even over the panties thing?" I grimaced and shook my head again. Bridget studied my face. After a moment, she relaxed back against the couch again. "In that case, I can't decide between the underwear or the front. You pick, but tell me *everything*."

I did. She was as shocked as I had been that the junior sales associate position had been a cover-up for an illuminant enforcer position (after I explained what an IE was, which she was thrilled by). I told her about Kyle and seeing him glow, and she immediately wanted to know if I could glow that bright, too (not unless I was set on fire). I told her about the imps, and she was appreciably awed and frightened, loyally agreeing she would have ended up on the floor, too.

"Only, after I flashed everyone, I probably would have run screaming," she said.

"I wanted to, but Kyle took care of the imps."

"Took care of them as in he snuggled them up in a blanket and fed them?"

"The way a mafia mob boss would. *Poof.* No more imp."

Bridget's eyes widened as this sank in. "You mean, your soul-sight—"

"Has a purpose." I grinned at her round-eyed expression. I explained that as an IE, my duty was to kick evil-creature butt. When I said it out loud, it sounded completely insane, but Bridget never once questioned the veracity of my story.

"I always knew there had to be a reason," she said.

"Other than the pervy reasons?"

She rolled her eyes. "Wait, didn't you say you already almost got fired?"

I finished my tale, describing the portion of Roseville under my jurisdiction—Bridget was happy she lived in my region; I felt a little sick at the thought that I was now responsible for the well-being of her soul—the horror of the imp's attack, its impossible number of teeth, my pathetic reaction, and finally Mr. Pitt's rage.

"It's your first day on the job—not even that: It's the day you were interviewed! What does he expect?" Bridget demanded.

"Apparently most IEs have figured all this stuff out all by themselves by my age," I said. "So he thought I'd be ready to step into Kyle's shoes. Obviously I can't, which is why I have training tonight."

"Tonight?" Bridget glanced at her watch. "It's almost eight."

"The crotchety lady said she'd be by around ten. I got the feeling that she wanted to make me squirm awhile. Instead, I'm here with you, and this has been the highlight of my day."

Bridget raised her glass in a toast. "To finally finding your life purpose."

I lowered my glass. "Life purpose? This is just a job."

"Maybe. But think about this. You haven't been able to stick with anything since we met, and nothing's stuck with you, but the whole time you've had this ability to see the world in Primordium." She winked at me for her correct use of the new terminology. "And now you find out that you can do something with it. I don't think the universe could light up a bigger neon sign for you."

She had dropped her hand when I did, and now she raised it again. "To finding *a* new purpose," she amended.

I clinked my glass against hers and drank, my thoughts spinning.

"Don't look now, but there's a cute guy at the bar who's been staring at us for the last ten minutes. I think he's working up the nerve to come over."

I rolled my eyes at her, but that didn't stop me from trying to get a discreet glance.

Bridget flashed me a knowing grin. "Here he comes," she whispered. Much louder, she said, "I'm so proud of you, Madison. We should celebrate."

"If you're celebrating, maybe I could buy you both another drink," said a rough male voice behind me.

The man walked around the low table that held our nachos and into my line of sight. Bridget was right: He was cute, in a very disarming way.

He couldn't have been much taller than my five feet ten, though his gelled brown hair gave him an extra inch or so. I pegged him to be a banker or maybe a higher-paid office drone in management, judging by his well-pressed black slacks and light blue shirt with subtle gray pinstriping that matched his black and gray tie. His shirt matched his eyes perfectly. It was a very pleasing effect, and I wondered if he knew it.

He flashed us an unsure smile, his eyes darting between us. "Or maybe I'm interrupting?"

"Nope," Bridget said. "Have a seat. We're celebrating my best friend's new job."

The man eased into a chair across from Bridget. "Congratulations. What's the new job?"

"Bumper stickers," I said before Bridget could tell the truth. Just because she believed me often made her forget that others wouldn't. "It's not the most exciting thing, but at least it pays well."

"Oh, I don't know. I've never met anyone in bumper stickers before."

His easy grin made my pulse kick up a notch. Bridget caught my eye and cocked an eyebrow. I gave her a slight nod. Cute, blue-eyed man had made it through the first round.

We introduced ourselves, shaking hands with him. His name was Tim, he was new to Roseville, and he had large warm hands. He asked what we were drinking, then headed for the bar. All traces of his nervousness had disappeared as we'd introduced ourselves, and I found myself thankful once again to be on the receiving end of the traditional pickup. The guys had the nerve-wracking part.

The bar was still virtually empty, so Bridget and I had time only to solidify our exit strategies before Tim returned. Mine was set for me by Doris, and Bridget agreed that she'd leave when I did.

Bridget and I flirted our way through the next half hour, filling Tim in on the local scene, good places to shop and eat, and from Bridget, good places to buy a home if he decided to stay in the area. Bridget's enthusiasm for real estate was contagious, and while Tim had started the conversation seemingly more interested in me, by the end, he was fascinated with Bridget. She tended to have that effect on men. With her wavy red hair and large green eyes, Bridget looked guileless and sweet, but once men realized that she had more brains than the average woman, many found the juxtaposition enchanting.

"You're out of your mind, dude!"

The shout turned every head in the bar toward the pool tables and the circle of college kids that now crowded around two men, who had cue sticks clutched in their white-knuckled fists. Bridget trailed off, and Tim turned to watch the men, too. The last song on the jukebox ended, and the bar was unnaturally quiet as the bizarre fight unfolded.

"Linux requires you to *think*."

"You might as well be programming in DOS. The eighties called; they want their OS back."

"I can see how the simpleton interfaces of Windows pander to a poser like you," the first man countered.

"Right. Because ugly equals quality? I guess Bill Gates didn't get the memo."

"Bill Gates wouldn't know quality if it was shoved up his ass."

"I'll shove quality up your ass. Bend over!"

The men lunged for each other. The first got in a good jab to the other's gut with the thin end of his cue stick, but the other followed with a swing to the jabber's arm. The meaty sound of the cue stick hitting flesh made me flinch. In a flash, the bartender vaulted the bar, his wiry frame serving him well as he slithered through the small crowd, then dodged the flying cue sticks and fists to pull the two guys apart.

Bridget and I shared a wide-eyed look.

"That never happens here," Bridget assured Tim. We'd been coming to this bar for the last two years, and we'd never seen so much as a raised-voice argument. I peeked at the face of Tim's watch. "Shoot. We've got to get going."

"I'll walk you both out," Tim suggested.

"Thank you, but I've got to freshen up," I said. I might have accepted his offer a moment ago, but witnessing the fight had raised my danger radar. Tim was undoubtedly perfectly safe, but I didn't feel like walking with him to an empty parking lot now.

Bridget took her cue from me, and we bid farewell to Tim—after he got Bridget's phone number.

Five minutes later, we exited the bar and hurried through the crisp November air to where we'd parked our cars under a lamp.

"Call me and tell me how tonight goes," Bridget said.

"I'm sure it'll be a piece of cake."

5

Welcome to the Dark Side. Are You Surprised We Lied about the Cookies?

I GOT HOME WITH TIME TO spare, so after giving Mr. Bond attention and treats, I retrieved Medusa from the bottom of my purse and entered my friends' and parents' numbers. I considered once again calling my parents. I wanted to tell them I had a job, even if I couldn't tell them any specifics.

I'd hinted at my ability to see souls to them once as a teenager. They'd taken me to see a psychologist. If I let them know about my evil-fighting skills now, I was sure they'd make it their mission to get me back into therapy. When I told them about the job, it'd have to be the one that I had originally thought I'd been interviewing for. A nice, normal office job.

I considered calling to tell them at least that much—to avoid any well-meant meddling in my life, if nothing else—but then I worried Doris would show up in the middle of the call, and I couldn't think of a plausible explanation to be training in the middle of the night for a sales position at a bumper sticker company.

I didn't want to admit to myself, but I was anxious about Doris's imminent arrival. I'd cooled down since my outburst in Mr. Pitt's office, and now I was beginning to regret my rudeness.

"This is what happens when you let your mouth do the thinking," I told myself.

What if she didn't show up just to teach me a lesson? What if she came and was really mean?

"She sounded like a little old lady. How tough can she be?" I asked Mr. Bond. He batted at a rope mouse, pounced, and bit into it, shaking his head vigorously from side to side. "You're not helping."

Abandoning the mouse, he darted through the kitchen and back, racing behind the TV in a flurry of flying claws. I tossed him his mouse. He came out of hiding claws first. The mouse never stood a chance.

Since Medusa was still in my hand, I scrolled through all the people Rose had entered. I didn't recognize the majority of the names. I nearly dropped the phone when I saw Niko's name and number. Niko Demitrius. Mr. Dark and Deadly. Too bad I didn't have a reason to call him.

I spent several minutes imagining it was Niko instead of Doris I was waiting for, but when those fantasies began to stagnate, I decided to try my luck at programming ringtones.

It was easy to pick a ringtone for Bridget (Shakira's "Ready for the Good Times") and my mom and dad (Beethoven's Symphony No. 5). It took a little longer to select "Hail to the Chief" for Brad Pitt. Choosing a ringtone for Niko was the hardest. I needed something subtle, a song that didn't say every molecule of estrogen in my body went into overdrive when I saw him. After wracking my brain for several long minutes, logic prevailed over my imagination and over my ego: The likelihood of the modelesque elite enforcer of Northern California calling me was zilch. Which meant it didn't matter what I picked. After that, it took me only a moment to program Justin Timberlake's "SexyBack" as his ringtone.

I jumped at the sharp rap on my door and rushed across the room to open it.

"Third floor, eh?" a diminutive gray-haired whirlwind greeted me. She brushed past me into the front room. "Good thing I do spinning every day, or I might have had to play Romeo down there."

I shut the door behind her.

"Look, I'm sorry about what I said on the phone," I began.

"Water. Bridge. No worries, dear."

Doris made a beeline for Mr. Bond, who obligingly trotted up to sniff her fingers. She had the short, permed hair of grandmas everywhere, sneakers, elastic-banded jeans, and a sweater that had two felt old ladies holding up a banner that said "I Like to Get Knotty." Mr. Bond stuck his head in her enormous leather purse and meowed happily.

"Cute cat. Got a man?"

"No." The "not that it's any of your business" part of the sentence came through in my tone.

"Too bad, but I guess it makes this easier. I tried to explain what I did to only one of my husbands, and he tried to force me into a loony bin. Instead, I took his house and called it even. You should find a man, though. This job can be hard without the support."

"I'm sure I'll manage."

Doris snorted. "Is that all you're wearing? We're going to be out in the elements."

I gestured to my sweater and jacket lying on the back of my dining room chair.

"Good. Glad you're not one of those silly women who puts fashion before health."

Personally, I thought I looked quite fashionable in my sweater and coat, but that wasn't a conversation I was going to have with a woman who had felt people on her sweater. I slipped on my extra layers, gave Mr. Bond a farewell pat, and followed Doris outside.

"Whew—these stairs!" she exclaimed on the way down, but I had to jog to keep up. "We'll take my car. At least we'll be prepared that way."

Groaning to myself, I followed her across the dark parking lot, expecting a Buick or Cadillac. I was shocked when she stopped next to a car buried in the shadows of two minivans. The thing didn't even come up to my waist. A Buick suddenly didn't seem so bad.

I folded myself into the toy car. Doris was already in place, her seat pushed so close to the steering wheel that a thicker sweater would have gotten in the way.

"I don't think I've ever been in a car so small."

"Mazda Miata. Best car out there. Not like those metal death traps. It *reacts*." She laughed as she zipped out of the space. My seat belt caught, and I braced a hand against the dash. "Marilyn is like an extension of my body, like we're fused together when I drive. We're quick. And our average age is thirty-three."

I peered around me at the hubcaps of cars she rocketed past on the boulevard. *Please let us be more visible than I feel.*

"Brad seems to think you're still wet behind the ears, Madison, so I'll start at the beginning and you can stop me if I'm covering information you already know, okay?" Doris didn't wait for my response before launching into her lecture. "Evil, darkness, whatever you want to call it, is about as predictable in where it clusters as you'd expect." She downshifted before a corner, then floored it through the curve like a race car driver. I gripped the edges of my seat and checked the mirrors like I was the driver. "It grows in low-income areas, anywhere abandoned, near bars, tattoo parlors, and head shops."

"That sounds a bit stereotypical."

"With reason. It also forms in wealthy areas where corruption is not as visible to the naked eye, so don't think I'm a reactionary old woman. For training, we're going to the obvious areas."

I grabbed the dash as we slid between two SUVs.

"Sometimes I feel like I should be able to slide under those beasts," Doris told me gleefully. "They're like the dinosaurs of the road, and I'm the dragonfly!" She looked over at me and cackled. "You should see your face, girl. You need to lighten up if you're going to last."

"I'll keep that in mind."

She rolled her eyes at me, then thankfully focused on the road again. "Light, good—again, whatever you want to call it—grows, too," Doris said, picking up her lecture where she'd interrupted herself. "I spent many of my enforcer years as a real estate agent. Move a few good people into an area, and they can change the whole balance with very little effort on your part. And if a neighboring enforcer pissed me off, I'd stick 'em with the bad people."

"How can you tell if someone is really good?"

"You can see it in Primordium. You *are* an enforcer, right? So tell me what made you stop using it? What horrible event lurks in your past, kid?"

"What do you mean?"

Doris slowed to pull into a neighborhood. We cruised through evenly spaced streetlights on the quiet street. Everyone was inside, enjoying late-night TV or asleep in their beds, somewhere I'd like to be.

"Come on. I'm not stupid. Neither of us would be here if something hadn't spooked you in your teens. You don't get to be an ignorant old woman like you unless you've had a bad experience in the past.

Otherwise, you'd be training the next IE now, not me."

"I'm hardly old," I said.

"By the time I was your age, I'd transferred twice to tougher regions just to give myself a challenge. Out with it."

I thought about refusing to tell her, but there was something confidant-inspiring about the cocoon of the darkened car and the sleepy street. Especially knowing I was talking to someone who might understand.

"I was fifteen, no sixteen. I really liked this boy. He was seventeen. A senior. Real cute." God, Steve had been gorgeous. A football star with charisma. It was so cliché that I couldn't stand it now. Of course, then I'd been a bundle of hormones and thrilled to think my life might follow a movie plot—and I had thought I was head deep in the kind of love Shakespeare wrote about. "I couldn't believe he'd noticed me, let alone asked me to the prom."

By then I'd been using my soul-sight long enough to know what I was seeing. I thought I was getting pretty good at judging the level of evil in a person based on their soul. I couldn't correlate a particular shade of smut with any particular crime or immoral offense, but I thought I could tell who was really bad from who occasionally stole candy from the grocery store bins or lied to their parents about their weekend activities.

"Back then, I checked everyone in soul—in Primordium."

"No, tell me your word for it," Doris said.

"I called it 'soul-sight.' I know, it's corny."

"And only half true. You see people's souls in Primordium. You also see their health, their energy levels. It's more like life-sight. Sometimes a sick person can look as bad as an evil person."

"How can you tell the difference?"

"Practice. Something you've obviously been avoiding. Tell me more about the boy. I bet you he wasn't just white."

"Well, no. He was mostly white, a bit gray in the hands, but nothing alarming. So we went to the prom. Halfway through, Steve—that was his name—suggested we go to a party at a friend's house he knew in the city." I had been having too much fun with him to say no. I'd felt wild and adult. I'd felt ready. For *it*. Steve wasn't a virgin, and he'd been sweet to me all night. When we'd started making out in a quiet bedroom at the party house, I'd been an eager participant. Until he lowered his pants. His groin had been so dark in soul-sight it had looked like he was wearing oil for briefs.

"And?" Doris prompted, jolting me back to the dim interior of her car.

"Well, one thing led to another—"

"You had sex," Doris supplied. She grinned at my discomfort.

"No. Yes. I mean, we were going to. But while most of him was light gray, parts of him—important parts—were black."

"Ah."

"He didn't like it when I told him I wanted to stop, either." Seeing his black groin had worked like a bucket of cold water to the face, making me realize I was going too fast for my comfort. Steve, however, thought we weren't going fast enough. He'd held me down when I'd started to get up, and his light gray hands had boiled with black flecks that spread, coating his palms, bleeding onto me, tainting my soul around my wrists.

I remember screaming, terrified. I went wild, thrashing and fighting with strength I hadn't known I possessed. I'd landed a knee to his groin, which finally gave me the upper hand.

"I fought him off. Somehow the darkness on his soul got on me. It grew on his hands and stuck to me." I shuddered and pushed aside one of my least favorite memories.

"How did you get rid of it?"

"I didn't. Eventually it went away, faded with the bruises."

If only Steve could have faded from my life as easily. He made the rest of that year a living hell, and before he graduated, he'd given me such a bad reputation that none of the boys in my class would look twice at me. It was just another reason I'd been happy to leave Berkeley behind and head to Davis for college. The boys there had never heard of me, and when I did have sex my freshman year, I'd gotten so good at avoiding soul-sight that it never occurred to me to check the boy.

"And that was it? You were too scared to look in Primordium again?" The soft scorn in Doris's voice jarred me.

"Would you have wanted to? I watched evil form out of nothing on what should have been a good soul. I hadn't been able to tell he was evil until he was *naked*. I couldn't trust my soul-sight. I felt betrayed. I didn't need that kind of complication—being normal was already hard enough."

"But you could trust it. Steve wasn't all good." Doris waggled her gray brows.

"So what was I supposed to do? Ask everyone to disrobe for me?"

She let that one go. "You've never done anything with *lux lucis*?"

"I guess I'd know if I had?"

That earned me a snort. "You stagnated yourself. Child, you've got a lot of learning to pack in. Look at me." I looked. "No, in Primordium."

I blinked. Doris glowed a soft white, hardly brighter than the average person, though no gray tainted her soul.

"Tell me what you see."

"Well, you're rather dim compared to Kyle." I realized the moment I said it how rude it sounded. "I mean, Kyle glowed like a freaking search light."

"He's always been an ass. A stupid one, too. He was making himself a beacon. You could do that, too, if you wanted, but I can't think why you would. All he did was gather as much *lux lucis* into himself as he could hold, which made him a target for any scrap of darkness out there."

"What is *lux lucis*?"

"Light. Life. It's what you see when you look at people; it's their life force. All plants and animals have it. Without human influence, plants and animals are typically immune to evil, but humans are completely capable of corrupting their own *lux lucis*. Which is why your teenage fling had darkness in him. It was evilness corrupting his soul, his life force. If you'd looked later, I'm sure Steve's underlying evil would have been impossible to miss—without making him drop his drawers. Teenage years are formidable years; they set up the balance of a person's life force, or soul, as you called it. Using Primordium to judge a teenager's balance is always tricky because they can change so much—from good to bad or bad to good.

"Everyone naturally generates a certain amount of *lux lucis*—or if they're bad for long enough, *atrum*," Doris continued. "I guess it's like blood—you can lose or use some *lux lucis* and it grows back. Or you can take it."

"Like a vampire?"

"Not the blood, silly. The *lux lucis*. You can absorb it from the plants around you if you need it faster than it naturally replenishes—and you will. Evil creatures have *atrum*, which is dark energy just as *lux lucis* is light energy. You'll use *lux lucis* to overpower *atrum* when you take on an imp. Is this making sense?"

"Sort of. So Kyle wasn't radiating because he was a particularly good person?"

"Hell no. Before we get out, I want to explain a few things. Then we can get to the fun."

I looked around. I had been so captivated by the conversation, I hadn't noticed that Doris had parked. We sat in front of a row of two-story run-down apartments I could just make out in the gray-on-gray of Primordium.

"Use Primordium all the time. In the grocery store. At the office. In the car. Use it until you can see depth and colors in it, until it's as natural as your normal sight."

"Colors?"

"Oh yeah. It's not a black-and-white world. It's just not a world that relies on light to create color. Some creatures, good and evil, have color tints to them, like citos and dryads, but I'm getting ahead of myself. For now, just use it. All. The. Time."

"Primordium is my new friend. Got it."

"Okay, we shouldn't encounter anything worse than an imp or two out here tonight. Even if he was a prick, Kyle was good at his job. He left you a very clean region to start in."

"Hang on," I said, stopping her before she could get out. "I've never done anything with Primordium or *lux lucis*. So, I mean, it's not too late for me to"—I searched for the words—"give it up."

"Give it up?"

"On a permanent basis."

Doris turned from where she'd swung her legs out the open door to give me a long, considering look. "Child, there's no off switch. If you decided you didn't want freckles anymore, they wouldn't just go away. Your ability is like that—it's a sense, not a button you can turn on and off. You're stuck with it." She bounced out of the car and slammed the door shut behind her.

The quiet cocoon of the car pulsed in my ears. The shreds of hope to which I'd been clinging remained suspended in that silence, holding me frozen. The moment I exited the car, my life was going to change forever.

I willed my freckles to disappear and then glanced down at the back of my hand. It glowed butter white in Primordium. I blinked and held my hand up to the feeble streetlight. The freckles were still there.

Doris rapped on the window beside me and I jumped. I took a deep breath and opened the door. Who was I kidding? My life had changed the moment I'd accepted the signing bonus.

6

IF FOUND,
PLEASE RETURN ME TO REALITY

COME ON, GIRL. YOU'VE GOT a lot to learn and the night oil's going to burn up fast. Before you get out, take a good look at me. Can you see the definition in my face?"

I blinked back to Primordium, steadying myself with a discreet hand on the dash. "Of course."

"Good. What about this?"

"What?"

"I rolled my eyes at you. I could see that in Primordium if you did it, so don't think about it."

"Are you looking at me in Primordium right now?"

"You've got good color for your age. Don't be shy about it." She started to walk away, then turned back and squatted in front of the open door. "They did this experiment with kittens in the sixties or maybe the seventies."

"In Primordium?"

Doris waved my question aside. "Has nothing to do with Primordium. These were 'real scientists.'" She did air quotes around the words, like there really was no such thing as a real scientist. "These scientists put goggles on kittens so they saw only vertical lines during some key developmental phases in their lives. When they were grown, the scientists let the cats loose in the world, without their goggles. They fell over everything—off tables, walked into walls, missed stairs. They couldn't see horizontal lines."

"That's horrible! Why would anyone do that to a cat?"

"Because scientists need a way to get their jollies, too. The point is, you're like those cats."

"I have no problem seeing horizontal lines," I said, feeling dense, my mind stuck on the image of kittens wearing goggles.

"Of course you can. But you're missing all the nuances of Primordium. You're seeing only part of the world. You've got to take off those blinders you've so blithely been wearing and really view the world. Come on. And act natural, too. I don't want to have to explain this to the cops."

I wriggled out of the toy car and stretched, feeling ten feet tall. The cold air seeped down my neck and up my jacket's sleeves. Shoving my hands into my pockets, I moved around to the trunk to see what Doris was doing.

"Every woman needs her accessories," she said. She'd pulled on a black hoodie with a white skull and crossbones on the back. She opened a small kit in the trunk and selected a flashlight and a wand. "This place is pretty clean. We shouldn't need more than pet wood and our hands." She quietly closed the trunk. "We'll not stray too far, Marilyn," she promised her car.

I blinked out of Primordium to get a better look at our surroundings. Muted colors washed through the dark world and I steadied myself against the Miata. Only one light on the street worked, illuminating a fire hydrant and a patch of dead grass. Cars lined the street, and the sleek Miata stuck out like it had a "free" sign on it. Broken down 4Runners, rusted Mercurys, and dented Metros were more the norm. The apartments were in worse shape than the cars. In flickering porch lights, I could see ripped window screens and scattered trash, with torn-apart children's toys littering the walkway. I blinked, checking for signs of life in Primordium. A single spindly tree glowed faintly against the apartment building. No animals or humans were foolish enough to be out in this neighborhood at night.

Except me and a crazy old lady.

"Not the country club, is it?" Doris asked. "First lesson before we go anywhere: Gather *lux lucis* in your hands."

"In my *hands*?"

"Sure. Where else would you do it?"

"But I thought this was all about looking at things and, ah, zapping them with my glare."

"With your . . . ? Humph, give me your best . . . zapping," Doris said.

"That's just it. I don't know what muscle to flex." I squinted at her and thought about zapping that grin off her wrinkled face.

Doris guffawed. "That's pretty fierce."

"Feel anything?" I asked hopefully.

Doris's cackle echoed off the nearby walls.

"This isn't funny!"

"Keep your voice down," she sputtered around giggles.

I planted my hands on my hips and glowered. Doris crumpled over in laughter, leaning against the Miata for support. I watched her, feeling foolish without knowing why, which made me angry.

"Look. If this is your idea of training, maybe we should call it a night."

Doris got herself under control. Wiping at tears running down her face, she said, "You're strung tighter than a clothesline, girl." She held up a hand to forestall my retort, burst into giggles again, then regained control. "I see where you've had some, ah, confusion. Your ability to see the world in Primordium is just that—a sight. It's not telekinesis or telekinetic judo. Just like you can't pick up a rock and throw it by looking at it, you can't move *lux lucis* with just your sight. You've got to use your body."

"Oh." Was it dark enough to hide my flaming face? Could she see the red glow in Primordium?

Still grinning, Doris said, "Let's try again. Gather *lux lucis* in your *hands*."

"How?"

"Focus on your hands. Focus on the light glowing brighter." I watched as her hands gradually brightened, though the light didn't extend beyond the boundaries of her fingers. If she had been a flashlight in the real world, the edges of her fingers would have blurred as the light got brighter, but Primordium didn't follow the normal laws of physics.

I held my hands up. They glowed their usual butter white color. However, I hardly registered the dizzying sensation of looking *into* myself this time. Maybe it was the embarrassment.

Focusing on the light growing brighter in my hands seemed too simplistic and New Agey, but I concentrated nonetheless, keeping my eyes glued on my fingers, picturing my hands changing as Doris's had. At first, nothing happened. Then the glow gradually intensified.

"Look at that!" I'd done it! I was using *lux lucis*! I stared at my hands in awe.

"Congratulations. You figured out what every fourteen-year-old enforcer-to-be learns on her own."

I stuck my tongue out at her. I was still impressed.

"I'll pretend I didn't see that. Now remember that imps will recognize you. The more you manipulate energy and the more time you work as an IE, the more quickly they'll recognize you."

"Won't they recognize you, too?"

"Oh, sure. Tonight they will." Doris gave her car one more pat and took off at a brisk pace down the sidewalk. I lurched to catch up. "Lesson two, which is the most important lesson: To kill an imp—to kill any creature of the dark—you must force enough *lux lucis* into it to overpower its *atrum*."

"How?"

Doris grinned at me. "You grab 'em and squeeze real tight." She cackled. "Close your mouth, girl. I'll show you how."

"What about all the teeth?" There was no way I wanted to get within range of an imp's teeth again.

"All show. Well, if you're stupid and leave them attached to your soul, they'll drain you of your *lux lucis* and they'll create weaknesses for the dark to get in and take hold."

"Oh, is that all?" I muttered. The warmth of the car had dissipated, and I bounced from foot to foot to keep warm.

Doris flipped on her light. I stared in wonder—I could see it in Primordium! Like a normal light in the normal world, it shone through the darkness of Primordium, illuminating a circle in front of us. Of course, unlike real light, it didn't cast any shadows.

"You'll want to get yourself one of these. They're pretty handy. Aha! See. There's our first victim."

A tiny, adorable (in an I-know-you-have-crazy-teeth-and-want-to-eat-me-but-I-still-want-to-cuddle-you kind of way) imp scurried along the edge of the apartment wall. The moment the light fixed on it, it froze.

"Does it feel it?" I whispered.

"Speak normal, girl. You're not going to frighten it. And, no, the light doesn't hurt it. It's not *lux lucis*. It's just a different kind of light."

It occurred to me to wonder what the light looked like in normal vision, but I wasn't about to check while there was an imp in my sights.

"Watch and learn."

Doris turned off her light. There was no need to wait for my eyes to adjust in Primordium. I could still see the imp against the apartment, though I wasn't sure that I would have picked it out so quickly without the light. Doris took a step forward and crouched down. The imp cocked its head to the side, much as the little bugger that'd attacked me earlier had.

Doris's hands began to glow brighter. The imp scurried forward in quick, delicate hops. When it was about two feet away, it opened its mouth. I jerked back. Row after row of jagged teeth in a perfectly round mouth bounced toward Doris. She held out a hand toward it like she was offering her flesh up as food. In fact, that's exactly what she was doing. I held my breath as the imp pounced. Doris stood and turned to face me. The imp was attached to her wrist like a leech. She appeared unfazed. I swallowed several screams.

"Get a good look. It's nothing more than a ball of evil. Darkness coalesced. Which is nothing to be afraid of. Touch it."

"Touch it?" I repeated stupidly.

"Now," she barked, thrusting it in my face. I instinctively blocked it, and my hand slid through its inky little body. It didn't detach from her wrist. Goose bumps slid down my spine in one long shudder.

"Grab hold of it," Doris ordered.

I was working up the courage to wrap my hands around it—and trying to figure out how to hold something intangible—when she shoved it at my face again.

"Stop doing that!" I grabbed at the dark little body, cupping its weightless form with my hands. I could vaguely feel the imp; it was like dense air or very light water—not quite solid, but not completely vaporous, either. I couldn't tell if it was my imagination or not, but it felt cool against my skin.

"Use the *lux lucis* in your hands and push it into the imp."

I wasn't sure what she meant exactly, but I didn't want to touch the creature any longer than necessary, so I didn't waste time with questions. I thought about my hands getting brighter and that energy flowing into the imp. There was resistance as I pushed the light against the imp's body, then suddenly, like the pop of a bubble, the light burst through the imp. My hands flared like twin beacons.

I jerked back, letting my hands fall to my sides. They dimmed to normal brightness. White and black sparkles drifted between Doris and me. Feeling a thousand imaginary spiders scuttle across my skin, I met her gaze.

"Not bad, but you need control. If there are any more imps in the area, they're headed this way now."

"What happened to it? And don't ever do that to me again!"

"You disintegrated it like you were using a maxi pad on a paper cut."

I grimaced. "Did you have to shove it in my face?"

"If I'd waited for you to get your nerve up, it would still be sucking the life force from me. Clean your panties; we're on the hunt again."

I gathered my tattered ego and marched after her.

We didn't have far to go. As Doris had predicted, my hands had acted like the beacons they had looked like. We rounded the corner, sidestepped a mysterious puddle, and ran across three imps. They hopped like bunnies across the deadened ground, heading directly for us.

"I'll take two this time," Doris said.

She boldly strode forward into their cute, teeth-filled midst. I followed before I could second-guess my sanity. I wasn't going to be a coward this time. Two imps bounded toward me, but Doris reached out and snagged one. The other continued, oblivious to the particles of its previous companion floating in the air around it. *How can anything so cute be scary?* The imp grinned, all its tiny ebony teeth flashing. *Ah, yes. That's how.*

I reached for it the way I'd reach for a spider; the imp pounced. I yanked *lux lucis* into my hand and smashed it into the imp. There was the same resistance as with the first imp, then a spray of light and dark particulates. My hand glowed like a miniature star.

"Where was the control in that?" Doris snorted.

"So your second kill was perfect?" I demanded.

"Not by half, girl. But I wasn't in charge of a region at that time, either."

A healthy revulsion of anything made of pure evil made quitting, going home, and burying myself under a pile of blankets sound like a good plan. But there was this other niggling emotion, one that felt remarkably like enjoyment, that made me look around the vacant street for more imps.

"How old were you when you first started doing this?"

"Thirteen."

I rubbed my palms frantically on my pants when Doris wasn't looking, trying to get the strange, sticky feeling of the imps off me.

"It doesn't stay on you," she assured me without looking. "When they disintegrate, they're gone. Oh, good. There's a few more."

"You like doing this, don't you?" I asked. Once again, I found myself jogging to catch up with the elderly woman. I was getting used to looking at her glowing head and features in Primordium, and as an added bonus, it was harder to see the skull and crossbones on the back of her sweater in this vision.

"Oh yeah! I'd forgotten how much fun this is! But I'll let you have all the ones in the next batch."

"Gee. Thanks."

Luckily, the few more she spied ended up being only three again. I stopped beside Doris when she paused, but she gave me a firm shove in the back that sent me staggering toward them.

"Have at 'em, girl."

I knew I couldn't flinch or falter, not with her waiting to judge me. Feeling like I was walking into battle, I stepped into the middle of the street to meet the imps. The high noon showdown music played in my head. The little cuties bounded toward me. I let them come, widening my stance, testing my control of *lux lucis*.

The largest imp was the fastest, and it sprang for my throat from two feet away. I hadn't been prepared for that, but pride didn't let me jump aside. I threw my hands up to grab it. It swallowed my right hand to the wrist. There was no pain, only a slight tingle that quickly faded. Gritting my teeth to hold in a scream, I pushed *lux lucis* into the imp while staring into its glowing eyes. The teeth convulsed on my wrist. A little more *lux lucis*, and *pop*, there were only sparkles in the air in front of me.

Before I could congratulate myself, the next one attacked, this time aiming for my knee. I scooped it up and used two hands to press *lux lucis* into it. It sprinkled out of existence, and the energy flared in my hands for a moment too long.

"Not bad, eh?" I asked, turning to get Doris's nod of approval. I was learning fast.

"Yeah, except you've still got one attached to your ankle."

I glanced down. An imp I'd completely forgotten about was gnawing on my left leg.

"Ggnaa!" I shook my foot frantically, trying to dislodge it. "Off! Get off!" Hopping and flailing didn't shake the creepy chinchilla wannabe. I caught sight of Doris out of the corner of my eye: She was doubled over with laughter. A rush of embarrassment broke through my panic, and I forced *lux lucis* into the imp the fastest way I could: through my ankle. It popped in a shower of sparkles. Apparently, just as clothes were no barrier against imps, they were also no barrier against *lux lucis*. My ankle swelled with light.

"Ah, child. Good move at the end. And a lot of good moves before that. If I could learn a few of those dance steps, I'd knock the socks off the men in my salsa class." She gave her hips an experimental shake.

I assessed myself. Yep, everything was still intact. No thanks to Doris.

"Let's go find us some more fun." Doris gave me a cheerful pat on the back.

"More fun" ended up being a few streets away in the form of a small pack of imps. Doris challenged me to an "imp-off" to see who could kill the most first. I lost, but at least I was able to kill five to her eight. I also consoled myself with the fact that Doris had props. She used the wand she'd taken from her trunk, infusing it with *lux lucis*, then spearing imps before they reached her. When I asked her about it, she only snorted.

"One thing at a time, girl. If you can't control the *lux lucis* in your body, you're definitely not ready to start brandishing it around."

The whole point was to avoid contact with the imps, hence my interest in the wand and being able to kill from a distance. Still, I didn't push Doris for more information. I was learning a lot, and killing imps—even barehanded—wasn't as bad as I'd expected.

We roamed through a three-block area of dilapidated duplexes and apartments, killing stray imps as we went. Doris challenged me to different forms of attack, first allowing the imps to land on my body and binge-feeding *lux lucis* into them from whatever piece of soul they'd latched their teeth into, then having me rush a small herd and try to disintegrate all the imps before they could jump on me. Of the two methods, the latter was the hardest. The imps had no sense of self-preservation. Rushing them was the equivalent of ice cream leaping toward my mouth; they merely opened their jaws and started feeding.

It took over an hour for us to flush out all the pockets of imps in the small neighborhood.

"Why are there so many imps here?" I asked.

"It happens. There was a hit-and-run here a few days ago. They tend to congregate after bad events. They might have dispersed on their own, but this is such a bad neighborhood, it looks like they found a home."

I felt overwhelmed by how much I still had to learn—and how much I would be expected to do on a daily basis.

"When you were an IE, how many hours did you work each week?"

"It depended. If something big happened, it overwhelmed my life. But most of the time, I put in the normal hours, just not always at the normal times. You worried you won't be able to handle it?"

I shrugged.

"Don't. You'll get the hang of it. Let's cruise for a bit."

We backtracked to Marilyn, which was fortunately still there, then zipped back to Douglas Boulevard. Doris took us across the interstate to Dairy Queen, because she was hungry and "it was too late at night to be bothered with chewing." Since my last meal had been gelato—not counting the nachos at the bar—I ordered a salad. There's something massively unfair about eating a salad when your dining companion has ice cream, though.

Doris drove while she ate and parked at the outskirts of an apartment complex near the junior college while we finished our late-night snacks. An occasional car passed by, dark except for the glowing heads of the passengers visible in Primordium. The apartment complex was quiet on a Wednesday night, though I knew that this time on Friday would see most balconies crowded with smokers and drunk coeds.

Once Doris had scraped the bottom of her Blizzard clean, we roamed through the pathways of the complex without speaking, past doors with turkey-themed wreaths and balconies crammed with bikes and patio furniture. Doris walked with confidence, like she lived in one of the apartments and always took a late-night stroll. I kept waiting for the complex's security guys to find us and kick us out. Not to mention that it was creepy, moving between all the buildings filled with unconscious people, hunting evil creatures. Creepy, and cold. I'd forgotten the cold earlier when we had hunted through the run-down neighborhood. The adrenaline had kept me warm. Now the chill crept into my bones and settled there. Doris appeared oblivious.

I kept my hands buried in my coat pocket except for the two times I needed to take out an imp. Since there were so few in the complex, Doris let me have them all. I destroyed each one quickly, temporarily able to forget the cold during each satisfying kill.

"You look like you're beginning to have fun," she said when we returned to the car.

I hadn't realized I was grinning. "I think I'm good at this."

"I think you are, too. Don't get cocky, though. We've hardly scratched the surface of everything you need to know. But at least now Brad knows he's got a little more than bait on his payroll."

"Thanks. I think."

"You look tired. Let's get you home. I've got a plane to catch tomorrow and I still need to pack."

It wasn't until Doris mentioned it that I realized how tired I was. I checked the clock. It was nearly three in the morning. Doris still looked like she could run a marathon. I didn't need a mirror to know that I looked frazzled and exhausted. I could only hope that I would be as energetic as Doris when I was her age. Hell, I would like to be that energetic at twenty-five!

Of course, Doris hadn't just had the longest day of her life. It was incredible to realize that it had been less than twenty-four hours since I'd interviewed with Kyle. There was something to be said for the mind's ability to adapt. Yesterday I'd been an unemployed, unsuccessful used-car saleswoman avoiding my soul-sight. Today I was an illuminant enforcer, charged with destroying evil wherever I found it, and enjoying viewing the world in Primordium. I hadn't even known what *lux lucis* was twenty-four hours ago, and now I wielded it as a weapon against creatures I would have refused to believe existed yesterday.

Tired or not, I felt a tad badass.

Back at my apartment, Doris parked and then bounced out of the car while I was still fumbling to retrieve my purse from under the seat. It wasn't surprising that she was faster and more energetic than me; it was surprising that she'd gotten out at all.

"Thank you for the training," I said to the skull and crossbones as she strode toward my apartment. I switched back to normal vision to navigate the stairs, not trusting my compromised sight in Primordium when I was so exhausted.

"You've got a lot more to learn, but that's a good start. We've got one last thing to do."

My pride wouldn't let me fall too far behind as she trotted up the two flights of stairs to my apartment. I stuffed my key in the lock and let us in.

Mr. Bond bounded to greet us, sniffing our shoes and telling us about how happy or upset he was. It was hard to tell the difference. After he'd twined through our legs a few times, he raced to his food dish. If nothing else, he was predictable.

"You'll need protection," Doris said.

"Like a gun?" I asked fuzzily.

"Like a ward, girl. Keep it together." She snapped her fingers under my nose, and I scowled at her. "Watch." I blinked. Doris gathered *lux lucis* in her palms as we had done to kill the imps, only this time she spread it around the frame of the door. Wherever she touched, it left a faint smear of light.

"How are you getting it to stick?" I asked.

"You can do this with any inanimate object, but it won't last long. For now, you'll need to do it every night."

"What's that do?"

"Keeps out evil. You've just made yourself one big target, announcing yourself as an illuminant enforcer. Some of the dark creatures won't sit by and wait for you to come and get them."

"The imps are coming for me?" I giggled. Man, I was tired. I blinked to focus on my apartment again.

"Imps couldn't find a brain between fifty of them. No, it'll be the larger creatures that hunt you."

"Like what?" *I should be frightened,* I thought. Anything hunting me should make me scared, especially anything evil. *I'll be scared tomorrow,* I decided.

"Nothing for a while. The area's pretty clean. But you'd better get in the practice of placing wards now. Is there a window in your bedroom?" I nodded. "You ward that. I'll get the glass door. Anywhere there's an opening, you have to ward."

I stumbled off to the bedroom, followed by an insistently meowing Mr. Bond. Ignoring his complaints, I blinked to Primordium and gathered *lux lucis* in my palms. It took longer for the light to brighten my hands than it had earlier: Apparently my *lux lucis* was as diminished as my physical energy. Once my hands glowed, I smoothed them along the frame of my window. Before I finished, Doris had come to inspect my handiwork.

"Not bad. Well, good luck, kid. I'll check in with you when I'm back."

"Thanks again," I mumbled, trailing after her light form as she zipped to the front door. Mr. Bond looked as adorable in Primordium as he did in normal vision. He glowed a beautiful, bright white. After all the dark imps I'd seen that night, it was nice to look at something pure. It was going to be even nicer to curl up in bed and sleep.

I looked up when I heard the door open.

"You need to recharge," Doris said, eyeing me closely.

"I plan to," I assured her.

"It can be dangerous if you don't. It's one of the most important things to remember. And you live in the perfect place for it. Those trees are lovely."

I nodded and tried unsuccessfully to hold in a yawn.

"I'll check in with you when I get back," she repeated.

I nodded. Would it be too rude to push her out the door? Finally she waved a good-bye and I closed and locked the door behind her. I shuffled about the apartment, fed Mr. Bond, brushed my teeth, and stripped down. Mr. Bond darted into the bedroom with his fake fuzzy mouse in his mouth and tossed it about while I crawled into bed. I fell asleep even as I was adjusting the covers around my face.

The alarm went off all too soon, and I fumbled to snooze it. The sun slanted through blinds I had forgotten to shut, but that wasn't a problem. I slowly pulled the covers over my head. Two years of living with Mr. Bond had taught me slow movements allowed me to sleep longer; fast movements meant I was awake and ready to pet or feed him. I drifted back toward sleep, but a niggling sense that something was amiss prevented me from going under.

It wasn't new-job jitters. My first day had felt like the first week. If anything, I was ready to call in sick. I didn't have an appointment I was forgetting. Even snoozing the alarm wasn't going to make me late.

Trying not to wake up, I carefully cracked an eyelid. If Mr. Bond saw my eyes open, he would decide the day had begun, and there'd be no falling back to sleep. Everything seemed in place, except Mr. Bond. He wasn't on the bed. He was always on the bed in the morning, looming over me, waiting impatiently for attention.

I listened for sounds of food crunching or scratching in the litter box, but the apartment was quiet. I couldn't shake the feeling that something was wrong. Was he into the plants?

I opened my eyes wider and looked around the room. The tall plant at the foot of my bed wasn't looking so good. In fact . . . I sat up all the way, wide awake. It was dead. Not dying, with a few yellowed leaves. But dead. Brittle and dry. As if it hadn't been green and lovely yesterday. A shiver of premonition tingled down my spine. The small rubber tree on top of my dresser had dropped all of its leaves overnight. They lay brown and unsightly around the base of the pot, and only the spindly dried trunk remained in the soil.

Something was seriously wrong.

7

I ♥ My Cat

MR. BOND, WHERE ARE YOU?" I could hear the fear in my voice. I was through my bedroom door in three steps. Mr. Bond lay in a listless lump in the middle of the hallway. I knelt beside him, my heart in my throat. I ran my hand down his back, but he didn't so much as twitch to acknowledge me. My mind raced through possibilities while I carefully held Mr. Bond's sides to feel if he still breathed—gas leak? Life-stealing creatures I hadn't encountered yet? Poison? My heart started beating again when I felt his sides move faintly. He was cold, and his fur felt thick and gritty, like he hadn't cleaned in a week. I blinked, looking around for enemies in Primordium. Nothing moved. My gaze dropped to Mr. Bond. His brilliant white had faded to a dim, pulsing gray.

"No!" I started to scoop Mr. Bond into my arms, ready to run off to the vet, only to realize I was naked and unprepared. Cursing myself and Primordium, and praying for all I was worth in between, I blinked back to normal vision and raced about the house. I dressed in the first things I could find: jeans and a sweater. I pushed some toothpaste around my mouth with the brush in between shoving my feet into socks and shoes. Sprinting out to the porch, I grabbed Mr. Bond's carrier from the outdoor closet, spit toothpaste over the side of the balcony, and raced back inside. Mr. Bond still hadn't moved.

Throwing his favorite blanket in the microwave, I used the minute it took to warm the fuzzy cotton to rinse my mouth, collect my purse, yank my hair back in a ponytail, and check on Mr. Bond again. The microwave beeped, and I grabbed the blanket and stuffed it in the carrier. Then I lifted twenty-two pounds of Mr. Bond's dead weight into the carrier, trying to be gentle, but without his help it was difficult. I was crying by the time he was settled. Normally getting him in his carrier was an ordeal and a half. This time, he didn't even open his eyes.

"Hang in there, little buddy," I whispered. I hoisted the carrier in both arms and jogged out of the apartment, gaze snagging momentarily on the three front room plants, all dead.

I hardly remembered locking the door or the flight to the car. I was moving on fast-forward autopilot, all my attention focused on the small form huddled in the carrier. I took my time settling him gently into the front passenger seat next to me and buckling the carrier in, then sped out of my complex, cutting off two people and only caring that the blare of their horns might have scared Mr. Bond. I went sixty in a forty-five-mile-an-hour zone, and that was only because I couldn't go faster in the traffic. In minutes, I was unloading Mr. Bond and racing toward the doors of the Love and Caring Veterinary Clinic.

Luckily, there was no one else in the waiting room. I don't know what I would have done if they'd expected me to wait in line.

"I woke up, and he was like this . . . all . . . lifeless," I blubbered to the vet who had stepped out of the back at the sound of the door opening. "I haven't changed his food or his routine. He doesn't go outside. He was fine last night. He was playing with his mouse and—"

"It's okay, Madison," the veterinarian soothed in his deep voice. "Let's have a look at him."

I carried Mr. Bond to an examination room and carefully set his carrier down on the table.

"Can you look at him in there? I don't want to drag him out."

"Sure."

The vet opened the front of the cage, and for the first time in his life, Mr. Bond wasn't eagerly pressed against the opening, ready to race out.

"I heated the blanket because he was so cold. I didn't know what else to do," I babbled while the vet gently poked and prodded Mr. Bond.

"That was smart of you. I think we need to pull him out. Why don't you hold the carrier still for me."

I watched anxiously as the vet easily lifted my hefty cat and placed him, blanket and all, on the table. I held myself quiet, wringing my hands, while the vet finished his examination.

"I'm going to take some blood, okay? Are you going to be all right to watch?"

I met the vet's steady, calm blue eyes. Normally at the mention of needles I'd leave the room. "I would donate blood if that's what it took."

He rewarded me with a smile. With a jolt, I realized that the vet was none other than the attractive and charming Dr. Alex Love himself. I couldn't bring myself to care. If Mr. Bond was okay, maybe then, but right now, all that mattered was my little boy.

Mr. Bond didn't flinch when the needle pricked his skin. I watched the blood fill the syringe, staring as if I'd see answers in the red liquid. Dr. Love was gone barely a minute, during which time I petted Mr. Bond and told him softly how much I loved him and how he better be faking. The vet returned with an electric blanket that he gently wrapped around Mr. Bond.

"We'll send the blood to our lab, which will get back to us tomorrow, but there are a few preliminary tests I can do here based on my suspicions. Those results will be ready in about ten minutes," he said.

I nodded and swiped at tears. Dr. Love left again. I needed to do something. I blinked. Mr. Bond was still a dim, pulsing light. I wanted revenge against whatever or whoever had done this! Glaring about the sterile room, I silently dared dark creatures to show up. When none came out of the woodwork to be killed, I switched back to normal vision and petted Mr. Bond as calmly as I could. It felt like an eternity before Dr. Love returned.

"As I suspected, it looks like Mr. Bond is very dehydrated," he announced. "When was the last time you saw him drinking?"

"Yesterday." Even though he had a bowl of water, Mr. Bond always wanted to drink from the tub when I was going to the bathroom, and I always indulged him by turning the water on a trickle.

"That's very peculiar. By his blood results, it looks like he's been dehydrated for five or six days."

"Can you do something?"

"Yes. I'm going to give him some fluids. It's like an IV for cats, only a cat would never lie still long enough to leave a needle in a vein as it gradually pumped liquid back into him, so we have to do it in one dose. I'm going to inject the liquid under his skin here"—he indicated the spot between Mr. Bond's shoulder blades—"and it will gradually absorb into his body over the next twenty-four hours."

"How soon will he be better?"

"I think you'll start to see signs of him improving in maybe an hour or so. By tonight, he should be acting a lot like his old self."

I had to grip the table to restrain myself from leaping across it and hugging Dr. Love. I watched as he injected the liquid under Mr. Bond's skin until there was a golf ball–size bubble between his shoulder blades.

"Doesn't that hurt him?"

"Maybe a little, but there's a lot of loose skin here. By the time he starts moving again, the bump you see will be much smaller." Dr. Love gave Mr. Bond a gentle scratch under his chin.

My hands began to quiver as the adrenaline tapered off. I slumped into the plastic chair in the corner.

"Are you sure he's going to be fine?"

"Yes. You did the right thing getting him here so quickly. A few hours longer and I don't know that this would have been so easy."

I stared adoringly at the man who had just saved Mr. Bond's life. Dr. Love could easily have been a model with his spectacular bone structure and delicious physique. Yet, here he was, taking care of animals and their frazzled owners. He was being too nice and my nerves were too frayed. I began to cry all over again, embarrassed but unable to stop.

Dr. Love pulled his little round doctor's chair in front of me and sat down, reaching out to pat my knee.

"He's going to be fine. It's okay now," he said softly. His thick dark brown hair was cut almost military short, and as close as he sat, I could see blond sprinkled throughout it.

"I know." I met his earnest blue eyes, admiring the shallow laugh lines at the corners. I became abruptly aware of my appearance. Sniffing, I used my sweater to dry my face. I knew I looked horrendous, and I knew it was silly to want to look sexy after the ordeal I'd just been through, but I wouldn't have been a woman if I hadn't wanted to look attractive to a man like Dr. Love. "Thank you so much. I . . . I don't know what I would have done."

"Madison, it's people like you that make my day." At my questioning look, he explained, "You love your pet like a child. You've clearly taken good care of Mr. Bond. You make my job easy."

I found myself smiling crookedly back at him. When he stood, I stepped up next to him at the examining table. Mr. Bond already looked a little better. When I rubbed his cheek, he actually cracked an eyelid to look at me.

"What do you think caused this?" I asked.

"I don't know. Watch him closely for the next few days, but let me know if he's not better by tonight. We'll give you a call tomorrow to see how he's doing, too, and to let you know what the lab says about his blood."

Dr. Love lifted Mr. Bond back into his carrier and walked me to the front desk. At five-ten, I'm used to looking most men in the eye, but Dr. Love must have topped six feet by a few inches, because he made me feel petite. It was a novel experience for me.

He shook my hand good-bye. His hand was warm and engulfed mine pleasantly. Bridget and I argue on the matter, but I've always thought I could tell how good a man would be in bed by the shape and feel of his hands. Bridget maintains that she can tell by a man's posture. Based on either criteria, I found myself wishing that I'd been at the clinic for a different reason entirely.

I drove home sanely and left Mr. Bond in his open carrier when we got inside. Belatedly, I checked the time and then called the office to let Mr. Pitt know I would be in late.

"I'm sorry, Mr. Pitt," I explained to my new boss on the phone. "I had to take my cat to an emergency appointment at the vet this morning."

"I hope it was nothing serious," he said politely.

"It could have been, but I got him seen in time. He's back at home now."

There was a pause. "What were his symptoms?"

I explained Mr. Bond's complete lack of energy and dehydration. "Do you know what caused this?" I demanded.

"I'll explain when you get in." He hung up.

My heart did a funny lurch. I'd been right: Some evil creature had hurt Mr. Bond.

I put all the dead plants outside and opened the windows to air the house out, then reinforced the weak wards. Taking no chances, I emptied and washed Mr. Bond's food and water dishes and threw the comforter from my bed and Mr. Bond's kitty bed into the washing machine. When

I checked on Mr. Bond again, he had stretched out more comfortably in his carrier, his feet twitching in a dream. I crouched beside him for several long minutes, content to watch him. Then I brushed my teeth for real, grimacing at the frumpy image of myself in the mirror.

"Next time you do something crazy like that, Mr. Bond, make sure I'm all dressed up and looking sexy." I eyed his sleeping form sternly. "Better yet, never do that again."

I wanted to stay home all day with him, but Dr. Love had assured me it would be fine for me to go to work, and since it was only my second day, I grabbed my keys and promised Mr. Bond I'd be back during my lunch break to check on him.

I saw the message light blinking on my answering machine as I was headed out the door. Backtracking, I pressed the PLAY button.

"Hi, Madison. It's me." It was Mom. "Just calling to see how you're doing. We haven't heard from you very much since you were . . . let go. We're getting worried. Give us a call. Bye."

Guilt made me reach for the phone. I should have called my parents yesterday before going to meet Bridget. My eyes fell on the clock. It was nine thirty. I didn't want to be later than I was. Assuaging my guilt would have to wait.

It wasn't until I was nearly to my car that I remembered Medusa. Having a cell phone was going to be convenient.

I dialed my parents while I waited for the car to warm up.

"Hello, Fox residence," my mom answered.

"Hi, Mom."

"Oh, hi, Madison. Where are you calling from? I don't recognize the number."

I mentally sighed. Caller ID. Now they could reach me anytime. Having a cell phone might just have become decidedly *in*convenient.

"It's my cell phone. I had to get it for my new job."

"New job!" Predictably, Mom covered the phone with her hand and shouted for Dad. A moment later, a click announced that my dad had picked up the other phone in their house. "Madison has a new job," Mom declared.

"That's my girl."

"Where is it?" Mom asked on top of Dad's, "Do they have a good retirement plan?"

"It's called Illumination Studios. They make bumper stickers. It's about three minutes from my house, so we need to talk fast."

"She's on a cell phone," Mom told Dad.

I explained how I needed it for my new job.

"Are you on call?" Dad asked.

"No, but after I finish training, I get to make my own hours."

"Make your own hours? That's peculiar," Mom said.

"What about a 401(k)?"

In the recent years leading up to their retirement, Dad had become compulsive about reminding me of my own retirement plans. Thanking the universe that I'd remembered to ask about it when I'd filled out the company forms, I happily reported that I was going to be able to retire in forty-plus years.

"What do you do?" Dad asked on top of Mom's, "Are you late on your first day?"

"That's not going to look good at all," Dad admonished before I could respond to either question.

I decided to avoid attempting to explain my job just yet and dodged that question. "It's my second day. I had my first, uh, training day yesterday. Besides, I had an emergency this morning: Mr. Bond had to go to the vet."

I cruised down Douglas Boulevard, telling my parents about my morning in fits and starts through their steady stream of questions. When I pulled into Illumination Studio's parking lot, I assured them again that Mr. Bond was going to be fine and I didn't need them to drop by to check on him today.

"I gotta go. I'm at work. I'll tell you all about my job soon," I promised.

"Okay. Bye, dear."

"Bye, Mom."

"Knock 'em dead, Son." I rolled my eyes, surprised that Dad's favorite nickname for me hadn't come up sooner.

"I will, Dad."

I hung up and stared at the phone. I couldn't avoid explaining my job forever. I needed to remember to ask Mr. Pitt or Rose about the day-to-day office work on the bumper sticker side of the business today so I'd have something I could actually tell my parents.

I peeked inside the doors along the lengthy hallway leading to Illumination Studios, catching glimpses of bored office workers in the half-empty mortgage company office and in the much busier temp agency. For the first time since my interview yesterday, I felt a surge of optimism. I may have had the most bizarre day yesterday, but at least I hadn't droned along behind a desk like all those people.

Of course, they hadn't been attacked by evil creatures or spent their late-night hours training in the worst neighborhood they could find. They also hadn't woken up to find their beloved pet near death's door. My smile faded.

Dwarfed behind the large reception desk, Sharon glared over the top at me as I entered. I smiled and said hello. Her expression didn't change; she didn't blink, and she didn't say anything. *Doris's description of her as a gargoyle is apt,* I thought. I had to resist the urge to twitch at the feel of Sharon's stare boring into my back as I headed for Mr. Pitt's office.

He was seated behind his desk, staring at his monitor. I was again struck by the unfairness of having a boss named Brad Pitt who could not have looked less like the movie star. If there was any star he resembled, it was Wallace Shawn, but only in height. Shawn didn't look like a balding poisonous frog.

"Madison, I just got off the phone with Doris. She said you guys had a successful night. She's about to get on the plane, but I want you to talk to her."

He bustled me out of his office and to the cubicle that Rose had said was mine. There was a computer set up on the bare desk, an abandoned overflowing pen cup, two staplers, and a tiered folder holder. The computer was already on. Mr. Pitt clicked on something and a box appeared in the center of the screen showing a picture of Doris. Mr. Pitt clicked something again, and the picture expanded to the whole screen.

"I've only got a minute," Doris said. I jumped. It wasn't a picture; it was a live video.

Mr. Pitt motioned for me to sit; then he left. I sat, feeling like a country bumpkin who'd time traveled to the future. A cell phone yesterday. A video conference today. Watch out, world. I might get a Twitter account next!

"Tell me about Mr. Bond," Doris said.

I eyed the old woman. If anything, she looked more peppy this morning than she had last night. Maybe it was the lack of the biker sweater. Maybe it was the camera. Behind her I could see the steady activity of an airport.

Editing out my emotional reactions, I outlined my morning's visit to the vet, ending with, "So I was right to guess this had something to do with the forces of evil?"

"Did you recharge last night?" she demanded.

"Yeah. I slept, what, four hours. It was plenty." It wasn't plenty, but I'd be damned if I admitted it to this elderly lady who had clearly had even less sleep and yet still seemed more energetic. And I didn't see what my sleep had to do with Mr. Bond, anyway.

"That's sleep. That's not recharging. Oh, dear. You don't know about recharging." She slapped herself on the forehead and I winced for her. "I should have guessed." She looked around, then stood and walked quickly to a corner of the terminal, the image from her laptop bouncing and blurring with each step. I closed my eyes against the sudden carsick sensation, opening them only when she spoke again. "Listen, child. What we did last night—using all that *lux lucis*—well, it pulls from your own life force reserves. You have to recharge. Use plants and trees for this. Touch them, and pull the life force from them."

"You want me to uproot plants? I don't think that's going to help Mr. Bond."

"Not uproot—take their *lux lucis*. Let me guess: All those plants in your house were dead this morning, right?"

I nodded. My heart clinched in dread as she continued.

"Since you didn't actively seek to refill your life force, your body did it passively while you slept. You sucked the life out of the plants first, and then you sucked it out of your cat. You're lucky he's not dead."

"I didn't do that to Mr. Bond!" I shook my head frantically. "I wouldn't!"

"You did. You have to replenish yourself—recharge—before bed, or anything living around you is in danger."

"Why didn't you tell me that?!"

"I did. I told you to recharge."

"How was I supposed to know what that meant?" I was trembling with anger and guilt. I thought of poor Mr. Bond lying limply in the hallway, drained of life *by me*. "I could have killed him! These are the things you tell a person you're training. Jesus Christ!" It hadn't been some evil creature. It'd been me. The person who was supposed to love and protect and care for Mr. Bond. If this is what I got for embracing my abilities, I'd give up my advance and tell Mr. Pitt to find himself someone with a different moral structure. Killing evil creatures was one thing. Becoming one was intolerable.

"I'm telling you now, girl. Yelling at me won't help."

I felt like crying, so I focused on my anger instead. "Tell me how to recharge, and don't leave anything out this time," I demanded.

"I already did. Pay attention. All you have to do to recharge is touch a plant and absorb its *lux lucis*. Trees are best. They have more life to give."

"Intentionally suck the life out of things? That doesn't exactly sound like the good side. No one told me anything about this!"

"No need to get all melodramatic, child—"

"I'll be the judge of that. You didn't spend this morning at the vet's with a nearly dead cat that you almost killed! And I wasn't touching him. I wasn't touching any of the plants, and they all died."

"You don't always have to be touching the plant; it's just faster. This isn't evil, either. The plants will give you their life force willingly. It's up to you not to take too much. If you were evil, you'd take it from animals and other people."

"But I *did* take it from Mr. Bond."

Doris sighed. "Your life force doesn't distinguish between what you morally feel is good and evil. It fed off the plants first because they were willing, but when you needed more, it fed off the next closest, weakest thing, which happened to be Mr. Bond. In a way, you're lucky. It could have been a neighbor's pet or a neighbor's child."

"How is that not evil?"

"It just isn't. It's a balance you've got to learn to maintain. It'll become like second nature." She looked over the screen, and I heard a loud announcement for the last call of a flight. "I've got to run. You're going to do fine. Always recharge after using *lux lucis*, especially before bed. Oh, and remind Brad you need some weapons. Good luck."

The video froze as she signed off.

"Bite me," I told her picture.

"Rough first day?" a deep voice drawled from behind me. I jumped and spun. I'd totally forgotten where I was. When my eyes fell on Mr.

Dark and Deadly—I mean Niko—I forgot everything all over again. *Good job, Dice. You looked like a wreck when you saw Dr. Love this morning, and now you're cursing at the picture of a little old woman in front of Niko. You really know how to impress them, don't you?*

"Uh, second day. Kind of a rough beginning to the second day," I stammered.

Niko was as heart-stoppingly drool worthy as he had been yesterday. His jeans fit his hips and thighs snuggly, and his tight blue T-shirt emphasized his stunning pectorals. He had his arms crossed and was leaning lazily against the wall of my cubicle. A hint of a smile quirked his sensual mouth, but his eyes were dark and serious. If he was the elite of the enforcers, I was sure there were many questions he could answer for me. If only I could formulate a single thought. Other than how nice it would be to rub up against him. *Down, girl.*

I stood, tripping over the wheels of the chair.

"I'm Madison," I said, extending my hand.

"Niko Demitrius." His grip was warm and strong. I made sure I didn't hold on. He passed my hand test with flying colors, but while Dr. Love had made me think of romance and long nights of languid passion, shaking Niko's hand had me scanning a mental map of the office for the nearest empty room with a door, no preliminary chitchat necessary. Honestly, my hormones needed a shot of sedatives around this man.

"It'll get easier," he assured me.

I blushed before I realized he was talking about the job, not my attraction to him. He flashed me white teeth, then walked away.

I relaxed my white-knuckled grip on the back of my chair. *Women don't swoon in the twenty-first century,* I told myself firmly.

"You've got a little drool on your chin," Rose said from beside me. I jumped and made a swipe at my chin before I realized she was teasing. Rose laughed. "Come meet the others."

She led me across the aisle to the group of four cubicles where she sat. A beautiful blond-haired supermodel lounged behind the desk across from Rose. She had the kind of hair I always tell myself only people with a team of stylists could maintain. It was thick, with a wavy curl that glistened in the flat fluorescent lights.

"Joy, this is Madison Fox. She's our new enforcer. Madison, this is Joy. She does a lot of our graphic design." We shook hands. Hers was warm and slender and I felt like a thick-boned Neanderthal in comparison.

In the cubicle beside her was one of the most pleasant men I'd ever seen. We were evenly matched in height, and probably in weight. Short, mussed brown hair gave his ageless face a boyish charm, and the smile he shone upon me made me like him instantly.

"William, this is Madison. Madison, William does much of our marketing and advertising."

"Call me Will," he said in a lovely British accent, tipping the scales from pleasant to attractive.

I blinked. I did it without thinking, with only the remembered voice of Doris in my head instructing me to use Primordium constantly. Who better to start with than my coworkers?

Will was more beautiful in Primordium than he was with regular sight. His life force glowed with the visual warmth of a small sun. It was all I could do to not reach out and touch him to see if he was as warm as he looked. Not wanting to be rude, I averted my gaze to Joy. Her life force sparkled, literally. Almost like someone had sprinkled glitter all over her.

"What Rose didn't tell you is that we're Illuminea," Joy said in a soft, musical voice.

"Illuminea?" I repeated stupidly. What was wrong with me? I wanted to touch Joy, too.

"I told you, she's totally ignorant," Rose said behind me. I turned to look at her. Her life force was a standard white, though abnormally pure for an adult. Unable to resist, I found my eyes drawn back to Will and Joy.

"You don't know what Illuminea are?" Will asked incredulously.

I licked my lips and shook my head. Niko I wanted to rub up against physically. I hadn't even thought about what his life force looked like. These two I wanted to rub my soul against. That definitely would be crossing the boundaries of personal space.

"We are highly evolved people who have chosen to step out of Primordium into this realm for a while."

"You what?"

"They're not human," Rose said behind me.

"Eh?" Why was this conversation so hard to follow?

"We're not nonhuman either," Joy said defensively. "We're just more advanced. When we feel the desire to help, or the desire for a physical form for a while, we come into this realm."

"They stick their noses into everyone's business and no one minds because they're all too happy to let them, is what she's trying to say," Rose translated.

"I'm sorry. You're not human?" I asked. Joy and Will shared a look and shrugged. "And what exactly is it that you do?"

"Add a little light to the world in our own small and humble ways," Joy said.

"I think you would be surprised how many nonhuman humans there are," Will said.

I was still trying to absorb the idea of nonhuman humans when I saw an albino imp at Joy's feet. It rubbed happily against her ankle, its glowing eyes watching me.

"There's an imp on your foot," I said as calmly as I could.

"Oh, that's Nemo," Joy said. "I named him after the fish."

"He's all white."

"Yep."

"You can see in Primordium?"

"We came from Primordium," Will reminded me gently. I looked toward his golden warmth, then back at the white imp.

"How is that possible?" I pointed to Nemo.

"Joy decided she wanted a pet," Will said with a shrug.

"Aren't the imps so cute?" Joy asked, reaching down to pet the imp. It bounced up to rub eagerly on her hand, nipping at her soul with sharp, white teeth.

"Until they feed on you." I was trying hard not to be rude, but I felt *way* out of my element.

Joy shrugged, as if a silly little thing like having your life sucked away was no big deal. "I just had to have one, and this guy was following me around."

"Imps do that to us. They can't resist us," Will explained.

"How is this possible?"

"It took a while," Joy began.

"Five months, three weeks, and two days," Will filled in.

"I fed him some *lux lucis*, a little trickle at a time, and he kept coming back for more."

"Of course he did. You're like chocolate cheesecake to him." Will sounded indignant.

"Not anymore. Now Nemo loves me, don't you, Nemo? Don't you?" Joy had reverted to a tone that I seldom used with Mr. Bond even when we were alone. She also didn't seem to notice the bites Nemo was happily taking out of her soul.

I met Rose's gaze above Joy's head. "If you think that's bizarre, think about how this looks to me," she said.

"Crazy." I meant the albino imp, but Rose eyed Joy and nodded in agreement. I blinked. Joy looked insane petting at the air near her ankle.

"If you couldn't guess, Will and Joy are brother and sister."

I eyed the Illuminea with regular vision but couldn't find a resemblance between the two nonhuman humans. From bone structure and height to coloring and facial features, they shared no trait in common. It was, however, much easier to look at Will now. With normal sight, I didn't feel the urge to cling to him. I still thought he looked very nice, and if he asked me to help him move from a fourth-floor walk-up or push his broken-down car, I probably wouldn't be able to resist.

"Rose! Madison!" Brad Pitt bellowed from his office.

"I think the boss wants us," Rose said.

"Nice to meet you," Will said, and Joy seconded it, still petting the air near her ankle.

As Rose and I walked to Mr. Pitt's office, I asked, "If they're brother and sister, how come only Will has an accent?"

"Oh, he's been around longer and lived in Britain for a while. You'll get used to them. Everyone's enthralled by Illuminea when they meet them. Most people don't know why, though. You've seen them in Primordium, right? Then you know why."

"How many Illuminea are there?"

"In the world? Who knows. In our area, they're the only two, but there's a few in Sacramento and more than their share up in the hills in the less-populated areas. They prefer areas with a larger plant-to-human ratio."

I had a thousand more questions, but we were already in Mr. Pitt's office. He had opened a thin cupboard on the side wall to a map of the greater Roseville area. It was hung a little low for me, but it was the perfect height for Mr. Pitt. He started talking without turning around.

"Something fuzzy is going on here." He jabbed his finger at a spot on Sierra College Boulevard. "It's been blipping on and off my radar for a few days now, and I think it's here to stay. Go investigate it and clear it out."

"Sure thing, boss," Rose said.

"Doris showed you what to do last night, right, Madison?" Mr. Pitt asked, turning to pin me with his dark eyes.

"Yes, sir."

Mr. Pitt snorted. He redirected his gaze to Rose. "Make sure she doesn't do anything stupid."

"That's above my pay grade."

8

GOT TOYS?

ROSE STEERED ME OUT OF the office. "Grab your purse. It's hunting time. I hope Doris crammed in a few years' worth of knowledge last night."

I waited while she collected her luggage-size purse and we walked out together. Sharon's eyes tracked us over the rim of the desk. Rose told her good-bye and I waved. Sharon didn't blink.

Anticipation warred with anxiety as we crossed the parking lot. I was eager to take out a few imps and prove to Mr. Pitt that I could be useful. I'd performed miserably yesterday, and it was a small miracle I still had a job. But was it a job I wanted? Doris had claimed that I couldn't get rid of soul-sight, but that didn't mean I was ready to barrel forward along this career path. I'd felt so righteous last night, cleansing evil from the world, but lower than a cockroach this morning for harming Mr. Bond. I had a wealth of ignorance and a pittance of skill. What was to say I wouldn't do more harm than good today?

Give this job a chance, I reasoned with myself. *And perfect recharging!* If I still didn't like the job in a few weeks, I'd quit then, after my bills were paid.

Plus, I *had* done very well last night, I reminded myself. Doris had said I was a natural. She may have added something about how I was as naturally gifted as most teens, but I took it as a good sign. If there were teenage IEs in charge of other regions, at least I was good enough to keep up with them. The only nagging problem was that I didn't know *what* I was supposed to be doing.

"What did Mr. Pitt mean, something was blipping on and off his radar?" I asked Rose when we were cruising along in my Civic.

"That's the warden's job. Brad lets us know where things are getting dark in our region and sends the appropriate people to fix it."

"It won't always be me?"

"Nope. We all pull our own weight. Like how today I'm along to make sure you don't end up rolling on the ground in terror. Again."

I decided to change the topic. "Is Mr. Pitt always so, um, eloquent?"

"Nah. He's in a mood today. The sooner you're performing up to par, the better. The fact that not knowing what you're doing doesn't slow you down will definitely help. Kyle was all about planning, doing research, developing a strategy, and thinking things through before jumping in. You must learn best by doing."

"Something like that." How did one go about researching evil, let alone developing a strategy?

"There's our spot."

We passed a construction site on the left side of the road, a landscaped divider forcing us to travel up the hill to the next light before backtracking. There were a plethora of "No Parking" and "Trucks Only" signs at the entrance, so I cruised beyond it again, finding parking on a side street nearly four blocks away. Rose and I got out and walked back, and I was cursing my heeled shoes before we'd gone two blocks. I'd forgotten to ask about a dress code, so I'd opted for business attire this morning, which meant I was overdressed in tan slacks, an emerald cashmere V-neck sweater with my black jacket over it, and black calf boots with one-inch kitten heels. Rose was even more dressed up than me in a tight, short black skirt with black stockings and a boatneck silk fuchsia top that strained across her breasts, but she sashayed along with no difficulty despite her stiletto heels.

Cars rushed by us at forty-five-plus miles per hour. My dark brown hair whipped around my face in stinging slaps, and I tried to hold it down with one hand. I'd pulled it half back again today to keep it out of my eyes, but now I was wishing I'd kept the ponytail I'd originally thrown it in for my rushed visit to Dr. Love. I hadn't expected to be marching in the wind today, and besides, I liked leaving my wavy hair loose to fall down my back. As Bridget was fond of saying, my ego was in my hair, and I needed a pick-me-up after my terrible morning.

Leaving my hair loose, the scent of my shampoo drifting around me, made me feel deliciously feminine, confident, and in control—traits that I sadly needed to be reminded I did occasionally possess.

I had a feeling that Bridget would have something pointed and insightful to say about my "ego" repeatedly slapping me in the face as I strode toward my first assignment. I chose not to think about it.

The sidewalk ended abruptly where the construction site began. The housing development was going up in stages. Three tiered levels of dirt lots ramped away from the main road, and I assumed more went down the back side of the barren, bulldozed land until it came up against the greenbelt and biking trails in the protected shallow ravine beyond. Houses were being built on the ridge of the property; the front tiers nearest the busy road were only flattened lots cluttered with equipment. I'd driven by this housing site many times before construction had begun, admiring the tall, old oak trees and beautiful rolling hills of wild grass. After they'd toppled the trees and scraped away the layer of life, I'd been disgusted by the sight but was a capitalist enough to want to buy one of the properties on the back side near what was left of the natural landscape.

A Jeep full of college guys roared past, the guys whistling and making catcalls at us.

I rolled my eyes.

"See anything strange?" Rose asked.

Reminded of our purpose, I blinked. The bright morning light swapped with darkness like I'd thrown a switch that turned day into night. My gaze was on the road when I refocused, and I was unexpectedly hypnotized by the streaming white lights of people as they seemed to float down the hill and past me in the loud, dark bodies of their cars.

"Is there something in the road?"

"Uh, no. Just cars." I turned my gaze to the construction site. The hills of dirt were gray mounds of dead soil. Near the top of the hill, easy for me to see without the glare of the sun or shadows of half-constructed houses, were the shapes of construction workers. I scanned the ground for imps, finding none. "I don't see anything. Let's get closer."

We wobbled along the side of the road, clinging to the edge of the pavement for balance. I should have had an easier time of it than Rose since my heels were negligible, but I lacked her years of experience.

When you're five-ten, you don't need three-inch heels to give you height. In fact, it'd only been since college that I'd become comfortable towering over people. Even then, I preferred my flats and tennis shoes for most activities.

After the fourth time tripping and scuffing the toe of my black leather boots, I blinked to normal vision so I could see the contours of the ground more easily. I had to stop and hold my arms out for balance at the rush of color and light. The cars barreling past close enough that my pants rippled from the buffeting winds no longer looked pretty or fascinating—they were just scary.

"After all this effort, there'd better be some cute ones. I'm not walking all this way for some beach ball–bellied balding men," Rose declared.

"Hear, hear."

We dodged out of the way of an empty gravel truck leaving the main entrance, and Rose boldly walked onto the private property like she had been invited. I followed after a brief hesitation. The workers saw us coming and stopped what they were doing to watch. Or more accurately, they saw Rose; I wasn't sure if I was visible next to her swaying hips and breasts—not that I wanted that kind of attention, of course.

I ran my hands through my hair, which was doing a much better job of staying in place now that we'd left the busy road behind, and I straightened my posture.

"Hi, there!" Rose called, waving a hand at her admirers.

It may have been early November, but there were still a few shirtless bronze-chested young men standing around with nail guns and pneumatic staplers. There were also a few leathery-skinned old men with their shirts off, but I chose not to focus on them.

"You seeing anything suspicious?" Rose asked me out of the side of her mouth.

Oh. Right. I blinked. We were almost upon the men, at which point I sincerely hoped Rose had a story for them, because I couldn't think of a good reason why two businesswomen would be roaming a private construction site in the middle of the day.

For the most part, the men looked like what I expected: mostly light gray souls with patches of darker shades. Two had dark oil running through the white of their souls. Doris had lectured a little about people's souls—or life force—while we'd been driving around last night. People could be good or evil, but most were a shade somewhere in between. Everyone was born with a white soul. Then little evil acts make the soul turn gray. Large evil acts make the oil-like black spots appear.

Doris hadn't given me a specific scale for what constituted a light gray consequence and at what point a negative action crossed the line to charcoal and black. She claimed that the more I used my ability to examine people, the better judge I'd become, and I'd develop an instinct for judging a person's proclivity toward evil. It'd felt like a cop-out answer.

However, Doris had assured me that adults were easier to judge and predict future choices based on their souls than teenagers were. Judging adolescents would get easier with time, or so she'd promised, but she'd agreed I shouldn't make any important decisions regarding teens for a while.

"If bad actions turn a soul black, can good actions clean it back to white?" I'd asked.

"You betcha," Doris had said. "The soul's constantly in flux. But by the time most people are in their twenties, their personalities—and the fates of their souls—are pretty much set. The amount of good and evil stays in relative balance from there on out, barring extreme circumstances and interference of evil minions or us good folk, of course."

Last night I'd been satisfied with her answer, but now I wondered about myself. I'd made my share of bad decisions and I wasn't a saint, but I couldn't see so much as a smudge on my soul. Could I simply not see my own failings, or did my soul's purity have to do with my ability to see Primordium and work with *lux lucis*? The latter made sense, given that all the souls of my coworkers were equally as pure. We were crusaders of light. You couldn't have a tainted soul and do that, too, could you? I didn't think so. And I was positive that if I told Rose I thought of us as "crusaders of light" I'd have to carry her back to the car because she'd be laughing too hard to walk, and then she'd never let me hear the end of it.

Remembering my task, I scanned the area around the men. Right away, I saw two imps, but they were farther up the hill, too far for them to notice me, especially not when there were several other easier victims between us. One of the oil-stained-soul guys had three imps attached to him, one at the elbow, two on his calf. I watched their ticklike mouths suck at his soul and felt light-headed. Squaring my shoulders, I headed for him.

"Where're you going?" Rose hissed.

"To save someone."

"Aw, shit."

"Hi!" I said brightly to the men around me. I blinked to focus on the terrain and tripped sideways into the nearest dusty man. He caught my elbow and I gave him an overly large smile.

"Can we help you?" one of the less dumbfounded, older men asked.

I searched for the man I planned on saving. He was the youngest in the group, covered in tattoos, and scowling at me fiercely enough to make me pause.

"I'm . . . I'm . . ." *Think, Dice!* "I'm a real estate agent. I wanted to come by and see the property." *Brilliant.* "This is my assistant, Ro—uh, Romaine." I tossed Rose an apologetic look. She glowered at me, then turned her full smile on the man who was questioning us.

"You gentlemen look like you're doing a fine job," she said, strutting up to place her hand on the questioning man's sweaty arm. The proximity of her ample breasts to his arm seemed to momentarily transfix the man, and I used the advantage to meander up the dusty, nail-strewn path to the house. I didn't beeline straight for Rebel Boy, not wanting to look too obvious. I peered inside the framework of the house and blinked.

There weren't any other imps inside. Just the three leeched to Rebel Boy. I double-checked the other man who had black streaks in his soul. Whatever he'd done had left him tainted but imp-free. I'd made it within a few feet of the guy when a booming voice stopped me in my tracks.

"What's going on here? Who are you, and what the hell are you doing on private property?"

I spun to see a large, solid gray figure barreling down the hill toward us. I didn't need to see a name badge to see *supervisor* written all over the guy. Nor did it take a genius to realize we were moments away from being evicted.

"Sir, we're here to check out the properties," Rose explained, cool and brisk. She stepped into the man's path and he obligingly stopped.

Rebel Boy adjusted himself and spat. He tossed a hammer idly in his hand, most of his attention on the scene unfolding a few feet away. Were we going to be fined? Thrown in jail? Fired? *Shit, shit, shit.*

I blinked while turning my head. The world spun toward my feet. I staggered, clutching my mouth to hold in vomit. Color rushed into the world, and I found myself staring at a gelatinous loogie. I sucked in air and blinked again, swallowing convulsively. I tripped when the world made an unexpected duck left. When my head cleared, I realized my hand was touching something warm. I looked up into the eyes of Rebel Boy.

"Oh! I'm so sorry! I'm not usually this clumsy," I said, feeling a blush rush to my cheeks. I stepped quickly back. Behind me I could hear Rose arguing with the supervisor. I stared at the imp attached to the guy's arm and grimaced. *Just do it, Dice!* I pushed *lux lucis* into my hands and grabbed the imp. It imploded the moment I touched it, and my hands flared brightly, out of control. Before I could think about it, I dropped to a crouch and grabbed, two-handed, for the imps on his calves. They imploded and I quickly released the excess light.

"What the fuck are you doing, lady?" Rebel Boy demanded, scuttling backward.

I blinked, steadied myself against the ground, then slowly stood. Rose was calling to me. The supervisor was shouting. I met Rebel Boy's eyes. He looked scared, and I was suddenly aware of how crazy I must have looked lurching at the air around his body.

"I . . . uh . . . I . . ." I turned and escaped toward the scowling supervisor and Rose. "We're leaving, sir. I'm so sorry to have troubled you." I grabbed Rose's elbow and trotted her along with me. "Won't happen again," I called over my shoulder.

Rose jerked her arm out of my hand when we were halfway down the hill.

"Who do you think you are? The karate kid? What were you doing back there?" Rose demanded.

"He had imps on him. Did I look totally crazy?"

Rose paused in the middle of the construction road and mimicked my slicing motions through the air, throwing in a kick or two that I hadn't.

"Not here! They can see you."

"They already saw your smooth moves, girl," Rose said, laughing. I tried to get her moving again, but she started chopping the air around me. "It was like you were grabbing at flies or something. Whoo-eee, Madison! You're a riot!"

The adrenaline tapered off, and even though I was blushing hot enough to break a sweat, I giggled. Rose started walking, but every time I stopped laughing, she hacked the air around us, making us laugh all over again.

We were almost to the car when she stopped chuckling. Shaking her head, she said, "You can never trust an alpaca."

"Excuse me?"

"The supervisor. He's going to die, trampled by alpaca."

"What? Why would you say that?"

"I get these feelings."

"You get feelings about how people will die?"

"Sure. It's sort of a hobby of mine. I can predict people's deaths."

"Accurately?"

Rose frowned. "Of course."

I couldn't tell if she was serious or not. I pictured Rose sneaking into morgues and memorial services, double-checking on people whose deaths she'd foreseen.

"Is that something all empaths can do?"

"Doubt it. The other guys' deaths weren't as obvious. Took a little time to figure out, but the guy you were scaring with your cha-cha skills will die bungee jumping, choking on his gum. The other ones were boring: tree felling gone wrong, mob hit, and avalanche."

"How is an alpaca trampling obvious?" A heart attack would have been my guess for the supervisor, if his girth and temper were anything to go by.

"Trust me, once you've met an alpaca owner, you'll recognize the next. That guy is hip deep in alpaca farming, but he'd get out if he had any sense."

I didn't even want to ask what crazy deaths she'd predicted to think that a mob hit was boring. That sounded like a bizarre way to go, the type of death reserved for cinematic characters, not real people.

Since we'd reached my car, and the conversation had veered into uncomfortable territory, I decided to change the subject. "You know, that would have gone a lot smoother if I'd had a wand thingy." I envisioned the *lux lucis*–filled stick Doris had used the night before. Rather than lurching around Rebel Boy like a drunken grope gone wrong, I could have waved my wand, pretending to point with it, or something equally sly and in no way embarrassing.

"A what?"

"You know, a weapon."

"I think you're dangerous enough all by yourself." Rose tossed a kick in the air, with a loud "Hee-yah!" then grabbed the open car door for stability.

"Not a real weapon," I corrected with a grin. "A *lux lucis* one."

"Oh, you mean you need accessories. Let's go shopping." Rose gave me directions to a place at the end of Douglas Boulevard in Granite Bay that made "specialty items."

The strip mall looked like an intercity transplant, not a shopping center in the most affluent zip code in the county. The stores had been built in the seventies and I doubted they had been repainted since. We bounced through uneven pavement to a parking space in front of a shop with the creative name Accessories and More. The windows were barred with wrought iron, the door had a cage of metal on it, and there was more neon in the window than five bars combined. Everything about the place screamed, "Go away, come in."

The interior of the shop was dim and packed so tight that we couldn't walk two abreast down the aisles. Everything from cell phones to purses to gum to watches was crammed haphazardly on metal shelving units usually reserved for mini-marts and gas stations. The white tile floor was smudged gray and the pattern was worn away from the door to the counter. The store had probably opened with the shopping center, and nothing inside except merchandise had been moved since.

There were no other customers, and all the other vehicles in the parking lot were bunched two doors down in front of the liquor store.

"Musad, Muhamad," Rose called to two men standing behind a glass-case counter that held the register.

"Rose. So good to see you," one of the men said. They were twins. The one on the left wore a red shirt, and the one on the right wore a striped orange and black shirt, but otherwise they were a mirror image of each other, both with thick black hair that was losing the battle against gray, rounded beer bellies, and dark skin. When they smiled at Rose, even their movements and mannerisms were identical.

"Who have you brought with you?" the man in the orange and black shirt asked.

"Fellas, this is Madison Fox. She's our new IE." My eyebrows shot up. Was I the only person in Roseville who didn't know about illuminant enforcers? Maybe the secret society I'd been initiated into wasn't a secret at all. Maybe I was just the last person to find out.

"Pleased to meet you, Madison. I'm Musad," the man in the red shirt said.

"And I'm Muhamad, the good-looking twin. You must be here for some goodies. What can I help you with today?"

"This girl needs everything," Rose said.

"Everything? Where did you transfer from?" Muhamad asked.

"Transfer? She's fresh off the boat."

Both men turned to give me a once-over; then they shared a quick look.

"You better not mention my age," I warned them. Identical right eyebrows quirked, silently voicing their unfavorable opinion of my delayed initiation to my career and my subsequent limited abilities. There was a slight possibility that I was feeling a tad defensive and reading too much into their facial tic. *No, not me.*

"I'm a quick learner," I added, feeling obligated to defend myself. *Speaking of things I'm supposed to be learning . . .* I blinked. I examined the twins first, surprised to see that even though they knew about IEs, appeared to be trusted by Rose, and dealt in "goodies" that I could use, they were not purely good. In fact, there were a few construction workers who could teach these two men a thing or two about soul cleanliness. I peered around the shop. No imps. No other life. Everything was as it should be. I blinked back and steadied myself on the counter.

"You'll need a flashlight," Musad said.

"And some pet wood," Muhamad said.

"Excuse me?"

"Pet wood," Muhamad repeated, looking at Rose in askance. She gave him an "I told you so" shrug. "And a knife. You probably haven't settled on a favorite weapon yet. Do you have a cell phone?"

"Her first ever," Rose said helpfully. She was enjoying my discomfort.

"Let me guess: most expensive on the shelf?" Muhamad asked.

"Oh, yeah. Those salesmen saw 'sucker' written all over her."

"Hey! I like Medusa."

"Medusa?" all three asked at once.

I blushed and pulled out my pretty green phone, wishing I were anywhere but here. Rose gave me a very eloquent eyebrow raise. Musad snatched Medusa from my hand.

"Hmm. At least it's not an iPhone." He flipped it on and began pressing buttons. Muhamad rolled his eyes at him.

"Take a look at these." He gestured toward the end of the glass case, and I obligingly peered through the glass at several yard-long rods and a fanned array of knives. "You can't get more simple than pet wood. Stick some *lux lucis* in it, stick the wood in an imp, and voila! Disintegrated imp!"

Based on that description, *pet wood* equaled *wand*. I was in the right place.

"How exactly do you know about these things?" I asked.

Muhamad tapped the side of his nose. "We've seen a few things in our time." I glanced at Rose. I wanted to demand more of an explanation from Muhamad, but Rose shook her head. "Now the knives are obviously shorter, but they have the added benefit of causing physical injury along with"—he fluttered his hand, looking for the word—"spiritual injury."

"Physical injury? No thanks!" I thought about Rebel Boy. He really would have freaked out if I'd started stabbing the air around him with a knife.

"But, Madison, you'll need—"

"No. Thanks," I repeated firmly. "Let me see the, uh, pet wood."

"She's only worked with imps," Rose said from behind me.

"Oh dear."

I ignored them. I wasn't going to get a knife, and that was final. I hardly trusted myself with my kitchen knives; there was no way I was going to start carrying a knife as a weapon. I'd probably end up hurting someone, and it would most likely be me.

"Why is it called pet wood?" I asked.

"It's like petrified wood, only not as old. Unlike dead wood, which can hold a bit of *lux lucis*, the lifelike plant properties in pet wood make it highly conducive for *lux lucis*."

That made a certain amount of sense. The wood around my windows and door had held the *lux lucis* wards, but it was as if the energy sat on top of the surface. I couldn't have pushed *lux lucis* through the wall if I'd tried.

Muhamad placed an array of rods on the glass countertop. They ranged in thickness and length. I hefted a few of them, not knowing what I was looking for. In Primordium they looked the same: like dead wood. I experimented with *lux lucis*, gathering it in my hands, then touching my hands to a rod like Doris had shown me with wards. The wood retained a faint glow. I picked up a rod and pushed *lux lucis* into it like it was an imp. It began to glow as bright as my hands. I continued to feed it *lux lucis*, fascinated. Suddenly a pressure inside the rod that I hadn't even been aware of broke, and the *lux lucis* dissipated, leaving the pet wood black.

"That was stupid," Rose said.

I blinked and looked at the rod I held. Its soft brown color was now charred black.

"I'm afraid I'm going to have to charge you for that one," Muhamad said cheerfully. "Good to see that you've got it in you, though. Try this one: It's a favorite of the local enforcers." He placed in my hand a rod I'd been avoiding because it was no longer than five inches; then he grabbed my wrist and flicked my hand. The rod expanded like an antennae to about four feet long.

"Nice." I blinked to Primordium and pushed energy into the wood, paying careful attention to the pressure pushing back against me. The rod held a lot of *lux lucis*. I poked at the ground with it. It'd be really nice to not have to get so close to the imps. "I'll take it," I said.

"Excellent choice."

"You said you have Primordium flashlights?"

"More than you'll find anywhere else," Muhamad said with pride. He led me to the back of the shop where every flashlight ever invented was displayed on shelves and hooks. Gesturing, he said, "This row works only in Primordium. This row works in both worlds."

I checked the prices. The flashlights that served double duty were triple the price. Since I could find a regular flashlight anywhere, I opted for the ones that shone in Primordium only. It took double-A batteries, so I grabbed a packet hanging from a display near the counter.

"Are you sure you don't want a knife?"

"Very sure."

"If knives aren't your style, we have swords, staffs, spears, canes—I think we even have some arrows around here, and we could order you a custom bow."

"Uh, no. Thanks, though."

Muhamad shrugged at Rose. Rose shrugged back. "I tried," he said.

"Yep. She's as thickheaded as every enforcer."

"With no experience?"

"Zip."

Muhamad shook his head. I frowned at them.

Musad set my phone on the counter.

"I've made a few necessary modifications, added an app. Now you can take pictures in Primordium." He showed me how to navigate the menu screen and switch the camera from regular light to "Pri pics." Then he had me take a few pictures of the shop to make sure I knew how to use it. I took a picture of Rose and let her see how she looked. It obviously was not the first time she'd seen herself in Primordium. She was more interested in pictures of me, and she played with Medusa while I paid for my new toys.

"One thousand six hundred twenty-five dollars," Muhamad announced.

I tried to keep my face neutral when I handed him my ATM card. I looked at my three items—well, four, if you counted the rod I'd burnt out. Enforcer business wasn't cheap.

"Are they human?" I asked Rose when we were back in my car.

She shrugged. "As far as I know."

I didn't know what to make of that. "Did you pick up anything from them? You know, empathically?" I wiggled my fingers at my head and she gave me a dark look.

"They were very pleased with the sale. They would have been more pleased if you'd gotten a knife. I would have been, too."

"What about how they're going to die?"

"Muhamad and Musad? No. I didn't get any feelings from them."

It seemed callous to be disappointed, so I said nothing.

Rose waited in the car when I parked at my complex and ran up to my apartment to check on Mr. Bond. I found him curled up on my pillow. He cracked an eye at me and stretched when I scratched his chin. The lump of liquid between his shoulder blades had gone down in size, but it still looked like a grotesque growth. I checked his food bowl and saw that he'd eaten a little. Reassured, I gave him one last pat before leaving.

"As your official babysitter, I decree it's time to get some food," Rose announced when I returned to the car.

My stomach grumbled in agreement, so I decided not to take exception to the babysitter comment.

"At least Mr. Pitt will be happy when we get back," I said once we'd settled at an orange plastic table at a nearby taqueria. Things were looking up: Mr. Bond was doing better, I had successfully completed an assignment, I was equipped for the next challenge, and I was about to consume a huge burrito loaded with guacamole and sour cream.

"What do you mean?"

"At the construction site. I took care of the evil, and it was even easy."

"You think a few mad Tae Bo moves cleaned up the area?"

"It didn't?"

Rose snorted. "If that guy was the evil Brad felt, then I'm Sofia Vergara. More likely, there's something else going on there, and those imps just saw some easy food."

"Oh."

"Don't go getting all depressed on me. You'll figure out what the real issue is. I'm sure your initiative and enthusiasm will win you a few points with Brad."

I ate my burrito in silence, my good mood punctured.

We reported immediately to Mr. Pitt when we got back to the office. I was determined to put a good spin on the outing and took the lead.

"We tried to take a look at the area, but it's a construction site, and we got kicked off by the crew," I said. "I've got a few ideas of how to get around them." I had no ideas, but I'd think of some.

Mr. Pitt waved his hand dismissively at my words. "Sit. Both of you. We've got a bigger problem. It's at the Roseville Hotel off North Sunrise. Something cropped up in the last two hours that wasn't there yesterday."

"Sounds big," Rose said.

"This much activity this fast . . . yeah, it's big. If Madison were Kyle . . ." He shrugged. "If Niko were here, I'd send him."

"Where is he?"

"Emergency in Shasta."

"Shoot."

"Hey, give me a chance, guys," I said. "I'm not completely useless."

Mr. Pitt and Rose didn't look at me. Mr. Pitt sighed.

"At least she's enthusiastic," Rose said. "Look at her. She doesn't have a clue what she's up against, but she doesn't let that stop her. She's fearless."

"I got pet wood today," I said, since Rose's argument didn't seem to be doing me any favors.

"You hear that, boss? She's got pet wood. What more could she need?"

Mr. Pitt dropped his head into his hands with a groan. "Okay."

Rose gave me a thumbs-up. The burrito churned in my gut. I was pretty sure we'd just talked me into a situation I was completely unprepared for.

9

ALL YOUR BASE ARE BELONG TO US

DON'T *DO* ANYTHING," MR. PITT said for the third time. "Assess the situation. That's it. You got your phone's camera fixed to work in Primordium, right?"

I nodded.

"Good. Take pictures. But don't do *anything* else."

"What about Joy and Will? Why not send them?" I didn't want to seem like a coward, but if there were more qualified people, it seemed wiser to send them.

"They're Illuminea. They're like walking lollipops for creatures of the dark. If they get too close to whatever it is, they'll be mobbed by the underlings."

At my confused look, Rose explained: "They don't fight back. They influence people. They're no good against the creatures of darkness. They're strictly people-people."

That sounded like a personal flaw.

"Which is why you're necessary, Madison," Mr. Pitt said. "You can fight back. Not that you're going to. This time you won't attract attention, right?"

"But what if there are imps—"

"Yeah, I know—the imps find you fascinating. They find a lot of light, bright souls fascinating. Try not to look right at them in Primordium, and they won't know you can see them."

I scowled at him. That wasn't what Kyle had told me when I took the job. "And if they bite me?"

"Be discreet." Mr. Pitt fixed us with a serious, bug-eyed stare. "This is strictly a recon mission. Once we know what we're up against, we'll formulate a plan."

"Sure thing, boss," Rose said.

I stood when she did, and we headed for the door.

If they think I can do this, then I can, I encouraged myself.

"Madison," Mr. Pitt called. I turned around. "Don't do anything stupid."

I'd fully restored my self-confidence by the time we got back to my car. After all, I'd been able to handle all the imps I'd encountered so far (the first one by the fire station didn't count), I had a new pet wood wand full of *lux lucis*, and I was doing what I was born to do, which surely was a plus on my side. Playing spy at a hotel would be a piece of cake.

What I didn't account for were all the nerds.

The Roseville Hotel boasted what no other hotel in the county could claim: enormous conference halls at a reduced rate, or so I assumed. Most conferences in the area were hosted in Sacramento, which was fifteen minutes away with a population triple the size of Roseville. Yet the Sixteenth Annual Gamers' Fan-tasy Land Convention had set up camp in the High Sierra conference hall on the second floor of the Roseville Hotel. The geeks, however, swarmed the entire grounds.

Rose and I were swept along in a gaggle of pasty, overweight, pubescent boys as we neared the entrance. We funneled through the lobby doors behind an obese teen dressed as some sort of Pokémon character and his scrawny Darth Maul friend. A clutch of pimply boys in matching Luigi outfits darted around the main crowd and ran, backpacks jostling, toward the elevators.

"Are you sure we haven't found the source of the evil Mr. Pitt felt?" I asked Rose.

"You'd think so, right?"

Through the lobby and to the elevators, we swam with the herd, deciding to postpone the floor-by-floor check we had previously planned in lieu of following the masses. Gamely, we crammed into an elevator that was filled over capacity, and I did my best to hold my breath: Not only had someone failed to teach these boys the value of outdoor activities, but they'd also failed to teach them about personal hygiene. Fortunately, the ride was short, and we burst out of the elevator onto the busy floor of the convention center, taking deep breaths of clean air.

I stepped to the side of the elevator to avoid being trampled by a trio of businessmen in slacks and ties and paused to take it all in. All the moveable interior walls had been removed so that a single, enormous room the width and breadth of the hotel was filled to bursting with gamer nerds. A clear grid of booths had been mapped out—there were even brochures at the entrances to help the foaming fans navigate. Every booth had a huge banner hanging from the ceiling over it and an enormous logo prominently displayed on the port-a-cube walls. Businessmen and a few businesswomen manned the booths, along with a collage of costumed characters, and the aisles swarmed with men and women of all ages and sizes, dressed in everything from homemade costumes and fanwear T-shirts to business attire. To add to the chaos, the conference center displayed more TVs, gaming consoles, flashing lights, and booming sound systems than most large electronics stores sold in a year.

"I heard the booth babes aren't as hot this year as they were last year," a spiked-hair, pimply faced teenager complained to his friend as another elevator-load of eager geeks rushed past us. "They made their clothing PG-13."

"But that's not accurate to the games!" his friend whined.

"Booth babes?" I asked Rose.

She pointed. At the entrance to the closest booth, a lanky young woman sauntered back and forth wearing little more than a bikini and some leg armor. A small crowd of men swelled in front of her, which she deftly formed into a line to enter the booth. A frenzy of cell phones and cameras centered on the woman, like the nerds were paparazzi in training. The bravest got a picture with her.

"That's sad. Sick. Degrading. And *so* not PG-13," I said, unable to tear my eyes away from the spectacle.

"At least her legs won't get hurt if she has to fight her way free."

"Always gotta make sure the vital body parts are covered before going into battle," I agreed.

Rose snorted. "Come on. This is definitely the place. My skin wants to crawl off."

"Oh, goodie."

All the open-door entrances were roped off and monitored by hotel staff, who checked tickets and bags. We were directed back to the lobby, where the attendant informed us that it would cost us seventy-five dollars each for the privilege of spending the day with video game dorks.

"This is extortion," Rose complained. "Why don't you pay for the both of us? It'll be easier for Mr. Pitt to reimburse only one of us."

I eyed her suspiciously and handed over my ATM card.

We suffered through another odorous elevator ride. I tried to be charitable: Maybe the smell wasn't my current companions but the residual stench of previous occupants seeping from the metal walls. Either way, I held my breath.

After handing over our tickets, being subjected to a pat-down and a purse search by security, and getting our hands stamped with a design that looked vaguely like an *H* with a stylized circle around it, we were admitted into the heart of the convention.

Rose pulled me into the crowd. The air inside the room was dank. There's no ventilation system yet invented that's capable of dispelling five hundred or more sweaty, excited men's body odor. Between the smell and the visual bombardment of so many moving screens and people, it was enough to make a woman sick. On top of that, the clamor of the crowd and competing sound systems battered against me at a level that was almost physical. I blinked to Primordium, hoping against hope that we were in the wrong place.

Imps scampered everywhere. I would have screamed, but that would have meant inhaling first. Instead, I settled for a death grip on Rose's arm.

"What'd you find?" she shouted.

"Imps. Everywhere," I whispered. It was harder than I thought it would be not to look at them. They bounced along in dark, seething clumps, following the whim of whatever thoughts entered their puny brains.

Rose must have read my lips, because she asked, "Are they feeding?"

I watched the herds discreetly. They ran along the aisles, passing around and partially through the feet and legs of all the fans, but only a few stopped to snack.

"That's strange. Most aren't taking a nibble." Maybe it was too large a feast for them to pick just one victim. Maybe it was a commentary on the food selection.

My hand twitched for the pet wood in my purse. It'd be so easy to kill the imps.

"Oh, no, you don't," Rose said, grabbing my elbow. I hadn't even realized I'd taken a step away from her.

I looked back at her in time to see a herd of imps bound down our aisle. Helplessly, I watched them come. It was one thing to be able to kill them. It was entirely another thing to watch impotently while the imps had their way with a defenseless crowd. I shuddered as the tangle of evil bounced closer.

"One or two?" I pleaded with Rose.

"You take out even one with that pet wood and the rest will know."

She was right. Even if I used my hands and was discreet, avoiding overcharging and turning myself into a *lux lucis* flare, the odds against my kill going unnoticed were slim.

The imps were almost past me when I made eye contact with one. It froze. I froze. It cocked its head and bounced slowly toward me.

"Shit, you're looking at one, aren't you?" Rose demanded, giving me a small shake.

Grimacing, I forced myself to tear my eyes from the adorable, horrible little creature, though I tried to keep it in my peripheral vision. "Not anymore."

"You look like you've got bad gas. Smile."

I thinned my lips, which was the best smile I could muster. From the corner of my eye, I watched the imp hop nearly to my feet before it bounded away to catch up with the rest of the herd.

A pair of booth babes walked by, so scantily clad I felt everyone should be able to see their souls as easily as I could. *Women, not booth babes,* I reminded myself.

"If one of them bites me, I'm destroying it," I warned Rose, gesturing vaguely down a crowded aisle at some imps.

"I don't think that'll be a problem. We're practically invisible with all these pesky clothes on."

"Not the men. The imps."

"Oh. No, you won't. Not here."

"What if one gets on you?"

"Vaporize it. Covertly."

I rolled my eyes at her back.

My skin felt twitchy as I followed Rose through the aisles. I switched back and forth between Primordium and normal sight nearly as often as I blinked, trying to see everything in both realms. If I staggered a bit more than I should have as I fought off the dizziness between visions, no one noticed in the jostle of the crowd.

Rose and I circled the outer perimeter first, looking for the main attraction, so to speak. I purposely avoided all speculation about the exact source of all these imps. It was clearly not the questionably sane masses of people. As bizarre and juvenile as I found the fans that filled the conference room, they weren't evil. Not at this scale. Whatever had attracted the imps, or whatever was allowing them to breed, was far worse than a few hundred horny men. I double-checked my assumption with Rose, and she agreed. Something larger was at work here. Since I didn't know what I was looking for, I concentrated on taking stealthy pictures of the imp herds and any door or booth they were attracted to. Maybe Mr. Pitt could make more sense of it than me.

The competition for the notice of fans was fierce, and the booths used every gimmick in their arsenal. Nearly naked women, I decided by the end, were the least annoying. They, at least, didn't assault my eardrums or, for the most part, my vision. I could even escape the flashing lights of all the monitors and displays in Primordium. The sound, however, was impossible to tune out. Each vendor was so close to the next that there was never just one song playing but a cacophony of songs that pounded against my skull. Somehow above all that noise was the drone of hundreds of voices. Though they all spoke English, it was not an English I understood, and it seemed to consist mostly of acronyms and excited squeals. Rose and I stopped trying to shout back and forth at each other after a few minutes and concentrated on pushing through the masses.

I think it was worse for Rose. Primordium, I could turn on and off. It didn't seem like empathy had a switch.

"Do you feel anything suspicious?" I asked Rose after we'd finished our first circuit.

"Nothing noteworthy, but if I start looking interested in these games, slap me. It's like all these boys are on a high. And if I turn into a horn-ball, it's not my fault either. There's *way* too much testosterone in here. I can practically taste it." She smacked her tongue against the roof of her mouth and grimaced.

"Horn-ball?"

Rose puckered her lips and blew me a kiss, batted her eyes at me, and ran her tongue over her upper lip.

"Got it. Horn-ball is bad. We'll rush you out of here."

A flash popped in our face. I glared at the guy holding the camera. He grinned at me and winked.

It took us over two hours to thoroughly investigate the entire floor, and by the time we were done, I felt like I'd been at an atrocious rock concert. I'd certainly seen enough leather, glow-in-the-dark apparel, and breasts that the ringing in my ears made the feeling only more authentic.

We stumbled back to my car in sunlight that was too bright in a world that had gone silent while we were inside. My nerves were frayed. I'd found myself reaching for an imp more than a dozen times before I remembered to stop myself. I'd had the pet wood out and fully extended no less than five times, and each time Rose had shoved it back into my purse. Against my body, it was invisible to the dark creatures of Primordium. In my hand, with me brandishing it like a sword, it looked exactly like what it was: a weapon.

Rose rubbed her arms and legs vigorously when we got in the car.

"Are there any on me?" she demanded.

I shook my head. I needed a shower.

Rose called Mr. Pitt while I drove.

"The place gave me the major heebie-jeebies. Madison says there are imps everywhere." Pause. "No. She was well behaved. Exactly what I wanted to see in an enforcer." Pause. "Yes. Many times. Which is my point. I don't want someone passive."

Back at the office, Rose showed me how to send the pictures from my phone to Mr. Pitt's email through my company e-mail address—an account I hadn't known I'd been given.

"This is it?" Mr. Pitt asked when we reported to his office. "Pictures of imps?"

"They were everywhere."

"You didn't see anything larger?"

I shook my head. "Maybe if you'd let me kill some."

"And then what? What would you have done if the imps had

mobbed you? Or better yet, if you'd fallen into a turbonis or attracted the attention of a demon?"

A demon or a what? I wisely kept my mouth shut.

"This was a waste of time. Go home. I'll figure something out. I want both of you back here at eight thirty tomorrow."

"Babysitter again, boss?" Rose asked.

Mr. Pitt nodded.

"Damn. Okay."

I slumped out of the office after Rose. I might not be sure I wanted this job, but I didn't like feeling like I was letting everyone down. Rationally I knew I wasn't capable of handling all the evil I'd seen at the hotel. I simply didn't have the experience. It was frustrating, even without Mr. Pitt's obvious disappointment.

I glanced in the direction of the hotel. Though I couldn't see it, it was almost like I could feel the swell of evil beyond the horizon. Evil that I'd done absolutely nothing about. What was the point of being an IE if I didn't get to save people from having their souls turned into snacks?

What good would you have done if you'd announced yourself as the tastiest snack of all? Killing a few dozen imps last night had wiped me out; I wasn't sure what attempting to kill a hundred or more would do to me.

"Hey, don't be hard on yourself," Rose said when we were in the parking lot. "It's only your second day. No one expects you to be able to do it all yet."

"Mr. Pitt does."

"He's just used to having Kyle. It'll do him good to have to do a little work. Anyway, I'm still horny. If I'm going to have to do this two days in a row, I need to spend some quality time with my main squeeze. See you tomorrow."

I shuffled to my car and slid behind the seat. The convention hadn't left residual feelings of anything good for me. My nerves were in tatters and my pride was bruised. The day had started badly and it'd only gotten worse. What little confidence I'd gained while out with Doris had all but evaporated. Mr. Pitt clearly didn't trust me with any big jobs, and every job was looking big at the moment.

I considered going straight home and calling it a night, but I was too restless. I grabbed a sandwich at Subway, which helped stabilize my shaking hands, but my insides still felt like they'd gone through the dryer with a pair of tennis shoes.

"Tomorrow's going to be better," I assured myself. "I'll make sure it is." Waking up tomorrow to Mr. Bond prancing on my stomach would make the day ten times better than today.

The thought reminded me of all the dead plants on my balcony. "There's a problem I can fix."

Feeling a little better now that I had a goal, I headed down Douglas toward Granite Bay, feeling like my whole life revolved around Douglas Boulevard lately. I peeled away from the homeward-bound commuter traffic and into the one-way loop parking lot at Bushnell Gardens Nursery, and some of the day's tension lifted from my muscles. The nursery sprawled across several acres just outside of Roseville, and though it was designed more for people with houses and yards to landscape, it still had plenty of indoor plants. It also had an enormous cage of tiny birds. It was to this cage that I went first.

In the midst of oriental plants, bridges, and yard decor, the huge round cage swirled with activity. The racket of the birds' calls and the flutter of wings was oddly soothing. I blinked to Primordium and watched the beautiful light shapes flutter around the aviary like a kaleidoscope. When I finally tore my gaze from their hypnotizing mass to look around, it was like looking at a winter wonderland. Plants of all shapes and sizes glowed with iridescent life. I wandered through their midst, admiring the beauty of so much pure, good life. After all the evil and darkness I'd seen today, it was a balm for my eyes and soul.

I roamed through aisle after aisle until the last of the day's tension ebbed from my shoulders. Only then did I get a cart and start piling it full of plants. In the end, it took three carts of plants and over four hundred dollars to achieve a sense of security. I was not going to take another chance with Mr. Bond's life.

An older salesman with a kind smile helped me spread the emergency blanket I kept in the trunk over the Civic's backseat; then we stuffed in plants where they would fit. They filled the trunk, backseat, and floorboard and dangled out the windows. Two more tall plants fit on the passenger floorboard, with the foliage bent back toward the backseat. The seat itself we covered with ivy plants and smaller pots. I wedged my purse in the middle of them. The salesman gave me a jaunty wave as I backed out, and I drove off into the sunset feeling like I was part of a moving rain forest.

The combination of soothing plants and the pensive time of day put the final restoring touches on my self-confidence. Just because Mr. Pitt had dismissed me didn't mean I had to stop doing my job. Any practice would help, and I was definitely going to need it if I decided to keep this job after my savings account was restocked. I turned off Douglas into a quiet older neighborhood and blinked to Primordium.

Nausea mixed with vertigo, and I lifted my foot from the gas pedal, belatedly checking my side mirror. Luckily, I was alone on the suburban street. Even at fifteen miles per hour, seeing the white lawns, bushes, and trees sweep by on either side with only a black road and empty, black sky before me created a tunnel effect, like moving through a vortex. In Primordium, I no longer had the headlights to point out things like stop signs and the sides of the road. I had to focus intently on the subtle shades of gray to see the difference between the asphalt of the road and the concrete of the sidewalk. The brilliance of the plant-filled interior of my car made it harder than it would have normally been, too. I couldn't see anything out my right window or rearview mirror. Of course, I couldn't see anything in those directions with regular sight, either.

My head nearly hit the roof and my teeth snapped together when I jostled over a speed bump I hadn't seen. I lurched to right a tall plant on the floorboard, which had bounced to obstruct my vision. A horn blared to my left, and the dark bumper of a car jerked to a halt just short of hitting me in the middle of an intersection. I swerved, bouncing the right tires up the dark curb.

"Eeek!" My elbow knocked into the door as my abused Civic canted to the left. I jerked the wheel, and my brain rattled in my skull as the right tires bounced back to the road. My vision cleared in time to distinguish the faint outline of a tall black plastic garbage bin against the charcoal black of the asphalt.

"Gnaah!" My reflexes weren't fast enough to save the trash. The plastic container bounced off the front bumper with a *crack* like a gunshot, falling to the sidewalk, then scraping down the side of my car. I fumbled for the brake. Another invisible speed bump tossed the contents of my car. When I landed, I blinked to normal vision.

A couple walking their dog on the opposite side of the street had stopped to huddle near a large tree trunk. I ducked my head down and, with the assistance of my oh-so-helpful headlights, took the next right and fled the neighborhood.

"Way to go," I congratulated myself. Perhaps I needed a little more experience before I tried Primordium while operating heavy machinery.

Disheartened, I considered my options. There really was only one. I couldn't afford to ignore or put off learning about my ability. I'd been passive long enough, and it had nearly gotten Mr. Bond killed. It cheered me a little to think that I was no longer merely a spectator in the world of soul-sight; I could take action against evil. I just had to figure out how to do it.

Figuring Mr. Bond would be okay by himself for a few minutes longer, I decided there was no time like the present to kick a little evil booty. I turned onto Sierra College Boulevard, made a U-turn at the top of the hill, and, ignoring all the "Trucks Only" signs, cruised into the construction site turnout and cut the engine.

I grabbed the Primordium flashlight from my glove box where I'd stuffed it earlier and pocketed the pet wood, Medusa, and my keys. Before I could think too much about trespassing alone in the dark and abandoning my illegally parked vehicle, I strode purposefully up the main road.

It was harder to navigate at night. I opted for Primordium since I had a flashlight that worked in that vision. As I moved away from Sierra College Boulevard, the quietness of the night settled around me until all I could hear was the crunching of my own steps on gravel and the muted rush of cars. I tried to keep my mind away from replaying horror movies and scary stories.

"The frames are just frames," I told myself of the looming half-erect houses that littered the landscape. "That's only my footstep echoing, not another person." Just in case, I thought I'd better stop talking out loud.

Come on, you're a big, bad illuminant enforcer. You can do this. Mr. Pitt's disappointed expression surfaced unbidden from my memory. I wasn't the failure he thought I was. I may not have done anything amazing yet with my life, but that didn't mean I lacked potential. I just hadn't had the right motivation—like getting paid to use my soul-sight and using it to fight evil.

I crested the top of the construction site's main hill and could see down the backside to the greenbelt. All the bright plants and soft arching lines of the trees looked far more inviting than the bleak, plundered construction property. I spun in a slow circle, looking for imps. The grounds were empty.

I took a dirt side road that led toward the greenbelt, systematically checking every house, peering through the two-by-four frames, shining my light in every nook. I was pleased with my purchase but rapidly getting bored when I stumbled onto a nest of imps. They were huddled on the backside of the last house in the row, one of the few homes that had sheet wood up. I had circled the building with the intention of heading back to my car. Now I found myself grinning at the swarming mass of imps.

"Come to Mama," I said softly.

As a group, the seething pile swiveled their heads, and dozens of glowing eyes stared at me. The hairs on the back of my neck rose. Slowly, I pulled the pet wood out of my pocket and flicked my wrist to extend it. The imps felt no compulsion to take their time. En masse, they charged. One moment, they looked like a bouncing flock of chinchillas, cuddly and fluffy black. The next, they opened their mouths, and it was like staring into the jaws of land sharks.

I forced *lux lucis* into the wood. It flared to life, and I jabbed the nearest imp. It popped and sparkled to glittering dust. There was no uncontrolled flare with pet wood. I simply had to keep feeding the wand *lux lucis*, mindful of its threshold containment, and the weapon did all the work. Two imps jumped for me at once. I caught one with a slash of the pet wood. The other landed on my stomach. I grabbed it around the throat and pulsed *lux lucis* into it. It exploded into sparkles of white and black. Grinning, I looked at the remaining imps. Formerly at the back of the pack, they had paused to watch me with identically cocked heads and curious glowing eyes.

"Anyone hungry?" I taunted. I stepped toward the imps. There were at least eight sets of eyes, maybe more. They charged as one. Hacking and slashing, I spun into their midst, feeding the pet wood energy as each imp died. It was over too fast, leaving me standing in a cloud of imp dust, laughing and breathless. "That's how it's done, folks." I examined myself to make sure none had gotten through my wild defenses. I was clean. I looked about the area but could find no reason why the imps had congregated in that spot. "Is that it? Is that all you've got?" I demanded of the darkness around me.

Something large moved at the edge of my vision, kicking a nail against a sheet of metal. I spun. A dog stood a few feet away at the edge of the house. It looked like a cross between a Doberman pincher and a pit bull, except it glistened ink black in Primordium, like wet blood in moonlight. It growled deep in its throat.

"Aw, shit," I muttered. It was definitely evil. It also had moved something in the real world. I looked at my pet wood and then at the dog. Something told me the pet wood wasn't going to cut it.

Oddly, it didn't rush me. It stood at the corner and growled. I maintained eye contact with the beast's large glowing eyes and fumbled in my pocket for Medusa. I needed someone who knew what they were doing. I needed Doris.

"Good evil doggie. Stay there for a moment while I figure out how to kill you." I silently thanked Rose for programming everyone's phone number into my contact list and selected Doris's name. After three long rings, she picked up.

"Hello."

"Doris, it's me. Madison. I've got a problem."

"I'm in LA. What do you expect me to do?"

"Coach me. I'm looking at a dog of some kind."

"Where are you?"

"Does it matter? There's this huge dog and it's black in Primordium and it's real—solid. Right now, it's looking at me like I'm its next meal."

"Ah. A hound. Must be a weak one if you're still standing there."

"Can we boost my confidence later? What do I do?"

"Did you get a weapon?"

"Pet wood. A flashlight."

"That's it? No knives?"

"This is all I've got." The hound took two steps toward me and stopped again, growling. "Look, can we hurry this up?"

"Okay, okay. What's it look like?"

"I told you. Hungry."

"No. Look at it with normal eyes."

I blinked. The dog was a dark blob against the dark building.

"Scrawny. Homeless. Like it hasn't eaten in a week." I blinked back to Primordium. "Why is it real? You know, physical. Solid. I thought all the evil creatures only existed in Primordium."

"Whatever gave you that idea?"

Crap. I'd assumed based on the one evil creature I'd encountered: imps. Of course, now I remembered Kyle saying imps were the weakest evil creature. My fear ratcheted up a level. The hound didn't look weak. If it attacked, its teeth weren't going to pass through my soul. They were going to shred my flesh. "Why didn't you tell me there were worse things than imps?"

"There are worse things than imps."

"Gee—"

"There are worse thing than hounds, too. Are you having second thoughts now?"

Hell yes! "I'm staring into the eyes of a starved hound. I don't have time for second thoughts. Tell me how to deal with it."

"Time to see what you're made of, Madison. I hope you didn't scrimp on the wood. Fill that pet sucker up with as much juice as it can take. You'll have to hit the hound with a lot more *lux lucis* than the imps. And your wood isn't going to sink into it like it does with imps. Oh, and when you go for the hound, don't let it bite you. Bites from a hound injure your body and your soul."

"They what?"

"If you get bitten, call Brad. See his doctor. You don't want the bite to fester in your soul."

I didn't want to get bitten. Period.

My heart hammered so loud I wondered that the hound—and Doris—couldn't hear it. I crouched down like a tennis player and fed energy into the pet wood until it was close to burning out. The hound lowered its front legs, too. We both readied for the charge.

Between the open frames of the houses, I saw the figure of a human coming down the road. His soul was smoky gray. He was holding something in his hand and approaching cautiously.

"Shit. I've got company." I blinked and squinted as the beam of a flashlight swept across my vision. When the light was directed away from me, I could see the man. "Crap. It's a cop."

"Where *are* you?" Doris asked.

"I'm not in Kansas, that's for sure. What should I do?"

"You're trespassing, aren't you?"

"Bingo." I was whispering now, afraid that the cop would hear me. If it wasn't for the hound, I could try to slip away. But I couldn't leave the cop alone with the hound. The academy simply didn't train cops to handle dogs turned into minions of evil. At least, I didn't think it did.

"Did Brad send you there?"

"Uh, sort of."

"Child, you're going to be in a heap of trouble." Doris chuckled. "I miss those days."

"I don't have time for a trip down memory lane. What should I do?" The hound's ears were flicking back and forth to listen to the cop approaching and my hushed conversation.

"Act remorseful and contrite. Trust me, you'll get away with a lot more if you don't give the cops attitude."

"I meant about the hound."

"You've got to protect the cop from the hound. He's seeing a dog. You're seeing the real evil. Now hang up and get busy. And remember, you're on the same side as the cop." The connection went dead.

"But he doesn't know that," I whispered. I pocketed Medusa. It was now or never. I couldn't exactly wield my pet wood in front of the cop without arousing his suspicion—or worse, his aggressive instincts.

"Here, doggie, doggie, doggie," I called softly. The hound's ears pricked in my direction. A long string of drool slid from the corner of its mouth. My pulse thundered in my ears, and my intelligent, self-preservation-focused inner voice told me to run. All the muscles in my body tensed. I forced myself to stalk forward one step, two, keeping the flashlight steady on the hound.

The hound circled to the right. I extended the pet wood in front of me like a glowing riding crop. It was too thin, too fragile. Why hadn't I picked a walking staff?

The cop rounded the corner. The hound glanced in his direction. I saw my chance. I lunged.

10

Earth First; We'll Log the Other Planets Later

"G O ON! GET!" THE COP shouted. He banged his flashlight on the side of the building. The hound jumped; I tripped. The hound took one last look at me and fled into the greenbelt. I watched it go, knowing I shouldn't have been relieved. It was still going to be out there tomorrow. I was still going to have to chase it down. Yet I felt like I'd been given a death-row reprieve.

"Are you okay?" the cop asked me.

He was approaching me cautiously, his flashlight aimed at my face. In Primordium, I could look straight at him, unaffected by the light that didn't exist to my vision. I took a closer look at his soul. There were no oily dark smears on his life force. His gray was honestly gotten from life experiences.

"Miss. Are you okay?"

Be scared, Madison. Be scared and remorseful. A damsel in distress. I didn't have to try too hard, either. I blinked, then quickly looked down at my feet, blinded by the flashlight in my eyes. How long had I been staring into it? Was he suspicious?

"Uh, yeah. I think I am," I finally answered. "Th-thank you for scaring the hou—the dog."

"What do you have in your hand?"

"Um . . . A . . . a cat toy. It was all I had handy." I carefully held the pet wood up for him to see, then pushed on the end to collapse it. It fell in on itself like an old radio antenna until it was no longer than my hand. "I don't think that dog found it too scary." I tossed the cop a trembling smile. He lowered the light out of my eyes.

"What are you doing out here?" He stopped a few feet from me, cautious, but he clearly didn't see me as a threat. That made two of us.

I had been scrambling for an answer to that question since I'd first seen the cop. *Keep it simple.* I gave him a sheepish look. "I'm thinking of buying a home out here and I wanted to get a look before anyone else."

"In the dark?"

"Well, there was still light when I got here. And I have my flashlight." I held up the useless-looking Primordium flashlight. I flicked the on and off switch. Nothing appeared to happen. "I think the batteries died. And then that horrible dog showed up."

"And you were going to scare it away with a cat toy?"

I gave him wide, Bambi eyes. "It was all I had and I was scared." True, and yet not the complete truth.

The cop adjusted his belt buckle and relaxed his stance. He was older, closer to retirement than rookie. He had the hard eyes that all cops develop, but his round cheeks had hints of dimples and his lips had a natural curl toward a smile. I found myself relaxing a little, too.

"This is private property. You're not supposed to be out here."

"I know."

The cop gestured for me to head back to the road, and he fell into step beside me. I made sure to slouch a little so that I looked contrite.

"We've had some problems around here lately. It's not safe for a young woman alone."

"Problems? Is it dangerous? Should I not move in here?"

The cop guided me around a pile of dirt and used his flashlight to peer around us. I blinked to check for imps. We were alone. I blinked back to normal vision and stumbled. The cop caught my elbow to steady me and I gave him a smile.

"So far it's a few punk kids up to no good. But that's how it starts, and these things can escalate quickly."

"What are they doing?"

"The usual. Trespassing and vandalizing. Most likely bored rich kids from across the way." He gestured into the dark across the tree-filled valley to the homes concealed on the other side. "I thought tonight was my lucky night."

It took me a moment to realize he meant he thought I was one of them. "Sorry to disappoint you."

"Me too. But we'll catch them soon. Before these are ready for residents, that's for sure."

I smiled at him, congratulating myself for having found the source of evil in this area. Finally I had something to go to Mr. Pitt with.

We reached the road, and the noise of passing traffic filled in the silence between us. Streetlights provided enough illumination for me to read the cop's badge.

"Thank you again for rescuing me, Officer Parker," I said, reaching for my car keys.

"Don't let me catch you out there again," he said.

"No, sir. Definitely not."

He walked me to my car and peered into the windows.

"That's a lot of plants you've got."

"Yep. I'm redecorating."

"Huh." He shone his flashlight into the backseat.

I touched a plant. The leaf deadened under my finger. I jerked back.

"This is your warning. If I catch you trespassing again, I will have to arrest you," Parker said, his voice all business, though he was clearly distracted by my full car of plants.

"Thank you, sir." I slid into the driver's seat, careful not to touch any plants, and turned on my car.

With an admonishment for me to drive safely, Officer Parker stepped back and slapped the roof of my car. I took that to mean I was free to go and wasted no more time. I eased into traffic and sped up to five miles an hour under the speed limit.

I obeyed every traffic law all the way home, including using a blinker to turn into my assigned parking space at my apartment complex. It was silly of me, but since I'd gotten away with one crime that night, I felt I owed it to Officer Parker to obey the rest of the laws. When I turned off the engine, I sat for a moment gripping the steering wheel and stared blindly at the dashboard.

My encounter with the hound had scared me more than I wanted to admit. I blinked and checked my surroundings. Two cats were having a face-off in the bushes in front of my car, but otherwise I had the parking lot to myself. My gaze fell on my hands still gripping the steering wheel. The creamy light of my soul was dim. How much *lux lucis* had I used on those imps and the pet wood? And when had I gotten so comfortable with looking at myself in Primordium? All I felt now when I looked at the back of my hand was concern for the color, not dizziness or queasiness. If I was going to be honest with myself, I was a little nervous, too. Last night, I'd recharged unconsciously—literally. I'd never done it intentionally. Having the plant's leaves die at my touch had unnerved me. I didn't want to kill to recharge. Feeding off Mr. Bond wasn't an option, either.

I pulled the pet wood out of my pocket. It shone more brightly than my hand.

Maybe I can circumnavigate everything, I thought.

I tried to pull the *lux lucis* back from the pet wood, but nothing happened. I pushed a little *lux lucis* into it, just to check. Energy slid easily from my fingers into the wood. I tugged it back again. When that didn't work, I imagined the *lux lucis* flowing from the tip of the wand back to me. It worked as well as making my freckles disappear by imagining they were gone.

Tentatively, I placed the tip of the pet wood against my left palm and gripped the other end with my right. Taking a deep breath, I eased *lux lucis* through the pet wood.

Pure, good energy oozed into my left palm from the pet wood. The faint trickle tickled. Grinning, I pushed more through. A rush of *lux lucis* flooded my left palm. The tickle turned to a tingle, like my hand was half asleep. The feeling rushed up my arm, and I fancied it was traveling through my veins, carried by the beat of my heart through my body.

For a moment, I thought I'd done it and had taken the energy from the pet wood back into my body. Then the rushing sensation hit my chest and swirled down my right arm. When it met the pet wood, it raced through the wand and back to my left palm.

I'd created a loop.

In five pulses of my heart, the racing *lux lucis* completed another circuit. Three pulses the next time. Two the following time.

My upper body numbed, caught in a whirlwind of energy. If it hadn't made me dizzy before to look at my hands, I was more than making up for it now. I closed my eyes, but that only made it worse. My lips began to tingle and my teeth chattered. The *lux lucis* had taken on a will of its own, humming through the closed circuit I had created.

I forced my gaze to my hands. The pet wood hadn't dimmed at all. If anything, it was glowing brighter. The same could not be said of my hands. They were a pale white, despite the *lux lucis* racing through them.

Enough, I thought, pulling the *lux lucis* to a stop. Only it didn't work. The cyclone of *lux lucis* didn't even slow. I flexed my right forearm to pull the pet wood from my left hand. The muscles refused to move, too numb to function.

Crap, crap, crap!

In desperation, I used my knee to knock the pet wood from my limp fingers. *Lux lucis* flared in my right hand, growing brighter and brighter as the whirlwind stacked up on itself.

My hand pulsed as if my heart had migrated to my palm. My left hand was so pale it should have been translucent. I hesitantly clasped my hands together. *Lux lucis* bled from my right to my left hand.

When everything stabilized, I collapsed back in my seat and shut my eyes.

"That was stupid," I admitted.

When I opened my eyes, I saw a soul much dimmer than it had been before my impulsive experiment.

Gingerly, I reached for the bright pet wood on the floorboard and collapsed it, shoving it into the depths of my purse. Resigned, I reached for a plant. The moment I touched its leaves, I felt better. Even as I watched, the life force from the plant raced through its branches into my palm. The stalk in my finger crumbled. I jerked back and blinked. Half of the plant was dead, the other half wilted. I turned on the car's dome light and double-checked, then stared at my hands in horror.

"How is this not a sign of evil?" I reached into my pocket to call Doris, then stopped myself. She would tell me exactly what she'd said that morning: The plants give their life freely. I had felt it this time. The plant had willingly sacrificed its life to replenish mine.

"I'll nurse you back to health," I promised the wilted plant.

I blinked back to Primordium and looked around. There were plenty of trees, shrubs, and lawn around the complex. Plant life glowed everywhere. I got out of my car and locked it behind me.

I headed for the grass first. When I touched it, it died in a perfect handprint. I jerked back. *Too fragile.* I walked over to the shrubs and ran my hand along the squared-off edges. *Lux lucis* rushed into me, and dead leaves fell off the branches to the ground.

"Goddammit!" I was a freaking vegetarian vampire! *Why didn't anyone mention this to begin with?*

Wouldn't you still have taken the job? my own thoughts countered. *Would you deny how right this job feels just so you could save a few spider plants or azalea bushes?*

I smothered the voice, not wanting to hear reason—or acknowledge that anything about using my soul-sight felt *right*—when I was working myself up into a good fit. "I'm only doing this temporarily for the money," I reminded myself, and I pushed aside nagging concerns about attracting imps—or worse—after I quit.

I stomped across the lawn to a cottonwood tree. Hesitantly, I placed my hand against the bark and pulled away. The tree looked fine. I place my hand on it again, and its *lux lucis* rushed into me through my palm. I rested my forehead against the bark but didn't close my eyes. If the tree started to look at all strained or dim, I was ready to jump away from it.

The tree's life force didn't even flicker. I felt the moment my energy level was full and I straightened.

"Thank you," I whispered to the trunk of the tree. My anger had evaporated. In its place was resignation. I was like a druggie. I'd gotten my fix, and now the method didn't seem so evil. *Okay, now you're just being dramatic.*

My feeling of peace was a familiar one, and I almost smacked myself in the forehead when I realized that this most definitely was not the first time I'd recharged. I'd been doing it unconsciously for years. There was a reason I loved to stand among the large oak trees in the clearing in front of my apartment, touching their bark, and it hadn't been just because they were beautiful to look at with soul-sight or normal sight. All this time I'd thought I simply found trees relaxing. Now I knew it was because they fed my energy.

Shaking my head, I trudged back to my car.

It took nine trips to get all the plants upstairs to my apartment. On my first trip, Mr. Bond greeted me at the front door, twined between my legs, and meowed. When I set the plants down, he trotted over and stuck his head in their pots and sniffed the leaves. If it wasn't for the decreasing knot of liquid between his shoulder blades, I wouldn't have believed that only this morning he'd been close to death.

After my last trip, I flopped onto the floor and waited for some strength to return to my noodle-like arms. All the plants I'd purchased covered the front room floor and turned the room into a jungle. Mr. Bond had a good time weaving between the pots and rubbing against the sturdier plants. Then he came over and perched on my stomach. I convinced him to lie down and distribute his weight on larger surfaces than the tiny pads of his paws. He happily stretched out on my torso, his sharp front claws on either side of my neck, his chin rubbing on mine. I petted him and told him how much I loved him, then pushed him off me when I began to feel asthmatic.

My phone rang. I checked the clock. It was 10:12. No one called me this late. I rushed to the phone, and when I saw it was my parents' number, I snatched it up, my stomach tightening with dread. The only reason they'd be calling this late was to share bad news.

"Is everything all right? What's happened?" I asked.

"Nothing, dear. I was calling to see how your job went."

"This late? Are you sure there's nothing wrong?"

"What time is it, Oscar?" Mom shouted to my dad, only partially covering the phone. I paced the room once, stepping around all the plants, then flopped into my chair. Of course nothing was wrong. Unless you could count the fact that they'd retired. All concept of normal, working people's hours and schedules had evaporated from their minds the moment they started receiving retirement checks.

"I'm sorry, Madison. The time got away from us," Mom apologized a moment later. "We were playing Trivial Pursuit—I won the first one, so your dad insisted we play two out of three. I'm still the Trivial Pursuit Champion of the Universe."

"Oh. That sounds like fun." It didn't. And I was too tired to make my comment sound genuine. It had been an incredibly long day after too little sleep and I was exhausted. This false alarm proved to be the final straw. I closed my eyes and reminded myself that some people weren't so lucky as to have both their parents. And those unlucky souls were already in bed, asleep.

"You sound tired. How's Mr. Bond?"

"He's good. Back to himself. I guess this morning was a fluke." I grimaced at the lie. How do you explain to your parents that you sucked the life out of your cat while you slept because you'd spent the night destroying evil and depleting your own reserves of life force? The answer is, you don't. "I am pretty tired, too. It's been a long, long day."

"How do you like your new job?"

I heard the click of a second phone being picked up. No doubt Mom had given Dad the sign language for "Madison needs us," and he'd rushed to grab the other phone.

"It's more interesting than I thought it would be," I said, trying to weigh how much I could tell them. "My coworkers are really nice. I have my own cubicle."

"Did you get to do any real work today?" Dad asked.

I smiled to myself. "Yeah. Some. I spent most of the day out of the office, though."

"Why?" Mom asked at the same time Dad said, "Is that normal?"

"Um, sure." *Shoot. What had made me go with honest?* Half-truths were definitely the way to go. "They're, uh, very interested in the community. There's a video game conference in town and they sent me and a coworker to check it out. We looked for opportunities for our business to, uh, do business." *Not bad.*

"That sounds like fun," Mom said.

Fun was not the word I would have used to describe it, but for the sake of ending the conversation sooner, I agreed. "Yeah. But it was a long day. I just got home a few minutes ago."

"Just now! Why so late?"

"Do you get paid overtime?" Dad asked.

"No overtime. I'm salaried. But I get bonuses if I do well."

"Don't let them get to where they expect you to work insane hours every day," Dad warned. "If they realize they can take advantage of you, they will."

"I'll be sure and do that. I've got to be at work pretty early tomorrow, though, so I think I'm going to head off to bed."

"Okay, dear. Just remember that there're plenty of jobs out there. You don't have to stay at one that makes you unhappy." This from Mom, of course. Dad was more concerned with how many jobs I'd had in the last three years. Oh, he wanted me to be happy and find something I felt passionate about, but he also had certain expectations for my career—expectations that I didn't necessarily share. Mom was more concerned about my day-to-day happiness.

I said good night after promising that I'd come over to their house soon, and shook my head at the phone. They'd been retired only five months. What were they going to be like after ten?

Mr. Bond helped me distribute the plants around the house, mainly by chasing after trailing leaves and racing between my legs at inconvenient times. I put four plants in the front room, five in the dining room, one in the kitchen, and the rest in the bedroom. I saved the hardier treelike plants for the bedroom just to be safe. Between my desk, dresser, nightstand, and the limited floor space at the end of my bed, I managed to fit eight plants in the room. I blinked to Primordium and checked the wards around my doors and windows. They were weak, and I reinforced them. Then I refilled the little bit of energy I'd used by carefully touching several of the plants. There were no dramatic crumbling dead leaves this time. In fact, I couldn't even tell that I'd taken some of their life force. I was getting the handle of this.

Fifteen minutes later, feet washed and alarm set, I was horizontal in bed. Mr. Bond settled next to me, with his upper body propped up against my legs. By the sixteenth minute, I was asleep.

I woke up ten minutes before my alarm. Usually I would have fallen right back to sleep, because everyone knows that there's extra restorative properties in those sacred minutes before the alarm goes off. However, the moment I realized Mr. Bond wasn't on the bed, I was wide awake and panicked. A quick glance confirmed that the miniature forest in my room was still healthy. I threw back the covers and raced down the hall. The plants in the front room looked fine, too.

"Mr. Bond, where are you?" I called, scanning the floor for his limp body. What if Doris had been wrong? What if I had sucked the life from

Mr. Bond first, before the plants? What if—

Mr. Bond chirped from somewhere in the dining room. I got down on my knees and looked under the table and between the chair legs. Mr. Bond meowed a full statement and I slowly stood. He was seated innocently in the middle of the golden pothos ivy I'd placed in the center of the dining table. Its long vines were crushed under his feet, and his tail was slowly destroying leaves as he wagged it happily at me like a dog. He wasn't *ever* allowed on the table. Nor was he allowed to get into the plants. Yet, I couldn't bring myself to yell at him, so I hefted him from the center of the table, cupped his purring bulk to me, and scolded him in a loving tone.

Twenty minutes later, I was getting out of the shower when the phone rang. I wrapped myself in a towel and checked the caller ID. *Love and Caring* showed up on the glowing screen. I snatched up the phone.

"Hello, this is Madison."

"Hi, Madison. This is Dr. Alex Love from the Love and Caring Veterinary Clinic. I was calling to check on Mr. Bond."

Suddenly I felt very underdressed. And warm. Dr. Love had a voice made for phone sex. And why could I think of nothing but all the corny puns and porno titles I'd come up with that involved him and his name?

"Is now a good time?" Dr. Love asked after I'd paused for too long.

"Oh no. I mean yes. Sorry." *Sorry? Sorry for fantasizing about you?* "Mr. Bond is doing so much better today. In fact, he's feeling well enough to get into trouble."

When he chuckled, I felt a little giddy. "That's good to hear. I thought he would make a complete recovery. Do you have any questions now that you've had a chance to relax?"

I didn't think I could work "Do you have a girlfriend?" into a question about Mr. Bond. "How long will it take for the liquid to fully absorb?" He'd already answered that question yesterday, but I wanted an excuse to listen to him talk longer.

"It should be all absorbed by tonight. Is he eating normally again?"

"Yes, he's back to herding me to his food dish. He doesn't miss many meals. But I'm sure you could see that, Dr. Love."

He chuckled again and my stomach did a little flip-flop. "Yes, we might want to think about a diet plan for him. Or maybe an exercise plan. I'd be happy to talk with you about it when you have time."

Tonight? Dinner? "Okay. I'll bring him back in when things settle down a little for me. I just got a new job." I wanted to bite my tongue. Dr. Love didn't care about my new job.

"Oh, really? Where are you working now?"

"Illumination Studios. They create bumper stickers."

"So I could be reading a bumper sticker you wrote soon?"

"Yep." In theory, at least.

"That sounds really interesting." There was a pause while I frantically tried to think of something to say. Dr. Love filled in the silence. "I called mainly to check on Mr. Bond, but I also wanted to check on you. You were very distraught yesterday, and I wanted to make sure you were doing okay."

My heart picked up to double time. *Don't read too much into it, Dice.* "It was one of the worst scares of my life. Thank you so much for treating Mr. Bond so quickly."

"It was my pleasure. I'm glad to have your cat as my patient. I look forward to seeing you again when you're ready to start Mr. Bond on a weight-loss plan."

"Me too."

We both said good-bye. I did a little dance around the front room.

"I got a call from Dr. Alex Lo-ove," I sang. "He wants to see me a-gain. Dr. Love's in love with me-e!" Which I knew wasn't true, but it made me happy to think it was. When my giddiness settled, I knew I needed a second opinion. Had I imagined the subtle flirting? Was it normal for the head vet to call to check on a patient? Wasn't that something typically left for the front desk people?

I called Bridget.

When she answered, I could hear traffic noises in the background. I checked the clock. It was nearly eight, which meant Bridget was almost to work and I needed to get hustling if I was going to make it to work on time, too.

"Digit, I've got Dr. Love news." There was no need for me to clarify who Dr. Love was. Bridget was well aware of my crush on the handsome vet. I told her briefly what had happened to Mr. Bond, letting Bridget know he was fine. Then I relayed my conversation with Dr. Love.

"Did he sound genuinely interested in your job?" Bridget asked.

"Yeah. And he chuckled at two of my lame attempts at a joke!"

Bridget laughed at me. "So when are you going to take Mr. Bond in for a fitness evaluation?"

"I'm thinking tomorrow would be too soon."

"Just a little. Are you sure he doesn't have a girlfriend?"

"No, but I'm determined to find out."

"I don't think many doctors with girlfriends make personal checkup calls to hot young women and ask to see them again."

"Do you think so?" I squealed and we both laughed.

"So how was your first full day?"

I groaned at the memory of all the nerds. "It would take too long for me to tell you now. But I can tell you this: I've killed evil creatures!"

"Killed? That sounds awfully . . . violent."

"You'd think so, but remember me telling you about all their teeth? That's not an evolutionary trait of a good creature. They're evil, with a capital *E*. Plus, the ones I killed existed only in Primordium, spawned by evil deeds and *atrum*."

"Sounds like you've learned a lot." The background traffic noise quieted, replaced shortly thereafter by the steady click of heels. "I knew there was a reason you can see people's souls! I really want to hear all about it, but I've got to go into a meeting."

"Yeah, I've got to get to work. I'll call you later when we have more time. Thanks for reassuring me about Dr. Love."

"Anytime. Give poor Mr. Bond my regards." She laughed as she hung up.

"Poor Mr. Bond will have to take one for the team," I told the obese Siamese in question. He meowed at me from where he lay next to his empty food bowl.

11

KEEP CALM AND CARRY ON

I ARRIVED AT WORK AT 8:29. Mr. Pitt was lurking at his office door and came hustling out when he saw me.

"Mr. Pitt, I would like the chance to prove that I can do my job," I said before he had a chance to get a word in. I'd rehearsed this conversation on the drive over. "Having my hands tied yesterday was unproductive." *Awful* would be a better word for it. I'd felt useless and frustrated. "You didn't hire me to be your spy. You hired me to cleanse this region and destroy evil. To do that, I need your permission to fight back."

Mr. Pitt looked past me at Rose, who had come up behind me while I made my case. "Listen to her. She's not even here three days and already she knows why she was hired and how to do her job *and* my job better than I do."

"That's not what I meant, Mr. Pitt—"

"I know what you meant, but you're in over your head on this one. Trust me. I really do know what I'm doing."

I blushed at his tone and tried to hide my frustration. The last thing I wanted to do was spend another day pretending I couldn't see imps. Now that I knew they existed, and that my ability to see—and use—*lux lucis* had a purpose, I didn't want to pretend otherwise. There wasn't anything worse than being idle in the face of evil when I had the capability of taking action.

I was wrong.

It turns out, there's nothing worse than being idle in the face of evil when I had the capability of taking action *while* wearing a friggin' costume.

"Tell me again why this makes sense," I said to Will forty minutes later.

He looked me up and down in the mirror—the bathroom mirror for the women's restroom for the bottom floor of the entire building, which he and Joy had blithely commandeered when Mr. Pitt had handed me off to them. Will's appraisal was flattering without being suggestive, and I fought off his easygoing Illuminea charm by crossing my arms and glaring back.

"You said yourself that you felt useless yesterday," he reminded me.

"And being dressed like some pubescent boy's fantasy will somehow be useful?"

"You'll have employee access."

"This"—I raised the lanyard with the attached forged employees' badge—"gives me employee access. This"—I gestured down my body—"is sexist. If I were a guy, I'd be going as a different type of employee."

"Yeah, like a bouncer, but you're not going to be able to pull that off," Will said.

"I think you look cute," Joy said.

I would have laughed at her joke, but it wasn't funny. "Where did you get this stuff?" I asked.

"Here and there," Will said.

I was beginning to wonder if the Illuminea were really evil spies. First of all, they enjoyed torturing me too much. Second, what innocent, good people have a spare set of minuscule, camouflage-print spandex shorts—complete with a British flag emblazoned across the butt—a matching spandex top (without the flag), and size ten, calf-high, lace-up, three-inch-heeled, black shit-kicker boots just lying around? I might have written the whole outfit off as a bad clubbing costume if not for the Lara Croft–style gun holsters strapped to my thighs and the slits in the boots designed to hold knives.

"It's early November. I'm going to freeze," I told Will.

"It's California. You'll be fine."

Wishing I'd shaved my legs that morning—or even the morning before—I tugged at the hem of the shorts, futilely attempting to gain more coverage. Abandoning the lost cause, I fussed with the holster straps on my thighs until they felt reasonably comfortable. Too tight, and my thigh fat bulged. Too loose, and they chafed and left red imprints when I moved. The Illuminea siblings had graciously allowed me to wear the sleeveless high-collared camo shirt that covered me from collarbone to waist rather than a black crop-top, but only because I'd compromised and agreed to wear the padded bra that inflated my breasts to two times their natural size.

"I can't see my feet."

"They're still there," Joy assured me. She finished braiding my dark brown hair into two French braids that ended at my shoulder blades. They both eyed a collection of pictures of video game characters from which they'd designed the costume, then me. The idea was for me to look like I worked at one of the convention booths, without anyone mistaking me for their employee. I slumped. Mission accomplished.

"Stand up straight," Will admonished. He handed me a pair of fingerless black leather gloves and shoved some fake guns in the thigh holsters. They were surprisingly heavy. I pulled on the gloves, then pulled out a gun.

"Please tell me this isn't real."

"It isn't loaded," Joy said.

I groaned. "I can't carry a real weapon into this convention."

"You'll be fine. No one will think they're real."

Crap. What had I gotten myself into?

Joy and Will argued playfully over my makeup. More than once I considered storming out—after grabbing a coat—but my curiosity to find out why all the imps were at the convention held me in place. Even if my outfit was degrading, cold, and highly inappropriate, it was going to get me into places that had been off-limits yesterday.

"I could have gone as a businesswoman working for one of the game companies," I said.

"This is the gaming industry we're talking about. If you were a businesswoman, you'd stand out like a prostitute at an inaugural ball."

"So instead I'm going in as a prostitute?"

"Besides, Brad insisted."

I met Joy's eyes in the mirror. She grimaced and shrugged. "He said you needed a little humility."

What I needed was a gigantic rule book to explain everything Mr. Pitt already expected me to know, along with a CliffsNotes cheat sheet for his rules of operation.

I gritted my teeth and examined the final effect in the mirror. Extra-large breasts made my waist look smaller. The guns made me feel a tad badass. Joy had done something to my eyelids so that my eyes looked slanted and a little catlike, and she'd made my naturally full mouth look downright pouty. *Damn it.* I wanted to be able to look at myself in the mirror and be as disgusted by the idea that I was going as a showpiece for men's sexual fantasies as I had been before I was in the costume.

"You like it," Will said.

"No, I—"

"You can't pretend with us. You're hot and you know it," Joy said.

I sighed. "I'm a hypocrite."

Joy laughed.

"At least I get a backpack." The siblings had supplied a small black backpack that fit my wallet, Medusa, and the pet wood. I slipped it on and tightened the leather straps.

I pulled the guns and struck the dramatic pose of a woman in one of the pictures. When I looked up at the mirror, I was taken aback by how authentic I looked, given what Will and Joy had had to start with.

"I'm so getting you guys to do my next Halloween costume."

We met Rose back at her cubicle. She took one look at me and grinned. "I'm glad you're the enforcer and I'm the babysitter."

"You don't have to wear a costume?"

"Nope."

I eyed the employee pass dangling from a lanyard at her neck, which was a matched set with mine, and then I looked to Will and Joy for confirmation. They shrugged.

"That's *so* not fair."

"Get over it," Mr. Pitt said from behind me. I turned, and with the added height of the boots, my fake boobs were slightly above his eye level. He took a step back. I smiled sweetly at him and stood a little straighter, rolling my shoulders back to emphasize the breasts, and enjoyed watching him squirm.

"You're going behind the scenes today, but your orders are the same: Look but don't touch. Think you can handle that?"

"Aye-aye, Captain."

Rose drove. I struggled with finding a comfortable position for the seat belt and tried to ignore the butts of the guns poking into my legs.

My only consolation was that in Rose's Hummer I was less visible to the people driving around us.

"You should have gotten a knife yesterday. It would have gone perfectly in those boot sheathes."

"Hmm."

"Where are you keeping the pet wood? I mean, there's not a lot of options, and I don't see it in the boots." Rose eyed the shelf of fake boobs. "It'd be rather inconvenient . . ."

"Don't even start. I've got it in the backpack."

"Mmm-hmm."

Once again, the droves of nerds caught me off guard. Their numbers had swelled. Gone were the businessmen, too, or so it seemed at first glance. The hotel was swarming with testosterone, and all of it was too nerdy for my taste.

I hadn't appreciated how invisible I'd been the day before in my conservative business clothes. Apparently businesswomen are not the stuff of video games. My ridiculously large chest, however, was. We barely made it through the hotel doors before gamer geeks began daring each other to get close to me. Several snapped pictures on phones that would have made Medusa jealous.

"You need to get that look off your face," Rose said. "All of this"— she waggled her finger at my body—"looks right, but unless you get control of your expression, no one is going to believe you work here."

I gave her my best grimace. Two men headed in our direction stopped and went the other way. I smiled smugly.

"That's a bit better. Remember, they may think you're here for them, but we know why you're really here." I looked at Rose to see if she was trying to push the right buttons to get me to work. "Besides, girl, you look hot."

"I agree," a man with a scraggly goatee next to me said. "Can I have your autograph?"

I started to say, "Shouldn't you be at work?" but Rose's sharp elbow to my ribs turned it into, "Sho— Sure."

The man handed me a small black book and pen. I almost signed *Madison Fox*, but I caught myself and scribbled *Elizabeth Firth*, which I thought at least sounded British. He snapped a shot of me, then held the camera in one hand to get a shot of the two of us together.

We'd drawn a small crowd in the lobby and a few more men pushed forward.

"Sorry, boys. I've got to get to work," I told them, indicating the elevator. Then, feeling supremely foolish, I rolled my shoulders back and stalked across the room. Rose scurried to catch up.

"Did they buy it?" I asked out of the side of my mouth.

"Hell, I bought it. Keep it up and don't forget the mission."

By some small miracle, we had the elevator to ourselves. I adjusted the gun straps and straightened the bra. With all the mirrors on the walls, it was impossible not to pull several poses. Rose laughed at me.

"That's exactly what you need to do out there," she said.

"The more ridiculous the better?" I grumped.

"If that works for you."

No, that didn't work for me. As we stepped into the thickening mass of men on the conference floor, I was more aware than yesterday of the women who had been reduced to the title of "booth babe." By their standards, I was conservatively dressed. At least everything from the tops of my thighs to my collarbone was covered. I watched the women, looking for behavior clues that would help me pull off this absurd charade. *It's all about the attitude,* I decided. *Own it.* I straightened my spine, grasped the butts of the guns, and glared around me.

What kind of person tells herself to "own it"? I giggled. Shit. I was nervous.

We passed through the entrance doorways after having our badges and bags inspected. The bored staff member didn't glance twice at the forged IDs, though his eyes did linger on the British flag stretched across my butt. His eyes weren't the only ones drawn by the bright red, white, and blue, either. Just like that, I was back to scowling.

"What does it look like today?" Rose asked. She was chaffing her arms, and I knew it wasn't because she was cold.

I blinked. My hands convulsed on the guns. Imps were *everywhere.* They moved through the crowds like visible currents of air. For a moment, they seethed around our ankles before the tide of darkness carried them away. But it wasn't the imps that made my blood cool. Clinging to the banners and swinging from booth top to booth top were monkeylike creatures of pure evil. They had the same general shape as monkeys and moved like monkeys, but I'd never seen a monkey with only three fingers on each paw, especially not fingers that ended in black claws as long as my palm. Those black claws glistened in Primordium the way the hound's fur had—like dark, wet blood. Their small round bodies were spiked and scaled, not furred, with no two creatures looking exactly alike. Long tails twirled behind them, ending in scorpion-like striking tips. When one looked in my direction, it smiled, and row after row of teeth glistened under brilliant, glowing eyes.

I turned away only because movement near the ceiling caught my eye. Atop two closely hung banners, a small cluster of the creatures fought, using their claws, teeth, and tails to tear apart one of the smaller, weaker ones. I shuddered.

"What? What is it? Stop staring!"

I looked down at Rose and took physical comfort in the pure white of her energy.

"You look like you've seen a ghost. Is it a demon?"

"How would I know?"

"You'd know. Take a picture!"

I fumbled into my backpack, vaguely aware of Rose shooing away eager men. I finally fit my hand around Medusa, bypassing the pet wood by sheer force of will. When I turned, one of the monkey creatures was standing at the corner of the booth watching me. I stiffened. My instincts told me to gather *lux lucis* and prepare to do battle. Instead, I turned enough to keep it in my peripheral vision.

"Oh, look at that booth," I said inanely to Rose, pointing, then taking a picture of a group of creatures an aisle away. I silently handed my phone to Rose.

"Crap. Vervet."

"What-vet?"

"Vervet. Monkey things." She tapped the phone. "This isn't a good sign at all."

"I figured that."

"How many are there?"

"You want me to take time to count?"

"So what's the plan?"

I stared blankly at Rose. Plan? What plan? Mr. Pitt had made it clear that he didn't want me taking out any evil creatures, and if I was honest with myself, I wasn't enthusiastic about getting close to the vervet.

Cute and cuddly mindless imps were one thing. Monkeys with razor-sharp appendages and some obvious intelligence were another. My only consolation was that vervet appeared as insubstantial as imps.

"Same plan as yesterday," I told Rose. *Only with better results. Hopefully.*

"Winging it. I like it. Kyle would have wasted half the day gridding this place out, planning something methodical."

I grimaced. Kyle's method sounded far more professional.

"All right. Let's get busy," Rose said, eyeing the room. "There has got to be a demon around here somewhere. Let's see if we can find it."

Anyone with a shred of common sense would have left after a statement like that. I followed her. I wasn't sure I liked what that said about me.

We roamed the floor. Or I should say Rose roamed the floor. I stuttered along after her, pulled aside nearly every other step by a geek who wanted a picture or a conversation with me. Fortunately, the more attitude and arrogance I used on the men, the more they liked it, which suited me fine.

I lost track of time, and I would have gotten physically lost just as fast were it not for Rose. The crowds engulfed me like sweaty quicksand. I fantasized of better days, better times, like this morning's phone conversation with the hottest vet in the county. I tried to picture Dr. Love's face superimposed over those of the pubescent boys who stopped to get pictures of me. It was a challenge my imagination wasn't up to. I didn't even attempt to picture Niko. I shook myself free of my downward plunge into insanity when I mistook a man an aisle over for Tim from the bar. No man that Bridget had a crush on would be caught dead at this convention. She had better radar than that.

The whole time, I obsessively alternated between Primordium and regular sight. I couldn't stay in Primordium for long, because it was too hard *not* to look at the vervet and imps, and I couldn't use my regular sight for too long because I felt a compulsive need to track the evil creatures. Whether it was the repeated blinking or the sheer volume of evil making me nauseous, I couldn't tell.

There were so many imps and vervet frolicking through the convention floor, it was difficult to determine their point of origin. However, after ruling out the booths, I noticed an ooze of *atrum* leaking under this particular door and re-forming on this side as imps and vervet. After watching them bound into the feeding frenzy also known as the gaming fans, Rose and I decided I should investigate the other side of the door.

Lucky me.

"I'm going to check out that booth," Rose shouted over the blaring music. "Be quick. It's past my lunchtime and I'm horny."

"You mean hungry."

She shook her head. I shot her a worried look.

Rose slipped through a crowd of Japanese boys with spiked hair and colorful skintight pants and disappeared into a neon-lined booth. I blinked to Primordium.

The door opened before I reached it and two men came out. Their souls were normal. The number of imps clinging to them was not. They were clustered around the men's stomachs, so many stacked on top of each other that it looked like a writhing mass of black maggots. My stomach flipped and I lurched into a table to steady myself and close my eyes for a moment.

Keep it together, Dice. Swallow. Think of Mr. Bond.

"Are you all right?" the man behind the table asked. He was short with curly blond hair. I must have unintentionally blinked back to normal vision, because I was seeing in color. I eyed the man's stocky torso, which strained against a too-small T-shirt, and straightened.

"Yes, thank you. I just need some water."

"Here, let me get you some." He started to race off, but I stopped him.

"I'm going to take a break." I waved in the direction of the evil-spawning door. "But thank you."

"Oh. Okay. Come back by if you still need a boost later. We've got a stash of energy drinks back here." His smile revealed two dimples.

I smiled back and blinked. He didn't look so bad in Primordium, either. A little short for my taste—and voluntarily working at this damned event, which was a huge mark against him—but he didn't have a single imp on him and he had a nice smile.

"Okay," I agreed.

Reluctantly, I turned back to the door. The two horrifying imp-covered men had moved away. I plastered on my best smile, gave my gun belt a tug, and sauntered over to the door.

"Badge," said the bored-looking muscle man at the door.

I pulled the thin lanyard and employee pass from my bag. I'd taken it off after the first man had noticed my real name on the card. The last thing I wanted was for someone here to know my real identity. The security guard scanned the badge's bar code with something that looked like a large cell phone. I crossed my fingers behind my back. The scanner turned green. He pressed a button on the door to let me through.

I brushed past the guard into the hallway beyond, knocking my breasts against the doorway and staggering to the side. That earned me a snort.

"Hey, they're bigger than they look," I said.

The corridor had several rooms feeding off it, all of them clearly marked with taped-up pieces of paper: break room, restrooms, supply closet, exit. It may have looked innocent enough in my regular vision. In Primordium? I swallowed. As Mom said, there were many professions out there. I didn't need to stick with this one, right?

12

Honk if You're Hot and Horny

IMPS BOUNCED ALONG THE EDGE of the corridor, bubbling out of walls thick with *atrum*. Half-formed vervet swung from the slick black molding over the open doors and spilled from the tops of sign placards, tumbling in balls of claws and teeth to the floor, ripping each other to pieces that disintegrated back into raw *atrum* to coat the floor.

Facing that evil-encrusted hallway, I tried to remain unbiased toward the video gaming industry. I'd always dismissed the reactionary statements that video games led to real-life violence, but maybe there was something to those paranoid news stories. This convention appeared to be a prime example.

Rose would have pointed out that most of the people at this event were good, normal people—well, maybe not *normal*—who were victims, not evil predators.

Yet, something had attracted the sludge of darkness that seethed in the employees' hallway, and it wasn't the hotel staff.

A group of bikini-clad warrior women sauntered out of the lounge. They weren't bad. One had dark soot on her soul, but the others were basically good. A rolling wave of imps chased their heels, taking tiny bites from their souls but not attaching.

The women kicked through a pile of twitching, detached vervet body parts that were slowly melting into the linoleum. My knee twinged. I tore my eyes from their *atrum*-smeared calves. My bare legs looked like snow against a starless night sky, marred jarringly by the soccer ball–size imp attached to my knee. I swallowed a shriek and stomped my foot to dislodge it.

The women's laughter died, leaving the hallway eerily quiet. I glanced up in time to watch a vervet drop from the doorway to the last girl's shoulders. It shimmied down her back and sank its teeth into her ass. The women were all staring back at me, faces frozen. Maybe it was because I was in such a cool costume and they were all envious. After all, I was nearly fully clothed while they had only tiny scraps of fabric covering their X-rated bits.

More likely, they watched me in wary silence because I was hopping around, stomping my feet like I was in a hoedown while staring at the one woman's butt.

They gave me wide berth, scuttling against the far wall like crabs in stilettos, sliding against all that raw *atrum*. My hand twitched toward the last woman's ass, and she raced through the door with a shriek, tossing me a wild-eyed look. The vervet waved at me, never losing its mouthful, before the door clicked shut.

"Shit." The vervet had noticed me watching it. "Shit, shit, shit." My cover was blown.

Cover? What cover? I was like a walking Popsicle in front of a swarm of starved two-year-olds. Two-year-olds with razor-sharp teeth and predatory tendencies.

Okay, Dice. Use that pretty little head of yours. I stopped jumping around and concentrated on my knee. The imp burst into glitter. My control was perfect. None of the other creatures looked my way. Apparently they'd all missed my friendly exchange with the vervet, too. Not wanting to question my good luck, I eased down the hall.

Medusa caterwauled. I yelped and jumped, then rifled through the small bag while the horrendous sounds ricocheted against the narrow walls.

"Hello?"

"Get your butt back out here, girl. Brad's calling us back home."

"What? Already? I haven't learned anything yet." *Other than I needed to pick a ringtone for Rose.* I peered down the hallway. Imps bounded ahead of me, disappearing around the bend.

"We confirmed that we're in way over our heads and that our suspicions of demons were most likely right. You're not ready for that."

"Just give me another minute." I forced my feet to trot down the hall. I glanced into the lounge on the way by. The small room had two refrigerators, four couches, two tables, a group of chairs, and three human snacks for a pile of imps and vervet. Would I ever get used to the sight of evil creatures feeding on people? I hoped not.

"No. That's it. We're leaving. Boss's orders. If I don't see you in thirty seconds, I'm pulling the fire alarm and blaming you."

"You wouldn't!"

"Don't test me."

I recognized my euphoric rush of relief for what it was: cowardice. I stalked back to the main door, my skin crawling with the feel of dozens of glowing black eyes on me.

Rose was waiting for me outside the door, glowing white and looking tense enough to levitate.

"Five more minutes," I forced myself to say. I wasn't a chicken.

"You've had enough fun for one day. It's time to go home."

"But—"

"No."

"We could—"

"No."

"How am I supposed to do my job if no one lets me!" It was whiny and childish, but it was the best I could muster. The evil hallway was scary enough; finding the source of all that *atrum* was downright terrifying. But that's what I was supposed to do. If Brad would only let me, I could wipe out all the evil creatures and save this mob of nerds.

In theory.

The security guard cocked an eyebrow at me. "Need help, ma'am?" he asked Rose.

She gave him a coy smile. "Thanks, sugar. I think I can handle Ms. Legs. I'll have to remind her who's boss when we get home, won't I?" She smacked my butt. I yelped and gaped at her.

The guard grinned.

Rose pushed me into the sweaty masses.

"What the hell do you—"

"Like I said, don't test me. I'm on edge."

I gave the nice, blond-haired man a weak smile as Rose marched me past him. It was a marvel really: The crowds parted for Rose where they would have clustered for me, and I knew it wasn't simply because I was in costume and she wasn't. It had to do with presence. If she hadn't been dragging me along behind her like a petulant child, I might even have enjoyed watching the acne-ridden geeks leap out of her way.

I was surprised to see the position of the sun when we exited the hotel. I peered at Medusa's clock. We'd been swimming with the nerds for almost four hours.

Rose didn't speak to me until we were in her Hummer. "Boy-howdy, I'm glad to be out of there! Are there any on me?"

"No." I glared at the hotel's innocent front. "You could have given me a few more minutes. I think I was close to discovering something really useful."

"Or close to getting hurt."

Or that.

"It's okay, you know," Rose assured me. "No one expects you to be ready for a demon on your third day. Hell, no one expected a demon to show up on your third day!" She sounded genuine, but I couldn't help feeling as if I were failing. "You might want to give your approach a little more thought, though. Kyle was an ass, but Mr. Pitt kept him around for a good reason."

"Is there a correct approach to being allowed to do nothing?"

"Hey, don't get snippy with me. I'm trying to help."

"Fine. I'll take it under advisement."

She snorted. I let the silence ride until we were out of the parking lot.

"So you think you can tell how people are going to die, right? Was I in danger?"

Rose took her eyes off the road long enough to flash me a quelling glare. "Enforcers are complicated. And even if I knew, I wouldn't tell you because you're my friend."

"That's convenient." I was a bit mollified that she considered me a friend.

We stopped at In-N-Out on the way back to the office. Rose threatened to make me go in if I didn't stop whining about our lack of progress. I shut up and she took the drive-thru.

"Still horny?" I asked Rose cautiously.

"Nope. My priorities are firmly back in order." She patted her stomach fondly and ordered an animal-style hamburger and fries. I couldn't get rid of the image of the imps moving like maggots on the stomachs of the businessmen, and I opted for my hangover food of choice: greasy fries and a strawberry shake.

While Rose drove back to the office, I forwarded pictures straight to Mr. Pitt in between bites of strawberry shake–dipped fries. I didn't wait for Rose to catch up once we were parked. Scrolling through all the pictures again had only reinforced my need to go back to the hotel. I couldn't let all those helpless people be harmed just because I wasn't a veteran enforcer. I told Mr. Pitt as much when I stormed into his office. He listened until I got to the part about the vervet biting the booth babe's butt.

"You saw *what*?"

"It waved at me."

"It waved!" Spittle sprayed the desk. I realized too late that I'd chosen the wrong tactic. Again. "What were you doing, looking right at it?"

"I—"

"Now the demon knows of you for sure."

"Isn't that a good thing? Now it knows someone protects this region."

"Twirling Twix sticks! Maybe I should keep running the ad if you're so determined to kill yourself."

"You haven't given me the chance to get killed yet!" I crossed my arms around my padded chest. That had sounded better in my head.

"Where were you last night?"

The question threw me. "Uh, home."

"You weren't by chance trespassing, were you?"

"Is that what Doris told you?"

Mr. Pitt didn't answer. I looked away from his florid face and accusing bug-eyed glare.

"I needed to blow off a little steam . . ."

Mr. Pitt sighed and deflated. "You don't know what steam is. You don't even know enough not to be caught by the police."

The way he said it made it sound like he'd seen toddlers commit crimes better than I had.

"It wasn't my fault. I was distracted by the—"

"Don't," Mr. Pitt interrupted. "No more. The only thing that's saving you right now is that you've got a fighting instinct. That, and I'm desperate. Don't push it. You blew the infinitesimal advantage we had."

"It's gone underground," said a voice behind me that made every nerve in my body hum happily.

Trying to be cool about it, I slowly turned to ogle Niko.

He stood propped against the doorjamb, looking as casual as a man with danger practically tattooed on his forehead can look. He was dressed in faded jeans that hugged in all the right places, a light green T-shirt with dark green at the collar, and a lightweight tan coat that he hadn't bothered to zip. The T-shirt was thin enough that it clung to his stomach muscles, and I forced my gaze not to linger.

Niko was watching Mr. Pitt, not me, and I took a moment to admire how nice frustrated looked on Niko's handsome face. I suspected there wasn't an emotion that didn't look good on him, and I was willing to be the judge.

Movement beyond Niko caught my eye. Rose was in her cube, either standing on her step stool or kneeling on her desk so she could peer over the top of the wall. She made a gesture at me to close my mouth. I wanted to stick my tongue out at her but caught myself just in time as Niko's gaze swept down to meet mine.

"A demon's definitely taken residence," he said, "and it's not being shy about it. The entire hotel is crawling with its underlings, but it wasn't home."

I smiled at Niko, happy to be the center of his attention. Then his words sank in.

I flew out of the chair and rounded on Mr. Pitt.

"You had Niko double-checking on me?" I was furious, and it was completely misdirected. Niko *should* be watching what I do. Better still, he should have been handling this one himself. Yet Mr. Pitt had sent me in, making me wear this ridiculous outfit, acting like I was doing important work. Fortunately—or unfortunately—I remembered that I needed this job, maybe even wanted it, and I clamped my mouth shut before I could tell Mr. Pitt where he could shove his managerial tactics.

Mr. Pitt watched the muscle in my jaw tic, then switched his gaze to Niko. "She blew her cover today. The demon knows what it's up against. Or not up against, in this case."

I turned to see how Niko took this news. He was eyeing me, and I felt a blush rush from my toes to my crown, following his toe-to-head perusal. Damn Mr. Pitt and this degrading costume!

"She's not dead yet," Niko said to Mr. Pitt while holding my gaze. I shifted but refused to look away first.

"*Yet* being the operative word."

Niko broke our staring contest and turned to Mr. Pitt. I swiveled to look at my boss, too. Silent communication passed between the two men. For all I knew, they were speaking telepathically. *You're paranoid, Dice.*

"Is that it?" I asked. "Am I off the case?" I didn't know if that was the right lingo, but it sounded good.

"Get changed, Madison," Mr. Pitt said.

I opened my mouth to demand a more concrete answer, took another look at the vein standing out on Mr. Pitt's forehead, and snapped my mouth shut. Niko moved aside so I could pass, then followed me back to my cubicle. I snatched my clothes out of the bottom drawer of an empty filing cabinet. Niko sat down in the desk adjacent mine and powered up the computer. His presence was the only thing that stopped me from stomping about my cubicle and slamming drawers like a frustrated child. I gathered the last shreds of my pride and tried to pretend I was invisible.

"Meet me out front once you're changed," Niko said over his shoulder as I slunk out of my cubicle.

I tripped and dropped my pants. "Uh. Okay." He could have said, "Meet me out front once you're naked" and I probably would have agreed. I snatched up my pants and did my best not to look like I was running.

You've really got to get a grip, I told myself, and felt ridiculously proud of the fact that I'd managed to berate myself silently rather than out loud.

I changed in record time in the large handicap stall. My jeans and lightweight long-sleeve buttercup-colored T-shirt felt bulky and as loose and relaxing as a muumuu after my miniscule spandex outfit. When I slipped my black jacket on, I felt comfortable for the first time all day. The fact that I could cross my arms over my chest again was the cherry on top.

I stuffed the costume clothing into my purse, but the guns, the holsters, and the gargantuan padded bra wouldn't fit. It was a choice between stuffing the bra or the guns in the costume's backpack. If it hadn't been for Niko, I'd have hidden the guns, or better yet, returned them to Will and Joy, but I didn't want to make Niko wait, and there was no way I was going to chat with one of the most attractive men I'd ever met with a nearly solid foam double-D bra dangling from my fingers.

I gave the businesswoman washing her hands at the communal sinks a fright when I walked out with a gun fisted in each hand and the holsters slung over my arm.

"They're fake," I told her, but I don't think she believed me, especially not when I whacked one of them into the wall as I tried to open the door, and it chipped the paint. I wedged the door open as she scurried toward the stall she'd just vacated.

Niko sat in one of the office building's lobby chairs. When he saw me, he stood and headed toward the doors. "I'm glad it's Brad you're upset with," he said, and I thought I detected a hint of a smile at the corner of his mouth.

I tried to downplay it, like carrying guns was an everyday occurrence for me. "They don't fit in my pockets," I said. I shrugged, and one of the holsters fell to the ground. I bent to retrieve it, scraping the gun against the sidewalk with a nails-on-chalkboard sound. Wincing, I tried to juggle the heavy weapons to one hand. Niko swiped the holster off the ground and handed it to me when I straightened. I said nothing and concentrated on dampening my blush as I followed him through the parking lot.

A glossy black, four-door BMW chirped, and Niko opened the driver's door. I eyed the expensive car, the cream-colored leather interior, then my reflection in the polished hood. I'd left my hair in braids because I knew it was going to look clownish when I finally let it down.

They made me look younger despite the amount of makeup I still wore. I rolled my shoulders back and stood a little straighter to compensate.

I met Niko's expectant gaze and waited for him to tell me whatever he'd called me out here to say.

"Get in," he said. He slid into the driver's seat and shut his door.

It took me a moment to get my legs to work. Niko was sexy as hell, and he made me nervous just looking at him. Not only did his stellar looks have a numbing effect on my thoughts, but he was also the epitome of everything I wasn't when it came to being an illuminant enforcer. There was no doubt in my mind that he could have taken care of every single imp and vervet at the convention—blindfolded and while eating with chopsticks. It was one thing to bumble along with Rose at my side and only three days on the job under my belt. But when I thought of how I must look from his eyes, my ineptitude was painful. He couldn't have been much older than me, and he'd already been promoted to the highest enforcer level. I cringed to imagine what he must think of me.

Niko popped the passenger door open from the inside, which I was pretty sure he'd done more to save his paint after having seen my dexterity with the guns than out of courtesy. I slid awkwardly into the seat and piled the guns, backpack, and my purse onto the floorboard at my feet. I pulled the door shut, then looked at Niko to find him watching me with an unreadable expression.

"Um, are we going somewhere?" I asked.

"I talked with Doris this morning," he said.

"Oh?" My mind raced. Doris no doubt told him how incompetent I am, which wasn't a newsflash to anyone. She also could have told him about the hound. It seemed she'd already ratted on me to Mr. Pitt.

"How long have you known what you can do?"

"Not just the vision but the whole *lux lucis*–manipulation thing?"

He nodded.

"Three days."

He turned on the car and buckled his seat belt. I pulled my own on and tried to guess what he was thinking. For all I knew, he could have been contemplating the diversity of his 401(k) portfolio or what he wanted for dinner.

"Doris said she did some training with you."

"Yes," I answered, though it wasn't a question. My neurons finally squirmed through the miasma of hormones and registered the obvious. "Are we going to train?"

"We've got work to do, but I guess it'll work as on-the-job training. All this time that you've been logging at the convention hasn't helped the rest of your region. Especially not with a demon in town."

"Oh, good. I'd really like to take care of some of those smaller problems," I said, thinking of the construction site and the hoodlums that were raising the evil in the region. Plus, the thought of cleansing that area and then returning to rub it in Mr. Pitt's face sounded pretty good right about then.

Niko cocked an eyebrow at me. "Doris also told me that you don't have anything in your arsenal more potent than pet wood, which makes me think those guns aren't loaded with anything special."

"Uh, no." That was an option? "They're props."

"Why are you leaving yourself so vulnerable?"

Confessing that knives scared me and that carrying around even unloaded guns made me nervous was out of the question. I was trying to project an aura of confidence, especially since no one else seemed to have any confidence in me. Plus, if word got back to Mr. Pitt that I was scared, I was pretty sure he'd take back that comment about keeping me around for my fighting spirit.

"I didn't think I'd need them." I realized that I'd admitted more than I'd wanted to and quickly added, "This soon. I didn't think I'd need them this soon."

Niko let that one ride without comment and finally backed out of the parking space. The parking lot was only half full since it was a little past four thirty on a Friday. I eyed the pink horizon and the warm glow of the setting sun behind the clouds.

It was shaping up to be a nice November weekend—not too cold and only a partial chance of showers. Normal people were cutting out of work early to head up to the slopes for some weekend skiing or to the grocery store for weekend supplies. Freed from the chains of work, people were headed out to movies or the mall or to mow the lawn or whatever homeowners did on the weekend. Not a single normal person driving the crowded streets was plotting how to remove a demon from their backyard or track down a roaming hound of evil and some wayward teens.

The streetlights flickered on as Niko pulled onto Eureka Road. He didn't look ready to talk, and I didn't want to put my foot in my mouth again, so I kept quiet and used the time to evaluate my feelings. Was I upset that I wasn't planning a weekend of fun with friends or that my evening was going to be spent doing work that most people would tell me was a delusional fantasy?

Niko turned to drive in the opposite direction as the construction site, and I got my answer in the form of a stab of disappointment. I'd been looking forward to tracking down the teens. I squelched my sigh.

The BMW's purr changed to a growl as Niko accelerated, pushing me into the soft leather. I tried not to compare the BMW to my Honda. My car was only five years old, and it was reliable and efficient, but it had not been designed with this sort of luxury in mind—or this kind of power. Mr. Pitt had mentioned bonuses for hazard pay, right? Surely a demon qualified. Would one demon captured equal a down payment on a car like this?

"Where are we going?" I asked. Better to risk embarrassing myself than contemplate how shallow my motivations were.

"There's a spot near the hotel that's seen increased activity. It feels like a spillover source."

"Do you think there'll be a hound there?" I asked, then could have bitten my tongue when Niko gave me a quick, knowing glance.

"It's a possibility."

He didn't add anything else, and I realized he was going to make me work for my answers. Annoyance helped clear the last of the proximity-induced fog of lust. "If there is, what do you recommend I do?"

"With pet wood? Not a lot. You'll need a net, for sure. If you don't have one of those, your best bet is a *lux lucis*–enhanced knife, preferably thrown so the hound can't get too close to you."

I blinked at his matter-of-fact tone and for the first time wondered about the things he'd killed and what sort of toll that had taken on his mind. The hound I'd encountered hadn't looked much different than an abused dog in normal sight. I didn't think I could kill a dog, no matter how evil it was. I also thought Niko was giving me a lot more credit than I deserved if he thought I could throw a knife at a moving target and hit it.

"What's so special about a net?" I asked.

"Hound nets are made with natural fibers that hold *lux lucis* better than metals, so you can charge them before you throw them over a hound. The *lux lucis* will hold them captive until you're ready to deal with them."

I swallowed hard at the thought of pinning a dog down before killing it. It seemed worse than killing it with a thrown knife. At least then it had a fighting chance.

What have I gotten myself into? I asked myself for the thousandth time.

To my surprise, Niko pulled into the Golden Goose's lot. The parking spaces close to the strip of businesses were full, but Niko parked even farther away than necessary. From across the long parking lot, I examined the bar. The other businesses were still busy with customers and employees, but the bar had barely opened its doors to the Friday-night crowd, and at a little before five, it was hardly more active than it had been on Wednesday night when Bridget and I had made our appearance. Wednesday felt like a lifetime ago.

"Give me the guns," Niko said, snapping me back into the moment.

I handed over the weapons and their holsters and Niko got out and put them in the trunk. I got out, too, and eyed the tacky yellow goose in the backlit sign above the bar's door. I blinked. The world turned off its lights. The Golden Goose was located in an outdated strip mall where even landscaping had been an afterthought. There were no trees or bushes to offer shade to the parked cars, and the only thing that relieved the nearly solid charcoal landscape in Primordium were the white and gray souls of people walking to their cars. Though I could see a few people through the windows adjacent the bar, it was still impossible to see inside the Golden Goose through its tinted black windows.

I dismissed the other businesses one at a time. I doubted that the local nerds or a demon would have had a need to visit the chiropractor's office or a Realtor. Farther down the strip was a tanning and beauty salon—which I ruled out, remembering the pasty skin and oily hair of the majority of men I'd encountered—and a dentist. Again, not a place you'd typically visit unless you're a local, doubly so if you're one of the soda-junkie fans from the convention. I wondered if the nerds even bothered to brush their teeth, and I shuddered.

The Golden Goose had to be the place, and everything looked fine from the outside.

"I don't see anything amiss," I said when Niko came up beside me. I took a moment to admire his soul, which radiated strength and confidence with nearly visible pulses of pure white. I blinked to normal vision to help pull my gaze from him.

Of course, Niko in normal vision was just as hard not to ogle. Especially his lips. I'd never known a man to have lips that fit the stereotypical "begged to be kissed" description before, but his brought the phrase to mind. They were also moving as he spoke, and I made myself focus.

"This is the place. I can feel it from here. You check inside the bar. I'll check the back. Try not to draw attention."

"Okay," I said to Niko's back. I shouldered my purse and marched toward the bar. I wasn't sure what I was looking for, but I figured I'd know it when I saw it. Since the outside looked clean, that meant I could watch Niko walk away without a twinge of guilt.

I happily admired how well he filled out his jeans until I ran into the hitch of an exceptionally long truck.

"Oww!" I stifled the urge to kick the hitch to let it see how it liked it, but since I was afraid the truck's owner might misconstrue the gesture, I hobbled along, embarrassment making me pretend that nothing had happened. I consoled myself with the fact that if I could walk on it, my leg wasn't broken.

Limping up to the front door, I checked Niko's status. He was about to slip down the side of the building, but he'd paused to watch me with a puzzled expression. I straightened and gave him a jaunty wave, then rushed inside the bar.

A band was setting up a stage and equipment on the right side of the bar, and all the empty couches and chairs had been rearranged to accommodate the loss of floor space. The pool tables were similarly deserted, and the bartender was futzing about the garnish station. The TVs were on and muted, and the lights were low. With the tinted windows blocking the outside world's fading evening light, it was impossible to tell the real time. No one had bothered to turn on the music yet, which lent a strangely intimate feel to the place, like I'd interrupted everyone during nonwork hours.

Only two people sat at the bar.

Shockingly, I knew one of them.

"Madison? What are you doing here?" Tim asked.

I strode across the floor, secretly pleased that Tim remembered me and that he was standing so he could greet me with a friendly hug. His golden brown hair had received an expensive cut in the last few days, like he'd upgraded from a hairdresser to a movie-set hair stylist. He was dressed much the same as last time, in light gray slacks, a white shirt, and a gray and blue checkered tie—and once again, he'd found a blue that matched his eyes, though I'd swear that this time his eyes were darker, closer to navy than sky blue. They practically twinkled as he pulled back from the hug.

The smile he flashed warmed me, and I shook my head at my rampaging hormones. Tim should have paled in comparison to the last man I'd seen, but when I smiled up at him, I had a hard time remembering exactly what Niko looked like. I congratulated my decision to not remove the makeup Joy had so artfully applied. I probably looked ten times better than the last time Tim had seen me, if you disregarded the braided hair.

"What a surprise to find you here again," I said, avoiding Tim's question.

"A pleasant surprise, I hope," he fished.

"Of course." We smiled at each other a moment longer; then I took the seat beside him at the bar and he eased back onto his stool, brushing against my knee as he did so. The touch distracted me, and when I looked up, Tim was signaling to the bartender for a drink for me.

"Oh, I'm not—" I caught myself before I finished the sentence and admitted I hadn't come to the bar to drink. What other reason could Tim assume I'd be there for? I couldn't exactly confess I was there to check out some possible evil creatures in the area. Even in my head, the idea sounded preposterous. I did squirm a little in my seat, wondering how I was going to explain this to Niko when he arrived.

Tim was waiting for me to finish my sentence.

"Ah, I'm actually waiting for a coworker," I said, giving him a weak smile.

"Oh? A new friend from the new job? Sounds like things are going well."

"They are. I work with some really nice people."

"I've been curious since we spoke: What does working in a bumper sticker company entail?"

"So far, not much," I said ruefully. "Mostly training and odds and ends." I didn't feel like talking about my job, partially because it reminded me that I was rather bad at it, but mostly because it reminded me that I should actually be working and not talking with a handsome man. "What about you? How's . . . what was it again? Marketing?"

"I'm about to close a big deal, if I'm not mistaken, and I don't think I am." He winked at me, like I was in on a secret.

I felt myself relax. It was nice to flirt and chat with someone normal. No talk of demons or hounds or evil or souls. Just ordinary get-to-know-you casual conversation.

Tim glanced around the bar, and I took the opportunity to study him. My memory had not done him justice. He wasn't at Niko's or even Dr. Love's status, but he was nothing to scoff at either. Realizing I was staring, I made myself look past him. I followed his gaze toward the back of the bar and wondered how Niko was doing and if he'd found anything. If he had, I was sure he could take care of it by himself. Plus, he'd told me to blend in, and I'd arouse suspicions if I abruptly abandoned Tim now.

I took a sip of my drink. Tim had ordered me a peach margarita, one of my favorite drinks. More points for him.

"Where's your friend tonight?"

"Bridget? I don't know. This is more of a work thing."

"That's right. When did you say your coworker was getting here?"

"Any minute now."

"That's too bad," Tim said, making a production of looking at his watch. "I've really got to be running." He stood and pulled a twenty from his wallet. "Hopefully I'll see you again soon," he said, and there was a definite leer to his grin. "By the way, I really like what you've done with your hair."

"Thanks. Bye." I watched him leave and was surprised to note that I was glad he was gone. His final glance had rubbed me wrong.

Shaking off the whole encounter, I turned back toward the bar to check to see if he'd left enough to cover my drink or if I needed to add any money. I was pleased to find my drink and tip were covered.

"He was the best-looking one we've had in here all week, and you had to go and run him off," said a voice two stools down.

I turned to look at the only other customer in the bar, a bleach-blond woman in her late forties, fighting a winning battle against aging. She was dressed in standard office apparel: a pencil-thin black skirt that was just this side of being too short and a button-up blouse that had probably made use of a few more buttons when she was still at the office.

"I've seen better," I said, thinking of Niko.

I remembered my purpose and blinked, annoyed that I'd allowed Tim to distract me. It would have been interesting to see what his soul looked like.

It was a good thing the blonde had turned back to the TV and her drink, because I got a good look at her soul, and my face contorted the way I imagine it would were a slug to swim across my tongue. She was covered from neck to knees with imps, each of them twice the size of my fists, all attached like leeches to her soul, sucking away with stomach-churning greed.

She wasn't the only victim. The bar had been dipped in *atrum*. It coated the furniture, bar, and floor. Imps sucked on the band members, three vervet danced among the liquor bottles behind the counter, and a fountain of imps erupted from the plastic cushion of Tim's vacated stool. How many had left clinging to Tim? How many were attached to me?

I leapt to my feet and did a quick inspection of myself. Two imps clung to my left foot and another to my knee, my hands were smudged with black, and a sharp cold feeling behind me told me I likely had an imp or two clinging to my rear end.

All those wasted hours at the convention finally paid off, and I clinched tight against the need to scream and jump spasmodically, but it was a close thing.

Unattached imps drifted like dust bunnies on an unseen breeze across the floor, swirling around my feet and the base of the blonde's stool. Several small imps broke away from the herd and latched on to me. Even more leapt for the other woman. The rest drifted away toward the band members.

I clung to the lip of the bar with a white-knuckled grip and tried to figure out what to do. Mr. Pitt hadn't let me kill the imps at the convention because he hadn't wanted to raise the suspicions of the demon and he didn't think I could take them all out before . . . I didn't know how to finish that thought. *Before I was overwhelmed? Pulled under? Killed?*

Now's not the time to think about it, I told myself, but I couldn't get the picture out of my body of being dragged to the ground under a wave of imps and sucked dry, until all that remained of me was a mummylike corpse of *atrum.*

"Can I get you anything else?"

I jumped and whirled to face the bartender. A vervet perched on his shoulder and licked the man's cheek, leaving behind a slimy black trail.

"Are you okay?" the man asked, taking a careful step back.

I couldn't tear my eyes away from the vervet, but I fought for control of my expression. It wasn't easy. I managed a smile that had the bartender backing up another step. "I'm fine."

I whirled toward the door and slammed into a blazing white, imp-free chest.

"Niko!" I breathed with such relief it sounded intimate.

Niko took in the scene with one glance. "What are you doing?"

"Panicking," I whispered, too happy to see him to try to play it cool.

"I see what you mean," said the blonde behind me. It took me a moment to realize she was referring to my earlier comment: Tim didn't hold a candle to Niko's macho-modelesque good looks.

Niko met my gaze. We were separated by only the few inches I'd bounced back after slamming into him. He had one hand on my arm to steady me, the other resting at his back, where I guessed he probably had some sort of weapon concealed. He was taller than me by a good five or six inches, but with him looking down at me from so close, I could almost reach up and plant a kiss on his lips.

His eyes darted over my face, and the corners of his mouth tightened. Apparently kissing was not on his mind. With a warm hand to my back, he guided me away from the blonde toward the couches.

"What have you done so far?" he asked quietly.

I gave him a blank look. I doubted he wanted to hear about me flirting with Tim.

"I didn't know what to do," I said. "At the convention, Mr. Pitt wouldn't let me touch anything. Can I do that here? I'm afraid the others will notice, but I need to get these things off me! They're disgusting! I don't know how much longer—"

"Whoa, slow down. Yes, we're cleaning up the place, so you can take out whatever you like. Start with the ones on you."

I didn't wait for him to finish. I gathered *lux lucis* and pushed it into the imps I could see on my feet and knee and more carefully into the ones I couldn't see on my behind. Then I pressed against the smudges on my hands. The black blotches of raw *atrum* didn't want to disintegrate, and my soul looked taxed from my exertions once it was clean.

"There's a couple of trees out back. Go recharge, then go to my car and get a net." He pressed his keys into my palm and my fingers convulsed around them.

"A net?"

"A hound's been here recently, and I want to be prepared. Do you have your pet wood?"

I rummaged through my purse and pulled it free.

"Not the handiest location for your only weapon."

There wasn't anything to say to that, so I used a diversionary tactic. "How do we get the imps off the woman?" Aside from doing some karate around her. While it'd worked for the few imps on the construction worker, I didn't think the lady would sit still for a full-body fondle conducted about an inch above her skin. At least not by me. I eyed Niko again. She would probably sit through anything he asked.

"I'll show you. Remember, though, you only want to attempt this if you can handle all of imps in the vicinity. You wouldn't be able to do this right now."

As true as I knew his words to be, I didn't like hearing them.

"Don't stick around too long, either," Niko said. "Once you understand what I'm doing, go recharge and get that net. Don't let any more imps stay on you."

I nodded to show I understood and swallowed my sarcastic comments. It wasn't Niko's fault that I couldn't do my job as well as he could, but it felt like he was rubbing salt in a wound with each cautionary statement.

Niko sauntered over to the bar, casually brushing his hand along the back of an *atrum*-tainted couch along the way. *Lux lucis* spread from his hand outward across the couch, eating away at the *atrum* until the couch was a normal nonlife charcoal color in Primordium.

Cool trick, I thought. The only thing similar that I knew was a ward, but the wards that Doris had shown me how to make stayed only where I placed the *lux lucis*. The energy hadn't spread at all. Tentatively, I touched the back of a nearby chair that was smeared with *atrum*. I gathered a trickle of *lux lucis* into my fingertips and pressed it to the fabric. When I lifted my hand, five white dots remained in the middle of the *atrum*, and they began to fade even as I watched. I put my fingers back to the fabric and tried to push *lux lucis* out the tips, envisioning it flowing down the chair.

My hand flared bright white, and nothing happened to the *atrum*. Niko glanced my way, and I quickly clasped my hands together behind my back and willed the *lux lucis* to redistribute, all the while trying to look innocent. Niko's lips twitched.

He selected Tim's old stool, casually brushing his hand across the surface first, like he was dusting crumbs away. Again, *lux lucis* washed across the plastic top and down the metal leg, burning away *atrum* and neutralizing the vicinity. He did the same with the counter of the bar in front of him, creating an oasis around himself.

The blonde had already turned to engage him in conversation. Niko turned his full smile on her, and I thought I was about to witness my first-ever swoon. Niko placed one hand on the bar and gathered *lux lucis* into it, letting it grow brighter and brighter, like a fluorescent bulb warming up. In seconds, it was bright enough to be difficult to look at, reminding me of Kyle's sun-god trick. Just as the imps in Starbucks had been unable to resist Kyle's beacon of light, the imps on the blonde were unable to resist the call of a brighter soul. Like moths to a flame, they leapt for Niko, and one at a time, he extinguished them wherever they landed on his body.

It's a bit like watching a lux lucis *vacuum,* I thought, fascinated. It wasn't until Niko waved his other hand behind his back at me that I remembered my mission. I did a quick check for imps, thankful to see none had crept up on me while I'd been mesmerized, and made a beeline for the door.

Stepping outside into the cool night air felt like an escape. I took a few deep breaths and surveyed the parking lot. Nothing hinted at the evil housed inside the Golden Goose. Most of the businesses had closed while I'd been inside, and the parking lot was slowly emptying as workers trickled out.

I eyed the BMW and considered grabbing the net first, but one more glance at my dimmed soul had me turning toward the back of the building. I thought it was a bit ironic that aside from the Dumpsters and scattered storage piles stacked near the back exits of the businesses, the alley behind the strip mall was more attractive than the front. Large pine trees marched between the back of the strip mall and the back of the Walmart it butted up against, making a natural fence. The Walmart side had an additional row of hedges and a few large-leafed flowering plants.

The alley and Walmart's loading dock were quiet. I trotted over to the nearest tree and pressed my palm to its rough bark. *Lux lucis* jumped from the tree to me, and I effortlessly removed the lingering stains of *atrum* from my hands and arms. Feeling like I'd had a shot of caffeine, I stepped away from the tree.

A low growl brought me up short. I swiveled to my right. Bared teeth, raised hackles, fur composed of spiky *atrum*. Yep, the hound had found me.

13

HAVE YOU HUGGED YOUR DOG TODAY?

THE HOUND SNARLED, SCRUNCHING ITS nose to expose sharp teeth half parted. A long string of drool slid from a bared canine. Tension tightened its muscles until I could trace the tendons beneath its skin with my eyes.

I eased back a step, then another. A quick blink confirmed that the hound was a mutt. It looked identical to the one I'd encountered at the construction site, over five miles away. It was in pretty bad shape—scrawny enough to count its ribs and vertebrae, with grungy fur liberally pockmarked with fresh and old cuts. I wasn't fooled by its appearance, though. A starved wild dog was more than enough to make me leery. Add in the fact that it was a creature of pure evil, and I was its natural enemy, and I wouldn't have trusted the hound if it were a Chihuahua.

I blinked back to Primordium and debated my options. One, I could run—and probably be tackled from behind by the much faster hound. Two, I could stay there—and be tackled by the hound. Three, I could slowly move around the side of the building, then run to the BMW, call in a miracle or two, and grab the net out of the trunk—and be tackled by the hound, who would then take gleeful chunks out of my flesh and soul.

None of the options sounded good, and two of them involved leading the hound to a more populated area, which was out of the question. Aside from how bad I'd feel if other people got bitten due to my incompetence, Mr. Pitt would fire me, and Niko would be disappointed. All three outcomes made me cringe.

The hound growled. The hairs on my arms stood on end.

"You don't want to mess with me," I warned it.

It snarled, giving me a spectacular view of its glistening fangs. It could tell a lie when it heard it.

I scavenged through my purse, cursing myself for having ever let go of my pet wood, especially after Niko's admonishment. The moment I took my eyes off the hound, it started for me.

"Hold on, doggie," I pleaded. I clutched the pet wood and yanked it free of my purse, extending it with a flick of my wrist. "Good doggie. Stay."

It charged.

I slammed *lux lucis* into the pet wood and brandished it like a sword. The hound swerved at the last minute, whimpering and growling. We circled each other in the alley.

"Okay, Dice. You wanted to do something. Now's your chance." I gathered more *lux lucis*, this time in my left hand. *Now just grab the slobbering attack dog of evil*, I urged myself. Maniacal laughter echoed in my skull. Niko's lack of faith in a pet wood's effectiveness against a hound replayed in my head. Yet, even face-to-face with a homicidal hound, I still didn't wish my pet wood were a knife.

The hound lunged for my throat. Sheer self-preservation brought my arm up in time to knock its head aside before its body slammed into mine and I stumbled to the side.

Now!

I slapped my hand into the off-balance hound, flipping it on its side. It snapped for me and its mouth closed around the pet wood. *Lux lucis* sank into the hound as if into a void. For the briefest second, the hound froze, and I jumped to straddle it, grabbing it by the scruff and abandoning the drained pet wood to its jaws. With a yelp, it dropped the stick and writhed in my grasp, trying simultaneously to escape and to bite me. I hung on, shoving its head into the pavement, and pushed *lux lucis* into it through my hands the way I would an imp.

Nothing happened. No puff of glitter. No flare of *lux lucis* in my hands. It was like I was feeding *lux lucis* to the air for all the effect it had.

The hound bucked beneath me, almost latching its teeth around my ankle, unfazed by the *lux lucis* I poured into its throat.

I was trapped. I couldn't let go of the hound and get away unscathed, and the *lux lucis* wasn't working.

I considered, for one irrational moment, attempting to call Doris or Niko, but my purse was several yards away and it would have been impossible to get Medusa out and hold on to the hound anyway.

It lunged for my left leg, teeth snapping on a flap of my jeans before I tore free and wrestled for control again. The foul stench of its breath accompanied the next growl. I suppressed hysterical laughter. I'd begged all day for the go-ahead to fight evil, and now I wished I were anywhere but here.

Desperate, I thrust *lux lucis* from me, aiming for the pavement beneath the hound. It arced from my hands into the overwhelming *atrum* of the hound. The slick black taint didn't so much as flicker. *Lux lucis* that would have disintegrated a hundred imps disappeared into the hound without a trace.

My arms quivered and my muscles grew heavy with fatigue, but I didn't have a choice. I poured a steady flood of my energy into the hound, hanging on to his fur with cramping hands.

Something in the hound popped. One moment, it was a dark void sucking the *lux lucis* from me; the next the fur under my palms glowed white. I jerked and nearly lost my hold before shoving more *lux lucis* into the hound. In moments, the hound's shoulders were white, then its back, until the *atrum* drained from its fur, from its soul, like someone had pulled a plug in its paws. The dark substance pooled beneath our bodies, eddying outward.

The fight went out of the hound with the last of the *atrum*, and it lay still beneath me. I continued to pump *lux lucis* through it, watching the white energy slide out the paws, chasing the *atrum* across the asphalt until we were surrounded by an evil corona. The area beneath us was clean, though, and that was good enough for me. I broke our connection and fell back on my butt. The hound and I panted in rhythm.

No. The hound was gone. Left behind was a normal malnourished, neglected mutt. Pride rushed through my veins in a fizz of euphoria. This was what I was meant to do—I was meant to fight evil. I was *made* to fight evil. And I had done it! I was an illuminant enforcer by nature and now, officially, by deed.

Nothing else I'd ever done had felt so *right*.

The dog lifted his head to look at me, and his eyes glowed a normal, animal glow. I gave him a tentative pat and his tail thumped against my legs. He closed his eyes and leaned back against my thigh.

I blinked and examined the dog with normal sight. The sun had fully set, and the only illumination came from the yellow lamps above the back doors of the building, but even in the indistinct lighting, I could tell he was the most pathetic mongrel I'd ever seen. The pads of his feet were raw, and along with the cuts I'd noticed earlier, I could now see that he had eaten away his own fur around his hips. The rest of him was matted gray and grimy.

The dog pricked his ears and I followed his gaze. Niko stood propped against the corner of the building, arms crossed, watching us.

"He was a hound," I explained, and pointed stupidly at the dog. My breathing was almost back to normal. The dog seemed as content as I was to remain seated on the dirty asphalt.

"I know." He pushed away from the wall and retrieved my pet wood and purse. The pet wood was coated with slobber; when he handed it to me, I held it delicately between my thumb and forefinger. Niko crouched beside the dog, only to have the mutt cower and try to hide behind me. I scratched his neck, and his eyes partially closed in bliss. When I looked up, Niko had cleared away the *atrum* circling us.

"That was a pretty stupid stunt," Niko said.

I gave him an unfriendly look before turning my attention back to the dog. "What would you have had me do? Trap it and kill it? Even if I'd had the net, I wouldn't have done that. My way worked fine."

"No one said anything about killing. The net is to hold it captive until it can be safely drained of *atrum*. Hounds, like wild dogs, usually run in packs."

"Oh." Charming. I'd jumped to the worst conclusion. But wait; Niko wasn't done making me feel bad.

"You got lucky with this one. He made a pathetic hound. A bigger one could have drained you until you were too weak to fight back."

I blinked and examined my soul. I could see Niko doing the same thing. I looked worse than I had after I'd gone training with Doris and then nearly killed Mr. Bond.

"Why didn't you come get me?" Niko asked. "The hound clearly didn't intend to attack until you threatened it."

"You've been watching since the beginning!" I blinked to normal vision so I could properly stare at him in indignation. He didn't look the least bit remorseful. Finally, I said, "I didn't want the hound getting any ideas. I was the only person back here, but there are a lot more people out front."

Niko smiled at me, a real smile, not the charming flirty one he'd turned on the blonde inside. It warmed me to my toes. I looked away so I didn't do anything foolish.

The dog had a collar, and I read the tag. It was tarnished silver in the shape of a pit bull's head, and it said *Max*. There was no address or phone number to contact.

"What now?" I asked, beginning to feel foolish sitting on the ground in the middle of the grungy alley.

"We've got some work left to do inside. That bar has seen something pretty bad recently, or else it's quite the hangout for the people from the convention. You need to recharge. Again."

I selected a different tree. I didn't know how much *lux lucis* a tree could give before it grew weak, and after watching the plants die under my fingertips, I didn't want to take chances with one of these large trees. Max glued himself to my side like we were tethered together. I wondered how many fleas were jumping onto me, but I couldn't bring myself to push the dog away.

Niko waited while I recharged, and his gaze roamed up and down the alley, ever vigilant. I wondered if he expected more trouble. If so, he was welcome to handle it all on his own.

We stopped by the BMW next. I thought that Niko might want to leave Max inside, but instead he pulled a leash out of the trunk and snapped it onto Max's collar before the dog could shy away from him. Niko pointed out the net while the trunk was open. It looked like a normal net, made of a twisted rope material, with small, finger-size openings. It wasn't holding any *lux lucis*, but Niko had me feed a little into it to feel what it was like. The net absorbed *lux lucis* like Max had, seeming to soak it right from my fingertips, and the white light raced down the network of paths, glowing brighter at evenly spaced intervals where disks of leather reinforced the netting.

The net wasn't the only item in the trunk either. The sides and back of the trunk had been fitted with customized heavy-weave open-top storage bins that neatly divided everything into its own place. The center of the trunk was empty. My guns and holsters were packed in a side cubby on top of a blanket roll. That side also had a row of small loops holding a flashlight, two knives, and several oversize pet wood–like objects. On the other side was a first aid kit and an ice chest that looked to be the perfect size for a six-pack. I tried to picture Niko at a grocery store picking out some Corona and a small bag of ice, but the image didn't fit with the obsessively organized trunk.

The trunk was abnormally shallow, and I didn't ask Niko what the false bottom concealed.

Niko handed me Max's leash, and I tied him to a handicapped signpost near the door to the Golden Goose. Max whined when I walked away, but he wouldn't be allowed inside the bar. Feeling like a jerk, I left him cowering against the bumper of a minivan.

A few more people had straggled inside while I'd been out back, and the band had finished setting up, though they weren't playing yet. I didn't see any imps or vervet, but *atrum* slime still coated most of the surfaces. The blonde was gone, too, which was the most impressive change. I figured nothing short of a crowbar would pry her from Niko's side after he'd sat down next to her. I was about to ask Niko how he'd done it, but he'd gone into instructor mode, and I decided it wasn't the right time.

"Let's sit in the corner while you figure this out," Niko said, gesturing to seating at the side of the stage. He swept the *atrum* from the table and our chairs as I'd seen him clean the stool earlier.

"Did you get rid of all the imps that quickly?" I asked. I'd hardly been outside five minutes before he'd come to watch me tackle the hound. Even though I knew he was a thousand times more competent than me, I was still amazed.

"For now."

I remembered the imps and vervet bubbling out of the *atrum* in the inky black hallway at the convention and pretended to adjust my seat across from Niko to disguise my shudder.

"For the *atrum* to soak into the furniture and floor like this means some strong evil was here, and it'll likely be back."

"So you don't think this was the ner—ah, guys from the convention?" With no arcade games, scantily dressed women, or free Wi-Fi, I would have guessed this bar to be safe from a geek invasion.

"This wasn't humans," Niko confirmed. "People, whether good or evil or anywhere in between, don't leave a residue like this. At least not in a public place. For humans to generate this much *atrum*, they would have to have done some horrific things here, and since the cops haven't busted any human trafficking or shooting sprees here, it's a safe bet that we're dealing with an evil creature. Or the hosts who brought the evil with them."

"Hosts?"

"Regular humans carrying evil. Like Samantha was."

I gave him a blank look.

"The lady at the bar. If she'd left here with all those imps attached to her, she'd have been a host, and she would have tainted wherever she went with *atrum*."

"On this scale?"

"No, but she's just one person tainted by visiting here."

"So you mean all those people at the convention…?"

Niko nodded. "Hosts."

Damn Mr. Pitt and his look-but-don't-touch orders. All those hosts. Walking through my region. Making *atrum* pits of evil to spawn imps and vervet and who knew what else. I stared at the inky interior of the bar and swallowed down my rising despair. Illuminant enforcers did this all the time. I wasn't the first to have an evil creature taint her region. In fact, my job was based on evil creatures popping up and making a mess of normal humans' lives.

I tried to think proactively, but the first question that came out sounded like a whine. "*Lux lucis* doesn't stick around like this, so why isn't the *atrum* dissipating?"

"Usually it will, but there's so much here, it's like it's breeding itself stronger. Left unattended, there's enough *atrum* for imps to spawn from it. And if people with tainted energy come in during that time, they could easily help spawn a couple more vervet, too. It's a perpetuating cycle. Evil begets evil."

"Good begets good?" I asked hopefully.

Niko nodded.

"Then how do evil creatures feed on *lux lucis*? Shouldn't they eat *atrum*? I mean, I use *lux lucis* to kill imps, but that seems to be their favorite food source, too." This paradox had been a nagging question at the back of my mind, but I hadn't had a moment to ask anyone until now.

"System overload," Niko said. "Creatures like imps grow stronger by turning *lux lucis* to *atrum*. In essence, they cycle *lux lucis* to *atrum* the way you or I, well, turn oxygen into carbon dioxide."

"There's some *atrum* in *lux lucis*?" I asked, confused.

"You mean like there's carbon dioxide in the air we breathe? Maybe that was a bad analogy. I was trying for something PC, but . . . here's how it was explained to me: imps eat *lux lucis* and shi—poop *atrum*. Only they don't 'eat' and 'poop' as much as inhale and exhale."

I grinned at his discomfort. "So when I push *lux lucis* into an imp, I'm giving it more food than it can, ah, exhale?"

"Exactly. Imps can't convert the amount of *lux lucis* you feed them, and it overloads their bodies and they explode. Creatures with form, though, like the hound, are more complicated. As you saw, the *lux lucis* eventually takes over where the *atrum* was."

I sat back with a grin. I finally felt like I was getting a handle on my new, bizarre world. Niko was giving me information and answers, I'd successfully cleansed a hound, and I'd gotten rid of a few imps, too, before Niko had sent me outside. I was a woman in charge of her own destiny, and soon, hopefully, her own region—in more than name only. Plus, sitting in an intimate setting with Niko and receiving his full attention was doing wonders for my libido—I mean, for my self-confidence.

"So how do we get rid of the *atrum*?" I asked.

"Have you created anything with *lux lucis* before?"

"Just a ward. Doris showed me how."

Niko made me demonstrate by warding the table.

"That's about as basic as you can get," Niko said, eyeing the glow around the rim of the table. "All you're doing is pushing *lux lucis* out of you. *Lux lucis* will stick to any surface for a while, but it will fade, and it fades faster from objects that were never alive than it does from wood, leather, and fabrics like hemp and cotton."

"So even if it's dead now, if it was once alive, it'll hold *lux lucis* longer?"

Niko nodded. "But a ward won't get rid of existing *atrum*. To do that, you have to manipulate the *lux lucis* first."

"Make it hungry?"

"What?"

"You know, somehow make it so it wants to eat the *atrum*, like you did before."

Niko smiled. "I never thought of it like that. Watch closely."

I blinked to Primordium and watched as Niko gathered *lux lucis* in his right hand. Like I'd seen many times before, his hand grew brighter but settled at a white barely twice as bright as the rest of his body. I waited a moment before looking at his face expectantly.

"Are you watching?" he asked.

"Uh-huh." I peered closely at his fingers. It took me a moment to see it. When I did, I gasped and poked at his fingers. *Lux lucis* was *moving* beneath his skin. It looped over the top of his fingers, reached the tips, then slid back toward his palm on the bottom side, only to reach his palm and curl back over the top of his fingers. Touching him, I could feel the cycling *lux lucis* tickle against my skin.

"How are you doing that?" I reluctantly pulled away from his warm fingers.

"You can do it, too. Give it a try."

I held my hand up and gathered *lux lucis*. I pushed it to my fingertips, and at the last minute, pulled it back. My hand flared brighter, then dimmed, but the *lux lucis* didn't start looping through my fingers.

"Refine it down to one finger first," Niko instructed. "The more control you have, the better you'll do with larger amounts of *lux lucis*."

I obediently focused on my pointer finger.

The server came by for our drink orders, and Niko ordered us both a Coke. I didn't bother to glance at the waitress, and I'd be just as surprised if she noticed me, what with Niko to admire.

"Feel the force of the *lux lucis* first on top of your finger, then on the bottom. Top, then bottom," Niko instructed after the server walked away.

I squeaked a little when I felt the *lux lucis* flare at the top of my finger, then sink to the bottom.

"Good. Now move it forward and backward. It's all just energy, and you can shape it and move it however you like in your body."

Niko's deep voice was hypnotic. I sank into my body, lost my awareness of everyone around us, and focused on my *lux lucis* and Niko's instructions. He guided me step by step through the process until I had a minute swirl of *lux lucis* circling the length of my finger.

"Good job," Niko said, and his light tone broke my trance. I glanced up. The bar had filled and the band was starting to warm up. I blinked at Niko and switched to normal sight, feeling a little light-headed. I shifted in my seat. From how numb my butt was, I'd been concentrating for a lot longer than it had felt like.

"Now what?"

"Now, while it's moving, you transfer the *lux lucis* into the *atrum*. By starting the *lux lucis* rolling within you, you can make sure that it continues to roll when you release it. That way it'll roll over the *atrum* and, like you said, eat it."

We stood with our drinks in hand, and I followed Niko to an empty couch coated with *atrum*. I blinked back to Primordium and watched him again. This time, I was aware how much he must be deliberately slowing himself down so that I could see what he did. The first time he'd cleansed a couch, I hadn't even seen his hand flare.

Niko got his *lux lucis* spinning through his fingers at a much faster rate than he'd shown me at the table; then he pressed his fingers to the couch and the *lux lucis* rolled off the tip of his fingers and spread like wildfire through half the *atrum*.

"Your turn," Niko said, indicating the remaining *atrum*.

I got my *lux lucis* spinning again, though it took me a good two minutes; then I placed my hand on the *atrum*. Nothing happened.

"Give it a push," Niko said.

I pushed. *Lux lucis* flared and eradicated the *atrum* under my palm, then died back down. Niko didn't say anything. I tried again, this time attempting to work with the *lux lucis* rolling in my fingers. When the cycle of light energy reached my fingertips, I flipped it from my fingers, picturing it doing a barrel roll down the couch.

A tiny patch of *lux lucis* the width of my fingers rolled two inches through the smear of *atrum* and stopped.

I giggled. "That was sad."

"Try it with a little more umph."

Determined to not look completely pathetic in front of Niko, I shoved *lux lucis* into a rolling wave through my fingers. My entire hand blazed with light, and I heaved the *lux lucis* from my fingertips. It hit the couch cushion like a camera flash, bright and fast, and rushed through the remaining three-foot square of *atrum* faster than Niko's had. When the *lux lucis* ran out of *atrum* to devour on the couch, it rolled down a stubby wooden leg and iced across the dark floor, leaving an uneven patch of clean, evil-free linoleum. My cushion shimmered under a coat of *lux lucis*, where Niko's was a plain charcoal gray.

"Too much umph?" I asked, sheepish.

"You'll learn better control with practice."

"Is that okay?" I indicated the stain of *lux lucis*.

"Completely. Whoever sits there will feel especially refreshed when they get up."

After that, we made quick work of the Golden Goose. Niko told the server we'd lost our car keys, and we made a big production out of looking for them, using the opportunity to remove the evil taint from all the furniture, walls, and floors in the process. The server helped us look, for which I felt a little bad, but I figured she was happy to help Niko, especially after she learned Niko and I were simply coworkers, not dating.

Even with all the practice, my control was erratic, but we both could tell I was getting better by the time the bar was clean and Niko "found" the keys hidden in a couch cushion.

When we exited the bar, Max's mangy form was huddled under the bumper of a massive lifted truck, head slumped on filthy paws. The moment he saw me, he leapt to his feet, and his wagging tail nearly knocked us both down as I untied him. He was starved for affection as much as food, and I paused to rub the matted hair under his collar. My apartment had a tiny balcony, which got blazing hot in the middle of the day. Maybe if I installed a pet door—

"We'll take him to a shelter," Niko said. "There's a local one that takes most of the hounds we turn."

My heart lurched, the fantasy shattered by Niko's matter-of-fact pragmatism. I didn't have the space for a dog, let alone the time. It wouldn't be fair to Max. I looked away from the dog's soulful, trusting eyes, and led him across the parking lot on wooden feet. A shelter would be good for Max. He'd have the chance of being adopted into a family with a yard and kids to play with.

"Most?" I asked, forcing my mind away from visions of taking Max to the dog park on the weekends.

"Not all hounds-turned-dogs are able to be rehabilitated. Dogs that have been hounds for too long can take to it. You've heard of dogs getting a taste for blood, right? It's like that. They get a taste for evil and start acting out in ways that taint their souls all over again."

"But I thought that animals were naturally good."

"They are, but they can be corrupted just like humans. It's simply harder with animals."

Niko spread the blanket from his trunk over the BMW's backseat, and we loaded Max into the car, then piled in ourselves. Niko cracked the back windows to draw Max's special funk out of the car and make it breathable again. The BMW hummed to life, and I was content to sit cocooned in its silence for a while. It was depressing to picture animals turned evil. I was glad I'd saved Max.

We merged onto the freeway and headed south toward Citrus Heights. I was surprised to see the traffic moving at almost normal speeds. Usually Friday-evening traffic was bumper-to-bumper, crawling along at thirty miles per hour or less. I eyed the dark sky, then the clock, and was amazed that we'd been in the Golden Goose for nearly two hours. It hadn't felt that long.

Niko took the Madison Avenue exit and made a left over the freeway into the urban sprawl that stretched from Roseville to Sacramento. The cities in between had long since blurred together. We could have been in Carmichael or Citrus Heights or Fair Oaks; the dividing lines between each had been reduced to small welcome signs on major crossroads. Strip malls, apartment complexes, gas stations, and car lots clustered on both sides of the six-lane road. Every once in a while, I got a peek down a side street into packed subdivisions.

I wondered what enforcer worked this region. It was so dense with humanity that there was hardly room for parks and parking lots. At least in my region I had patches of open space left wild, with huge sections of sprawling properties, an abundance of parks, and winding greenbelts around the marshes and bike trails.

Were the regions here smaller? Was the ratio of evil to good greater? Where did enforcers recharge? What sort of creatures were out there, waiting to be cleaned up? Hounds? Vervet? Evil things I hadn't yet learned of? Were the enforcers here stronger? Better?

Of course they're better, I thought with a tinge of bitterness. The enforcers here were fully trained, had probably been working with Primordium since they were toddlers, and knew the answers to all my questions.

I peered into the backseat at Max. His blanket had slid to the floor during one of the many stops and starts of traffic, and he had gone with it. His emaciated body fit behind my seat, and he had his head resting on the middle hump of the floorboard.

"What corrupts a dog to make it a hound?" I asked, continuing our dropped conversation.

"They turn evil the same way everyone does: through evil deeds or by absorbing evil. Where humans more spontaneously commit evil acts, animals have to be taught. Pets have it worse, though. When owners of pets are evil—especially owners of very loyal pets—the animals will feed their *lux lucis* to the owner and take on the owner's *atrum*. It lets the person stay 'good' longer."

"The animals do that consciously?"

"Who knows."

I wondered if there was anyone I could ask who would know, anyone who could talk with animals. It didn't seem particularly far-fetched, given I was now wielding *lux lucis* and Rose could feel other people's emotions just by being near them.

"I think Max is the same dog—hound—I saw the other night," I confessed.

"The one that Doris said you encountered?" Niko asked, confirming my suspicion that Doris had ratted me out to him, too.

"Yes. But I was way over off Sierra College at the time. Do you think he could have traveled that far?"

Niko thought about it before answering. "He looks neglected and hungry. It's a possibility. And he could have felt drawn to the demon, and we just happened across him along his way."

"Do some hounds look well loved?" I asked, finding it hard to believe that a person could simultaneously love a dog and turn it into an evil hound.

"Definitely. Max is the weakest hound I've seen in a long while. Which is why you were able to overpower him."

"Yeah, I heard you the first time."

"I'm not going to lie to you and tell you you're stronger than you are." Niko took his eyes off the road to pin me with a hard look. "I'd be setting you up for a nasty surprise if I did. You got lucky with Max. Don't let it go to your head."

"I don't think I'll get the chance," I muttered.

It took over an hour to get Max checked in at the shelter—only after I'd verified it was a no-kill shelter. Niko wrote out a sizable check to cover Max's expenses for the next three months, during which time the dog would hopefully be adopted by a loving family. I watched Max be led away by the shelter handler, his tail clamped between his legs, his head swiveled so he could watch me with big, pleading eyes that begged me not to leave him. My vision blurred as he rounded the corner out of sight, and I was very careful not to blink as we walked out to the car. Niko slid into his seat first, and I used the moment to dab at my eyes to make sure my tears hadn't spilled over before I got into the passenger side.

"He'll be well cared for here," Niko assured me, clearly not fooled by my attempt to appear stoic. "They're familiar with the types of dogs we bring in."

"Do they know they were hounds?"

"No, but they can tell an abused dog when they see one. They think I'm part of a private organization like the Department of Animal Care and Control, and I told them you were a new employee."

"How do I prevent this? How do I stop evil from growing in my region, from corrupting innocent animals like Max?" It came out harsher than I intended. At least people brought it on themselves. They made choices they knew were good or bad, and their souls reflected this. Animals either didn't have a say—if they were loyal pets, like most dogs—or they had to be taught to be evil, and the thought sickened me.

"You can't, not completely," Niko said. He pulled out into traffic, taking Hazel Avenue toward Roseville rather than going back out to the freeway. "The best you can do is eradicate the evil you do find."

"Like the demon at the convention. Only Mr. Pitt won't let me touch it."

"Not all evil is so large and blatant. Take the construction site."

"What do you know about that?"

"Brad filled me in this morning when he was telling me about the demon."

"About how I'm incompetent bait," I said, feeling sorry for myself.

"About how you keep trying to take on more than you're ready for . . . and how you got caught by the cops."

I sighed. "I may have gotten caught, but now I know what the problem is." I paused for effect. "Kids."

"All of them, or just a few in particular?"

"There's been some vandalism on the property. The cop thought it was a few teens. Would that be enough for Mr. Pitt to somehow sense the evil?"

"He said it wasn't too large, so that fits the description. You'll learn to judge that soon, too."

"I'll be able to sense evil from miles away?"

"Not quite. Brad can feel the movement of *lux lucis* and *atrum* throughout his region. But you should be able to feel *atrum* when you're near it."

That sounded cool. And useful.

"I need to be able to do that now. How else am I going to track down those kids or prevent another Max from being created?"

"Give it time," Niko said. He followed his useless comment with a smile, so I restrained my snarl. "You're new. Cut yourself a little slack."

I didn't want to complain to Niko, so I kept my mouth shut for the rest of the ride.

I stopped by the grocery store after Niko dropped me off at my car and picked up a carton of Ben and Jerry's Half Baked ice cream, drove home, recharged, showered, then collapsed into my single recliner chair—after feeding Mr. Bond—and devoured the whole carton. I reached the bottom before I decided whether or not today counted as a successful day as an illuminant enforcer. I had taken out more evil today than the last two days combined, but I'd left a gigantic ticking evil bomb at the hotel.

I had a hard time falling asleep, reliving Max's scared and pleading expression as he was led away at the shelter, and my dreams were haunted by imps feeding in a writhing, maggot-like mass on my stomach.

14

Stop, Drop, and Roll Doesn't Work in Hell

THE NEXT MORNING I DRESSED in the day's business attire—spandex top and bottom, gun holsters, and self-braided hair. I couldn't work the same makeup magic Joy had applied, but I did my best. Then I covered most of my body with a long coat and scurried to my car before my neighbors could see me.

I was fully prepared to kick some evil butt, especially after my training with Niko, but Mr. Pitt had other ideas. Again. With Niko on speed dial, I worked the floor for most of the day, looking for signs of new demon activity while Niko did something I was sure was far more effective. I knew busywork when I saw it. It didn't help that Rose was no longer on babysitter duty. I'd chafed under her watchful eye, but I quickly discovered I'd underestimated the benefit of having one sane person to talk to.

It was a long, irritating day. I snapped and snarled at any male who approached me—and considering it was Saturday and the convention's biggest day, there were quite a few men who escaped with singed egos. I spent a lot of my time contemplating evolution in the twenty-first century, which developed into a fantasy in which I was given free rein to thin the herd of the weakest members. I knew exactly where I'd start.

Near closing time, I defied Mr. Pitt's orders and made my way to the employees-only door. It wasn't unprovoked defiance. It was desperation. My nerves were so frayed my skin itched, and a pulsing headache had long since lodged behind my eyes. My discomfort was only infinitesimally related to humans, too.

I hadn't thought it possible, but the convention floor looked worse today. While the number of imps seemed to have diminished, the number of vervet had swollen. They no longer confined their activities to the higher positions but now scampered through the crowds, pausing frequently to sink their teeth into unsuspecting victims or crawl over them to choicer parts of their souls. There were no hounds, though, which I took to be a good sign. There might be more evil here than I'd dealt with earlier, but there was nothing as tough.

The guard at the employees' door eyed me with one cocked eyebrow. "Where's your keeper?" he asked.

I gave him a blank stare before remembering the embarrassing scene Rose had made when we'd left yesterday. I blushed, which made him laugh. When he finally opened the door, I slithered through, cursing Rose under my breath.

The door closed behind me and I flinched. With the added evil on the convention floor, I'd hoped the more confined behind-the-scenes space would be clear and I could relax. I'd also looked forward to more easily being able to kill any creatures that attached themselves to my soul; out on the floor, I'd either had to surround myself with men—which sounded a lot more exciting than it had been—or I had to find a corner mostly concealed from vervet eyes, which was easier said than done at a convention where every booth was designed for maximum visibility, especially from the rafters.

However, instead of a personal sanctuary, I'd found the missing hordes of imps. Like drifts of dirty snow, they piled in the corners and eddied in the wake of employees striding through the hall. There were more people here than last time, too. Everyone was collecting their personal items and preparing to leave, unaware that they carried seething masses of soul-sucking creatures with them. And wherever the imps weren't, the vervet were. They clung to the walls and leapt from person to person like it was a game of human hopscotch. Some people seemed to be tastier than others, and the vervet squabbled over them. I stared in horror as a dozen monkeylike monstrosities clung one-handed to the belly of an overweight woman and ate from her soul the way starved hyenas might, tearing into each other when they were jostled.

The woman gave me a dirty look and knocked into my shoulder when she passed.

It occurred to me that I looked like a shining beacon of tasty *lux lucis* amid a depleted group of humans right before the same thing occurred to a clump of imps. They swarmed around my ankles and knees, and hundreds of sharp teeth sank into my soul. I pumped them full of more *lux lucis* than they could handle, snickering when they popped into glitter. When I looked up, every vervet in the hall was staring at me.

Crap. There goes an entire day's worth of stealth. Mr. Pitt would be so proud. I prepared myself for a full assault as best I could—how do you prepare to be overwhelmed by *lux lucis*-leeching creatures when you're armed with only pet wood, fake breasts, and unloaded guns?— and ignored the strange stares I was receiving from the people in the hall.

After the longest second of my life, when the entire world hung on my held breath, the remaining imps flowed away from me down the hall. A moment later, the vervet scampered after them.

"Well, I'll be . . ." I said, straightening from my crouch. Maybe they were scared. And maybe my name was Hillary Clinton.

People gave me a wide berth as I eased down the hall. I must have looked like a madwoman, but I was getting used to that. To normal folk, it looked like I was stalking a blank wall where the hallway took an abrupt left beyond the doors of the employee lounge. Of course, if the normal folk could see what I saw, they'd have run screaming in terror long ago.

Not such a bad idea, that little voice of reason said. *We could be home, safe in our bed, in less than twenty minutes, and no one would be the wiser.*

And how many more animals would be hurt in the meantime? I reasoned with myself. *How much more evil would spread through my territory?* I replayed Max's forlorn look as he was led away, and my resolve firmed. I also realized I was having a conversation with myself. *Loony bin, here we come. Or is that "here I come"?*

Did I just answer my own question?

I rounded the corner, leaving behind all the wary human glances. I was alone in the new hallway—except, of course, for the seething masses of imps and vervet. I stopped asking myself about the wisdom of my actions, and I didn't attempt to count the evil creatures. If nothing else, all these imps and vervet were no longer feeding on the people I'd left behind. Better, the likelihood that I'd have something useful to report to Niko and Mr. Pitt tipped from zero to hopeful.

The imps swarmed through a set of double doors, oozing through the cracks, defying the laws of physics. The vervet followed after a few jaunty waves, their insubstantial bodies pouring like liquid through the tiny openings. For the first time, I understood why Doris had insisted on the wards in my house. Pure *atrum* creatures didn't need an open-door invitation. They'd just ooze their way in.

I paused with my hand on the door handle. I'd been working for Illumination Studios for four days. In that time, I'd trespassed, lied to a police officer, falsified my identity, and was in the illegal possession of firearms. The thought stopped me where I half crouched. This was not a good sign. If I could be persuaded to break that many laws in four days, what would I be doing in ten days? In a month?

I almost turned around. I may not be proud of my job history, but I'd never committed a crime before, let alone a crime in the name of my job. Then again, I'd never done anything as important as battle evil. My other jobs had been meaningless or boring—often both. At least as an enforcer, I was positively influencing the very balance of good and evil. That had to outweigh the minor transgressions I'd made along the way, right?

Isn't there a saying about hell and good intentions? asked that tiny, annoying little voice.

Contemplation for another time, I answered it. *One when I'm not hunting herds of evil.*

I eased opened the door marked HOTEL STAFF ONLY, then shut it soundlessly behind me. Slinking forward, I rounded the corner and froze. An enormous bullmastiff blocked my path. It was easily large enough for me to ride, and its coat glistened with a familiar wet-blood darkness. The rest of the hall was empty.

The hound growled. A liquid chill of fear slid through my body. I hated for Niko to be right, but Max looked like an emaciated puppy compared to this hound.

I backed up, simultaneously fumbling for my pet wood. I seized upon the hope that it was merely Primordium making this pony-size hound look so scary. For all I knew, it could be as pathetic as Max in normal vision.

I blinked. The sterile hall was blindingly bright, pale beige walls and white linoleum tiles lit for practicality not ambiance. After the dimmer no-source lighting of Primordium, I had to squint through dizzy vision to see the hound. It still looked like it'd had three square meals a day, interspersed with weight training. The only improvement was that with regular sight it had normal fur that was brown with black flecks, like it had run really fast through a black-paint sprinkler. It also had ordinary golden eyes and regular long, white teeth. It was a measure of the growing insanity in my world that I was relieved to see its ordinary bared white teeth. One row. Mostly rounded.

My hand finally found the pet wood. I closed my fist around it and realized I didn't have a clue what to do next. If I pulled it out, the hound would know for sure that I was an enforcer, or at least someone who should be attacked. I could only guess that the reason it hadn't charged me yet was because it was still trying to decide if I was a threat. A hound this large wasn't going to pause at the sight of my slender pet wood. I also wouldn't be able to wrestle it to the ground; if anything, the hound weighed more than me, and it was all muscle. I hadn't thought to stop by Accessories and More for a net this morning either.

The hallway beyond the hound was devoid of potentially helpful humans. It ended in another set of double doors through which the swarm of evil creatures I'd been following had disappeared. If I could make it to the doors, I could slip through, continue my mission, and leave the hound behind.

Okay, Dice. Think action heroine. What would I do if I were a heroine? Well, first off, I'd probably have real bullets, a few more backup weapons, and a black belt in something. Second, I'd have on a lot more protective clothing, especially if I was used to battling against creatures with such sharp teeth. *This isn't helping. Focus.*

I blinked to Primordium. The blinding hallway was reversed like a negative to black, only I was beginning to realize that there were many different shades of black. The hallway was heavy-shadow gray. The hound was black. Black-black. Blood black on a dark night.

I pulled the pet wood slowly from my backpack, keeping it tight in my fist to hide it. The hound's ears twitched. It stopped growling and looked over my shoulder.

I tossed a quick look behind me. The hallway was empty. I whirled back to the hound. A second later, a swarm of vervet dropped from the ceiling. I screamed and flailed with my arms.

The monkeylike creatures scurried over my body, and unlike the woman who had knocked into me earlier, I didn't have the luxury of not feeling them. Tiny cold spots pricked my skin everywhere their claws sank into my soul. It felt like there were thousands of them, though more than a dozen couldn't have fit on my body. I swung at them with my hands. It was as ineffectual as stomping an imp off my leg. They had no physical form, so no physical action touched them.

I backpedaled, instinct kicking in, making my legs retreat from the larger foe while I dealt with the smaller ones. If the imps felt like spiders on my skin, the vervet felt like chicken-eating-size tarantula—with fangs. One of the vervet pressed its mouth into my thigh, and I could feel the razor-sharp teeth like cold pins and needles in my flesh. Shrieking, I grabbed the hideous little creature by the neck. It rolled its eyes up to look at me and I swear it smiled without removing its teeth. A blast of *lux lucis* created a puffball of glitter out of it.

The hound lunged. Pure luck saved me. I twisted to the side to grab one of the vervet clinging to my shoulder. The hound's jaws snapped at the air my neck had occupied a second earlier. Its body slammed into me and I careened off the wall. The hound smashed into it face-first.

If I really had been an action heroine like I'd been pretending to be all day, I would have kicked the hound in the side of the head at that moment, maybe even brained it with the butt of a gun. Instead, I ran.

I'm not a sprinter—my body's built for endurance. Even then, I'm no speeding bullet. But there was nothing like a hound of death on my heels to give me an Olympian-worthy boost.

I pounded down the hallway toward the double doors with the hound's hot breath panting against my legs. I didn't have a thought or energy to spare for the vervet that still clung to me. I slammed through the doors a step ahead of the hound, turned at the next corner, and was racing down stairs almost before I saw them. I heard dogs barking behind me, and I hazarded a glance back as I used the railing at a corner to fling myself down several steps. Two smaller Doberman hounds had joined the bullmastiff.

In my terror, I missed the exit for the ground floor and was at the basement door before I knew it. I flung it aside, then slammed it, but the nose of the lead hound pushed through before the door closed. Cursing, I kicked the snout. It fell back with a howl and I slammed the door shut and grabbed the handle to hold it closed. The door bounced as two huge bodies flung themselves against it. Lucky for me, it opened from the inside out. Unless those evil dogs had opposable thumbs, they weren't getting in.

As the hounds barked and scratched at the bottom of the door, I turned to survey the room.

A hysterical scream lodged in my esophagus. I'd found all the imps and vervet.

The room was large, though it was hard to tell the exact dimensions through the bubbling mass of evil creatures. It was probably the storage room for the kitchens. It looked like a slice of hell. Even if I'd had my back to a hundred-year-old oak tree, I wouldn't have had enough *lux lucis* to take out all the creatures.

I slid down the wall to sit on the floor. What was the use? I couldn't make a dent here. I couldn't get out. I was stuck, and I was either going to die by hound or I was going to leave a very changed person.

I'd forgotten about the vervet clinging to me until one scrambled onto my head and hung in front of my face to look at me upside down. I froze, wide-eyed. Slowly, so that I could see how much pleasure it got out of my fear, it lowered itself toward my neck. One of its claws traced a line down my front, its insubstantial paws going through the fabric and padded bra to trace intimately against my soul. My chest throbbed like a plucked guitar string, vibrating with a chill close to pain, not sound.

I snapped out of my trance with a scream of denial. Using both hands, I grabbed the vervet and disintegrated it. Without pausing, I slid my hands down my body, disintegrating two vervet on my back and a third on my leg. When I was sure I was clean, I glared, panting, at the swarms of evil creatures. What had seemed impossible a moment before while the vervet were feeding on my soul looked merely improbable now.

Miraculously, the pet wood was still in my hand. I sprang it open, stood, and planted my feet wide. The way back wasn't an option. I needed another exit. Chancing it, I blinked to normal vision, twirling the pet wood in front of me. With any luck, anything that attacked while

I couldn't see it would be snuffed out of existence on the pet wood.

There were only two lights on across the room, lighting up another exit like a beacon. Between me and the other door were three rows of shelving, bins of food and supplies, and more evil than I could shake a stick at. Literally.

I blinked back. Nothing had moved toward me. The imps bounced and bounded in cute little herds around the room, and the vervet swung from their perches and darted around the floor, but nothing approached me. I congratulated myself on my wood-waving tactics.

The door vibrated behind me as a hound threw itself against it.

I reached into my backpack and grabbed Medusa. It was time to admit the truth: I needed backup.

I glanced at the display illuminated in Primordium, thanks to Musad. No signal. Double damn. I snapped three quick pictures of the room, setting them up to forward to Mr. Pitt as I had been doing all day. Still nothing approached me. Maybe I could sneak through. Maybe they were blind to me now. Maybe I intimidated them.

The glittery dust of leftover vervet had vanished. I took a deep breath and headed for the shortest route. The moment I stepped away from the doors, the imps and vervet turned as one to watch me. I almost froze, but once I'd started moving, I didn't want to stop. With my heart fluttering in my throat, I picked up my pace to a jog. It was impossible to keep the whole room in my sight. Part of me—the part that was fond of my sanity—was okay that I couldn't see all my enemies. It made them less real, made my attempt to escape seem more plausible. The other part of me wanted to run, screaming, and never stop.

The creatures parted like a black sea. As grateful as I was, a cold feeling in my stomach told me it wasn't a good sign. Especially when I noticed how they flowed in to fill the space behind me. I was being herded, and there was nothing I could do about it.

I crossed the storage room and bounded up the stairs on the other side. My fear was dulling. There were too many of them and too much time had passed to maintain elevated levels of adrenaline. I climbed the center of the stairs, constantly scanning both sides where vervet clambered on the railings. A herd of imps hopped up the steps behind me. If it hadn't been for their sharp teeth and claws, I might have forgotten the danger I was in; the imps reminded me of dust bunnies

I'd found under my bed and the vervet made me feel like I was on an Animal Planet show. The sharp teeth, however, were the reason I kept Medusa out, Niko's number pulled up, and my finger over the CALL button, ready to press it the moment I got a signal.

I cracked the door at the landing to the first floor. A ruckus of barking hounds made me jump. I yanked the door closed and listened to the baying for a moment. Surely someone who worked at the hotel would hear the dogs and come investigate. Unless that person happened to be a hound whisperer, I shuddered to think what would happen to them. I needed to get somewhere with cell phone reception.

I started up the next flight of stairs when a door opened somewhere above me. I paused. The vervet turned and scrambled over one another, fleeing back toward the basement. I watched them go and smiled. If the vervet were scared, then it had to be good.

A quick check of Medusa's screen showed a single bar. I pressed CALL. Niko was going to want to hear about this immediately, not to mention I needed at least five nets for the hounds. Perhaps a little assistance with those hounds, too, if I was being honest.

I listened to the rings, feeling optimistic for the first time all day. I collapsed my pet wood and shoved it into the knife slot in my boot. I was trotting up the stairs again when I saw it, dark as the night sky between stars. There was a vastness to it, or a vacancy. It was disorienting to look at, like I was falling into or toward it. And that was just from the knees down. Oh, yes. I'd found my first demon.

I reversed direction, fumbling with the railing as I backed up, but not quickly enough. It rounded the turn of the stairs to the landing above me. It was human. Or maybe humanoid. Male, taller than me by an inch at the crown of his head, and not particularly bulky. It was the razor-sharp mutated deer antlers that rose like claws from his head that gave him an extra two feet in height and made him overwhelming.

I dropped Medusa back into my bag and spun to run, only to grab on to the railing to prevent a headfirst fall into a sea of imps. The demon may have been the bigger evil, but there was no way I'd survive wading through that many imps.

The fluffy bits of evil and teeth jumped for my toes. I lunged back a step, whirling when a man's hand settled against my spine.

He filled my vision, the darkness sucking at my very sight. I blinked, thinking that if I couldn't see that dark, absorbing soul, I could concentrate.

"Holy shit," I breathed. He was beautiful in the way men's underwear models were beautiful: all wide shoulders, strong jaw, faint stubble, steady gaze. And I knew him. Tim gripped my arm and smiled into my eyes.

15

GUNS DON'T KILL PEOPLE; BULLETS DO

I RAN MY HAND UP TIM'S chest. Oh, yeah. There was solid muscle under his expensive white button-up shirt. I licked my lips. Would it be too forward to kiss him, or would it be sexy? It's not like he was a stranger. We'd practically had two dates.

My eyes dropped to his firm lips. He had the hint of a dimple and a slight cleft in his chin. How had I not noticed how attractive he was before?

"Are you lost?" Tim asked me. His voice was deep and smooth. I would have rolled naked in the texture of that voice if it were possible, wrapped myself up in it as a tempting treat for him.

"Not anymore, big boy," I said.

Big boy? Who had taken over my mouth and why was I unbuttoning his shirt? Embarrassment cooled the flush of lust coasting through me. I took an unsteady step away from him to the side, because I didn't want to step back.

There was an important reason not to go down a step. At least a more important reason than the fact that I wouldn't be able to continue to rub Tim's bicep.

Rub his bicep? I shook my head to clear it and hesitantly pulled my hands back to my own body. I didn't want to touch him, right?

He stepped forward again, keeping a light grip on my upper arm. His smile cut through my confusion.

"What are you doing back here?"

"Looking for someone. But I've found you now." My words made me shiver. What was wrong with me?

He laughed, and I wanted to rub up against him again. I noticed my hands were back on his arms. When had that happened?

"I had my suspicions, but I couldn't believe that you're really who they sent against me. You actually fooled me about the bumper sticker company. You're a very convincing actress but a terrible enforcer."

I shook my head in confusion.

"Did you come here to harm me?" His question was leading, as if he wanted me to remember an answer.

I smiled up into his charming blue eyes with their crow's-feet and dark-lash adornments. He was perfect. Even his flaws were perfect. I started to shake my head. I would never harm him. What was he talking about?

A cold sensation against my arm distracted me. It was a familiar feeling that I couldn't place. I glanced at his hand against my bare flesh. He had big, strong hands. Perfect for holding me, caressing me . . . My gaze traveled boldly down his silk-clad torso to the front of his gray slacks. Yep, he had to be an underwear model.

He turned to lead me up the stairs, still chuckling. I trailed along, eyeing his ass. Again my gaze returned to his hand on my arm and the strange cold feeling. It was as if his fingers were ice. I closed my eyes to concentrate and blinked when I opened my eyes.

Five sharp claws protruding from the demon's hand were buried in my flesh, piercing my soul. A blizzard of fear crystallized my lust. Without it, I could feel each claw like a paper cut on my soul. How could I have been thinking such horribly intimate thoughts about this monster? What had just happened? How could Tim be the demon? He hadn't had this bizarre effect on me either time at the Golden Goose.

I planted my feet. The imps were still behind us, a few steps away, like an adoring throng following their idol. The demon stopped, pulled short by my halt. Slowly he turned to look at me. I made myself look at his face. Gone was the strong jaw and attractive crow's-feet. In their place was a narrow chin; a nose that was part beak, part flesh; and eyes with the glow of nuclear sludge. The knife points of his antlers loomed above me.

He smiled at me, this time with sharp teeth that should have been too long to fit in his mouth. It made my heart race in a completely different way than his previous smile.

"Do I no longer please you?" he taunted. His voice was still the same. Rationally, I knew it. But he was so physically repulsive that it made his voice nasty, too.

I tried to pull my arm free, feeling panic set in. He tightened his hold and yanked me up the stairs to the landing.

"Let's go somewhere more comfortable."

"How about not." I gathered *lux lucis* and pulsed it through my upper arm. He jerked back with a hiss.

"Oh, you've got a little fight in you, do you?" He smiled again and grabbed me with both hands, sinking his claws into my shoulders.

I fought him like a cornered lion, physically with my fists and fingernails and feet and also with *lux lucis* against his hands. I used moves I didn't even know I had, twisting and turning, kicking his shins, stomping on his toes, pulsing *lux lucis* repeatedly into his hands as he adjusted his grip. Through it all, he held me at arm's length and tsked like I was a misbehaving kitten.

My fight didn't last long. I ran out of physical energy, and my soul dimmed at an alarming rate. Panting, I stilled. Nothing seemed to have an effect on him. *Shit. Conserve energy, Dice. We'll attack again when he's not expecting it.* I wished I believed myself.

"Impressive," he mocked.

I glared, my mind empty of witty repertoire.

"Now that we've gotten that out of the way . . ." He jerked me close to him with a vise grip on my left arm. It hurt, and not just from the cold claws digging into my soul. It was going to bruise. If I lived long enough.

I struggled feebly as he dragged me up to the door on the third floor. We exited into a bland hotel hallway filled with the usual floral carpet, two-tone walls, and evenly spaced cookie-cutter art. It was surreal. The world should not look normal when you're being dragged by a demon.

The demon stopped at a bank of elevators. The doors sprang open to our left and two women stepped out. One had an imp attached to her heel, happily leeching light from her soul. The other wore a vervet like a deformed stole. They were both booth babes dressed in plastic armor bikini tops and leather bikini bottoms with capes sewn on the back that drooped to their knees. Were their butts the superheroes?

The demon turned to smile at them. Both women leaned forward, like the demon had a stronger pull of gravity than the earth beneath their feet. I received a single glance from the pair that should have incinerated me. In the space of two breaths, the women transformed from normal to slutty, tossing hair, pressing their breasts forward, licking their lips, and running their hands slowly down their own bodies. It was partially reassuring that I wasn't the only woman who behaved like an ass at the sight of this man-thing. It also explained the hateful look.

"Excuse me, ladies," the demon said in his too-smooth voice.

The women twittered and stepped out of his way. As we passed them to step into the elevator, the demon reached out and ran his hand across the shorter one's cheek. A smear of *atrum* followed the trail of his claws. I shuddered. Neither of them noticed how hard I dug my heels in or how I clung to the edges of the elevator frame. The demon peeled my fingers away from the metal with sharp, quick snaps that left me cradling my hand to my chest, blinking away the sting of tears.

My mind raced in circles around thoughts of escape but found no answers. I glanced around the tiny coffin of death that was the elevator. No other evil creatures had boarded with us. I couldn't muster the energy to care what they were doing to other people now. I was selfishly thankful that I had only the demon to deal with.

The phrase *only the demon* set off mental hysterical laughter. I glanced down at my arm where the demon still had a death grip. Inky flecks of darkness were creeping along my soul like disorganized ants, reminding me of the dark smears that had been left on my hands after my encounter with Tim at the Golden Goose. Only these flecks of *atrum* were aggressively marching through my soul, not staying where he touched.

Oh, uh-uh. The thought of being soul-smeared by this hideous abomination rallied my fighting spirit. Prudently, I didn't attack the demon again. That had gotten me nowhere. Instead, I concentrated on the flecks of darkness. With greater and greater accuracy, I whittled away the *atrum* eating my life force, snuffing it out.

The *bong* of the elevator announcing our floor made me jump. The demon chuckled.

"Cute," he said, after peering at my once-again-pristine arm. "How long can you keep it up?"

"As long as I have to." It wasn't witty, but at least I'd gotten my tongue unstuck from the roof of my mouth.

He pulled me off the elevator onto the eighth floor, which was also the top floor. Roseville's more about width than height. Eight floors was a tall building for this city, one of the tallest, in fact. The hallway that we stepped into was not the bland hallway of the third floor. This one had real plants, a cluster of plush leather chairs near the elevator, and doors that must have hidden more than a set of twin beds and a bathroom given how widely apart they were spaced along the hall.

It also had hounds, which I was pretty sure were not part of the hotel's normal decor.

Five hounds paced the length of the hallway. They were tall and scrawny, like English hunting dogs. In weight, I could probably win a wrestling competition with one of them, but once the teeth, claws, and pure evil souls were thrown into the mix, I knew I was outstripped by one hound, let alone all five.

They bounded toward us, wagging happy tails at the demon, barking and growling at me.

This is it, Dice. This is where your throat gets ripped out. Wait: wrong thought. What would Cesar Millan say? I threw my shoulders back, lifted my head slightly, and tried to project confidence.

I doubt it was my actions, but the hounds came to a stop a few feet from us. The demon gave them an order in a language that was not a derivative of the Romance dialects. Something told me that it wasn't Russian either. *What made you think his native tongue was something nice, normal, and human, anyway?* The hounds whined and circled us, then resumed pacing the hall.

Realizing I'd been given a minor reprieve, I focused on the next important step: surviving. I needed *lux lucis*.

I touched the first plant we passed, pulling from it as much life as I could in the two seconds my hand rested on it. It might have been my imagination, but it felt like the plant fed me *lux lucis* faster than any plant had before. I did the same at the next plant, and at the next, until the demon noticed. He stopped, which meant I stopped, and turned, which meant I turned. Together, we looked back down the hallway. I was shocked to see that all three plants I'd touched were completely dead.

"You're being a naughty girl." He waggled a claw-tipped finger at me like I was a misbehaving four-year-old.

He pinned an arm around me from behind and held both my arms against my sides. We marched the last few yards with my entire left side pressed against his right. The sensation was nauseating. His darkness sucked at my soul, tugging it sideways while I tried to pull in the opposite direction, until I felt drunk and lopsided within myself.

When we reached the door, he used his key card and thrust me inside. I tried to decide if a demon having to use a key card was comical or not, and it took me a moment to focus on the room. *No. Definitely not,* I decided.

It was a suite, as I'd guessed, with a full front room, an opening to the bedroom on the left, and a large bathroom tucked farther around to the left. *Atrum* coated every surface, turning the normally charcoal surroundings to a black well of despair.

Not helping, I told my inner narrator.

The door clicked shut, and the absolute silence told me we were alone. Had every fiber of my being not already been screaming that I was in the wrong place at the wrong time, it would have then. I was alone in a hotel room with a strange man—worse, a strange demon. This was a bad horror movie.

I turned to look at the demon. He was warding the door with a blanket of *atrum* that sparkled with a red current. It figured that the first color I saw in Primordium would be evil. "What's that?" I asked stupidly.

"That, my sweet, is death to you." He grabbed my hand, lightning fast. With a sharp tug, he yanked me to him and shoved my hand into the red and black barrier. A thousand insects chewed through my fingers. I screamed and fought against his hold. An eternity later, the demon released me. I stared at my blackened fingertips in horror. When I flexed my fingers, I could feel that the flesh and bones of me were still whole, but the fingers of my soul looked like they'd been dipped in ink. "If you try to get through there, it will eat you alive."

He sauntered past me. I kept him in my sights but mainly I examined my fingers. I gathered *lux lucis* and pushed at the darkness staining them. Unlike the flecks that had been on my arm, the darkness on my fingertips didn't wink out of existence with minimal resistance. This *atrum* peeled back like a glove of sap, slowly, and feeling like it was removing a layer of flesh with it. I was sweating and weak by the time my hand was clean. The demon had fixed himself a drink and settled on one of the two couches in the front room to watch me.

"You've got a little something here," the demon said, gesturing to his left side.

I examined the rest of my soul. Besides looking weaker than a sputtering candle flame, my entire side was coated with patches of *atrum* from being pressed up against the demon. I looked at those splotches and felt utter despair. I couldn't do this. I didn't have it in me to continue to fight. I was going to be overwhelmed with evil slowly or quickly. Either way, it was out of my hands. The demon was clearly the one in charge. Some enforcer I made. I couldn't even save myself.

The thought spread a chill across my skin. It was inevitable. I should give up and let him kill me. I was practically dead already. The flecks of *atrum* were eating away at my soul. I would be evil soon. Or would I be lifeless? I'd never gotten the chance to ask what happened to good people whose souls were turned completely to darkness.

Mom would be so disappointed. I could hear her voice in my head, warning against negative thoughts. *"The universe brings about what you think about. Thoughts create things, dear. Thoughts create your reality."* I needed a better reality fast. Death would be awful enough. Being turned evil would be truly horrifying.

Latching on to the one last shred of what I hoped was sanity, I forced myself to think of something happy. *This universe thing better work quickly,* I warned my inner mom voice. *Something happy. Something happy. Bring about a solution. Think, Dice.*

I snuffed out the larger dark spots on my leg and arm. No happy thoughts were coming. Not a single one. I was going to die. Then Mr. Bond would be homeless again. He'd been a nearly white fluff ball of a kitten when I'd found him abandoned at my apartment complex. I'd nursed him back to health and watched him grow from a tiny kitten that fit in my palm to a gigantic dark Siamese cat that took up most of my recliner when we shared it. I loved him immensely, and I wanted more than anything to go home and bury my face in his fur and forget all about the demon in front of me.

I can do the next best thing: I can take out this demon, then go home to Mr. Bond.

Huh. Look at that. I'd found a happy thought after all. Impossible, but happy.

No, not impossible. Challenging.

There was that hysterical laughter again.

I straightened my spine and strode across the carpet. I imagined Rose with me, telling me that Kyle would have formulated a real plan of attack. Tough. I'm not Kyle. I had my own enforcer style, if you could call "winging it" a style. It was better than listening to my inner voice wail in despair.

The demon watched me with amusement.

"Nice tits."

"They're definitely crowd pleasers." It was stupid, but talking was better than nothing. I could sound a little stupid if it meant prolonging my life.

"I can't say I remember you being so well rounded yesterday."

"I don't remember you having antlers yesterday, either, so I guess we're even." I cursed myself for having not checked out Tim in Primordium yesterday when Niko had been right there.

I strode to the window and pulled back the drapes. I'd never looked at the world in Primordium from eight stories up. It was a beautiful thing to behold. All the trees that dotted the greenbelt gully that ran beside the hotel shone with pure light. Tiny light dots sped along in cars on roads that were black smears of deadened ground between light patches of sidewalk landscaping. Buildings were grids of darkness, but the people in them near the windows and moving through the parking lot were fascinating bits of light.

My eyes slid back to the huge trees in the gully. They were so close, yet impossibly out of reach. It would have been more practical to have the ability to fly. If I could fly, I could break the window and leap through to safety. Of course, if I could fly rather than fight evil, I wouldn't have been in this situation to begin with. That made two strikes against whoever was in charge of doling out secret abilities.

I forced my hands from the window and turned to face the demon again.

"So what's the plan?" he asked me. "Is this where you pounce on me and kill me?"

"Could be. What's your plan?"

"First, I'm going to find out what's real and what's show under those clothes. Depending on how that goes, you might be a meal or a mate. I've never sampled a brand-new enforcer. We'll just have to wait and see."

I should have kept my mouth shut. Time to change the subject.

"Where are all the imps and vervet?"

"Feeding. This area is ripe for harvest. I suppose I have you to thank for that."

"I wasn't the one who invited that nerd herd here."

The demon chuckled and swirled his drink. He appeared relaxed and in no hurry to get on with the meal-or-mate test. That suited me just fine. Eventually the thoughts scurrying around in my head would coalesce into a plan of action. Until then, we could chat. *Another positive thought: I appreciate his leisurely pace.* On the heels of that thought was, *I hope he underestimates me.* Then I refused to think a follow-up thought, because they were all negative.

"So, where're ya from?" I asked with a Southern California accent.

He blinked at me, then threw back his head and laughed. "Remind me to do this again. You newbies are fun."

I eyed the horns, the black and red door, and the faraway trees. I did my best to school my features to calm. *Think Sarah Connor under pressure.*

I made myself walk across the room so that I could hide my face for a moment while I regained my calm. Tim shifted quickly in his chair and I disguised my jump by leaning forward for a glass from the bar.

"Are you going to answer my question?" I asked. I filled the glass with water. This was getting ridiculous. I needed an out. Or a little mouse hole of my very own to hide in. Somewhere the demon couldn't get to me while my soul recharged. If I could unconsciously recharge in my sleep from plants I wasn't touching, maybe I could teach myself to do it while awake. *And maybe I'd feed off people,* I reminded myself darkly.

Tim smiled, exposing sharp teeth. "I've been in LA most recently. A friend mentioned this delightful region, ripe for a transfer. He was right: It's a wonderful place to put down roots." He petted the dark leather of the couch. I watched his hand glide back and forth and wondered how I had even for a moment fantasized about those sharp-clawed paws doing naughty fun things to my body. Of course, at the time they'd looked like regular human hands and he'd been doing some sort of demon voodoo on me. Still, it was repulsive.

"A friend?" I asked.

"How could I not stay once I met you, Maddie? May I call you Maddie?"

I hated that nickname. I hated it more that my weakness and inexperience were the reasons he'd settled in this region. It made me feel responsible for something that I had no control over, a misplaced guilt that could eat away at my soul. What was left of it, at least. I stared at my legs. A few days ago, looking at my own soul had made me sick with vertigo. Now my stomach churned with worry over how dim I was.

When I looked up, Tim was behind me and I hadn't even heard or seen him move.

"Enough talk." He reached around me to take my glass from my hand. It was now or never.

I threw the glass over my shoulder at him and whirled to race across the room. I felt his claws slide through my back, but my thin polyester shirt slipped through his hands. I darted through the furniture arrangement and gripped the back of the couch. Tim was still near the bar, watching me with patronizing indulgence. He flicked water off his shoulder and stalked toward me.

"That wasn't very nice. Where're you going to go, Maddie? There's no escape. Nowhere you can hide." He stepped in the middle of the furniture arrangement. There was only a coffee table and the couch between us.

I'd played this game of tag as a child with my cousins at family reunions. The person who is "it" tries to outsmart the other people and dart around the furniture to tag them. I was never good at being "it," and I'd been even worse at escaping. Of course, my life hadn't depended on it then.

"Why don't we dispense with these games?" Tim asked. He reached for the edge of the coffee table with one hand and flung it against the windows. They rattled but didn't break.

I made a small noise, more hamster than human.

"Ooh, do that again," the demon purred. He stalked to the right. I eased left. He lunged at me over the couch. I ran for the other side of the room, grabbing the lamp as I passed and hurling it blindly at him. A meaty *thunk* told me I'd hit some part of him.

There was nowhere to hide in the bedroom, and the door on the bathroom wasn't going to stop this demon. Resigned, I turned to face Tim again, this time with the other couch between us.

He crouched in the middle of the room, looking carnivorous despite the antlers. Or maybe because of them and their wickedly sharp edges. There was a gleam in his eye that riled my anger. He was having *fun*. His dark soul glowed wetly with what I assumed was excitement. Or anticipation. I must have looked tasty and helpless from his perspective.

I ran my hand down my side in a reflexive gesture to wipe the smears of *atrum* away and I brushed up against the butt of a gun. Desperation made me draw it. Seeing too many movies made me feel falsely empowered.

"Stop right there," I commanded with a surprising amount of authority.

Tim paused. He eyed the gun. When he gave me a full, sharp-toothed grin, I knew I'd run out of options.

"Bullets can't hurt me, Maddie—not for long." He took a step toward me.

"Infused with *lux lucis* they can."

He paused again. "True. But if you had *lux lucis* bullets, you would have used them on me already, wouldn't you have?"

Good point. If I hadn't, his patronizing tone would have pushed me over the edge now.

The hounds in the hall started barking. Neither of us breathed for a moment as we listened. The dogs were running toward the elevator, their baying growing fainter. Hope made my skin tingle, and I shoved it down behind a layer of sarcasm.

"We've got company," I said. "Friends of yours?"

Tim lunged, leaping onto the sofa cushions. I flailed backward, heaving the heavy gun at him. It smacked into his shoulder, spinning him slightly.

He staggered to the side. I ran for the door. I made it two steps before he tackled me from behind. We both went down, my padded breasts cushioning our fall. I kicked at him and tried to scramble out from underneath him. I couldn't get a purchase on the carpet. The demon grabbed the back of my neck and smashed my face into the carpet.

I'd barely registered the pain before the demon flipped me over as if I were a rag doll. I used my knees to land a few blows before I was pinned again, this time facing those glowing putrid eyes and sharp horns. He straddled me, one knee crushing my left wrist and a hand immobilizing my right arm.

When I realized none of my squirming was helping, I stiffened, trying to conserve energy. Yep, I'd been right; he was enjoying himself. The evidence was pressed firmly against my thigh. The demon grinned at me and I couldn't help it—I began to struggle all over again. With those teeth inches from my face, it was impossible to think rationally.

"You could just look at me," the demon said. He was breathing hard, too, but he wasn't having trouble holding me down. "You'd even enjoy yourself."

I didn't like the reminder of how easily he'd overpowered me earlier when I'd switched to normal vision. It was terrifying, and I didn't want to feel fear. I wanted anger.

"I don't want a mind fuck." I spat in his face.

He slapped me, and the blow bounced my head off the floor. The impact did something to my eardrums. I could hear the blood pounding in them like a hammer. I blinked and tried to focus. The demon lowered his face to my neck.

"There's room for only one vampire in this room," I growled. I gathered *lux lucis* and forced it through my hands into his body. The demon hissed against my neck. His teeth pressed against my fragile flesh. I screamed and pushed light through my neck, pulling from reserves in my life force that I hadn't known existed.

He flew off my body and landed next to me, rolling almost immediately to his feet. I stared in wonder at my own strength.

It took a second longer for me to make sense of the extra pair of feet by my head.

Tim stalked backward, hands splayed, ready to pounce on the newcomer. I scooted like a crab to press against the wall. It hadn't been my strength that had thrown the demon, I realized as I leveraged up against the wall while my rescuer stalked past me after the demon.

My eyes soaked in the fierce white of Niko's soul. After so much darkness and so much terror and despair, looking at him was like feeling sunshine after spending months underground. His soul was like no other's I'd seen. It wasn't merely pure like my soul. There was strength in it, a solidness that boasted of confidence and the physical abilities to back it up. I would have been able to pick Niko's soul out of a crowd from twenty paces.

The optivus aegis ignored me, his attention focused on the demon. I glanced back over my shoulder at the door. The painful black and red ward was gone. The door frame was gouged and splintered around the lock. The hallway beyond was empty. If a hound had somehow escaped Niko's notice, it surely would have come through by now.

The chime of metal on metal spun me back toward the men. From out of who knew where, both men had drawn long knives. Niko's shone white like energized pet wood. The demon's was a regular blade, dead in the world of Primordium. Of course, a regular blade was all it would take to kill Niko. There were no special added bits of evil needed.

I looked around for something I could use to help Niko and blinked to get a better view of the room. The sun had set and I'd broken the lamp in the main room. Light from the hall provided the only illumination. My gaze returned to the man who had rescued me.

Had there ever been a more delicious sight than Niko in full battle mode? He was dressed in army fatigue pants with a plethora of cargo pockets and a skintight sleeveless black shirt very similar to my own. Only, all the bulges in his chest were real. So were the defined muscles in his arms. Even in my sad state, my mind made nummy noises just looking at him.

His face was stern and focused. I held my breath as the men circled each other, jabbing and kicking. In a matter of moments, all the furniture had been knocked to the edges of the room. Niko fought conservatively, and the demon taunted him with jabs and feints that even I could see were more to test Niko's skill than to cause real damage.

Then my gaze collided with Tim's face.

He was beautiful—delicate and masculine at the same time. I itched to run my hands over his body. I dodged a roundhouse kick and sidled closer.

"Madison, stand back!" Niko ordered.

I stopped. I hadn't realized I'd moved. I stood two feet from Tim, two feet from Niko.

"Shit. Blink, Madison. Look at him in Primordium."

The men moved toward me at the same time. I shied away from the shiny blades in their hands, but I didn't shift too far. If we all could get along, this could turn out to be my best night ever.

Tim got to me first. I smiled at Niko and then turned into Tim's embrace. He was pressing a knife against my throat, glaring over my shoulder at Niko.

"Ooh, you like it kinky?" I asked. "I can be kinky for you."

"Move and she dies," Tim snarled at Niko.

Niko backed up, hands held up in surrender. I cupped my hand around Tim through his pants. He was no longer so happy. He'd been happy before, right?

"Drop the knife." I heard the muffled thump of Niko's blade on the carpet. One down, one to go.

"Blink, Madison, damn it!"

"She's so innocent. And *old*. What are you guys doing around here?" Tim asked.

"We could be doing so much more if you'd let me," I purred against his neck. I tasted him with my tongue. Odd. He tasted human. *What else would he taste like?* I rubbed my hand against his crotch while I thought, using the motion to help me focus. Tim turned us and I saw Niko over his shoulder. We were going to leave him behind. I fumbled to push the knife from my throat. "Wait. Stop. I want both of you."

Tim chuckled and slid his hand down my back to grab my butt. I continued to stare into Niko's dark, angry eyes. *Did I misread Niko? Is he angry he's losing me to Tim?* Was I making a mistake?

Yes! screamed a voice through the cotton in my brain.

Tim hauled me toward the door and Niko followed, but from a distance. I wanted him close. I knew it. I closed my eyes. My thoughts squirmed through a quagmire of lust, and I chased after them, pouncing on the loudest: *This is wrong.*

I didn't open my eyes. If I did, I knew I would lose my hold on that slippery, important thought. I ran my leg up Tim's side. He lifted my right butt cheek, half picking me up off the ground. I slid my hand into the knife sheath of my boot and grabbed the pet wood. Feeling like my actions were being performed by someone else, I pushed *lux lucis* into the pet wood. I slid my face up Tim's neck, slid my hand holding the pet wood under his shirt, and opened my eyes to Primordium. With all my strength, I plunged the tip of the pet wood into the demon's soft side.

He jerked, releasing my leg. I pushed off his chest, but he pulled me right back. The pet wood was already drained of *lux lucis*. I grabbed for it again.

"Madison, don't!" Niko shouted.

My hand closed around the pet wood and I slammed *lux lucis* into it. It was like pushing *lux lucis* into a cavern of *atrum*.

Tim looked down at me and smiled. "Why are you still fighting me, Maddie? You don't want this. You don't want to be an enforcer."

His words made me falter. Two days ago, I would have agreed with him. I'd taken this job for the money and to find a way to get rid of my ability. But changing Max last night had changed me, too. Given the chance, there was a possibility I'd still be okay with leaving humanity's fate in the capable hands of the already existing enforcers, but I couldn't turn my back on helpless victims like Max when I had a chance to prevent their suffering—or save them.

Staring at Tim, I now had a second reason to fight. The demon was an abomination, a creature that gleefully harmed and warped humans and animals alike; he was a being with no chance at redemption.

I redoubled my efforts, shoving my dwindling supply of *lux lucis* through the pet wood.

"I tried," Tim said with a shrug. Then, without moving his hands, he pulled *lux lucis* from my body through the pet wood faster than I'd been feeding it.

Icy dread drenched my scalp. I tried to halt my energy's drain. When that didn't work, I yanked my hand away from the pet wood, but my fingers had gone numb, much like they had when I'd accidentally created a loop with my own *lux lucis*, and they didn't budge. Inspired by the memory, I shifted to bring a leg up and break my connection with the pet wood.

The world tilted, blurring at the edges. Niko's voice washed against my ears, as unintelligible as the sound of the ocean in a seashell. I sagged in Tim's embrace. My last thought before I passed out was one of triumph, because Tim had let me fall, freeing me from the pet wood. Then the carpet crashed into me, soft as a down comforter.

16

PAIN IS WEAKNESS LEAVING THE BODY

I WOKE TO PAIN—THROBBING PAIN IN my head, arms, hands, and left leg; stinging pain in my elbows and knees—and a warm hand on my back. Had I felt only the pain, I might not have bothered opening my eyes, but the warm hand was large and male and pressed against my bare skin, and that realization snapped my eyes open.

I stared across the floor to where the flowered carpet met a cream-colored wall. This was not my home. I rolled to look behind me, but a second firm hand on my hip held me still.

"Don't move," Niko said.

Memory returned in a single pop of knowledge. I scrambled to my feet with the next breath.

"Where's Tim? What happened?" We were in the hall. Tim's suite was several feet away. Five dead dogs were crumpled at the other end of the hall.

Blood rushed to my head, chased by ice. I collapsed to all fours and threw up. Niko handed me a bottle of water and eased me back away from the foul-smelling puddle. I started shaking, then crying. I couldn't tear my eyes from the dead dogs. Niko pulled me around until I couldn't see their bodies, and he held me against him, pushing his hand beneath the back of my shirt again to touch skin.

"The demon fled after you blacked out," Niko said.

If the situation had been more intimate—if I hadn't just passed out, then puked in front of the handsome optivus aegis—I might have enjoyed being held up against him. We were almost hugging. As it was, I held myself stiff, trying to get my emotional bearings.

"You didn't kill him?" I asked, my voice raspy.

"I had to take care of you."

I blinked at the rough edge of anger in Niko's voice. I tried to pull back, but he tightened his grip.

"I'm not done," he said.

"What *are* you doing?"

"Giving you *lux lucis*. Enough to make it outside. You're lucky I got your call. And that you sent those pictures to Brad. If you hadn't, you'd be dead now."

I vaguely remembered dropping Medusa in my backpack right after I'd initiated a call to Niko, back when I'd been on the service stairs at my first sight of Tim.

"Thank you."

When Niko let me pull away from him, I kept my gaze turned away from the dogs, which meant I was forced to look at Niko. Like every emotion, anger looked good on him, firming his full lips, sparking in his eyes.

"What were you thinking?" Niko asked.

"Wait. You're angry with me?" I was the one who'd suffered a debilitating attack by a demon. If anyone was going to be angry, it should be me.

Niko's patronizing silence grated against raw nerves. "What was I *thinking*? You're going to have to be more specific. When I was being attacked by hounds? When I was facing a room of wall-to-wall vervet and imps? When I was under Tim's spell and then control?" My hands slashed the air around us. I was shouting, but volume control wasn't important. "I was *thinking* about survival. And how to save my region. And how useless busywork was."

"So you rushed up here to take on a demon all by your incompetent self because you were bored with 'busywork'?"

"I didn't rush anywhere. I was herded."

Niko made me explain what I meant. Grudgingly at first, then with greater apathy as my energy and righteousness fizzled, I told him everything that had happened between the time I walked through the employees' door and when he had arrived.

Niko called Mr. Pitt the moment I finished. Without offering an explanation and without Mr. Pitt demanding one, Niko outlined a plan that included several local enforcers called to the hotel, hound nets, and a floor-by-floor patchwork cleanup—whatever that meant. Niko assured Mr. Pitt that I was accounted for and the demon was not on the premises.

"Thank you for not ratting me out," I said when Niko hung up.

"There's no time right now. Mr. Pitt needs to get the other enforcers in place before more damage is done. They'll do what they can on the convention floor, but most of the people have already left. The demon won't be back tonight. But I *will* give Brad a full report when there's time."

I cringed. "He'll fire me." It must be delirium that made me concerned about losing a job that had nearly gotten me killed.

"I doubt it. But there'll be consequences."

I didn't want to think about it. "What should we do now?" I asked, gesturing toward the *atrum*-tainted room, then over my shoulder at the limp dog corpses.

"We need to take care of you. If you don't get some food and *lux lucis* soon, you'll relapse."

I realized I'd been avoiding blinking, so I made myself. Primordium revealed Niko's dim soul, which was hardly brighter than mine had been after taking on Max. Even next to his diminished light, my soul paled. I'd seen lit candelabras brighter than both of us combined. We were still the brightest spot in the hallway, though. *Atrum* pulsed in the doorway of Tim's room and trailed down the hallway. Niko must have cleared it near us, because we sat in a neutral circle. Every plant in the hall was dead. When I forced myself to look at the dogs, they were charcoal, the color of nonlife.

I swiped at my face, scrubbed my hands on my tiny shorts, and took another swig of water.

"You ready?"

I nodded and stood without his help. I was silent as we walked past the dogs. They'd died because of me. If I hadn't been in such a hurry to prove myself, and if I'd waited for Niko to take on the demon, I knew he would have saved them.

"Not all hounds can be rehabilitated," Niko said softly, his eyes on the corpses, and I couldn't tell which of us he was trying to reassure.

I wiped away fresh tears.

Niko didn't say anything else until the elevator doors slid shut behind us.

"I want to make it clear that what we fought up there was a demon."

"Yeah. I know." I frowned at him.

"Not a vampire."

It took me a moment to figure out what he was referencing; then I blushed. "You heard that?"

"It was hard not to. You were yelling."

Huh. That wasn't how I remembered it. I avoided his eyes and rearranged my scant clothing.

"If you knew it was a demon, what were you talking about?" Niko pressed.

I tried to think of a way not to answer. It was just too embarrassing. Nothing came to mind. I sighed. "Myself. Recharging. I feel like a vegetarian vampire," I mumbled.

Niko grinned at me, then threw his head back and laughed. I watched him, sullenly admiring his perfect white teeth and attractive laugh. It was only attractive, too. There was nothing about the sound that made me want to slip off my clothes and slip into the laughter. There were plenty of things about the *man* that made me want to slip off my clothes, but they were normal horny urges, not the compulsion of a demon.

Niko was still chuckling when we stepped off the elevator.

The lobby was quiet. Most of the convention's attendees had already exited, as Niko had said, but they'd left a trail visible to anyone who could see in Primordium. Dark smears of *atrum* oozed across the lobby in a wide arc from the elevators. Drearily, I contemplated the number of hosts who had left the hotel. Unaware of the evil they carried, they'd go to fast-food chains, comic stores, and Fry's, then home. Some were probably already on the freeway, miles from the borders of my region. At the airport, even. The horror reel played out in my head, with the hosts scattering across the continent, then the world, a pandemic of evil.

Just thinking about the cleanup made me tired. Where did I even start?

"Go recharge. Try not to harm the trees." Niko pointed to the greenbelt that backed up against the hotel's parking lot. "I'll meet you out there as soon as backup arrives."

I nodded woodenly. The boost of energy he'd given me in the hall was depleted. Lying down in the lobby for a nap sounded divine, but I forced myself to keep walking.

The blast of cold night air jarred me alert the moment I stepped through the sliding glass doors. It had rained while I'd been inside, just enough to make everything smell delicious. The clouds were already clearing away, revealing a few stars bright enough to compete with the city lights. I'd left my coat in my car when I'd arrived, and though I shivered in my tiny outfit, I didn't have the energy to walk two blocks uphill to my car. This morning, that far lot had been the nearest parking available, though now the hotel's closer lots had plenty of room.

So many hosts loosed on my region.

I stumbled to the edge of the blacktop near the greenbelt and half heaved, half fell over the three-foot metal fence that roped pedestrians and cars into the parking lot. My acrobatics earned a few stares. It wasn't every day that scantily dressed army-type women vaulted fences in these parts. As an added bonus, my exhaustion made me look drunk. I staggered to the nearest oak and planted a palm against its rough bark.

My skin felt saturated, like I'd spent too long in water, and the *lux lucis* seeped sluggishly into me. I wanted to pull it faster from the tree, but I held Niko's reminder not to damage the tree at the forefront of my fuzzy brain. I moved to the next tree after a few minutes, grateful that most of the trees close enough to touch were at least fifteen years old. I was afraid I'd kill a sapling.

I don't know how long I moved among the line of trees before Niko collected me. My hands, knees, and face were numb with cold, but my chest was plenty warm, insulated behind the enormous foam bra.

I climbed back over the fence, this time clumsy from cold rather than a lack of energy. The trees had done a pretty good job of resupplying me, but I still wasn't completely charged.

"Why am I not absorbing *lux lucis* faster?" I asked Niko as we walked toward the hotel again. His BMW was waiting by the front door with the valet hovering next to the driver's door. "It's never taken this long before. And one of those trees should have been able to handle filling me up with no problem."

"It's different when you've been drained like the . . . like Tim did," Niko said, choosing his words carefully now that we were back in hearing range of normal humans. It was weird to hear the demon's name come from Niko. Fresh embarrassment tried to flush my face, but I was too cold. What type of enforcer doesn't recognize a demon when he's right in front of her?

Niko tipped the valet, who then raced around to the passenger door and opened it for me before I could reach for the handle. I gave the teenage lad a wan smile, which was wasted on him, since his gaze was fixated on my chest.

I collapsed into the warm interior of the car, delighted when I found the seat's built-in warmer already turned on. The valet shut the door behind me. I pulled on my seat belt and resisted the temptation to recline the chair. Niko slid behind the wheel, took one look at me, and turned the heater off.

"No sleep yet. You'd be a hazard to everyone around you in your state."

He didn't add anything more, and he didn't need to. I'd already had my scare with Mr. Bond. I didn't want to be rushing anyone to the emergency room because I'd been selfish enough to fall asleep without fully recharging.

"You'll be better after you get some food. Your *lux lucis* levels got so low that recharging alone isn't enough to sustain you. Your body needs raw, physical nutrients. You should start keeping yogurt in your car. It's got live bacteria in it, and that can be an additional boost."

Suddenly the six-pack ice chest in the BMW's trunk made sense. "Do you have any on you?" I asked.

"Sure, but you're beyond the help of a yogurt or two. We're going to Mel's."

It wasn't until we reached the diner that I considered the ramifications of being dressed like a booth babe. "I can't go in like this," I protested when Niko started to get out of the car.

He let his gaze roam over me from top to bottom, then grinned. "I don't think it'd go over well if we switched clothes, and I've got nothing else with me."

I giggled at the image of Niko suctioned into these tiny shorts and suffocating under the balloon-size breasts. The laughter buoyed me.

"Come on. No one will notice," Niko said.

Neither of us believed him.

At nearly ten at night, the diner was doing brisk business. The startled hostess who sat us didn't seem to know where to look, between my atrocious attire and Niko's stunning good looks. The rest of the patrons in the small establishment gawked like country folk in a big city. Honestly, hadn't they seen a video game action heroine come to life before?

If I'd been thinking straight, I would have left the guns behind. They clanked against the table when I sat, causing the hostess to jump and scurry away. For the first time, I wondered if Niko was as okay as he appeared. His soul was the weakest I'd ever seen it, and I was pretty sure that if he'd been thinking clearly, he would have put the guns in the trunk.

My fake breasts rested on the surface of the table once I got myself situated in the booth. It was hard not to sag against them, the sensation not unlike having a pillow to lean against. However the chilly plastic seat pressed against the back of my thighs was enough to remind me not to nod off.

The waitress, a plump lady in her late forties who clearly thought I was a tramp and Niko not much better by mere association, took our orders. Niko selected Cobb salads for both of us—without bacon!—plus four large sides of grilled vegetables.

Screw that. I'd almost died tonight. I deserved something better than rabbit food.

"With some fries and a chocolate milkshake," I added before the waitress could flounce away.

"Those aren't going to help you," Niko said.

"French fries are natural restoratives," I told him.

"Says who?"

I pointed to my stomach, but with the positioning of the Dolly Parton bra, it looked like I was pointing at my breasts.

"I didn't know they had their own opinions," Niko said, straight-faced.

I let it drop. As long as I got my fries, I wasn't going to press the issue.

"Are you ready to admit what you did today was stupid?" he asked.

"I thought I already did."

He shook his head and waited.

"You're really going to make me say it?" My temper, which had melted away beneath my exhaustion, burned back to life. "Fine. It was stupid. Happy now?"

"Why was it stupid?"

I stared into his blank face and ground my teeth. Hadn't I been through enough today? Why was he heckling me on this issue? I attempted to cross my arms over my chest and ended up punching the padded bra by mistake—making the biker at the bar who'd been leering at me nearly fall off his stool. Frustrated, I clasped my hands in front of me on the table, which meant I was basically hugging the fake breasts. I leaned forward a little and said in a snidely sweet voice, "It was stupid because I nearly died."

"And?"

"Why are you doing this?" I gestured between us and ended up hitting my breasts again. I gave them an aggravated hoist to get the bra back in place and growled under my breath. How I'd ever let Mr. Pitt talk me into this ridiculous outfit in the first place was beyond me, but to have dressed myself in it for a second day in a row clearly indicated a lapse in mental clarity.

Niko ignored my brassiere troubles. "I need to hear you explain it."

The waitress returned with my milkshake and a water each. I snatched up the cold drink and, with some finagling of the straw and cup, managed to get a large gulp without spilling any on myself. The chocolate milk and ice cream slid down my throat, triggering a starvation button along the way. Suddenly all I could think about was food—the smell of it, the taste of it, how long it was taking for our salads and my French fries to arrive. With ravenous glee, I sucked down the entire shake before my cold headache registered.

I set down the empty glass and clutched my forehead, pinching my eyes shut until the pain abated. When I could think again, all I could focus on was the hollow pit that had replaced my stomach.

"I'm starved," I said.

Niko looked like he was trying to hold back a smile and keep his stern face on. I replayed the last few minutes in my head to remember what we'd been talking about. I waited for my anger to resurface, but there was no room for it *and* the hunger, and the hunger definitely won.

"You want to know why everything I did today was stupid? No"—I shook my head before he could say anything—"you want to know if I realize the mistakes I made, right?" At Niko's nod, I sat back, hugging my hollow stomach under the table, and evaluated the day. I didn't think I'd made that many bad decisions—aside, possibly, from taking the job in the first place—and I wasn't going to confess to any just to get him off my back. "Okay, I disobeyed Mr. Pitt. That was stupid because he's going to be mad."

"An enforcer should always listen to her warden."

I kept forgetting that was the term for Mr. Pitt's position. I made a face at Niko, then nodded. "It seems like it could save a little trouble."

He snorted. "Anything else?"

"Sure. I should have had a bundle of hound nets on me. That would have saved me some hassle. Of course, getting captured is never intelligent, though it wasn't intentional, and you'll agree that the circumstances leading up to that moment didn't offer me a way to avoid it."

Niko sighed. "Do you like your job?"

"Not if I'm going to nearly die every day."

"Aside from that."

"Right. Aside from that little issue. Is this about what Tim said?"

Niko didn't respond. He was very good at having his silence speak for him. It had a pressure all of its own.

The waitress came by with our salads, vegetable sides, and my fries. My mouth watered, but Niko's silence held me still. The waitress left, and I forced my eyes from the food back to Niko's face. I felt I deserved a medal for the effort.

"I like preventing animals from being hurt," I said. I'd already come to that conclusion, but I could see from Niko's face that it wasn't answer enough. He wanted a definite answer to whether or not I was on board with being an enforcer . . . an answer I had been avoiding thinking about.

I'd taken the job to rid myself of my ability to see in Primordium, thinking that if evil creatures thought I was a normal person and I couldn't see people's souls, I'd be able to live a normal life. I tried to picture myself back in an office job, working nine to five, dating whoever I wanted without necessarily knowing the moral contents of his past, living for the weekend, and saving for a mortgage I didn't yet have. I'd tried to maintain a normal life ever since I was a teenager and learned of Primordium. I sucked at normal.

I didn't exactly excel as an enforcer. But I'd never experienced the rushes of adrenaline I'd had in the last few days at any other job. I'd never experienced a satisfaction equivalent to what I'd felt the night before when I'd saved Max. Whatever else Niko or Mr. Pitt wanted to say, I had a knack for tracking evil—though maybe they'd word it as *attracting* evil. Plus, I was really good at killing imps, and I *liked* doing that. Add in good pay and no hint of monotony anywhere in sight, and there wasn't much to complain about.

Ignoring the obvious terror and near-death experience I'd had an hour ago, of course, I reminded myself. But sitting in Mel's diner, food before me, the region's sexy optivus aegis across from me, death seemed very far away.

"Yeah, I like being an enforcer," I said. Niko studied me a moment longer before nodding his satisfaction. "Plus, it pays well," I added with a wink.

Finally he smiled, and I dug into my meal.

The fries, of course, went first. They were hot and salty and easy to eat around the enormous breasts. They did nothing to quell my hunger. The enormous salad tasted like it'd come straight from the farm, crisp and fresh and far more delicious than it deserved to be. I chewed through it with single-minded determination. It wasn't until I'd polished off the two-portion salad and started on the side of vegetables that I felt like something was actually reaching my stomach. I considered Niko's earlier words about the milkshake and fries not helping me while I crunched through the last of the zucchini. I'd assumed he meant my figure, which was none of his business. Now I wondered if he'd been referring to something else.

It wasn't until I ran out of food that I realized I'd seen eating contestants who were better dining companions than I'd been. Fortunately, Niko didn't appear to care. Sliding his fork around the edges of his salad plate, he scooped up the last shreds of lettuce and blue cheese, then pushed his empty plate aside.

"Why didn't the fries help?" I asked. Greasy hot potatoes and sugar-laden ketchup were my cure for pretty much everything.

"There's no *lux lucis* left in them. They were dead before they got to the table. Same with the milkshake. Unless you're drinking the milk straight from the cow, you're not getting anything useful from it, at least not as far as your *lux lucis* levels are concerned. Did you check out your salad before you inhaled it?"

I shook my head.

"You need to pay more attention to what you eat. Your body needs more than the energy you get from touching plants. Especially if you want to become a stronger enforcer."

As great as all the vegetables had tasted, I grimaced at the thought of making every meal a salad. "This is my life now?" I asked, forking a piece of lettuce that had escaped my notice and eating it.

"You'll survive," Niko said without an ounce of sympathy.

I leaned back in my seat, relaxed now that I had a full stomach. Niko didn't appear in a hurry to leave, so I figured he had more lectures for me. I jumped in before he could start.

"What's our plan now?" I asked.

"That's for Mr. Pitt to decide."

I veered away from that delicate subject. "Was this the first demon you've encountered?"

"No."

"The strongest?"

"No."

"The shortest?"

That got me a smile. "No."

"How long have you been an enforcer?"

"Since my late teens. I was promoted pretty fast and passed the optivus aegis test when I was twenty-two."

I was surprised he'd offered information. "Why? What made you get strong so fast?"

"Lots of practice and paying attention to my wardens."

"You're not just saying that?"

"No."

"This job's got a steep learning curve." It wasn't quite a complaint.

Niko didn't answer. He reached down beneath the table and came up with a knife nestled in a leather sheath. Judging by the sheath, the blade was at least eight inches long. He set it on the table between us, then looked at me.

"Things would have gone a lot differently if you'd been carrying this tonight."

Yeah, I thought, *I might not still have all my fingers and toes.* I folded my hands in my lap beneath the table. My happy full-stomach glow cooled.

"You need to be able to take care of yourself and your region without backup."

"I've got pet wood—"

"Remind me how well that worked against the hounds tonight, against the demon."

I snapped my mouth shut. My aversion to getting a knife of my own spoke volumes about how I felt about using one. I didn't need to point out to Niko that I couldn't kill a hound with a knife knowing that it was a helpless dog who'd had no say in its transformation. Niko had probably guessed as much. What scared me more was the thought of plunging a sharp blade into a human-looking demon. If the demon had looked like a vervet, I might not have had a problem. But the demon was Tim, a guy I'd met at a bar. He was real, flesh and blood . . . and antlers and *atrum.*

"What if I'm not cut out for this job?" I whispered.

"You have doubts?"

I nodded.

"Is this the same woman who turned a hound last night with her bare hands? The same one who embedded her pet wood halfway into a demon?"

I squirmed at the reminder. "It's the same one who followed brainless imps to a trap. It's the same one who fell under Tim's spell."

"Everyone makes mistakes when they first start."

"What? After all that crap you gave me, you're going to shrug it off now?"

Niko grinned. "I don't condone some of the decisions you made, but I have no fault with your instincts as an enforcer."

I pulled my mouth closed with effort.

"Besides, you should have seen some of the stupid things I did when I was younger." Niko shook his head in rueful remembrance.

"Like what?"

Our waitress chose that moment to clear the table and bring the check. She hesitated when she saw the sheathed knife, then rushed away with our dishes. I waited for Niko to continue our fascinating conversation, but he shook his head.

"Something tells me you won't need the encouragement of the stories of my wilder—and stupider—days."

"You're just afraid of scaring me off," I taunted.

"Maybe."

Not the answer I wanted. It would have been nice to have more than Niko's word that he hadn't always been perfect.

I stared at the knife on the table. It looked much larger without all the plates and glasses around it. I blinked. The hilt and sheath looked like any other inanimate object in Primordium: charcoal.

Niko's color was still not up to full strength, but it blazed brighter than mine did. I wondered if it always would. He was the elite of the enforcers; I was the latest-blooming enforcer ever seen, or so everyone told me. Beneath my lashes, I eyed his strength, that subtle glimmer of *more* that his soul had. I eyed it, and coveted it. I didn't want to be weak. I didn't want my region to suffer for my weaknesses. I wanted to shine with a strength I wasn't even sure how to obtain.

Tentatively, I reached for the knife and pulled it halfway from its sheath. The blade glowed faintly, a soft white that was akin to a reflective shine. When I pushed a trickle of *lux lucis* into the hilt, if felt like I'd caressed a smooth piece of glass or stainless steel, something incredibly soft and cold and slick. The hilt remained charcoal, but the blade glowed a little brighter.

"I thought metals didn't hold *lux lucis* very well," I said.

"They don't. This knife has a core of bone."

I slid the blade home and rested my hands on the table. "Bone of what?"

"A cow's rib. And, no, to answer the question on your face, I didn't kill the cow. A butcher did. The meat was sold, and the bone was purchased by a knife manufacturer."

I let that sink in. The blade looked normal. It wasn't thick and round like the rib bones I'd seen.

"How does the *lux lucis* get from the bone to the outside to"—*harm, destroy, kill*—"banish *atrum*?"

"The bone holds *lux lucis*. It'll hold it longer than pet wood will. And it radiates the energy out to the sharp edges of the blade, sort of like water flowing in the easiest direction. That's why the knife is double-edged, and also why the hilt doesn't hold *lux lucis*. Which means that as long as the blade is sheathed, most *atrum* creatures don't notice it. A weapons expert could tell you more, but that's the gist of it."

"Do I know any of those?"

"Any what?"

"Weapons experts."

"Closest one is San Francisco, so probably not."

I blinked to normal vision. "How long did it take you to learn it all?"

"You never learn it *all*."

"Humor me," I said, not in the mood to play word games. I was sitting on the tip of the enforcer iceberg, and so much unknown was floating out of sight. How many creatures, good and evil, were out there that I didn't know about? What else was there that I didn't even know enough to ask about?

"How fast you learn is up to you, but if you want to catch up fast, stick with Brad, keep your ears open, and ask questions. That's the best you can do."

"Got anything more concrete than that?"

Niko let his silence ride. I wondered if we'd exhausted his week's worth of words. Was he normally a talkative man? It was hard to picture. He was so self-sufficient, he probably usually didn't need words to converse.

I would have loved to sit there and pick his brain for the rest of the night, especially for details about his life, his past, his present. Where did he live? Had he always worked in Northern California? Did he have a girlfriend in another city? A girlfriend in every city? A dog? Parents, or was he spawned from pure *lux lucis* like the ultimate good creature? What was his favorite sexual position?

I gave myself a little shake. If my hormones were back online, I was feeling good enough to go home. Especially since my hormones usually made me look like a fool around Niko.

The knife was large and menacing on the Formica table. I glanced down at my hands where they rested on the table on either side of my inflated chest. My right wrist was circled with a darkening bruise from where Tim had held my hand in the *atrum* barrier over the door. He'd been stronger than me physically and in Primordium. Even if he hadn't had the element of surprise or his lust magic, I wouldn't have been able to fight my way free of him. He'd pinned me easily to the floor in the end, and it'd been only Niko's fantastic timing that had saved me from becoming demon food.

The hilt fit easily against my palm, and the weight of the blade surprised me. I slid the knife into my costume's backpack with a shudder.

Niko pulled out his wallet and placed some money with the check. The butts of the guns scraped loudly as I slid from the booth. I caught the right one on the table as I stood. The table screeched in protest, drawing everyone's attention.

"Is that Lara Croft?" I heard a teenage boy whisper to his friend.

"She looks better in 3-D," his friend said.

"No kidding."

I checked to make sure my shorts were still covering my butt cheeks and walked out with my dignity trailing in my wake.

17

Spay and Neuter
Animal Abusers

NIKO DROVE ME TO MY car, then followed me home. We didn't speak again about the knife or the demon.

"Check with Brad tomorrow to see what he wants you to do," was the last thing Niko said to me.

I tried to take heart from Niko's belief that Mr. Pitt wouldn't fire me. For all that I'd finally admitted I wanted to keep my job, the fact was, I also still *needed* my job. If Mr. Pitt fired me now, I'd make rent and the Civic was paid through the month, but it would mean another frantic job hunt.

I recharged fully with the help of a huge oak tree in my complex. With nutrients in my stomach, the tree's *lux lucis* was more than enough to restore the remainder of my expended energy. Niko waited until I walked up the stairs to my apartment to start his car. When I peeked out my balcony window, he was pulling out of the lot.

I fed Mr. Bond on autopilot, meticulously replaced the wards around the doors and windows, tossed the costume in the washer for what felt like the tenth day in a row, and showered. Once I'd changed into some lounge pants and a soft old T-shirt, I flopped into my recliner. Mr. Bond decided that he had several days' worth of neglect to make up for, and he pranced around my lap while I petted him.

I didn't turn on the TV or radio. The only sound in the apartment was the soothing hum of the refrigerator and Mr. Bond's ecstatic purr.

My hands began to shake. Something wet was on my face, and I was surprised to realize I was crying. I closed my eyes and saw Tim's beautiful human face with twisted antlers tipped in *atrum* blades sprouting from the top of his head. I snapped my eyes open and stared at Mr. Bond.

My job as an assistant to Eliza Turner had been demeaning and frustrating, Catchall Advertising had been tedious, and being a used-car saleswoman had been disastrous, but none of those jobs, or any others I'd had, had been life-threatening. My biggest work-related concerns used to be about meeting management monetary goals, pleasing the customer, and not succumbing to boredom comas.

Mr. Bond head-butted my chin and I resumed petting him. Gradually my cheeks dried and my tremors stilled.

It had been easy to be brave while in Niko's company, but sitting in my tiny, isolated apartment was another matter. My wards looked feeble. If Tim had followed me, he'd have no problem knocking down the door.

The thought held me frozen, listening for footsteps on the stairs. The door slammed shut in the apartment below me, and I jumped. Unperturbed, Mr. Bond laid down and began to knead the blanket I had spread across my lap.

"If only you knew, you'd be more skittish, too," I told him. I scratched his forehead and focused on relaxing.

I tried to imagine what I'd be doing if I'd never heard of Primordium, never seen a soul. It wasn't hard. I'd already gotten a glimpse of that life when I was trying to ignore what I was. It was dull, uninspired. Why had I been trying so hard to go back to that life?

Oh, yeah. Because no one was trying to kill me then.

Max's happy puppy-dog eyes and wagging tail swam behind my eyelids. *No one was being saved then either.*

If I lost my ability to see in Primordium, I'd always wonder if a dog that snarled at me was coated with *atrum*, if the attractive man who made my insides flutter was a demon, if the people standing next to me in the elevator were unwitting hosts—if *I* was a host. I finally accepted what I'd known all along: There was no turning back, no giving up my sight. It was a part of me, and having seen the world of Primordium, I could never pretend it didn't exist, just as I couldn't *not* take action against evil now that I had the power to fight back.

The insurmountable task before me—of capturing and killing Tim, of cleansing my region, of fighting evil for a living—should have kept me awake. I slept like the dead.

I dressed the next morning in the camouflage outfit, shaking my head at myself in the bathroom mirror. I'd have to check with my parents to see if insanity ran in the family.

The outfit accentuated my injuries: the yellow and purple bruise on my left leg from running into the truck hitch; the raw red rug burn on both my knees; a matching puffy red burn on my elbows; an ugly bracelet of a black and blue bruise on my wrist; and the splotchy yellowing bruises on my upper arms. I'd put up a good fight against Tim and it showed.

I'm supposed to be some sort of army woman, I thought, *so maybe all my injuries make me look more authentic.*

"You really do need professional help," I told my image in the mirror. We grimaced at each other.

As I drove to work, I prepared my defense against anything Mr. Pitt might say. Everything I'd done had been prompted by an urge to rid the world of evil, which was exactly what an enforcer was supposed to do. That should count for something, right?

I'd been selfish these last ten or so years. I'd run from my ability out of fear. Had I been a little braver, a little more persistent or curious or even had a different first experience, I might have already saved countless lives from being corrupted. How many Maxes were out there because I'd been too afraid to trust myself?

I had a lot to make up for, and I'd only just begun. Mr. Pitt was sure to agree.

"You're the most brainless enforcer I've ever met!" Mr. Pitt bellowed in greeting. He pulled me into his office, pacing back and forth behind his desk, alternately yelling, then gesticulating in speechlessness. After ten minutes, I gave up trying to get a word in and sat stiffly in a black leather chair, savoring the sensation of clenching my jaw so tight it felt like my teeth were fusing together.

"Do you realize how close you came to dying? Without Niko, you'd be dead! A corpse. And I'd be out looking for another enforcer. Again! What were you thinking? Oh, that's right; you weren't. I get the only baby-strength enforcer who's carrying around an extra three pounds between her ears for no good reason."

"Maybe if everyone didn't dole out knowledge like it was a scarce commodity, I would have known better," my mouth said before I could stop it.

Mr. Pitt whirled to pin me with his beady eyes. "If you did what I told you, we wouldn't have a problem."

"If you explained why you had me do things, I'd be more likely to stick to your rules."

"I'm your warden, Madison. I don't have to explain anything to you."

"I know that I nearly got killed last night because no one bothered to explain to me about demons! How was I supposed to know that looking at them with normal vision would cause me to get all lusty?"

Mr. Pitt threw his hands in the air and flopped into his chair. "Fine. Here's your lesson in demons. Not all demons are the same. This demon didn't leave a strong signature from which to determine its type until late yesterday. We discovered it feeds on lust about the same time you did. And it's been feeding and gaining strength in *my* region for almost a week now. Thanks to you, it's still out there." He slammed his hands down on his desk. "Starbursts on a cupcake, we've been after it for days and it's *still out there*!"

"How do I take it out?"

"How do *you* . . . ?" Mr. Pitt sputtered, his face flushing alarmingly bright. "*You* don't do anything. *You* stay as far away from the convention as possible today. It's the last day of that gumdrop nerd event, which means it's our last good shot at taking out the demon. *Niko* will handle it. We don't need *you* messing everything up. Again. Everyone hardly finished cleaning up after *your* last catastrophe. I'm out of favors and deep in debt now, not to mention a laughingstock."

"If I don't learn how to take out a demon now, what's going to happen the next time one gets in our region?" I asked, trying for reason, clinging to my temper by my fingertips.

"There'd better not be another demon any time soon," Mr. Pitt growled. He leaned back in his chair and studied me while the color in his face returned to normal. "You're too jelly bean green right now. But you'll learn. You'll get more training. You'll get more practice. With a lot of luck, you'll get stronger. But not today. Today, I'm pissed at you. Today, you need to go home. Stay away. Don't mess this up. Come back tomorrow."

I ground my teeth and stomped from the office. I didn't want to take on Tim alone again. I knew it was foolish. But I also wanted to be part of whatever Niko and Mr. Pitt were planning. I hated being treated like I was incompetent. Worse, I hated feeling that Mr. Pitt's decision to exclude me was justified.

At least he'd not mentioned firing me. He hadn't even hinted at it. Slim consolation.

I wrestled my seat belt around the fake breasts for the third day in a row. I could go home and spend the day watching TV and doing laundry. It was Sunday. I could even call up Bridget and hang out at her house.

Instead, I headed up Douglas to Accessories and More. Mr. Pitt might not have wanted me in the office or near the convention center, but he'd said I needed to get stronger, and the only way to get stronger was to practice. To practice, I needed another pet wood.

"Where's the hoochie war?" Musad asked. Muhamad grinned at my breasts, then my legs.

"These are real guns, boys," I warned.

"They're not loaded," Muhamad guessed.

"They make great cudgels." I pulled one from the holster and held it by the barrel menacingly.

"Whoa, careful with that thing. You'll give my other customers a fright," Musad said.

I glanced around the empty shop.

"You might hurt yourself," Muhamad said.

Since that was highly likely, I slid the gun back in the holster.

"You want a twin blade to the one you got there?" Muhamad asked, nodding toward my right boot.

I'd slid the knife Niko had given me last night into the boot's sheath without any intention of using it for anything other than a prop. I couldn't even draw it without attracting attention from anything that could see in Primordium. Or really anyone who could see—most people tended to take notice when you started waving an eight-inch blade around. I didn't like having it on me either. Some people might have felt more badass or more protected. I felt like I had to constantly be on guard against it, like I'd trip and it'd fall out and stab me in the heart. Sharp things and I have always had a cautious relationship.

"Nope," I said. "I burnt my pet wood out on a demon. I need another."

The brothers shared a glance. Musad poked my bare shoulder with a finger. "Not an apparition," he told his brother.

"Come on. It's not that unlikely that I'd survive an encounter with a demon."

They shared another glance. Their eyes inventoried my visible injuries.

"Where's Niko today?" Muhamad asked shrewdly.

I shrugged and tried to look like I didn't care.

"Ah," Musad said, placing a finger beside his nose like he had a secret.

"Ah," Muhamad echoed.

"Look, I want to spend some money. Do you want it or not?"

I left with a slightly more expensive pet wood than the first one. This one extended just like the previous one, but it could hold more *lux lucis*. I also purchased a hound net. I wanted half a dozen, but they were twelve hundred dollars a pop. I checked the price tag on a knife similar to the one Niko had loaned me while I was there. Two thousand dollars. I knew I couldn't permanently accept his knife, but I would have to wait for a paycheck to replace it. The enforcer business was not a cheap one. I wondered how much the twins marked up their prices. If they had a monopoly on the niche market, they could charge whatever they wanted. I made a mental note to ask Rose what other enforcer shops were in the area. It might pay to do some price checking. Especially if I continued to go through pet wood as fast as I had. In less than a week, I'd spent nearly all of my signing bonus on supplies. Things weren't looking good for my wardrobe-expansion plans.

I cruised aimlessly back toward my apartment. It was a bad sign that I hardly noticed the press of the guns into my thighs and the unnatural cut of the seat belt high across my neck, held far out from my body by the bra. My thoughts kept circling back to Tim, the Golden Goose, Max, and finally, Mr. Pitt's restrictions of where I couldn't go today.

I was 99 percent positive that Max was the same hound I'd encountered at the construction site. Of course, I couldn't go back to check, because if I got caught again, I would face criminal charges *and* Mr. Pitt would surely fire me.

He needed a full-fledged enforcer. I needed to *be* a full-fledged enforcer. Someone like Niko. Someone who could handle the whole region and whatever evil threw at me. I wasn't up for the big assignments. Mr. Pitt, Niko, *and* Tim had made that clear. But that didn't mean I wasn't ready to tackle something a little smaller.

"Mr. Pitt can't stop me from practicing," I said aloud to see if I believed myself. "Besides, this is my job." I was almost convinced, and *almost* was good enough for me. If Niko claimed to have gotten his strength from practice, then that's what I'd do.

I headed for the greenbelt that backed up to the evil-plagued construction site. I had to park over half a mile from my destination at a gravel parking lot near the paved bike trail that wound through the protected environment. It was late in the morning, but down in the hollow through which the greenbelt and its accompanying stream flowed, the world was cast mostly in shadows.

Chill November air kept most people off the trails this time of year, but a few cyclists sped past as I pulled my courage together to get out of the car. Taking a deep breath, I blinked. The world lit up. All the trees and bushes glowed with purity. Birds and bugs flitted against the dark sky like fireflies in every size. The crisp white limbs of trees and shrubs against the dark, dead-grass hillsides looked like paper cutouts. I soaked in the beauty. This beat being stuck in an evil-infested convention with half the country's gaming geeks.

I got out of my car, grabbed the small backpack, and stuffed the flashlight into its already overcrowded pouch. When the icy breeze sliced against my bare arms and legs, I considered going home first to change. I'd left the house without my coat this morning, busy planning what I thought was a semi-decent explanation for the way I'd botched my run-in with the demon. By the time I'd realized I'd forgotten my coat, I'd been at the office.

I had plenty of time to go back for it now *and* get dressed in real clothes. I hesitated with my hand on the Civic's handle. I remembered how Max had leaned into me after I'd removed all the *atrum*. He'd been starved for good, clean affection. I scanned the ridgeline, where the dark shapes of houses hid behind trees. Someone here had abused and tainted the poor dog. I couldn't shake the feeling of urgency now that I was close to the culprits.

I locked the car behind me and marched purposefully down the trail. *Let people think what they want.* Plus, embarrassment came complete with its own heating system.

I was five minutes into my walk before I remembered that I was illegally wearing guns strapped to my hips. I debated returning them to the car versus the odds of running into a cop. Deciding the odds were in my favor, I continued. Besides, the guns weren't loaded.

"We're all on the same side," I reminded myself optimistically. As long as I didn't have to explain that to a police officer.

I trooped along at the edge of the trail, keeping out of the way of the occasional startled biker, giving a neighborly wave to the gawking people walking in the other direction when I really wanted to duck into the bushes in embarrassment. For the most part, though, I savored the balm of being surrounded by *lux lucis*. All the positive energy knitted my confidence back together. A demon might be squatted on my territory a few miles to the west, but this small surge of evil near the construction site I could handle.

My heels were rubbing painfully in my boots and the balls of my feet throbbed from the abuse of three days in heels by the time I approached the hill opposite the construction site. On my left, large expensive homes crested the rise, their long backyards sweeping down steep hills to the edge of the bike trail. Most homes had pools; all had expensive landscaping. Fortunately, it was too cold for people to be lounging outside.

On my right, dense undergrowth filled the valley, topped by enormous trees. Through the trees' bare limbs, the scraped-raw hillside and squared-off half-built homes were easily visible.

The complete lack of *atrum* was similarly blatant.

I marched along the trail, vigilant for signs of misguided teens, until it dipped under Secret Ravine Parkway. The construction site was long out of sight. Finally, I admitted to myself what a long shot the whole trip had been. Just because kids were vandalizing the construction site didn't mean they were from the homes on this hillside, like the cop had thought. Even if they were, the odds that they were outside, audibly plotting their next indiscretion at this precise moment were pretty darn slim.

The walk back to my car was twice as long, or at least it felt like it. I did my best not to think about my feet and the blisters I knew were rubbing into my heels and toes. Full-body shivers helped; it was hard to hold on to a solid thought when my entire body felt like it had been set on vibrate. Sheer willpower and a very strong visual of a hot bath kept me moving.

I thought about calling someone to pass the time but nixed the idea as soon as I thought it through. I couldn't call my parents because they'd have questions I couldn't answer, especially once they heard my teeth chatter. If I called Bridget, I'd have to admit how stupid I'd been. I didn't want to call Doris or Rose. Niko was out of the question.

I rounded the final curve and trudged up the hill toward the parking lot with a frosty internal cheer of relief half drowned out by the rumblings of my stomach. I hadn't bothered to switch from Primordium for my entire walk, figuring I was at least getting some practice out of my exercise in self-torture. My car was where I'd left it, the only vehicle in the gravel lot.

It wasn't, however, alone.

Two shapes crouched beside it, teenage by their size. One was half inside the car, his knee on the seat, his hands busy at the center console. The other had my purse, which I'd stuffed under the front seat, and was rummaging through its contents.

"Hey!" I yelled.

Both boys spun and froze at the sight of me.

"What do you think you're doing?" I demanded.

"Am I really seeing this?" the boy with my purse asked the other. He waved a gray hand in front of his face.

"Yeah, I'm real. And that's my car!"

"Crap!"

The one inside the car gave a final yank to my dash and came free with my stereo. The other tossed my purse back inside. Both sprinted away, gravel flying.

The little buggers had been robbing me while I'd been breaking every bone in my feet trying to find them! There was no way I was letting them get away now. Before, I'd been trying to prove something to Mr. Pitt. Now it was personal.

They tore off straight down the grassy hill in front of my car, toward a meadow and the construction side of the greenbelt. They had surprise on their side, but I had fury on mine. I sprinted after them, my blisters forgotten, leaping the crest of the hill with a war cry. The slower one looked back over his shoulder, then shouted something to his friend and they both doubled their speed.

I blinked to normal vision to see the terrain better—and nearly face-planted from a wash of vertigo. Some fancy footwork kept me upright, but I lost ground on the thieves. They blasted through the meadow and into the dense underbrush near the creek, not slowing. I might have lost sight of them as they dodged down an old deer trail if not for the slower boy's shock of copper red hair. The other was taller, dark-haired, and clearly in better shape as he outdistanced the redhead even with the added weight of my car's stereo.

I dodged a tree root, ricocheted off a tree trunk, and smacked aside limbs with both arms, cursing when my rug-burned elbows scraped bark. The trail made a sharp curve and then began a steep ascent. My high-heeled boots, which were not ideal for running in to begin with, didn't improve my performance during the climb. By the time I reached the top of the hill, my legs and lungs were burning and I was barely jogging. I'd lost sight of the boys. Though the trail continued in only one direction, the undergrowth was thick enough that opportunistic teenage boys with agility and fitness on their side could hide away in it while I bumbled along on the trail. The thought made me pause.

I bent over at the waist to catch my breath, hands planted on my knees, feet throbbing in reminder of burst blisters and bruised bones, and scanned the undergrowth. Nothing moved. I held my breath. This close to the creek, I could hear the burble of water over rocks. Gulping in a breath, I switched to Primordium, and still nothing moved. Even the birds were quiet.

I pushed myself into motion again, spurred on by the thought of the boys getting away, or worse, by them looping back around to finish looting my car.

The pause had helped me regain my breath, and I could hear my footsteps again over my breathing. Just when I was thinking I should start running again, that the boys had never stopped running and were long gone, I spotted them.

If I'd had only normal sight, they probably would have gotten away with it. They'd hidden tight against an outcropping of rocks, curled up near its base in its shadow. It was only the solid lines of their light gray souls against the dark, dead rock that gave them away.

Not wanting to have another chase on my hands, I considered my options. My lips pulled into an unfamiliar wicked smile when an idea came to me.

I pulled a gun from my holster and marched into the underbrush. In a few steps, the bushes opened to a clearing at the base of the rock outcropping, and I glared down at the crouched boys.

"Holy shit, Connor, she's got a gun!"

"Get up and stand still," I ordered.

The boys eased to their feet and pressed back against the rock. Imps the size of large rodents bounced in a confused mass near their feet, and several smaller imps fed from their wrists. The taller, faster one—Connor—had a few extra imps at his throat and shots of *atrum* arcing up his arms like bad tattoos of lightning. The redhead had only blotchy gray bits on his soul. I eyed them both down the barrel of my gun and realized I didn't have a second step in this plan.

To give myself a moment, I blinked to normal vision and took a look around the clearing. Two grungy backpacks and a box sat near the rock behind Connor. My stereo was sticking out of the top of one backpack; spray paint cans peeked out from the unzipped second backpack. The rock face behind the boys was covered with layered graffiti tags in garish pink and orange. The bushes around the clearing looked to have been indiscriminately sprayed, and even in normal vision, I could tell the toxic paint was killing them.

"What're you going to do now?" Connor asked. It's hard to be brave when you're staring down the barrel of a gun, even when the person holding it looks like she stepped straight out of a video game. Or maybe especially because of that. Even so, he did a pretty good job of looking nonchalant.

Good question. "I want my stereo back," I said, then added, "and anything else you took."

"Or what? You're not a cop."

"I think you should do what she says," the other boy said.

"Shut up, Sam," Connor said.

"No, I think Sam's right," I said. "Hand it over."

Connor kicked the backpack at me. The contents crunched from the impact of his foot, and the bag sailed to land near my feet. I didn't have to look to know everything was broken. I clenched my fist and swallowed my anger. I needed a clear head to figure out what I was going to do.

Cold slices in my ankles and calves distracted me. I blinked back to Primordium. The imps had no fear of the gun, and they'd decided I made a tastier snack than the boys. Negligently, I dissipated the entire group. When I looked up, I saw that removing some *atrum* from the area had taken the stiffness out of Connor's shoulders, and he dropped his challenging stare when I raised an eyebrow. I knew what I had to do.

"You're not the sharpest tool in the shed, are you, Connor?" I asked him. I advanced on Connor, kicking the backpack aside as if my broken stereo meant nothing. "Vandalizing, stealing, getting your petty high on these small-time crimes." I was less than three feet from him.

"Shit, shit, we're in so much trouble, shit," Sam chanted, inching away from Connor. The scent of musky deodorant and sweat rolled off the boys.

I pinned Sam in place with a look, then took the last step and slammed my empty hand into Connor's chest. Up close, I could see the scared youth peering from behind those hard eyes. Connor couldn't have been over fifteen. Older, and he'd have a car of his own and he wouldn't have been hiding out off a bike trail. Still, he'd already had his first big growth spurt, and I could feel muscle under my hands. I didn't wait for him to recover his bravado and try something stupid. I slammed *lux lucis* into him.

The energy raced across his chest and down his arms, pushing at the lightning bolts of *atrum* until they were washed away and the imps on his wrists exploded.

"You were right before. I'm not a cop. I'm an enforcer, and you're fucking around in the wrong territory." Connor's sneer had faltered when I touched him, and it slid right off his face when I cussed. I holstered the gun and slammed my other hand into Sam, feeding him *lux lucis* at the same time, dissipating the imps on his wrists. I had a height advantage, and I used it to lean on them, pressing them into the boulder. "If I catch you stealing— or vandalizing—in my region again, I'm not going to go easy on you."

I pushed off their chests and took several steps back.

"Holy cow! That was awesome," Sam breathed.

With the lack of a gun to look at, both boys' gazes dropped to my chest.

"I don't want to ever catch you out here again," I said.

"No, ma'am," Sam said, watching me with worshipful eyes.

Connor was silent and sullen. I could tell my words were having no effect on him, even though his soul was clean. If they walked away now, it was no better than me cleansing a few imps off the construction guy. I'd have nothing to go to Mr. Pitt with.

"What happened to your dog?" I asked, inspiration striking.

Connor and Sam exchanged a quick, fearful glance. It was enough. In one look, they confirmed my suspicion that Max had been theirs and that I was looking at the culprits responsible for turning him into a hound. I didn't know what to do about it, either, and it made me sick.

"How'd you know we have a dog?" Connor asked.

"*Had* a dog."

"Max will come back, I know it," Sam said.

My stomach did a flip-flop. Sam sounded genuine, like he missed the dog. "Why would he? He could roam anywhere he pleased. Why would he come back here?" I gestured around the paint-encrusted scenery. The fumes from the multicolored bushes had settled at the base of my nose, and I could feel the first tendrils of a headache unfurl.

"Because I miss him. He's the best dog ever."

Connor was back to sneering—though still staring at my breasts—but Sam was distressed.

"Is that why you starved him? Is that why his fur was coated with mange and fleas?"

"No! Dad wouldn't let me keep him. Not after we had to move to the apartment. They don't allow dogs, and there isn't even a porch. Dad said we had to take him to the shelter, but they were going to kill him, so I freed him. I couldn't let him die!" Sam was babbling, near tears.

I wanted to strangle Sam and hug him at the same time. What did I say to a kid whose heart was still good, though his actions had led to Max's suffering and transformation?

"He wouldn't let us keep the kittens I found, either," Sam continued. He darted around Connor to the box behind the second backpack. "Mr.

Brunsian ran over the mom with his car. Said I should drown the kittens, but I couldn't! They're so cute and—"

"You need to grow a pair," Connor said.

I, on the other hand, tried to control the urge to vomit. Sam held up a soggy cardboard box that reeked of urine and sour milk. Inside, perched on wet towels and coated with soggy cat food and dirt, were three tabby kittens, all no more than a few weeks old. Two clawed about the box, trying to get out. The third lay huddled in a ball in a corner, its soul a dim flicker in Primordium. I could count the ribs on all three.

"Why didn't you take these to a shelter?" I asked, my voice hollow.

"I didn't want them killed."

"There are no-kill shelters all over the place."

"Oh."

I reminded myself that Sam had only been trying to help. That he was a teen, misguided and uninformed. I thought it was helping until I looked up and saw their faces. Connor's arrogant stance had melted, and he eyed my hips, licking his lips nervously. I glanced down. My fingers were caressing my guns and I hadn't even been aware of it.

Hello to Psycho Dice. You're coming in loud and clear. Still, a little physical emphasis couldn't hurt. I took the box from Sam and pulled out a gun with my free hand. Sam flinched and backed away. I aimed the gun at Connor's crotch. The color drained from his face. *That's for you, Max, and whatever it was these boys did to you.*

"If you boys *ever* hurt an animal again—by neglect or any other reason—I *will* hunt you down and shoot you. The same goes for stealing and vandalizing. I won't go easy on you because you're a juvenile. This is your one and only warning. Max is being taken care of and so will these kittens. But if you want to reach adulthood as men"—I waggled my gun for emphasis—"you'll never, *ever*, harm another animal. Get out of here." They hesitated, and I realized they were frozen with fear. Good. I raised the gun to point at Connor's head. "Now!" I yelled.

They ran.

The box began to crumple around its soggy edges, and I hastily set it on the ground. Through the trees, I watched the now pristine souls of Connor and Sam race through the marsh around the creek and up the other side of the greenbelt on a well-traveled trail. They slowed to a fast walk when they reached the bike trail.

"Did she follow us?" Sam asked, his voice carrying across the quiet plant-filled gully between us.

"No, thank God."

"I didn't expect her to chase us from her car. Or to be so fast."

"No shit," Connor agreed.

"What's an enforcer?"

"Must be a crazy person. She totally had a gun on me!"

"She was totally *hot*."

"And scary insane," Connor said.

Sam seemed more awed than horrified, and I shook my head. I'd be coming back by this spot in the next few weeks to make sure I'd scared those boys straight. Right now, the kittens were far more important.

I tried to lift the box by its sides, and the cardboard tore off in my fingers. Had the kittens been lying on these cold, wet blankets since the night before? Longer? The unmoving kitten had me worried. I covered it with my hand and gently fed it *lux lucis* until its dim life force glowed half as bright as the other kittens'. I would have fed it more *lux lucis*, but it felt like it resisted, like the pet wood had at Accessories and More before I'd burned it out. Even with more energy, the kitten remained cold. It needed help, fast.

I couldn't bring myself to stuff the kittens into my backpack—that seemed like added insult to injury after the way they'd been treated. Plus, my tiny pack would hardly fit them if it was empty, which it wasn't. I didn't want to use the backpacks the boys had abandoned, either, after I saw the dripping paint cans and broken bits of metal inside them. Nor was my clothing loose enough to hold them in. I eyed the guns. And the holsters.

Two minutes later, the butts of the guns were stuffed in the pack with the barrels protruding out the top and I'd gently slid the two healthier kittens into their own, individual holsters. They fit perfectly, with their little heads peeking out. One tried to crawl out, but I gently shoved it back in.

"Don't go kamikaze on me," I told it sternly. It mewled and licked the leather with a tiny pink tongue.

I tried a few steps to make sure it would work. The kittens jostled a bit in their holster cups but otherwise seemed fine.

With great care, I bent over and lifted the limp form of the third kitten. I held it as close to my heart as the fake breasts would allow— propping it up on the provided shelf—and cupped my hands around it, painfully aware of how cold the November afternoon was. I promised myself I'd be back to collect the stolen items and give them to the cops tomorrow and to clean up the boys' mess. Getting the kittens to safety was my number one priority.

It was easier to follow the boys across the ravine than to climb through the bushes back to the deer trail. From the lack of tangled branches, I could tell this was a favored shortcut. By the time I reached the paved path, Sam and Connor were long gone.

A cyclist sped around the corner, eyes focused toward the next turn. His rhythm faltered when he saw me. I don't blame him. It's not every day that you see a costumed woman with cats for guns. I smiled as we passed and couldn't resist a drawled, "Howdy, partner."

"What the—" I heard his tires bounce off the paved trail to the dirt on the side, then some frantic pedaling. When I glanced behind me, he was back on the trail, but he kept looking over his shoulder at me.

I didn't encounter anyone else.

When I reached my car, I bundled my emergency blanket on the passenger seat and nestled the two holstered kittens in it. They immediately jumped to the floor and crawled under the seat. Sighing, I nestled the hurt one in the blanket on the now empty passenger seat. I shut all the car doors and performed a quick perimeter search of the Civic, finding the shell of my purse, my lip balm, and a sunglasses case—minus the sunglasses. I tossed it all in the backseat; then I got the car going and turned on the heat full blast.

I drove as fast as I dared to my favorite vet's office, paranoid the whole time that the kittens were going to crawl underfoot and be hurt by the pedals. My fear was unwarranted. When I parked and hunted for them, the kittens were nestled on top of each other under the passenger seat.

There was only one other car in the parking lot, a Volvo station wagon. I checked the time. It was nearly one thirty: lunchtime. The Volvo had to be the vehicle of the vet on duty. It was just as well. The fewer people to see me in my outfit, the better.

"Cross your paws that Dr. Love took the day off. Any chance of a date would go right out the window if he saw me now," I told the kittens under the seat. They mewled in harmony.

I pulled the kittens out from their hiding spot and stuffed them back in their holsters. They were sleepy now, and once resettled, closed their eyes and slipped back into their naps. I blinked and examined the final kitten as I picked it up. Its soul was at half glow. I gently pushed *lux lucis* into it. The extra life force made it temporarily glow brighter, but it didn't last long. I blinked back.

"Hang in there, little one," I pleaded.

Dr. Alex Love greeted me in the waiting room. My heart flipped. My stomach dived for my toes. How could I be excited and filled with dread all at the same time?

"Madison?" His eyes widened as they traveled from my face down my breast-enhanced spandex-clad body. He looked like he didn't know whether to smile or be horrified.

Act casual. He's only a hot guy. With a sexy smile. Who has dedicated his life to helping animals.

"Hi, Dr. Love." I glanced at the bundle of hardly living kitten in my hands and was washed in shame. There was more at stake here than my ego. "I, uh, found these kittens and this one needs immediate attention."

I thrust the kitten into his large, warm hands.

"What happened to it?"

"I don't know. I think it's dying."

He started walking even as he began his inspection, his large fingers gently manipulating the tiny tabby. I trailed after him into the first patient office.

I watched as Dr. Love injected various shots into the kitten. He paused long enough to ask me if the others needed attention, and I assured him they could wait. A few minutes later an assistant returned from lunch and—after giving me an incredulous look—jumped in to help Dr. Love. I settled into the seat provided for me, shivering when the cold plastic pressed against the entire back of my thighs. The shorts were far too short.

I pulled the kittens out of the holsters and set them on an office blanket in my lap, then contemplated the muscles in Dr. Love's forearms while most of my mind circled around thoughts of evil. I couldn't let this happen again. I couldn't let animals and people suffer. I needed to learn faster, be stronger. I longed to go straight to the convention center and kill every imp and vervet that crossed my path.

When Dr. Love and the assistant finished doing what they could to make the tiny kitten comfortable, Dr. Love did a cursory examination of the healthier two kittens. Without moving them from my lap. I took a deep breath and gripped the chair so that I didn't do anything embarrassing, like run my fingers through his thick hair. Beneath the initial wash of disinfectant, Dr. Love smelled like pineapples and vanilla—on the whole, completely edible. I was careful not to lean forward to get a deeper sniff since that would have pressed my padded breasts against the side of his face.

"I'm sure you've got a great story," Dr. Love prompted as he administered a shot to each kitten.

"Not really. I was out for a walk and found these guys." That was true. It just didn't include all the details that would have him calling the cops or the loony bin. "They were injured, so I brought them over."

"Do you always go for walks in November dressed like this?"

I blushed hot enough to hurt. "No, uh, no. I needed some fresh air and didn't feel like changing. This is, well, a work thing."

"I thought you said you worked for a bumper sticker company?"

"Yeah. We had a costume party."

Dr. Love gave me an assessing look. I wanted to reveal everything to him when I stared into his blue eyes, but I knew if I did, it would be the death of any future relationship. Sane people don't date crazy people. Maybe I was way out of my league.

"It's a good thing you found them," he said at last. "The little one wouldn't have made it another day. These two aren't looking so hot either. But they seem really fond of you." The kittens had fallen back to sleep on my lap, sprawled bonelessly atop each other.

"They're big fans of camo wear," I joked limply.

"And guns."

I jerked and reached over my shoulder. The barrels of the pistols were poking out of the backpack like accusatory fingers, one peeking over each shoulder.

"Uh, yeah. More costume stuff." I started to sweat.

"Well, I prefer kitten guns to real guns any day," he said with a wink. My heart fluttered in response.

The assistant came back into the room. I didn't remember her leaving. She took the kittens from my lap.

"Are you the owner?" she asked. She didn't disguise her disapproval.

"No. I just found them. I'll pay for everything, but I can't keep them."

"Oh. I see."

My feathers ruffled at her tone.

"We'll find a good home for them, I'm sure," Dr. Love said, patting me on the knee. His large warm hand on my bare leg completely distracted me from scowling at the prissy woman. I stood when he did. With the boots, I was close to eye level with him. My gaze slid to his lips and I stepped back, knocking into the chair. Dr. Love placed a steadying hand on my elbow.

"I, uh, I have to go," I stammered, staring at his hand.

"I'll walk you out."

I gave the kittens one last pet. The tiny limp one made my heart hurt to look at it.

"You did the right thing, again," Dr. Love said as he walked me through their waiting room. "Those animals are very lucky that you stumbled upon them." There were still plenty of questions in his eyes, but instead of asking them, he said, "I don't think I've ever seen anything so extraordinary as you when you came in here. If they ever create a comic book superhero that rescues animals, you're what she'd look like."

I blushed. "Thanks. I didn't really plan on going out in public like this."

"I'm glad you did. I'll never forget those kittens in your holsters. Ingenious!"

We shared a smile that warmed me to my toes. Was he flirting or just happy I rescued the kittens?

Dr. Love's gaze dropped to his feet and he shuffled. When he looked at me again, his expression made my breath catch.

"This might be very inappropriate, but would you be free for dinner sometime?" he asked.

For a second, I thought his question was another fantasy; then I realized he was waiting for a response.

"Yes." I tried not to grin like an idiot.

"I'll call you tomorrow."

"Okay."

I had the inappropriate compulsion to lean in and kiss him, so I forced myself to push the door open. The November air that blasted across my skin didn't feel nearly as cold as before. I gave Dr. Love one final smile, then floated across the parking lot to my car. I'd cleansed the stain of evil from part of my region, saved three cats, and had a date with one of the most handsome men I knew. I was an enforcer extraordinaire!

The sight of the tossed contents of my car and my busted dash with a hole where the stereo should have been dampened my euphoria, but it couldn't completely squelch it.

18

Don't Worry: There's Enough of Me for Everyone

THERE WAS NOTHING LEFT FOR me to do, especially not dressed as a booth babe, so I drove home. Mr. Bond was thrilled to see me and made a big production of sniffing my shoes. I tossed my clothes straight into the washer, wiped down the holsters just in case the kittens were carrying a transmittable disease, then hopped into a steaming shower. Fifteen minutes later, I emerged wrinkled and warm. I dressed in worn jeans, a soft long-sleeve muted gray cotton top that had been black at one point, and a lightweight green fleece.

My feet were as bad as they had felt. I applied ointment and Band-Aids to two burst blisters, then warmed a pair of socks in the dryer before putting them on. I microwaved a frozen burrito and took it with me on a plate to the front room.

"I'm in heaven," I told Mr. Bond when I flopped into my recliner to devour my lunch.

Ten minutes later I was full and bored. I grabbed the phone book and the phone and squished back into my chair beside Mr. Bond, who'd attempted to steal it the moment I stood up. He begrudgingly relinquished half the chair to me and then pretended to sleep.

I called around to several automotive and stereo shops and found a place that could repair my dash and install a new stereo the following week. The heater hummed away, keeping the apartment at a balmy seventy-two degrees. I ran my fingers through Mr. Bond's fur, and he purred softly. Propping up the foot of the chair, I curled on my side around Mr. Bond and waited for Niko or Mr. Pitt to call me to say Tim was dead.

I woke to a tinny rendition of Shakira's "Ready for the Good Times." Mr. Bond was sitting a paw's length from my costume's backpack, eyeing it curiously. A quick glance outside showed I'd slept past sundown.

I wrestled Medusa out of the backpack on the last ring and answered. "Hi, Bridget."

"Hi, Dicey-baby," she slurred.

Dicey-baby? I checked the clock to be sure. It was only six thirty, and Bridget was drunk. Bridget never got drunk, not anymore. She claimed law school had saturated her with so much alcohol she was now impervious to becoming intoxicated. Obviously she'd been wrong.

"What's going on?" I asked.

"I'm having the best time here and I miss you," she said. "You can't believe all the cute ones that are out tonight. And I know who I'm taking home with me." Her voice grew fainter. "Don't I, baby? You'll take me home, right?"

"Sure thing," a muffled male voice responded.

"Ah, Bridget," I said, trying to regain her attention.

"You are the most handsome devil I've ever met," Bridget said. "Your eyes are so gorgeous they've got to be illegal. Let me know if you ever need a lawyer. I'd work pro bono for you. I'll be the pro, you be the bone-oh!"

I rolled my eyes, partially amused but mostly appalled on Bridget's behalf. "Bridget!" I yelled into the phone.

"Oh, darling, where are you? Get your fine booty in your car and get down here."

I really didn't want to go anywhere, especially not a bar. I was home and comfortable and still shaking off the cobwebs of sleep. Bridget was a big girl and could take care of herself. She was happy with her one- or two-night stands, and she didn't need me there to monitor her behavior. Of course, Bridget also never got drunk before picking anyone up. I hadn't seen her drunk in public since I'd turned twenty-one. I hadn't seen her drunk at a private party since she was twenty-three. Furthermore, Bridget didn't go out on Sunday nights. She worked them, either at home or at the office. I'd always admired and pitied her work ethic, which called for six-day workweeks and ridiculous amounts of overtime. But that dedication, and a good deal of brains, was the reason Bridget was one of the youngest, most successful lawyers I knew. Or rather, knew of. She was the only lawyer I knew, since I refused to let her set me up with anyone from her office.

"I'm at home," I said. "Which is where you're normally at on a Sunday."

"Pshaw! I work too much. I need to have more fun. Mr. Hunk here agrees, don't you, sexy-pants?"

"Where are you?" I demanded. I was wide awake now. Bridget didn't understand the concept of "work too much." I trotted down the hall for my shoes, wincing as my bruised feet hit the carpet.

"A bar. The one with the bird."

My hands froze over my tennis shoes. "The Golden Goose?" I guessed, heart sinking.

"That's it, darling. We've got a link thesh tight. A bond. Like sisters. Tell me what I'm thinking right— Hmm? What's that, hot buns? Oh. Hang on. Dice?"

"Yeah?"

"Mr. Sexy wants to talk to you. You remember him? We met him the other night. Oooh, pushy, pushy, hunkalicious. Gimme a kiss and I'll give you the phone."

There was a loud, wet smack, then a rustle as the phone exchanged hands. I remained frozen, crouched over my tennis shoes, dread doubling gravity's pull.

"Hi, Dicey-wicy." Tim's smooth voice made my fingers spasm around Medusa. "I know you're there; I can hear you breathing."

Black dots danced in my vision. "If you hurt so much as one hair on her head—"

"You'll what? Stick me with another pet wood? I've been replaying that moment over and over again in my head all day, Maddie. The way you looked at me, the way you tasted . . ."

In the background, I could hear Bridget say, "I like the way you taste, Mr. Hunky-dory."

"Don't touch her," I ordered.

"If only it were that easy, Maddie, but you know how women can't help themselves around me."

I closed my eyes. If Tim's pull was anywhere near as strong as it'd been yesterday, Bridget would be all over him. She'd be lucky to escape with only the slime of *atrum*. I forced my eyes open and finished reaching for my shoes.

"What do you want?" I ground out.

"You really hurt my feelings yesterday," Tim said. "I thought we had something going, and then you tried to kill me." He tsked. "You owe me an apology."

"I'm sorry," I said. I cradled the phone between my ear and shoulder and shoved my feet into the sneakers, ignoring the throbbing fire of scraped blisters.

"Hmm." Tim made smacking noises like he was sampling the air's flavor. "Nope. Not quite what I wanted, I guess. I think I'm hungry for something more." He purred the last word, and my spine tingled.

"I could fill you up," Bridget said, loud enough in my ear that I knew she had her body pressed against Tim's. "Why don't we go back to my place?"

"Oops. Gotta go," Tim said.

The connection went dead. "Shit, shit, shit," I chanted. I threw Medusa aside and laced my shoes with fumbling, frantic fingers. I picked her up a moment later and scrolled through the numbers in her contacts while I shrugged one arm into a jacket. I selected Niko's number.

It rang through to voice mail.

"It's Madison. I got a call from Tim—the demon. He's got my best friend Bridget. Meet me at the Golden Goose."

I clicked Medusa shut, stuffed her in my back pocket, and ran for the front room. My new pet wood was in the backpack. I stuffed it in my other back pocket. My eyes fell on the boots and the knife sticking out from the top of its sheath.

"Niko, you'd better be on your way already," I said as I slid the knife into my purse after sheathing it in its original leather case. I was out the door less than two minutes after Tim had hung up on me.

I drove like a bumblebee in flight down the streets of Roseville, dodging and weaving through traffic, riding my horn when I got stuck behind someone. I was the biggest jackass driver I'd ever seen, and I vowed to remember this moment the next time some idiot cut me off. "My best friend is going to boink a demon!" I shouted by way of apology to the truck driver I screeched in front of to make a sharp right through an empty bank parking lot. If touching Tim had left me coated with *atrum*, I didn't want to contemplate what rolling around with him naked would do to Bridget. "Nothing. It will do nothing, because it's not going to happen," I promised myself.

I screeched into the parking lot, using my emergency brake as I squealed into a parking space at the sidewalk. I shot free of the Civic and into the acrid plume of burned rubber. Coughing, I darted the few steps to the bar entrance, blinking to Primordium along the way. There was no way I was going to take a chance of falling under Tim's spell.

The door bounced off the frame when I flung it open, drawing every eye in the bar. I spotted Bridget immediately, but it was the rest of the bar that stopped me in my tracks.

A cluster of women loitered at the pool tables, cue sticks in hands. They didn't look like they'd done much pool playing, given the placement of the balls. Already, they had turned away from me to cast flirty glances across the bar toward Tim. Their body language shouted intimate invitations, but even the men seated at the bar ignored them. I guess having a roomful of women focused on one man wasn't an ego booster. Almost as one sullen entity, the men staring at me swiveled back to hunch over their beers and watch the game on the TVs over the bar.

The humans may have all gone back to what they were doing, but the evil creatures continued to drool over my pristine soul. The walls, floors, and furniture were coated with *atrum*, thicker than before Niko and I had cleansed the place. In eddies around every human were clusters of imps, and crawling along the walls, furniture, and humans were vervet. At some signal from Tim, the creatures went back to feeding, lowering the *lux lucis* levels one bite at a time.

Bridget waved cheerfully from her seat on Tim's lap, her black-smudged fingers fluttering within an inch of Tim's razor-sharp antlers. Were they tangible but invisible, or did they exist only in Primordium? I'd never had the chance to check, and I hoped today would be equally void of opportunities. Bridget looked dreadful. Her soul was normally one of the cleanest I'd ever seen, aside from my own. It was even a point of pride with her, and she'd cajoled me more than once over the years to describe its pure, white lines to her.

Given that she was dressed skimpily enough to get cold at noon in July, it wasn't difficult to get a good reading of her soul. If I didn't know better, I would have said Bridget and Tim had already spent some time rolling around naked together. My best friend was smeared with tarlike *atrum* from the tip of her scalp down to the toes that peeked out of her self-proclaimed sex-me-up pumps. If she could see her soul now—and drag her attention away from Tim—she would be devastated.

I wanted to run across the room and tear her from Tim's arms before beating the demon to a pulp. Unfortunately, in my haste, I hadn't considered the ramifications of a public encounter. My weak plan would get me arrested for sure, if not pulled apart, limb by limb, by the women at the pool tables first. Not to mention that I doubted Tim would hold still for me to pummel him.

Indecision held me rooted in place. Tim gave me a knowing smile filled with razor-sharp teeth, clearly enjoying watching me realize I was impotent. When he winked at me, nausea churned up my windpipe.

"Take a fucking picture." A man jostled my shoulder as he pushed past me. He had his girlfriend—no, that diamond ring meant wife—by the arm and was dragging her from the bar. The man stopped. "He's good-looking, but he's nobody. What's so special about him?" he demanded.

His wife didn't answer, too busy straining around me to keep Tim in sight.

"Oh, my card," she exclaimed, and her free hand dug through her purse, though she never took her eyes from Tim. When she located a business card, she struggled against her husband's grip on her arm. "Let me give him this," she pleaded, still not able to tear her eyes from the demon's vision of perfection. "He looks like he, uh, might need my expertise."

"It's a pheromone thing, isn't it?" the man said, and I realized he was talking to me.

"Something like that. Get her out of here and she'll be fine."

"Fucking scientists." The man grimaced and tugged. His wife tugged right back. A string of mouse-size imps circled her neck; her husband had a vervet gnawing at his shoulder. There was nothing I could do about the evil creatures at the moment, but as the man pushed through the door, I realized there was *something* I could do.

"Hey," I called. I think he was surprised that I could look away from Tim, and it made him pause. "Go easy on her," I said. "She's not herself, not in control of herself."

"No shit, lady."

He peeled his wife's fingers from the doorjamb and the door slammed shut behind them. I turned back to my own personal hell.

"Dicey-poo! Come here!" Bridget called.

On leaden feet, I went. Bridget patted the cushion beside where she sat on Tim's lap. I ignored her and perched across from them on a different couch, far enough away that I hoped to avoid Tim if he attacked. Before I sat, I cleansed the seat of *atrum*, defiantly meeting Tim's gaze when I finished.

"New trick?" he asked. Whatever Niko had done to wound him after I'd passed out hadn't left so much as a scar. Looking at the pit of darkness that was his body made me feel light-headed, and I gripped the couch cushion against a rush of vertigo. A day of distance between our encounters hadn't done anything to improve his appearance in Primordium, either. If anything, his beak nose seemed sharper, his chin pointier, his antlers longer, and his mouth much more full of teeth. If only I could show Bridget—and the other women at the bar—the real Tim. They'd run screaming, but at least they'd be safe.

"What now?" I asked.

"We should go back to my place," Bridget suggested.

"All of us?" I asked, surprised despite myself. I shook my head, reminding myself not to be drawn into her drugged and drunk world.

"It's not a bad idea," Tim agreed.

I liked the thought of being somewhere private with Tim, but not for the same reason as Bridget. I tried to picture us piling into Bridget's Prius, the stilted conversation on the drive to Bridget's house. Nope. Wasn't going to happen. There was no way I was going to let Tim know where Bridget lived, let alone travel through that much of my region, tainting it as he went.

"I just got here. But you can leave any time you want, Tim."

"Not without me."

I glared at Bridget. She flipped her hair back over her shoulder and glared right back. Her hand slid up Tim's arm, and she turned to smile at him. When she lifted her hand to run it through her hair, she spread *atrum* along her scalp.

"I think you've had a little much to drink, don't you?" I asked her, trying to sound reasonable. "Why don't you come sit over here by me?"

"Way over there?" She wriggled a little, giggled, then shook her head emphatically like she was five years old, biting her bottom lip.

"I'm sure Tim could use a little air," I tried again. "Maybe he'll even go get us another drink."

"You could join us," Tim offered. He leered at me. "You would have yesterday."

Bridget licked a line from the base of Tim's throat to his ear, then whispered something to him.

"Bridget. Bridget!" I raised my hand toward her, trying to get her to come to me.

Tim walked his sharp fingers from her collarbone down her chest, and she giggled. I clenched my fists in helpless anger, watching his claws pierce her soul, replacing *lux lucis* with *atrum* at each puncture. Trying to reason with Bridget was useless. I knew from yesterday's experience that she wasn't listening to anything but her swarming hormones.

"I'll join you," I said desperately. "But you have to let her go."

Tim looked like he was considering my offer. "Bridgie-widgie, would that be okay with you? Maddie doesn't want you to be with me."

Bridget shook her head again, tears shining in her eyes. "Don't you like me?" she asked Tim.

"Oh, yes. You're wonderful." He leaned toward Bridget, and I had to look away from all those sharp teeth puncturing Bridget's soul in a revolting mockery of a kiss. When I looked back, the demon was watching me, his glowing eyes filled with mirth.

"Did you know this place has a back room?" Tim asked.

"It does?" Bridget squirmed in delight. "Let's go!"

"I don't think so," I said.

Tim stood, dumping Bridget to the floor. I sprang to my feet and grabbed for Bridget's flailing arm. I caught it and pulled her toward me. She held on to Tim with her other hand. I reached for Bridget's face and turned her to look at me, trying to keep Tim in my sight at the same time.

"Come on, Bridget. Time to go home. We'll come back tomorrow, I promise."

She shook her head and tried to tug free of my grip.

"Tim's a very bad man. He's not who he says he is. Please, let's go." If I could get myself between Bridget and Tim, I knew I could get Bridget to safety. I wasn't sure how, but it was as good as any plan I'd come up with in the last five minutes.

"Are you a bad boy?" Bridget purred to Tim.

Tim had been waiting patiently, holding Bridget's other hand like a boyfriend. Now he jerked my best friend's arm. Bridget tore free from my grasp and collapsed against Tim's chest. She gave no indication that Tim had hurt her wrist, but I knew it was going to leave a bruise.

"I'm a very bad boy," Tim said. Bridget shivered and tried to crawl up Tim's body. The demon stepped around her and clamped his hand down on my wrist before I could move. "This is getting boring. I'm ready to kill you."

"Oooh, *la petite mort*. Isn't that what the French call it?" Bridget giggled.

I put up a struggle, but it was a weak one. I couldn't take out Tim in public, and I couldn't let him out of my sight with Bridget. In the end, I walked as far behind Tim as his grip on my wrist would allow, settling for avoiding as much *atrum* taint as possible. Already, a black ring crept up my arm from his hand, radiating like a slow-motion solar flare of evil.

I tried to think of a plan. The only thing that came to mind was *run*.

My final hope for luck to save the day in the form of the bartender kicking Tim out for forcing his way into the private back rooms of the bar was dashed when Tim and the bartender shared a wink. The bartender didn't appear the least bit surprised, and I was nauseated all over again when I realized this probably wasn't Tim's first time taking his "date" into the back room.

The hallway to the back was lined with boxes after we passed the small kitchen. In Primordium, the whole hall was the black of inanimate objects coated with *atrum*. The only semi-bright light in the place was Bridget ahead of me. I didn't chance blinking back to normal sight to see better. A few bruises on my shins were worth not falling victim to a demon. Even Bridget had a hard time staying pressed to Tim *and* navigating the tight hallway. I tried to breathe normally, but my bravado had fallen away somewhere near the bartender. Only my fear of Tim killing Bridget kept me from screaming my head off.

Tim locked us inside a tiny office with a single desk and a cluttered mess of filing cabinets, boxes, and paperwork. As easily as I'd cleaned my cushion earlier, Tim raised a pulsing barrier of *atrum* across the door.

Déjà vu.

Raw fear iced my veins, settling in a knot in my stomach. I scurried to put the desk between us.

"Should I kill you first, or make you watch me fuck your friend, then kill you?"

"Oooh, I like option two," Bridget said. She shoved everything off the desk with a sweep of her arms. The resounding crash should have brought the owner back to check on us, but I wasn't going to pin my hopes on it. Bridget climbed up on the desk and sprawled on her side like a pinup girl in her short pencil skirt and loose blouse. When her hand reached to start unbuttoning her top, I grabbed for her. She wasn't expecting it, and in one heave, she dropped to my feet on the safe side of the desk.

"Tsk-tsk," Tim said, shaking his pointer finger at me.

"Hey! That wasn't nice!" Bridget clawed her way up my pant leg and shoved me to the side. I staggered against a filing cabinet, shock slowing my reactions.

"Let's give the lady what she wants. A fuck, and then you can die," Tim decided.

Bridget's head swiveled back toward him, her expression melting to adoration with an unnaturalness that made my skin crawl. Tim stalked forward until he was pressed against the opposite side of the desk. Bridget leaned forward, trying to get her knee up on the desk so she could crawl across, but she was hampered by her skirt. Not to be deterred, she reached for the back slit and ripped the skirt up the seam. I suddenly had an eyeful of bare, *atrum*-coated backside, from heels to thong-(un)covered buns. Her uncharacteristic lack of modesty finally snapped me into action.

"No, Bridget!" I threw a stack of paper at Tim. "Get back! Go away!" I threw the desk lamp at him, then a stapler, then a stack of paper-filled folders. They missed but made him duck and dodge.

"Paper fight!" Bridget cried. She scooped up the pieces that landed on the desk and tossed them back into the air.

Tim lunged for me, knocking the desk against our thighs. Bridget went down with a squeal, but I kept my footing. I grabbed anything I could get my hands on and tossed it at Tim, but it was a futile gesture. Eventually, I would run out of objects, and there was still only one thoroughly blocked way out of the room.

That eventuality arrived a lot sooner than I was ready for. My hands scrambled around the surfaces next to me, coming up empty. I didn't dare turn away from Tim to look for anything else. I knew the moment I took my eyes off him he would pounce. Either on me or Bridget, and neither option was a good one.

In desperation, I pulled out the pet wood, extending it with a flick of my wrist.

"I like the way you think, Maddie. Lay it on me. I can't wait." He spread his arms wide and puffed up his chest.

Bridget regained her feet and launched herself across the desk. I speared the pet wood at Tim and grabbed her knees. We went down in a tumble of limbs, sliding the desk back in Tim's direction. Bridget fought me with absentminded cruelty, shoving and pushing and climbing me to get to her demon. Her knee landed on my stomach, punching the breath from me in a painful rush. She used her advantage to push off my chest to her feet. I grasped at what was left of her skirt and it came away in my hand, tripping her at the last second. She sprawled across the dirty office floor with a shriek.

Panting, I scrabbled after her, pinning her in place with my body. She craned her head to the right, where she could see Tim's feet beneath the front wall of the desk, and she stretched for him with her free hand, mindless of me and the rest of the world in her urgency to touch him.

I gazed down at her sullied profile. This wasn't Bridget. This wasn't my best friend who I'd roomed with in college and told my darkest secrets to. This wasn't the intelligent woman who had breezed through law school while the rest of us were still doing undergrad work. This wasn't even a person with her own will. The demon had stripped it all from her—her identity, her personality, her morals and will and inhibitions. Tim had done so much worse than cover her soul with his evil taint. He'd made her a plaything.

My world narrowed to that moment, pausing for infinity on that second, pivoting as my thoughts realigned. I'd accepted what I was when I changed Max. I'd confirmed it when I saved the kittens. But in that moment, in that endless second, I knew what it was to be an enforcer. I saw the precipice of no return, hovered at its edge. Behind me was a normal life, or what qualified as one for me. A life where I could see how good or evil a person was, where I could watch evil creatures and people's evil actions taint the lives and environments around them. Ahead was a yawning abyss of possibility in which I could make the world a better place. It was scary and exciting. And required me to take action.

The second passed. Time resumed, blurring to catch up to normal speed.

I lunged under the desk where I'd kicked my purse. The knife practically leapt into my hand; then I shoved my feet against the front wall of the desk. The desk and I parted ways, sliding in opposite directions across the room. I came out of my slide already turning. Tim dodged the desk and stood beside Bridget, who was struggling to her feet. With a cry, I launched over Bridget and embedded the knife to the hilt in the demon's chest.

My jump slammed the demon backward. Tim staggered against the wall, shock etched in the inky features of his deformed face. Clutching the hilt, I shoved a whirlwind of *lux lucis* into the blade. A web of white light skittered across the demon's body. Tim scrabbled weakly at my hand, and I shifted to a two-handed grip on the hilt. *Lux lucis* poured through both my arms, gushing through the blade. It spread over Tim's body the way electricity might, in waves and arcs, radiating from the blade outward, the *lux lucis* made more powerful by the physical damage of the knife's metal blade buried to the hilt in his chest.

I knew the exact moment the demon died. *Lux lucis* backed up into the blade with nowhere to go, then backwashed into me, leaving me jittery like I'd received a caffeine jolt straight into my veins. The demon's body slumped to the floor. I released the blade and admired my handiwork.

"Dice?" Bridget's voice wavered, small and childlike.

I glanced back over my shoulder and watched as Bridget collapsed, a puppet whose strings had been cut. The sound of her hitting the floor jolted through me. The horror of what I'd done smothered my elation.

I scrambled backward, knocking into the desk and falling to the side, crab-crawling until I collided with the wall. My feet continued to push against the tile, flattening me against the wall. If I could climb it, I would have. I knew I should check on Bridget, but I couldn't tear my eyes from the dead body on the other side of the room.

The hilt stuck obscenely from the demon's chest. The body was slumped half upright against the wall, like he'd fallen asleep, though the knife screamed otherwise. Looking at him was no longer like looking into a consuming void. Nor was he charcoal, the color of nonliving things. He was black, solid *atrum*. But even as I watched, *atrum* bled from him, pooling first beneath the body, then spreading like blood across the floor. Unlike blood, *atrum* climbed the wall behind the demon, too, defying gravity, oozing outward in all directions from the limp body.

When the edge of the pool touched Bridget, she moaned. I scooted across the floor, kicking the desk to the side, and dragged her limp body back with me to the farthest corner of the small room. Keeping one eye on the expanding stain of *atrum*, I took off my coat and covered Bridget from her waist to her knees. Her skirt was in tatters under the desk next to my pet wood.

My legs were shaking too much to stand, so I crawled under the desk and grabbed the pet wood. Numbly, I evaluated my soul.

"You're not looking so hot, Dice," I said, and the raw sound of my voice scared me silent.

I checked Bridget's pulse. It was steady. Her breathing was relaxed. Without the draw of lust from Tim, Bridget had finally succumbed to intoxication. Not even shaking her got more than, "Again? I'm sleepy. You start and I'll catch up."

I slumped in place and stared at the demon's body. I needed to think. I needed to find a way out of here. But I couldn't bring myself to do it yet. The door, our only option, was still blocked by the *atrum* barrier. Not even Tim's death had brought down the soul-eating blockade.

Tim's death. I was already thinking about it in the past tense, distancing myself from it like it had happened to a stranger. But it hadn't.

I watched the encroaching *atrum* with numb dread. I knew there had to be a smart way of handling the situation, but my brain was short-circuited. Instinct was all I had left. Gathering *lux lucis* in my hands, I spread a ward in front of us on the floor and crossed my fingers.

When the tide of *atrum* slithered against my ward, the white line weakened, but the *atrum* turned aside, taking a path with less resistance.

I strengthened the ward. The *atrum* slid along the curve of my ward until it hit the wall. Then it climbed the wall and rushed straight across the vertical surface toward where I'd leaned Bridget. Hastily, I smeared a ward in an arc on the wall until we were completely circled by *lux lucis*. *Atrum* washed against the ward. It held. The tide of evil shifted and crawled up the wall. I took a deep breath and let it out.

Danger averted, I looked back at the body, drawn by those dead eyes that stared back at me. Tim . . . the demon . . . I'd killed—

I rubbed my hands together. The sensation of the blade sliding into the demon clung to my skin. Over and over again, I felt the blade slide without friction through flesh and organs, before catching against the spine.

I would have thrown up, but I didn't have the energy left.

Atrum breached an internal barrier in the demon's body, and the remaining evil gushed from Tim in a tidal wave. I regarded Tim's final, postmortem attack with dull fear. As far as tidal waves go, it was pretty insignificant, a mere foot tall, but it rushed up the walls and across the roof in a gravity-defying act no real tidal wave had ever accomplished. It also came straight at my barriers across the floor, and in my weak, exhausted state, it might as well have been a ten-foot wave.

I held my wards by sheer willpower and carefully doling out my limited *lux lucis*. When the tide receded and equalized in a thick layer about the room, I collapsed sideways across Bridget. I'd lost at least two square feet of clean space, most of it along the wall behind us. As long as I didn't sit back against it, I would be fine, and Bridget, where she lay up against it, was safe, too.

Against my will, my gaze slid back to the body. It looked fragile now in a way that Tim had never looked, in normal sight or Primordium. The antlers were blunted and gray, the beak nose and wide-staring eyes softened and blurred, like I was looking at the demon through a soap opera dream screen. The only thing solid about him was the knife hilt protruding from his rib cage, a hard black line of a handle and a dull, light gray of a blade.

I thought my mind was playing tricks on me, amplifying my sense of guilt by making me see things that couldn't be possible—like seeing the blade buried in the body. Then the knife shifted.

I screamed.

It was a tiny whimper of a scream. I didn't want to draw the body's attention.

The body was beyond caring. As I watched, the blurry, dreamlike edges of it collapsed, folding down on itself like a pile of dust that had lost its structure. Then it fell into the depths of the *atrum* coating the floor and disappeared. The knife clattered to the linoleum, only the slight shine of the blade visible across the room. I strangled another scream.

The demon was gone. I didn't dare blink to normal vision to check, but I knew that any human who walked into the room wouldn't see a body. They wouldn't see *atrum* coating the walls and ceiling, either, turning the office into a solid black box of death, with one tiny, misshapen circle of *lux lucis* around two dim souls. They'd see a knife and two girls huddled in the middle of a tornado-strewn office.

From the ashes of the demon arose a bevy of imps, the dark side's single-celled amoeba, brainless, with the drive only to feed and propagate—*atrum*'s first evolutionary step.

You're losing it, I thought. *This isn't a* Nova *show. It's your life.*

They bounced around in mass confusion until the first one spotted Bridget and me crumpled in the corner. As one, the others turned to look at us. With bounds and leaps, they approached.

I looked down at my dim body. It would be ironic if I killed a demon, only to be taken out by imps.

When I looked back up, the imps were dancing to Justin Timberlake's "SexyBack." I bobbed my head with them, acknowledging that I'd finally tipped over the mental edge.

"Your ass is ringing," Bridget mumbled. "I'll get it."

She groped me. I jumped, coming out of my trance.

"Medusa!" I scrambled to pull my cell phone from my back pocket.

"We should go clubbing," Bridget said. She raised one arm and waved it in the air, smacking me upside the head. "Oops. Sorry!" She giggled.

I unlocked Medusa with a shaky finger. "Niko?"

"Where are you?" Niko demanded.

The strength in his voice made my last shred of courage crumble. My hands started trembling so badly I supported my left with my right to keep the phone to my ear.

"Staring down a pack of imps. I think they're going to kill me." The imps had stopped inches from my feeble barrier.

"Tell me where you are—"

"Tim's dead. I killed him," I confessed.

"Good, now—"

"Does that make me a bad person?"

"Stick with me, Madison. I'm in the bar. *Where are you?*"

"You're here? Oh, thank God!" I smiled, and my face felt like it would crack under the strain. I turned to look down at Bridget. Her soul was coated with *atrum*. She hadn't moved more than her arm from her fetal position. But she was awake. Drunk and awake. And safe. "We're going to be okay," I told her.

"Make your butt sing again," she said.

"Okay. Niko, call me back."

"Madi—"

I clicked the phone off, then stared in horror at what I'd done. The phone rang, playing "SexyBack" at full volume. Bridget grabbed the phone from my fumbling grip and struggled to stand so she could dance.

"Wait! I need that! No, don't put your hand there!" I wrestled with Bridget to keep her within the confines of my ward. She laughed, holding the phone out of reach.

"I love you, you know," she said in a wash of cosmopolitan fumes. "You saved me." She lurched toward me to hug me, and we both went down in a sprawl of limbs.

The door splintered, and Niko burst into the room. Through the veil of Bridget's hair, I watched him pause, take in the room, the imps, my ward, and finally Bridget mashed atop me, her bare, thong-clad butt exposed to the world. "SexyBack" was still playing in Bridget's outstretched hand.

"Hey, is this Mr. Dark and Deadly?" Bridget asked, pushing up to straddle me with a complete lack of modesty. "You're right. He's *hot!*"

I tried to morph into a piece of linoleum.

Niko pulled his phone from his ear and ended the call. Medusa went silent.

"Aww. What'd you do that for?" Bridget asked.

The imps abandoned me and rushed Niko. Or the open doorway. I wasn't sure which. Either way, their lives were short. Niko turned and laid down something across the doorway. A sheet of *lux lucis* rose across the opening, blocking the encroaching *atrum* from exiting.

With the confidence of an optivus aegis, Niko strode across the *atrum*-coated floor, leaving footprints of *lux lucis* behind that the *atrum* oozed back over. He scooped up the knife, then took the two remaining steps to the edge of my ward.

"Hi, I'm Madison's best friend Bridget." Bridget raised her hand to shake his.

"I can see that." Grinning, Niko shook her hand. *Atrum* smeared across his palm from Bridget's, only to be wiped clean a moment later. He bent down and did something to my ward. The faint line sparkled with energy and expanded two feet in every direction, eating *atrum* as it moved.

Finally Bridget remembered she was sitting on me. She swayed to her feet, and I scrambled up beside her, snatching my jacket up and wrapping it around her lower half, using the sleeves to tie it tightly in place.

"'SexyBack'?" Niko asked.

"What other ringtone do you give Mr. Dark and Deadly?" Bridget asked.

"His name is Niko."

"Mr. Dark and Deadly by any other name is still—"

"Shut up, Bridget."

19

WELL-BEHAVED WOMEN RARELY MAKE HISTORY

N IKO TOOK PITY ON ME and helped my drunk, traitorous
friend and me across the *atrum*-coated floor without asking any
more questions. Walking through the sheet of *lux lucis* perked
my energy up a little. For Bridget, it was like walking through a shower;
when she reached the other side, most of the *atrum* had washed away,
leaving patches of darkness in the areas where she'd lingered against
Tim.

Niko called Joy, who said she'd meet us out front, well clear of the
interior evil minions who would have gleefully feasted on her pristine
and shimmering soul. Niko would remain behind to clean up, and he
set another *lux lucis* barrier at the main entrance to prevent anyone
from leaving as an unwitting host. By the time we'd hustled out of the
bar, Bridget's intoxication had turned on her. She sagged against the
storefront, one hand on her head, the other on her stomach, while I filled
Niko in.

Niko made me describe, in minute detail, how I'd used the knife
and how the body had disintegrated, until he was reassured the demon
was well and truly dead. I skipped over how Bridget had lost her skirt.
I didn't mention that I could still feel the impact of the knife against
Tim's—against the demon's—spine. I emphasized how I'd tried to
follow protocol and orders, but with my friend's life in jeopardy, I'd had
to act when I did. Surprisingly, Niko agreed.

"You had a busy morning, too, I hear," Niko said.

"I did?" It took enormous willpower to recall twelve hours earlier.

"Brad said you went back to the construction site."

"I didn't. I went— Wait. He knows? How?"

"He's a warden. He can sense what happens in his region."

I groaned and pinched the bridge of my nose. "There's no such thing as enforcer jail, is there?"

"Another unauthorized adventure?" Niko guessed.

"Not exactly."

"Brad told you to do it?"

"Not exactly."

Niko laughed. "You're lucky you were successful. Brad didn't know if he should tie you to your cubicle or commend you."

"Really? He was pleased?"

"*Was.* Partially. I'll let him know you did really well here. Maybe that will help."

Neither of us expressed our doubts about the good that would do me. I had directly defied Mr. Pitt. Again. There was going to be more yelling.

I decided now was not the time to think about it. Instead, I savored the fleeting glow of Niko's approval.

"There's one thing I don't understand," I said.

"Just one? You do learn fast."

"About Tim. The demon. Why was he so much more attractive now?" I stopped myself before confessing to having met Tim the day I was hired— and again on Friday—and not recognized him for what he was. For the first time, I had performed like a competent enforcer in front of Niko; I didn't want to give him a fresh reason to think I was an idiot.

"You looked at him with normal sight tonight?" Niko asked.

I shook my head. "But the other women in the bar did. It was like no one else existed but the demon."

"It's part of a demon's makeup: The more they can corrupt a region, the more power they gain. In this demon's case, he used his power to make himself irresistible to women. I imagine that made it a lot easier for him to spread his corruption, too."

I shuddered when I thought of how impossible it had been to think when I'd looked at Tim with normal vision at the hotel. Niko had a point. Whatever magic Tim had used to change his appearance, he'd used it well to exert his dominance over my region. It was comforting to know he was no longer a threat.

My hand tingled with the phantom feel of the jolt of the knife hitting the demon's spine. I wiped my palm on my pants.

Joy arrived while I was around the side of the building with Bridget, holding her hair back while she emptied her stomach. I convinced Bridget to let Joy drive her Prius, and once we were in Joy's company, Bridget was happy to do whatever the Illuminea wanted. Fortunately, it wasn't much, but it did include slipping on a pair of pants Joy had brought with her. As per Niko's instructions, I found myself at Mel's diner for the second night in a row, this time with my best friend and Joy. I didn't need Niko's reminder to order a huge salad and vegetables. I ordered the same for Bridget, who protested she wouldn't be able to eat anything, right up until the moment the food arrived; then she ate with the appetite of a starved wildebeest. I didn't comment, too busy stuffing food into my own mouth. Joy daintily sipped a lemonade and maintained an endless stream of meaningless comments that managed to soothe rather than be annoying.

The presence of the Illuminea also appeared to make Bridget forget the unpleasantness of her encounter with Tim and his demise at my hands. Or maybe it was the lingering side effect of the copious amount of alcohol she'd consumed. I didn't question it. If she never remembered this night, her life would be better. I also took solace in the fact that by the end of the meal, Bridget's soul was nearly clean. Mine still needed some good recharging, but I felt like I could handle a few imps again, if necessary.

Joy took me back to my car, then drove Bridget home, who was now too tired to keep her eyes open. Joy wouldn't let me follow them, either, to bring her back to her vehicle. It was impossible to argue with the Illuminea, and I half suspected that Joy didn't need a car to get around anyway.

I longed to drive home and curl into bed, but Niko had informed me that Mr. Pitt was waiting for me at the office. At nine o'clock at night. I wondered if Mr. Pitt lived at the office. Maybe he had a bed hidden under his desk. It didn't seem that far-fetched.

I tried not to think about how mad Mr. Pitt was going to be. At least this reaming had a silver lining. I'd taken out the demon. I'd successfully defended my region.

So rather than cruising down Douglas toward the comfort of my apartment, I turned left on Eureka Road and into the office complex of my new home away from home.

The parking lot was empty except for two vehicles parked near the front door. I parked to the left of them, blinked to Primordium, and scanned the lot and glass-fronted lobby for any evil creatures, finding none. I stuffed the knife Niko had given back to me in my purse—I'd think about the ramifications of not feeling safe without it later.

The building's lobby was empty, darkened and hushed. All the offices were closed along the long hallway until I reached Illumination Studios, where the double doors were open, the lights blazing. Sharon eyeballed me from behind the rim of the reception desk. I wasn't surprised to find her there. Sharon was as much a fixture of the office as her desk.

"Mr. Pitt is ready for you," she said.

"Thank you."

Less than a week ago, I'd been ignorant of everything: that I was supposed to do something with soul-sight, that my ability was much more than mere observation, even that the job I thought I was applying for was only a ruse.

Five days had changed a lot. I had a date with Dr. Love, a man I'd had a crush on for the last three years. I had a job, one that paid well for the first time in my life, even if I still wasn't sure how I was going to explain it to my folks. I'd saved the life of four animals, all who now had a chance at long and happy lives.

I'd almost killed Mr. Bond, but I knew better now.

I'd killed a man.

He'd been a demon, too, but I'd known him as a man first.

I'd embraced who I was, and it had changed everything. I'd become an illuminant enforcer.

I didn't allow my footsteps to slow as I crossed the threshold of my boss's open office doorway. With everything I'd accomplished, Mr. Pitt couldn't be too mad at me, right?

Note to Readers

Although Madison Fox and I share many things in common, such as the town she lives in, the cat she lives with, and even her apartment (which is based off a place I used to live), that is where our similarities end. I am a lifelong gamer, I worked in the video game industry for many happy years, and I enjoy playing video games on every platform yet created. In other words, I would be one of the fan nerds that Madison holds in such low regard, and so would my husband and most of my friends.

Of course, Madison is a fictitious character, welcome to her own fictitious views of what qualifies (or doesn't qualify) as worthy forms of entertainment. The rest of us don't have to agree with her.

Acknowledgments

This book would be a two-act mess without the feedback of so many wonderful writers and readers. Thank you, Kate Abbott, for introducing me to NaNo WriMo and subsequently changing the way I write. Your feedback was essential to shaping the scenes and sentences of the first draft into an actual book. I've enjoyed so many great writing discussions with you (and still don't understand how you can write without an outline). Jennieke Cohen, thank you for your amazing ability to see the big picture, including the huge plot gap I missed completely; it was a painful fix, but the book is so much stronger for it.

Carrie Andrews and Brooke N. Hall, thank you for the wonderful edits! You both make my novels shine.

Sara, thank you for being the best big sister I could ever ask for, and for always being interested in my story rambles and writer woes, for celebrating with me when I complete a draft, and for willingly reading multiple iterations of the same book.

Mom and Dad, thank you for reading all my early stories, including that first painful book when I didn't have a clue what I was doing, and still asking to read my next book. And the next. And two decades later, still asking about my writing, still interested in all the details of my daily process. Thank you for giving my dreams importance.

Cody, a sentence, a page, a book cannot express a lifetime's worth of gratitude for your love. Thank you for always believing in me, especially in my darkest moments.

THE ADVENTURES OF MADISON FOX

A Fistful of Evil

Madison just learned that her ability to see souls is more than a sight:
It's a weapon for fighting evil. The only problem is she doesn't
have a clue what she's doing.

A Fistful of Fire

In the midst of an uncharacteristic flare-up of evil and with fire-breathing
salamanders blazing unchecked across the city, Madison must determine who
she can trust before her region and career go up in flames.

"Rebecca Chastain has a hit series here, one full of humor,
danger and amazingly awesome characters!" –*Tome Tender*

GARGOYLE GUARDIAN CHRONICLES

Magic of the Gargoyles

In a race to save the lives of helpless baby gargoyles, Mika must jeopardize
everything she holds dear, including her life.

Curse of the Gargoyles

Rescuing a gargoyle from a sadistic invention should have been simple for
Mika, until it ignites a chain reaction set to destroy the city, the world, and
magic itself.

Secret of the Gargoyles

In her brief career as a gargoyle healer, Mika has faced some daunting
challenges, but none have stumped her—until now.

"I loved every minute of this series." –*Feeling Fictional*

Tiny Glitches

Dealing with her electricity-killing curse makes living in modern-day
Los Angeles complicated for Eva—and that was before she was blackmailed
into hiding a stolen baby elephant and on the run with Hudson, a sexy
electrical engineer she just met.

"I laughed out loud too many times to count." –*Pure Textuality*

**Books That Hook*
www.rebeccachastain.com

About the Author

REBECCA CHASTAIN is the international bestselling author of the Madison Fox, Illuminant Enforcer series and the Gargoyle Guardian Chronicles, among other works. She has found seven four-leaf clovers to date, won a purebred Arabian horse in a drawing, and once tamed a blackbird for a day. Writing stories designed to amuse and entertain has been her passion since she was eleven years old. She lives in Northern California with her wonderful husband and three bossy cats.

**Visit RebeccaChastain.com
for updates, extras, and so much more!**

**Join Rebecca on Facebook and Twitter
https://www.facebook.com/rebeccachastainnovels
@Author_Rebecca**

www.ingramcontent.com/pod-product-compliance
Lightning Source LLC
Chambersburg PA
CBHW031233120726
47905CB00002B/584